# SAM D. PAKAN

D1279906

# JESSE'S
# SEED

# Jesse's Seed

by

## Sam D. Pakan

**BOOK I**

ATHANATOS
PUBLISHING GROUP

*Jesse's Seed*
  by Sam D. Pakan

      www.sampakan.com

ISBN:  978-1-936830-79-4

Copyright 2015, Sam D. Pakan.  All Rights Reserved.

Published by Athanatos Publishing Group

      www.athanatosministries.org


Cover designed by Julius Broqueza.
      Copyright Athanatos Christian Ministries, 2015.  All Rights Reserved.

*Jesse's Seed* won first prize in
Athanatos Christian Ministry's 2015 Christian Novel Contest.

# Acknowledgements

It seems too little to say "thank you" to you, Dorothy J. Clark, my faithful critique partner and good friend. You taught me the difference between showing and telling, and, on many appropriate occasions, gently reminded me that I still didn't have it straight. How you had the patience, I'll never know. I promise I'll get it right eventually.

Then my friend, Curtis Shelburne; I would never have believed anyone could suffer more from grammar neurosis than me. (Or is it "I"?) You are a phenomenally accomplished musician, writer, and copy editor, and an even better friend.

I also owe an immense debt of thanks to Chester Beasley. I wish this book could have been written during your life here, but I suspect you know how grateful I am. Your experiences inspired me to move this novel halfway around the world, from the Pacific to Europe, and to create a character named Bear who resembles you in several ways. I deeply admire your courage. Truly, you were not ashamed…

To the aviators and administrators of the Commemorative Air Force, I offer my sincere gratitude. While many were helpful, two were amazingly so: Jim Dennison, B-17 pilot, flight instructor, and patient explainer; and Hartland (Bud) Ukes, CAF curator, storyteller, and all-around great guy. You both went the extra mile. Thank you so much.

Then there is Kit, my go-to guy for things that fly. Thank you, Mr. Sanders, for your input, your checking and re-checking.

Lastly, but most of all, I want to thank my mother, Minnie Lee Pakan. You believed in me when you had no reason to, and never stopped encouraging me to do all that was in my heart, even after the darkness came. I so look forward to seeing you again. Fast falls the eventide.

Sam Pakan

# Chapter I

## August 1941

A squeal quivered on the heavy air. David sank his ax into the cedar, turned to see a colt skitter along the road, black as tarnished silver, every line an echo of perfection. Out front and partially hidden by the pines, a big-boned gray strained against the lead rope blazing white and new as the sweat on his cheek.

The shiver settled in his gut. Morgan, bringing a colt this time, beseeching the old man's discipling, most likely. Not that he hadn't seen Jesse defeat horses, too. He'd ridden more than a few, all afraid of his every move. And he'd sat through countless meals listening to stories of the big sorrel or the Thoroughbred mare, but they'd been only words. Nothing flesh or bone about them. A yearning rose to his throat, as urgent as a smothered breath, that this one would stay unbowed, would know its mind, would stay proud and sure.

A chill rippled beneath his sweated shirt, and he felt his mother's finger trace his spine, turned and faced the house. Jesse sat on the porch, his stare piercing the shimmering stillness. David pulled his ax from the cedar and set his mind to his work, though not wholly. He summoned the look he knew was on the old man's face, the loss Jesse wore for all to see, sucked in the heating air and swung.

He was a part of his father's loss. Just one more thing that hadn't turned out the way the old man wanted.

* * *

Jesse gripped the push rings in his stiffening hands and wheeled himself to the edge of the porch, stared across the rigid precision of the kaffir corn where the boy's hewing shook the morning calm. The ax made a furious arc, ripped into the nearer of two cedars and fanned bark into the early light. He closed his eyes, remembered the double-mindedness that had played in him before the fall, the joy of hardness in his arms and fever in his breast, hills leveling to plain beneath his step. He breathed deep a clover morning sharp with some past autumn, the cool prickling beneath the sweat gathered on his chin.

It wasn't that he'd loved the cedars so dearly. They'd sprung up without his notice, had become a part the place by season and endurance. Still, he felt their absence, even before the first was topped, and vowed to let the hollow in his gut be his consolation.

He clenched his jaw, watched the ax head flicker. David was a stump of a man, broad at the shoulder and narrow at the waist, but for all the boy's strength and readiness for work, he had a woman's heart. Not that he hadn't seen the weakness all along. David knew nothing of what couldn't be undone, didn't see the loss of each step taken, each curled chip flying from his ax never to be replaced.

Something stirred beyond the cedars, and he squinted against obscurity, stared beyond the panicles splayed in dress formation in the direction of the pines. A gray horse, heavy-boned and coarse, dragged a thrashing colt. The rider bobbed between long shadows on the road, holding hemp to saddle horn as the colt fought the limits of the rope. Jesse let the air from his lungs and raised his chin, damned the gall of whoever it was for putting his worthlessness on display.

As quickly as it came, he let the fire subside. He eyed the colt, black and frothy, frantic against the staid complacency of the gray and spotted the apologetic chin and narrow shoulders hunched above the swell as the gray cleared the elms. Morgan again, no doubt in want of something.

A picket grin appeared beneath the black, curled brim. "I've got one for you, Jesse."

He stared into the darkness of the long shadow. "There's nothing I can do."

Morgan pulled up the lathered gray heaving in the morning calm. "I

2

want your head, Jesse, not your legs."

"Like I said, there's nothing I can do."

"Then let me use them pens. You ain't using them no more, and the boy won't be weanin' calves for a while. Ain't doctorin' no cows, now is he?"

Jesse surveyed the trembling withers, saw the signs blood left in an animal that made it special. The legs, fine and straight, the deep heart-girth, the rounded croup, the wide, intelligent eyes. He waited, considered his words. "You'll feed him, or he'll starve. The boy has money to make and won't be bothered."

"Done." Morgan spurred the gray and dragged the struggling colt toward the pens.

David stood silent as the cedar, his sandy hair brandished by the breeze. Though his eyes were dim, Jesse knew the contempt of the stare. The boy had learned too much of things that didn't matter and too little of things that did. It was the schooling that filled him with a love of words and mysteries about figures and music with no melody you could hum to yourself. The woman had insisted on putting those things in him. And for what? So he'd be unable to stand the peace of the hills at nightfall?

He spat across the porch and wheeled himself over the worn sill. It was an unnatural thing for a man's life to be constrained by walls. Three rooms, two beds, a table, an empty icebox, a salt barrel half full of bacon and side meat, and four chairs he could no longer use. The woman's dishes still in the cupboard. And David's door— always shut.

He reached to close the front door, to wall his thoughts into the past where all was fixed and sure, but the colt squealed and let the sound dwindle to a hollow grunt. He stopped, bound by what he heard, held himself from caring that the black had been spared the knife. Still it seemed fitting for such a creature not to have desire cut from his loins, to grow content with oats and easy days like some old man who'd outlived his usefulness.

\* \* \*

David had gloried through the morning at the knotting of his arms hard from the labor of the ax against the tree. Now the sun burned hot, and the promise of cold biscuits and beans gnawed at his plans for the second one. He sank his ax into the stump and started an even plod down the turn row.

3

The morning hadn't been bad. He'd gotten the first of the pair of cedars out. Next year, there'd be no spindly growth from the furrows near the trees, just perfect rows, quarter mile and longer to the east, straight and clean. He crossed the snake-like tracks left in the sand by Jesse's wheelchair, climbed the ramp onto the porch, and shuffled past the old man. He stopped at the blue-chipped water basin and yielded to the gnawing in his gut knowing his words were apt to be turned back on him.

"That was Morgan this morning?"

Jesse stared in the direction of the lone cedar. "You saw him."

"What'd he leave the horse for?"

"He's a colt. Two-year-old. Three at the most."

David glanced above the dingy towel. "You going to help break him?"

"Nope. Tie a rope to his tail and teach him to drag me around."

He slapped the towel across the peg, stepped through the door and toward the sink before he felt the restrained moan of the threshold beneath Jesse's wheelchair. "Is he gonna pay for the use of the pens?"

"You want to pay every time we use his truck?"

It galled him, Jesse bringing up the truck again. "It was your truck till you gave it to him. And we pay plenty every time we do business with him." He shuffled to the salt barrel, looked back.

Jesse nodded, agreeing with himself over something. Seemed to be all the concord the old man ever needed. "I owed him."

He drove his knife into a slab of bacon, held his tongue. There was no way they'd owed Morgan the worth of that truck, near new at the time. But arguing with the old man was senseless.

* * *

David took his honeybread and coffee in the dark, trudged to the pens at first light. If he hurried, he just might be gone before Morgan came. It hurt to see the horse so poorly tended. On the days Morgan stayed, threw a Hoolihan over the slender neck and caught a wrap around the center post, he found work beyond the pines that drowned the strangled squeals.

He led the first mule to his traces just as Morgan rode in. No way to avoid what was coming, so he dipped his chin in civility. "Morning."

Morgan returned a toothy grin and nodded toward the colt. "Noticed you ain't been stickin' around. Don't want to see how it's done? About to

4

get the silliness out of him."

He turned away. Morgan had always believed the old man a minor god of the minds and wills of horses. Worse, the man seemed to think his discipleship an entitlement to speak to him the way the old man did. He shrugged, caught the squinty stare. "Maybe, if you don't ruin him first." He slipped the chain into the hames.

"If he ruins that easy, I don't want him."

An instant rage rose within him, demanded voice. "Then you don't want him. Whatever breathes ruins easy."

Morgan rubbed the stubble on his chin. "Well, I had been thinkin' to sell him."

He snapped the chains into the singletree, watched from the corner of his eye as the rope slapped first against Morgan's thigh then the center post groaning from the strain. The hooves shook the ground. Some rhythm, ancient and beyond thought, drummed in his chest. A quick buzz and the loop went tight. The colt's eyes were wide and rimmed in white, his nostrils flared to barrel in air that wouldn't pass his throat. But the eyes...

"How much do you want for him?" The words rose unbidden.

"You'd hitch a horse like this to a plow?" Morgan's grin appeared within a cloud of dust.

"You'd kill him?" He detested the shiver in his voice. Likely, Morgan heard it, too.

The teeth again. "Hundred dollar bill."

"You don't really expect..."

Morgan approached the colt, moved hand over hand along the singing hemp.

"All right." He caught his breath, presented his chin as if he felt no shame. The deal would be talked about for days at Morgan's store. "I'll give you the hundred, but I'm taking out some for the alfalfa you've been feeding him."

Morgan coiled and struck, grabbed the colt's lip with his left hand, threw his right arm above the mane and wrenched the colt's ear, pulling his head toward the ground. "If you don't let me twitch you, I'll string you up, you high-headed son of a..." The curse faded into dust.

"You've got your hundred, Morgan. Why don't you just leave him be?"

Morgan squinted into the shaft of sullied light. "What's the matter with you, boy? It's only a horse trade."

"I'm good for it. Just leave him alone." He wasn't apt to hear the end of this anytime soon, but the black was as desperate as he was beautiful, and the old man with his cow ponies and Bible stories would never understand that. He'd think he'd won, too. "I'll bring you the money. Just let him go."

"Hard part's over. If you want him, you can have him tied. Same money as he'll cost you loose." Morgan dawdled, seemed to want the moment to last, maybe to have more to tell about how Jesse's boy was squeamish, had no heart to him.

"It's my money, Morgan. Just turn him loose."

"It's your old man's money, but it don't make no difference to me. Untie that end. When I get my hand in the loop, you slip that stringing. And build a fire in your breeches." Morgan wrenched the ear, bringing it to his mouth to vise between his teeth. The colt stepped forward, threw his head, and sent the gaunt figure flying backwards. Morgan shook, rolled to his feet and spat red-streaked saliva.

David squelched a smile. "Doesn't appear to be ruined yet, though."

Morgan's grin was gone. "Hundred dollars, boy. Have it to me by Saturday or I'm coming after him."

"You'll get it. You know that." The smile broke free. Fact was he'd be gaining either way, Morgan coming after the colt or leaving the poor thing in peace.

Morgan spat, mounted the gray and rode through the gate. The twisted brim of his hat floated on a shaft of light shielding the face beneath it from the waking eye of Jove. Adam come again, spitting, hissing, banished from the garden to the pines below. David breathed deep, his heart some freer. It pleased him to see Morgan in the old man's way as something fallen, but it pleased him more that the seeing of it held no power over him. He eased toward the railing.

The colt stood, his ears pinned, watching his every move.

"Come on, boy. You won't be bothered now." He stared into the eyes, all blackness and fear, then turned back to the mules. He snapped the last set of trace chains into the singletree and trailed them to the field an hour behind his usual time.

The rows stretched from everlasting to everlasting, the plow points turning weeds to die by measure before an indifferent sun. David gripped the handles and trudged behind, each step a battle with his will to return to the pens and start the colt.

The sun had burned its way into the sand before he loosed the mules, fed them, and stood before the black in the growing dark and watched him pale to shadow. "You don't trust me yet, boy, but we'll be friends. You wait and see." He shoved away from the rails and walked to the house, strode past the washstand and went inside, washed his face and hands at the sink. Jesse leaned from his chair, his lips parting to form the familiar sneer.

"What do you expect to do with him?"

The old man's voice brimmed with the delight he showed at the promise of failure. His gut clenched. He'd been found out, most likely when Morgan picked Jesse up on the way to get mail. He buried his head in the towel.

"Won't be worth much if he's not broke. If you want, I'll help you halter him." The old man's voice had softened.

A frail anger rose at Jesse for breaking the comfort of their contempt. He'd wanted the horse to quiet his secret hunger, was sure the old man knew it. His weakness, floating to the top again like a dead skunk in a cistern.

"Set up some panels. Run him up into the chute to feed him a few mornings. Get him used to your touch before you try anything." The old man spoke into the corner, entertaining some ghost from his past.

He should have thought of the panels himself. Why was it he needed the old man to supply him with answers? Even now. "I need that other cedar out of there. Need to be planting wheat. Haven't prowled the cattle in a week. I've got no time for that fool horse."

"He's a colt. Coming three at the outside." Jesse's chin rose, his face steeled. David knew the look. He despised himself for refusing the old man's tender, but he couldn't chance letting Jesse in with so much held over him. He stepped outside, let the door slam shut.

7

\* \* \*

David pulled the buckboard loaded with seed wheat to the edge of the field and covered it with a tarp. He stared across the wheat ground, clean and freshly tilled. The summer still blistered, had been a hard one, but the land was ready, showed the effort he'd put in. He hitched the mules to the grain drill then followed behind, trudging between the wheels as the mules plodded the soft earth. Hour after hour the field narrowed indiscernibly, the drill grew lighter, and the sun dragged toward evening.

An hour of light remained when he surrendered and returned to the pens. He told himself the mules were done in, but something more beguiled him, something he needed as surely as the team needed rest. When he reached the shed and saw the colt, the black, icy edge of the horse's stare, he knew what it was that had lured him home, but it had no name or reason to it.

In the sand before the tack shed, a pair of thin tracks switched their way to the pen where the colt stood cautious, nostrils flared, waiting for the whirl and snap of the rope. Just beyond the chute, the tracks turned and plowed back to the house.

He pulled hard from the cooling air, dreading to find in Jesse's eyes something shared where there had been only emptiness for as long as he remembered. Since his mother died.

She'd been gone so long, had left in him only the faintest of images he had no power to conjure— the slender neck, the airy scent, the brightness of her auburn hair, the supple whiteness of her hand as she lifted and piled the tresses in a knot at the top of her head. But the contempt was comfortable now, part of the certainty between him and the old man. The colt could destroy that, bring something to the surface that would have to be tried, contended for, nurtured.

Still the horse drew him, refused to let him loose— the eyes brimming with mystery and kinship. And desperation. The blackness thrilled him like terror, like the darkness of the lake that had bewitched him as a child. And drew him still. He stared at the horse, wondered again what it was that things of beauty shared, ratcheted his courage to go inside.

"Where you been?" The old man stirred in his chair, cleaned his glasses with his shirt.

"Checking on the colt." He knew the tone, stared at the lone cedar, waited.

"He still where you left him?"

He held his peace. Jesse would have his taunt regardless.

"He's not apt to leave with the gate shut. The gate shut?"

"Yeah." He ceded the loss, stretched his neck and wished for the old man to return to whatever he'd been reading. "Need to ride through the cows sometime. Haven't checked them in over a week."

"You said as much the other day. Your chatter's not apt to get it done." Jesse returned to the narrow kerosene glow. A letter from Naomi, his sister in Grimsland, lay open on his lap.

He shuffled to the sink to draw water for the tub. Best to give Jesse a wide berth when he was like that.

David lay on the floor still fresh from his bath, awake and waiting for the first shadows of the moon to soften the room grown hard with knowing. He settled beneath the mantle of his lamp, descended into a new Steinbeck he'd ordered from Brighton, one causing some sort of row over Steinbeck's plea for socialism.

His books had offered relief once and remained his most prized possessions. But his work, his plans, seeing the land change beneath his hand, gave his days purpose, even joy. It was the nights that were so hopelessly the same.

He looked into Jesse's corner, listened to him mouth Naomi's words. It struck him there, in that moment, what the colt could mean. He'd understood the horse could be ridden, could carry him faster than nightfall away from the house. But he hadn't thought, until now, how he could ride free of the muttered prayers and that room grown foul with loathing.

"I'm going to bed." He breathed in the darkness, waited. The old man's susurrations held their rhythm and strength. He waited, stared, then slipped behind his door.

The night passed in a fevered vision that gave no rest. He stared into the black-eyed mystery of the colt; it understood the fire within him, and they were one. He saw it asleep and awake and somehow in a place that was neither.

Gray light urged him from his bed. He boiled his coffee as the old man slept and sensed a freshness as from a rain, though there'd been no rain, stepped onto the porch, sipped his steaming brew rich with cream, and stared across the field until the lone cedar captured him. It looked sad standing beside the stump of its mate. The notion brought a shiver, and he turned away. He had no time for thoughts of a cedar standing alone against the winter, for imaginings that would have him breathe a spirit into it or life into the hills. That was the old man's way, finding magic behind things where there was nothing but the shadow of the thing itself.

Jesse needed all that to feed the melancholy he poured into his letters to Naomi, to wear on his chest like a badge. He held the dregs for a moment behind his tongue, swore an oath to the ceiling joists, they being as high a thing as he could see, that he'd never hold misery like a wife or gloat on his failures like a cat too proud of its kill to eat it.

* * *

The colt breathed his impatience into the blue, wheeled at the sound of footsteps and hurled into the mist. David stopped, felt the first fear return, sensing the distance between the night's dream and the morning.

The black thundered into the sameness of dawn. He took the bucket from the tack shed and scooped in oats, approached from the side most chilled hoping the scent would draw the tensed, black figure.

"C'mon, boy." He let the words flow softly, felt for a moment his mother's hand tousle his hair. "Step up now, boy." He placed the bucket in the opening of the chute and stirred the oats until the nostrils flared. The black stood, determined either in fear or will. "Here's your feed, boy, whenever you're ready."

He stayed too long waiting out the black, would have to ride one of the mules through the cows another day. The sun was well above the pines when he harnessed the team, the colt flinching with every slap of leather, and trailed them to the field.

The team plodded the rows in even succession dragging a complacent sun across the sky, David trudging behind. The oats would do the trick, he was sure. Tomorrow would be easier, the next day easier still, to lure the

10

black into the chute where he could be caught. There he would soothe him, inure him to touch and voice and, before long, halter him. It was only a matter of time. The horse would come to trust him, to expect his tenderness. To know his heart.

He didn't wait to unharness the mules when he came in, just hawed and ran to the colt, hoped for something different. The black stood in his usual place, ears pinned and nostrils flared. The oats were untouched.

\* \* \*

David ate his shredded beef but left most of the molasses and cornmeal mush for the old man. It was Jesse's favorite, and little seemed to be left for him to enjoy. He stared out the window, watched the blue light fade. The silence was unbroken save for the clinking of Jesse's spoon mining what molasses remained in the jar.

"When you're ready to work with that colt, boy, I'll help you run him into the chute."

He flinched at the suddenness of the words. The offer laid him bare. The old man had likely seen the oats and knew that he'd failed to win the colt over. Jesse would never have tolerated such coddling, would have forced the horse into the chute or let him be choked down at the end of a rope. But to conquer the colt would destroy what he needed most from him, and the old man would never see that.

"All right." It was all he could think to say. But he knew he wouldn't ask for help. The black was his, and the last thing he wanted was to see him ruined, too.

\* \* \*

The dream brought a promise of freedom that made Jesse's mutterings intolerable. David escaped the house, stood in the wind and watched the moon move out of the pines. Under the deception of its half-light, he saw himself atop the black moving in perfect rhythm. But the fancies and deceptions grew old, and he walked to the pen and talked to the horse, stood near him so that at least his scent and voice would be familiar.

When he returned to the house, Jesse sat staring at the stove, his Bible in his lap. "You make me remember when I was young." The old man offered no preamble. "I worked hard and most of the time that was

11

enough. But sometimes, like on Sundays, I'd get to thinking too much and get on my horse and ride. Just ride was all."

He choked at the old man's proffer. For all his willingness to counter, he had no words and let the silence cover them like a heavy blanket.

"You need to break that horse, boy." Jesse's voice flickered as if it might go out.

"I've got no use for that horse." His response was forced and lacked conviction.

"Maybe if you were to put a little sugar in his feed so he'd get to craving it, then always carry some with you, rub a little on your hands for a while so he'd smell it on you..." The old man raised his Bible almost to his glasses and mumbled breathlessly against the dark.

"Maybe so." He winced at the meagerness of it, willed to offer more. "Sure sounds like it'd be worth a try."

# Chapter II

Light flowed in ineffective rinsings along the wall, warped and twisted from the water trails on the windows. David rolled over, pulled the sheet back and reveled at the hushed sibilance of rain. The sustained, gray dampness made him think of mold and field mice that built hollows in the alfalfa and left the tack shed smelling of urine. And of Brighton, the trips occasioned by rainy days when he was small, and the smell of gasoline that seemed to travel with the truck like a ghost of the farm. Most of all, it made him think of his mother, the softness of her face, her freshness sitting beside the old man who was neither old nor silent then.

He swung his feet to the floor and pushed the hair from his face. Jesse had been an imperious figure, his jutting chin and wavy hair more black than gray in those days. And his eyes, dark and inscrutable. Every feature suggested a power scarcely held in check. But his father's hands were his strength, heavy and wide as his back when Jesse lifted him from the truck.

The rain whispered against the roof just as it had then. He pulled the least-faded pair of jeans from the drawer and relived the anticipation of Brighton, the gripping that was almost a fear. When they reached the hill stubbled with short cedar, his mother had always pointed to the endless lines of buildings and said: "See, David? Aunt Sarah lives just over there, just over that steeple there, see?" And him, always wanting to cry out for them to stop, to go back because he couldn't stand the falling thrill in his stomach. But he never did.

The pot had reached a low boil before he heard the old man sliding from his bed to the wheelchair. Something, a mystery more vague than

13

rain, called him to Brighton. He'd use the hackamore as an excuse, the headstall weakened by mice hungry for the salt sweated into it by one of the old man's memories.

He poured coffee into Jesse's tin cup, handed it to him as the old man emerged from his room. "I'm going into town. I'll need another three-ring hackamore for the colt." He moved quickly, hoping his keenness might squelch the old man's protest. "Can't work today, with the rain and all. I'll be back tonight. Beans and biscuits are under those towels."

Jesse shook his head. "Seems a waste. Can't you fix the old one?"

He raised his hand to show his haste, swallowed his coffee without allowing it to cool, and slid his scalded tongue behind his teeth. Outside, the morning cool was thick with the taste of pine, the air cleaner away from the house. He poured oats into the trough and looked back to see the colt drive into the shadows of the long pen in front of the shed, slide to a stop, wheel and kick.

"I'll be back, boy!" He turned and ran until his lungs burned, reached the blacktop and continued north to the top of the hill. Trucks were slowed to a crawl there by the grade, and once they started down, they wouldn't be inclined to stop. He hadn't been waiting long when a bobtail Dodge Brothers loaded with alfalfa hay ground to a halt.

"Need a ride?"

He nodded, stepped onto the running boards and opened the door.

"I'm needing directions." The driver was wet with sweat and covered in alfalfa dust. "Know how to get to 79?"

He pulled himself into the cab. "You'll cross it close to where I get out."

The man rested his arms on the steering wheel, an air of quiet weariness about him, cleansed by his work. David caught it in a glance, the mind put at peace by labor.

\* \* \*

The truck plowed through the morning heaviness above Brighton. David found the steeple and looked beyond, his memory covered in a dream that curled between the houses and flooded the streets with a cattail-cotton sleep. He'd hoped the drizzle would last so that Elise would be waking to the needle-whispered drops as he came into town. He needed to share at least that with her. He stiffened, scrubbed the back of his neck. What he hadn't let himself see became instantly clear— he'd come to tell her of the horse.

The brakes squealed, and he pivoted on the seat. "You'll turn left at the next light. I appreciate the lift."

He dropped to the street and ran beyond the green light, struck by the disparity of Jesse's place and Brighton, and slipped into the pretense of belonging.

He tramped past derelict buildings, a few abandoned, until he caught something new in the distance, an air of crystalline delight, a Runic rhyme keeping time, a tintinnabulation of the bells. Tintinnabulation. The music of the syllables matched the rhythm of his step until the ringing dulled in the morning peace. His thoughts turned to Elise again, and, this time, to James.

He'd first talked with James after a lecture, "Loss of Innocence in Shakespeare's Later Plays." He'd formed an instant bond with him. When James introduced Elise a few days later as his friend, they had seemed an unlikely pair, and he'd feared he might have shown his surprise. Months later, when she ran across the commons to greet him after class, he knew it was more than surprise he'd felt that day.

He looked past the buildings, listened for the music withering in the heavy air.

"David, I had to show you first." She was breathless, her face flushed with the bloom of spring.

She'd wanted to show him first. That was all he heard. "What is it?"

She dangled her hand before his face, a small diamond glittering in the suddenly jaundiced sun. "James gave it to me. He did it, Davey. It was just so— I mean, who'd have guessed?" Something in her face. What was she saying? That she wouldn't have— "It's beautiful, don't you think?"

The earth shifted on its axis, and he knew in that moment it would never be righted. "I— it is, Elise. It's beautiful."

"Davey? Are you all right?"

"Yeah. I— well, sure. Congratulations, Elise."

"Then you're okay with this?"

He stared. Nothing was okay. "I don't know. It's not..." He looked into her eyes. She seemed to be waiting for something. "Elise, if this is what you want, all I can say is, James is the luckiest man on earth."

She smiled, her eyes welling full. "Thanks, Davey." She spoke so quietly, he wasn't sure if he'd heard her or imagined it.

David slowed his pace, traced the silver sheen at the edge of a cloud, and remembered the delicate line of her face, the set of her mouth and the soft sculpture of her green eyes balancing her beauty with mischief. The silken angularity of her cheek, the golden sweep of her hair. And that vulnerability that always took him by surprise. But she was all the more captivating for it.

James was tall, round-faced, cherubic in his collar, and weighted by an ambivalent drawing of the brow. An unruly crop of blond hair fell in flagrant disregard of stylishness. Whether a blessing or a curse, his face was extraordinarily revealing, for he was both wise and confounded, perpetually surprised by human frailty no matter how often he saw it. Elise anticipated failures, waited for their exposure and found their every appearance a delight.

All that seemed so long ago, distanced by experience in a way even time couldn't soften a thing. To his thinking, he should never have had to meet James or Elise at all. Like the old man or the colt, they seemed to have always been a part of him.

He drove his feet into the clearing fog and looked around. He was in the flats, the Negro section of town, had been over the bridge that marked the beginning of graffitied walls and silhouetted doors less than a dozen times in his life. An old Crown Victoria oozed past, the front laden with Black men in slick suits and fedoras. In the back, red and yellow blossoms bobbled above the heads of the women. Another man, stooped with age or labor, his suit too heavy and large, met him on the sidewalk, stared. He nodded and passed, felt no obligation to explain his presence. He fit as well here as the old man's place. Or hers.

The suits, the bells, the flowered hats. He stopped, let it settle in. He'd come on a Sunday. There'd be no place open to buy a hackamore. He'd have to repair the old one. Another victory for the old man.

Notes reached him first, then phrases. The music lifted on a holy breeze, swelled from a clapboard church. The wood beneath the white-chipped paint was cracked and gray, but the air was alive, the strains a part of him as if he were the dreamer of the same dream. But they were rising from a tomb, sealed with the dust of blind and desperate truths. Some things, it seemed to him, had no connecting places, as James had no connection to a bloodless God. Why would a man so full of life and love choose to revel in parched imaginings? It was beyond his understanding.

David slunk across the wooden sidewalk blanched by seasonal torrents of law and gospel, found a perch on the top step, sat down and surrendered to the memories charged by the voices that filled the breeze. They jolted him like terror then melted just as quickly to a warm comfort.

His enchantment with Elise had grown almost without his knowing on the afternoons he walked across campus from his rented room behind McKelvey's Grocery to the student chapel. He listened there, sometimes for hours, to James play first the piano then the organ. He and Elise sat and laughed about James' "evening sabbaticals" at the keyboard when his music took him far away from them both. But the hope was born on the fall afternoon he stood beneath the choir loft held by the beauty of the piece James played.

"What was that?" he'd asked.

"Beethoven," James replied. "He called it 'Für Elise.' I would have, too."

He'd stared at his friend, found no words to cover his shame, knew beyond a doubt that James had seen what he'd been hiding. "I know, James. I would, too."

Since that day, he'd yearned to distill something flowing and pure, to take all the magic he'd seen, put it into one whole and give it to her, to his Elise, to James' Elise.

But he wasn't an artist like Beethoven, or even like James, though he saw the magic of the colt's prance, and, even then, was a part of the passion flowing from the church. He felt the spirit in the breeze and knew, for all his distrust, that something more than myths and stubborn, lonely lives swelled the music with power.

The voices strained, wove a magic in the breeze that stirred an aging cottonwood to bend low beneath the sun. David listened, rhythmed silent words, fit them to the saintly timbre swelling the air.

The preacher droned, the words more music than understanding until something sure took shape within the flow. What was certain, he said, was the Word, for the Word bore faith, was the substance of things hoped for, the evidence of things not seen. He let the notion sink beneath his understanding and watched the stirring in the trees. It pulled within him, and he hoped it might be true. The unseen substance took up his fancy, filled it with spirit and life. The preacher droned on, his words a holy breath lifting the cottonwood.

The Word was present, the preacher said, at the beginning of the worlds. It was the Light that was the Light of men. The Word brought Truth, and by its shining we have all come to know that what is, is. The preacher grew quiet, the organ died, and the breeze stood still until he spoke again. That Light, he said all hushed and low, was *alive*.

David caught his breath, wondered if it might be so for he'd seen it in the trees and felt it in his breast.

The Word became flesh and dwelt among us. The preacher burned hot. He had no notion of how the Word might be flesh, but if it were alive and rousing the cottonwood, then perhaps it was so. The thought thrilled him though he scarcely knew it as a thought at all, but as a knowing all its own. The preacher thundered on, but he remained, was taken with the might of the Word and watched a holy breath incite the leaves to dance.

The music waned in a trailing sadness that would have had it go on forever. A few worshipers breathed "Praise Jesus!" into the sacred stirring, and, as a tribute to the moment and the light dying with the strain, he whispered praises too, and let the moment end.

He rose from the steps, marched past the graffitied walls and climbed the boundary between two worlds. His steps were sure if his heart was not, so he vowed to steel himself against the doubt that would rob him of seeing her, of seeing them both.

He strode across the campus, followed the still-familiar path as though it were yesterday that he had hurried to listen to James play, to sit with Elise and taste the music of her smile. Those were the best days of his life.

\* \* \*

"David!" Elise was beautiful, smiling, holding to the open door, stand-

18

ing in a princess-styled, maroon suit, undoubtedly her Sunday best. He felt all the more shabby for it.

"We never see you anymore, Davey." She gave him a warm hug. "You should have gone to church with us this morning. James was brilliant." She turned and walked into the kitchen. "I tell ya, it's tough being married to a genius." She spoke as if Jesse's place had no hold on him and their lives now didn't form a barrier as wide as the bridge that partitioned the white-chipped doors and the magic a world away.

James walked from the study, abandoned his youthful step, extended his chest and assumed the posture of Elmer Gantry. David knew the role before he spoke. "We all have our crosses to bear, Mama." He extended his hand. "How are you, son?"

"Fine, Reverend, and yourself?" The uncertainty was gone. He grinned, glad he came.

"What are you doing in town?" Elise moved quickly from one cabinet to the next, speaking over her shoulder.

"Oh, they found oil on my Dad's place a few weeks back. Leased every acre he had." He inspected an apple. "He bought a new Packard and ran off with a prostitute. I'm in town to buy a new truck with some of my share. Thinking about buying a bigger ranch, too."

Elise spun around. "You're kidding, right?"

"Yeah, so what have you two been up to?"

She rolled her eyes. "Nothing quite that exciting."

"I didn't think so."

James, still the salvationist, gripped his shoulder. "Son, it seems to me you are in desperate need of past-o-ral counseling." The words were filled with tent revival intensity. "Now about those millions you stand to in-hay-rit."

"Whew, yes!" Elise suspended a hand above the baked beans and stirred with the other. "I can feel it!"

"We can forget the little pay-rish, honey. We gonna start our very own dee-nomination. Now, son," James turned back to him, "how would you like to be a bishop or something?"

He held his smile. "Well, you see, Brother James, the problem is, I'm an agnostic."

"That's all right, son. Ya' parentage don't matter so long as you're willing to commit your assets."

The laughter came free and easy. He was part of them again.

"You two! We can't just go off and start a dee-nomination on empty stomachs, now can we?" He glanced at Elise, caught his breath. She was in control of her charms and him in the bargain. "Daddy, you set the table, and Davey, you help me with the food."

"I really didn't intend to just drop in on your lunch. I guess I've lost all social graces living back there."

"It's no great loss, really. You were never very graceful, socially speaking." Elise batted her eyes. "It's good to have you home, Davey."

"Thanks." He edged out of the way. James stacked dishes, silverware, and serving plates to carry into the dining room.

"How are you, really? You know I've missed you two." He hated the sound of his voice, the melancholy that made him hear the old man. He hated it even more because it made Elise shrink from him.

"Yeah, well, we have too. I mean there doesn't seem to be much to look forward to these days with the war in Europe and all the saber rattling." She handed him a serving plate covered with roast beef. "There you are. Cut it up."

The radio screeched and whined as James fidgeted with the dials.

"You're going to stay and listen to the speech with us tonight, aren't you?"

His skin prickled at the expectation in her voice. "Speech?"

"Roosevelt's address. They think he'll take a stand on our moving back toward an alignment with the League of Nations. One of those accusation and denial dialogues with the Nazis, I'm guessing. I wish Congress would understand that he's got to take a stand. With the fascists in China and Spain, and now this Tripartite thing with the Japanese and them next door to the Philippines and that ship off Greenland— what was the name of it?"

"I don't remember." He'd heard nothing about a ship off Greenland. He picked up the serving plate and followed her into the dining room.

"It really scares me." Elise stopped and looked at the table.

In Jesse's place, Nazis weren't real. Coy men didn't make veiled threats. Here he couldn't account for the need for hardness in his arms or fever in his breast, or of yellow lights melting cool between rocks and pine into the night. Brighton wasn't a fitting place for phantom hooves slicing sharp and quick against the moon, of him and the black, smooth and flowing in a single motion. It would be more fitting to tell her what he'd learned of faith, perhaps, the flowing passion in the breeze, but then he'd want her to know how she was a part of that for him, and he couldn't tell her that.

"I've got a new horse. He's beautiful. Black as night. I'd love for you to see him." He turned to her and held her stare. "He's really special."

"Horses were more your dad's area of expertise, weren't they? You were always talking about poetry or airplanes. I never did see the connection there."

The words stung for a moment. "His eyes, Elise. If you could see him..." He hoped she understood more than he could tell her. "He just knows things. Senses them, you know?"

\* \* \*

David dropped from the running board and stared above the trees. The morning blazed in a violent consanguinity of earth and sky. He was tired, worn from all he'd seen since he last slept. Still he hungered for the beauty and the calm. And all he saw made him yearn to weave a song of colors from the pine and wild verbenas and Indian blankets, from the earth and burning sky, to compose his own "Für Elise," to hold it all in one piece and give it pure and whole to her.

The hills had a nearness to them that the voice on the radio didn't have. When Roosevelt spoke, James scowled and paced the floor. Tears flowed down Elise's cheeks for the hopes she had in men who spoke with cautious eloquence and for the tenor of the failing voice saying it would have her be strong despite the piracy and rattlesnakes on an ocean far away. She had turned to him then and told him of the hope, and he returned, for a moment, to the way things were before.

The beauty of the morning was all he saw before the house appeared. Too soon. David braced himself to go inside.

"Where you been?" The old man twisted his face into a pout. "I've been awake all night wondering what you'd gotten yourself into." His voice was thick and his eyes glazed from having been awakened.

21

He pushed past the questions. "There's trouble with Germany. It's all you hear on the radio. Nazis fired on one of our ships. Twice. Said there was no way it could have been a mistake."

The old man growled and shook his head, but he was sure Jesse couldn't put a meaning to it, either.

"Roosevelt said we would shoot any Nazi rattlesnake on sight in the Atlantic. And Winchell says boys, men he said— younger than me by five years, some of them— are lining up to enlist in the Navy. Sure looks like we're getting into it."

The war seemed no more real for the telling. Still, he understood that lives beyond his own might not always allow him to live in disregard of them. Men with polished tongues who spoke shadow words could hinge their jaws and crush his life, could stop the flowing passion of the voices behind the white-chipped doors. They could voice with eloquence the virtues of destiny and dominance, of natural order and the redistribution of wealth, of Fatherland and supremacy, and people would lose their worlds and spill their blood-red dreams.

The house grew quickly stale, and David stepped outside. The colt squealed his stallion squeal and thundered across the pen.

He whistled in return. "Better learn that whistle, boy." He walked to the tack shed to fill the bucket with oats and sugar. "Step up now. Got your breakfast for you."

The colt moved forward dropping his hooves with each footfall as from a momentary pointe. His caution seemed more game than fear.

"Come on, little dancer." He extended his hand, caked and sticky. "Little Dancer." He spoke it aloud, trying the sound of it. "My Midnight Dancer." The colt threw his muzzle forward in a quick jab to motion him away from the trough.

"Not this time. You'll have to come to me first."

The black took a tentative step, stretched to smell the oats and sugar on the extended hand. He pulled back but didn't run.

"Good boy. That was a good start." He brushed his hands and eased back toward the railing.

"That's a fine animal. Don't you go and ruin him, make a pet out of him!" The old man hollered from the porch. The colt broke free and ran to the far end of the pen. He had seen it before. Jesse seemed angered by his fondness for the horse, was intent on keeping the black fearful. Affection, the old man always said, should be reserved for people, for family. For him.

"There's no chance of that with you around! You afraid I might do something you couldn't do?"

"I'm your father. Don't you talk to me that way! You of all people. If I had talked to my father that way—"

"Your father died. You couldn't talk to him that way."

Jesse wheeled himself toward the pens. "So you want me to die. Is that it? You want me to die so you can have this place."

"I don't want your place. I've got enough things to hold me back now."

Jesse stopped in the shade of the tack shed. "That temper, David. Why? And why at me?"

"Why can't you let me be?" He glared into the shadows.

The old man turned back toward the porch shaking his head, pushing furiously against the chrome rings. "Why have I been given this in my old age? Lord, why?" Spit flew in bright penumbras against the morning sun as he pushed through the heavy sand before the house. Jesse slowed, raised his head against his silent God. "Why would you do this to me? Give me a son like this?" The old man slumped in his chair.

David leaned against the railing and watched from the corner of his eye, fearing the severing that would take the old man and leave him without a center. Hate, he was sure, was as great a bond as love could ever be.

"Go on inside." He squeezed the words, choked them into civility. "I'll come in after a while and fix us breakfast."

The old man breathed as if some great pain were falling away. "You've got a meanness to you, boy—just like your mother's."

"Yeah, I know." He bit his lip, wished for Jesse to let it go and waited until the old man was behind the door. Still he stood, pushing what had happened from his mind, willing the horse to return. After a few minutes, he eased toward the colt.

"Come on, Dancer. Come on, boy." His words flowed soft and gentle. "It's just you and me now."

Dancer circled and watched as he narrowed the distance between them.

23

The colt backed, forced his hooves hard against the earth. He edged closer. Dancer retreated, dragging his hooves. A step away from the wire and the jagged planks, the colt froze. He watched the throbbing pulse in the horse's neck, smelled his fear. The black was sensing a trap, likely waiting for the rope.

"It's all right, boy. I'm not going to hurt you." He extended his hand, caked in sugar. Dancer reached to smell, jerked back and wouldn't smell again.

He eased forward. A flash, the dark rippling of muscle beneath black sheen, a jolt as the powerful shoulders moved over him. Something popped, distant and indistinct, but his alarm was spent, and he groped in a dark comfort. All that remained of his fear had drained away. Hooves thundered at the far end of the pen, circled back. A frost came, blew against his face, and the comfort left as quickly as it had come. He lay in the dust warmed by a hot breath, opened his eyes to see Dancer, poised and wary, nostrils flared and ears brought forward in a curious gaze. David raised his head. A searing throb followed him to his knees. He crouched staring at a piece of splintered railing lying in the dust spattered with blood. The colt snorted and backed away.

"Pretty quick, old Dancer." The words surfaced on soft, slow breaths as he worked to cover his weakness, even from the black. He drew himself to his knees, steadied and stood. The horse wheeled and ran to the far end of the pen. He tongued the salt-metallic taste of blood against his teeth and drew his arm across his face. The sleeve came away red and wet, spotted at the edge with manure. His legs trembled. Dancer ran from one end of the pen to the other, his neck wet and frothed and his rump streaked with lines of sweat.

He extended his right hand, approached at a cautious pace, but Dancer turned again and ran. He opened the gate in the corner of the pen and slipped back. The colt thundered in, and he threw the gate closed behind him. It was a small enclosure, barely large enough for Dancer to turn. Still he spun.

"It's over, pretty boy. It's over. Everything's changed, now. I'll treat you right, boy, but this is the way it's got to be." He reached to smooth the frothy neck, but the colt fought his touch. "They won't let you just run these hills and collect mares, boy. Those days were over a long time ago." He slipped the noose from the gatepost and pulled the gate into the horse. With all his draining strength, he wrapped the lead end of the halter to the far side of the chute. "If you let me, I'll be your friend, but you got to let me, boy. I can give you a home, but your freedom's gone. You were born to this, same as me."

He looped the halter wide around the silken neck, and the colt threw his head against the limits of the tether. "Now we'll get to know each other, old Dancer. You'll find out I have a will, too." He reached again to soothe the lathered neck, but the black squealed and flung his head against the rail. The soft skin of his muzzle split and bled. With a sudden hope, David ripped the blood-wet sleeve from his shirt and tied it through the halter and across the bleeding muzzle. Dancer threw his head and snorted furiously at the scent he couldn't escape.

"Take it easy, now." He steadied himself, rose to the top of the make-shift chute and slid his left boot through the railing on the opposite side. With his leg extended above the black's withers and neck, he held himself with his right arm, reached inside to find a knowing for the colt and found instead the cold edge of fear. He stepped down with his right foot, positioned it on the middle rail and looped the halter over the flailing head, threw the lead around the top rail and pulled the colt's head to his chest. He waited for the horse to still and released his grip a little at a time until his right hand was free, pulled slack from the rope and took a careful wrap around the gatepost. A squeal filled the hollow of his gut. Still he strained, grew wet with sweat, held the head until the storm subsided. The colt eased, the calm purchased with draining strength and will. He breathed hard against the quivering jaw, hooked his left arm around the fine-boned face, patted and soothed the underside of the neck.

"Now you know my will, don't you? We'll be friends, though. You just wait and see." He held the head that wouldn't yield as the minutes drained to weariness.

* * *

Jesse minded the struggle from the doorway, shook his head and snarled at the pathetic display.

"Boy, get in here! It's time for breakfast."

25

David remained perfectly still perched atop the railing astraddle the black, a foot on either side of the chute. He shook his head. The boy held that animal like he would a baby, as revolting a display as he'd witnessed since the day he'd had to show the boy his weakness.

"C'mon, boy! Come fix our breakfast!" He clenched his teeth behind the words and swallowed down the bitterness. The boy couldn't have been much more than ten when it happened, twelve at most, but of an age to learn what work was. They'd found a missing cow they'd been prowling for, David riding that worthless paint mare he'd gotten for a song, and him on the big sorrel. Stout horse, he was, and rough. The cow was fevered, mastitis about as bad as any he remembered, her calf starving. Looked half dead, the both of them. And the boy? My God, the boy couldn't take his eyes off that starving waif. Until he made him.

Had to rope the cow, trip her. Put a second loop on a hind leg to keep her down. She was a mean one, too. Hadn't been much hope of her being useful after that, near no hope of saving her calf. But he ordered the boy to strip her udder, her still fighting mad, three feet free. Only way to save her.

Jesse grunted, shook his head again. The boy couldn't do it, couldn't make himself move in close. He'd run at her all right, but she'd bellow and kick and David would go running back to that paint. Had to be shown. If the boy was ever to become a man, he had to know that someone would always pay when he couldn't do his job. So he shot the calf. The boy had to see.

He'd never forget what David did then. Stood there beside that cow, not ten feet away, as if he all of a sudden had no fear. The boy looked him in the eyes, tears running off his cheeks, and demanded to be shot himself. Now why would he do that? What was wrong with a boy that would want to be shot over some near-starved calf?

He clenched his hands, rankled at the injustice of having a son with a woman's heart. "Boy, get in here! Quit fooling with that horse! It's time for breakfast."

* * *

David felt the hot coal of anger burning in the hollow of his gut where there had been only the rattling echo of Dancer's grunts. He couldn't holler back for fear of bringing a change to the steady tremble of the head.

That was what the old man wanted, for him to have to fight the horse into submission, and so he remained silent, forcing down his rage.

When he heard the ring of metal wheels against the earth, closer and stronger with every breath, he knew the old man wasn't going to let him win. In seconds that he counted away with loathing, the sound was just beneath him.

"What's the matter with you, boy?" The words exploded from between the old man's teeth, and Dancer's head, quick and sure as a hammer, slammed into his chest. David clawed for rail or post but found no purchase, slammed against the earth and drew hard for air beneath the flashing fury of the colt. He wanted to curse the old man, grab him and pull the air from the gristled throat. He captured a partial breath and struggled to his knees.

Jesse sat in his chair peering down, the ire gone from his face. David followed the old man's stare, raised his hand to his cheek, the skin parted and wet, drew his fingers before him red and tacky. He looked at his father. Jesse drew a breath, seemed ready to say something but stopped. If the old man feared for him, he'd lost the way to tell him so.

"Are you crazy? You ought to have more sense than to try a fool stunt like that! Anybody'd know better!"

He held the squinted stare. "Damn you!" It took all the air he'd gathered, and he paused to fill his lungs.

The old man cried, shook his head. "How can you talk to me that way? I'm your father!"

"Damn you!" His words were full of loathing. "You had to have your breakfast now? Just when the black was beginning to settle down?"

"You'll ruin that horse trying to make him a lap dog! You hear me? You'll ruin him!"

He found breath and strength to stand, stared down at Jesse as the old man had once stared down at him. "Just stay the hell away from him!"

Jesse shook his head, his face twisted. "You'll ruin him! You'll never be able to trust a horse that doesn't fear you." The old man leaned from his chair, his stoutly quivering finger jutting upwards.

David stood erect. "That's all you've ever wanted, isn't it? To be feared. Well, the dreaded Jesse Dremmer is riding a wheelchair. So who's going to fear you now, old man?" He turned away, hated himself for saying it, and the old man, too, and the morning, and the colt. He was sick of a world gone yellow with decay, wanted only to be free of life. He closed his eyes and wished himself wormed into the sand before the wind howled even his stench away, to cede nothing of his having been but a hollow in the grass. He seethed at God, if he was there, for having allowed him to be, for creating him weak, unable to do anything but dream.

He left the old man staring pathetically up at him and stormed to the tack shed to get his ax, shoved himself into the morning, thought of something the old man quoted from his Bible and laughed. He'd known the truth and the truth hadn't freed but bound him, had held him tightly in the grip of what he was and would always be.

His steps grew heavy, sinking into the furrows, and somewhere between the pens and the cedar, the fire went low. He wanted no more of killing, sank beneath the tree and lost himself in hearing the wind in the cedar, a rain crow in the pines. The fire flickered, went out and he thought of how he'd always felt a kinship with all around him, with the wind and the cedar standing alone against the winter. He felt so much for all he didn't know but loathed the old man whom he knew so well.

* * *

Jesse watched David kneeling beneath the cedar thumbing his ax and wondered what it was that ruined him, for the boy was surely ruined, a colt that had run wild too long and refused to learn. Headstrong, fighting discipline, knowing only what he wanted, not taking instruction. And the woman, always comforting her little man after he'd shown him the proper admonition of the rod. It kept the boy from seeing that he was wrong, kept him from submitting. So now his son was a spoilt colt, a lap dog with no heart. That's why he'd had to show the boy what he was, that he would never amount to anything— but all too late for remedy.

He shook his head and pushed his chair into the darkness of the house, tasted the bile of injustice. God would make amends. He comforted himself with the certainty of it, for God would surely break the boy.

He leaned from the chair, pulled a slab of bacon from the salt barrel, looked through a tear in the screen, and watched as David moved the way

28

he did, half trotting, half shuffling toward the pens. He remembered the story of the prodigal son; his heart grew full, and his eyes spilled over. How he longed for the boy to come to him and seek forgiveness. Then he would show David his heart, take the boy in and instruct him in the proper ways of being a man.

# Chapter III

David plodded behind the mules, cut the sparse heads and made a game of spilling them against the sideboards of the wagon. The summer had burned with a desiccated howl that ripped across the hills, blistered the withering leaves and held fall at bay for weeks. When it was finally spent, it left the sorghum spindly and poor.

With only the hiss of mule tails as they swished flies and the tiny bursts of kaffir heads, he thought of Elise and lamented the poverty of having no way to share the richness of all he saw. Still, it was preferable to being like the old man whose greater poverty left him with nothing but shadow words to fill his empty soul.

The sun burned color into the air heavy now with autumn and evening. He hawed the mules, spread his arms and stretched his back, looked up. A dove descended just beyond the mules, hovered clean and pure against the sky— perfect, white and frigid. It was suspended against evening as if it were light itself. The moment slipped from time, and he stood frozen as a blackness he'd never known covered all he saw. It overwhelmed him, made him shrink from all around, even from himself. He was sullied, too, riddled and foul, captured by the inescapable certainty of his lack. More than lacking, he was sick and miserable and running down.

He held to the back of the wagon, his knees sinking in the loose earth, staring at the bright perfection. It was more than beauty. It was purpose. And, pinned in stark relief from a blood-red sky, the dove held out a promise he couldn't dismiss. He stared, forced himself to breathe, held the brightness until it cooed and lifted into the heavens.

* * *

David eased the wagon across the ruts, held the brake as the mules tottered into the dry creek bed. His last load of milo. The deal with Morgan was set. Thirty percent of the sorghum for half its weight in cotton seed, plus another twenty percent for grinding. Come winter, he'd be hauling the ground feed back out to the cows, sacked and mixed with the cotton seed. He stretched his neck, stared across the cane field, made another rough estimate of the bundles. They were due a hard winter. A few heavy snows and the cattle would be short of feed.

He squinted into the evening sun, braced his feet against the dash rail. Morgan had gotten a contract for the remainder of the grain. Wouldn't say who bought it or when he was shipping it out, ignored him when he'd offered to help load the truck. He straightened, the fire rising in his gut. Forty cents a bushel was all Morgan offered. Kansas City price was fifty-three. There was the trucking to be added in, of course, but it was likely Morgan had gotten more, pocketed the difference, hoped to have it shipped out without him catching word of it.

He let it go, eased back against the seat. As little as there was, it wouldn't matter. And he and the old man didn't need much. So long as they could cover the cost of seed in the spring. And he'd be selling calves off wheat pasture come March. They'd do better. He wouldn't have said so, but he was glad there were no more days to spend behind the wagon. Now he could start the colt again.

He looked across the sorghum field, fixed the spot where he'd seen the dove and felt a chill run down his spine. So beautiful and full of promise. But what had it meant?

* * *

David took his honeybread and coffee and sauntered out to Dancer searching the murky gray, jabbing his nose into the first light, hoping to catch the scent of sugar and the one who brought it. The black had grown accustomed to his voice and touch, seemed settled with things.

He stepped to the tack shed, scooped oats into the bucket, whistled and warmed at the colt's approach. "Hey, boy. What's on your mind, this morning?"

Dancer moved from the half-light, pawed at the shadows then wheeled

31

and thundered across the pen for the sheer joy of the power in his legs. David smiled. He felt it too, the power that made his pulse quicken as if he were thundering across the earth kicking away the shadows.

The colt circled back and stood. "You ready for school, pretty boy? Or just here begging sugar?" He edged close, stirred the oats. Dancer steamed his desire into the shapeless blue, pranced forward and extended his muzzle.

"Here you go, boy. Got your breakfast."

He watched as Dancer ate, traced his lines in the half-light and remembered the frosty clarity of the dove hung across the ruby sky. Below the frigid clarity of the bird, he and the earth were one, decayed and running down. The image intrigued him, so haunted him with promise that he would have cried out for an answer if he thought he might be heard.

* * *

David held a coffee cup in one hand. With the other, he pushed a skim of ice as light and supple as cream on fresh milk off the water trough. He straightened, placed his cup on the corral post and moved toward Dancer, ran his hand across the slender neck and withers, touched the elegant curve of Dancer's back. The coat was growing thick, losing the silk of summer. He patted the shoulders, full and sure now. Dancer turned to nuzzle his hand, and he wished for a moment that all mysteries could end so well.

He frowned, stroked the fine-boned head and scratched beneath Dancer's throat latch the way the horse liked. The north winds had brought a distance between the hills moving them further from the concrete swells and tintinnabulations. And from Elise. He ached to tell her of his dreams in the morning, to share what had blossomed in his sleep. But more often now he summoned the dove, took pleasure in its pledge, its promise haunting him.

But Dancer filled his days. He'd taught the horse his gaits and turns with a whip, snapping before or behind or to his side while voicing commands, certain that Dancer could sense the whip wouldn't be used against him.

The colt moved close, nudged in expectation of sugar and petting. He grinned. "Getting used to this, aren't you, pretty boy?" He slipped the brush from the wire hanger he'd attached to the top rail and swept it across

32

the black's neck and shoulders. He ducked beneath the colt's head and saw the old man glaring from the porch. Dancer stood patiently submitting to his requests, yielding his front feet. He edged to the hind legs, reached to run the brush down them.

"Don't you trust that horse, boy! No telling what he'll do." The old man's voice was sharp and charged.

Dancer flinched.

"Easy, boy. Everything's okay." David patted and soothed.

"A horse with no fear can't be trusted!" The old man's words were edged with bitterness, like the horse's ease was a thing of shame. Or maybe it was his ease that provoked Jesse. He held his tongue, continued to brush the colt, but Jesse's demand for reverence from a creature too pure to know shame filled him with a slow fury.

\* \* \*

"I tell you about breaking the roan mare?" Jesse stared through the window into the cold that David had come inside to escape.

"Yeah, you told me." It wouldn't matter. The old man would tell him again, had already set his mind to, he was sure. He poured himself another cup of coffee and reached inside the cabinet for the cream he'd ridden a mule to Morgan's to retrieve.

"Now she was a hard one. Wouldn't yield. I'd about given up on her making a saddle horse. Decided to harness her with old Barney. Laziest mule I ever owned. Hooked the both of them to the buckboard loaded with creek sand. She did the pulling for the both of them, I can tell you that. Took them right across that field." Jesse pointed across the kaffir stalks. "Fresh plowed, too. When she couldn't take another step, I threw a saddle and that rawhide hackamore on her. When I climbed on, I thrashed her all the way to the barn with a cinch strap." He shook his head and smiled. "She learned aplenty that day."

The strap burned across his back and words erupted from somewhere beyond his will. "There's no shame in being what you're born to be. No need to whip her for it."

"She had to learn. I taught her so she'd remember. Creatures aren't born to this earth knowing all there is to know, boy. Not even you. And who are you to be telling me?"

"Nobody. I'm nobody." He grabbed his coat and pushed the door open, would drink his coffee outside. More comfort in the morning chill than in the house with Jesse.

His flare-up, he was sure, would be the subject of another letter to his Aunt Naomi who'd appointed herself moral governor of the family. He couldn't remember a time Jesse hadn't turned to her as judge. He pictured her lamenting poor Jesse whom she had relegated to wardhood though he was seven years her senior. She'd seemed to take the old man as her own after her gentle-spirited Henry died. That wasn't long after Jesse's fall. Almost three years now. They'd likely conclude that he was unregenerate, that he had inherited his mother's deficiencies. She'd been subject to inexplicable outbursts, too, and, like him, was incapable of fitting herself into the proper order of things.

He set his coffee on the porch railing, shoved his arms deep into his coat sleeves and settled it on his shoulders. Naomi had sanctioned Jesse's refusal to join a church while his mother was alive. After all, he had the truth of his Separatist childhood, a truth Naomi dispensed in all its purity in her weekly missives as she meted out condemnations for the libertines and Elamites running the churches amok.

He swallowed, splashed the dregs on the ground, couldn't comprehend not questioning. For all the awe and reverence Jesse exuded over Naomi's railings, he'd learned only to distrust her.

For the most part, he ignored her. She was a part of Jesse's world, perhaps its center, as Elise and James and Dancer were his. When she paid her visits, he was expected to show the same sort of doting admiration for her the old man displayed. As a child, when he followed Jesse's cues and accorded Naomi the respect Jesse required of him, the old man had actually seemed proud. That might have been the only time his father had approved of him. The memory brought no pain. Just another way he and Jesse were bound to each other whether either of them liked it.

He raised the fleece collar around his ears, pushed his hat down and headed to the tack shed. He'd never understood the old man's tie to Naomi. She had none of the softness, offered none of the affectionate displays his mother or his Aunt Sarah or the other women had. Yet the old man set her apart, found in her something he deemed worthy of a reverence he gave to no one else. Jesse's sense of family had somehow never been extended to him or his mother. Something like what he felt for Elise and James, maybe, though nothing of the divine inhabited that. The old man seemed unable to separate his past, his childhood in the Separatist Church, his dominion of the land and its creatures, and his reverence for Naomi from his spirit world, his land of smoky myths and Truth. From God himself.

* * *

The morning glaze on the water trough thickened. He broke and cleared it in the mornings, but on colder days, it re-formed by noon. Still, his work was light. He fed through the morning hours, occasionally caught and doctored a cow or calf. But after David had eaten his bacon and beans or shredded beef and biscuits, Dancer had his full attention. He saddled the colt each afternoon, drove him, pulling on the three-ringed hackamore, the leads strung through the stirrups. On the best days, Dancer turned and spun, enjoying the game of it, responding to the subtle tugs on the lead, sensing what he was signaling before he was sure himself. But more often now, the colt seemed bored by the simplicity of it all and was reluctant to go through his paces. It was time. He could no longer put off what had to be done.

He said nothing to Jesse of his plan to mount the black. The old man would recite all the reasons he wouldn't be able to stay with the horse who was, by Jesse's estimation, spoiled and an outlaw. Instead, he went out at his usual time but took no breakfast.

His whistle shattered the November chill. Dancer emerged from the gray to accept first the blanket, then the saddle. When he tightened the cinch, Dancer responded with his usual ill-humored grunt. But when he led the colt into the round pen and began to mount him, Dancer whirled in a sudden panic and backed away.

"Whoa, boy. You're all right, now. Just ease up." He crowded the horse against the pen wall. Dancer spun into him almost taking him off his feet.

"Hey, pretty boy. Easy, now. No need to make this a contest. Just trust me. There doesn't have to be a loser here."

Dancer wheeled and lunged to the end of the lead and spun again. He had no choice but to mount him in the chute then open the gate into the

35

holding pen. If the horse decided to buck, there'd be no holding him in an area that size.

He shivered. It might well be that this dream of oneness was nothing more than illusion, the fairy-tale-believing child in him wanting to see something more in the black's reactions than the desire for oats and sugar. He tied a knot in the rope, his fingers shaking and stiff, looped it over the top of the gate and the corner post. He led Dancer into the planked enclosure and pulled the gate behind him. The colt's eyes were wild, seemed near to losing the trust and calmness he'd gained.

"Easy, boy. This has to be done, now. You really haven't left me a choice."

He patted the slender neck, felt a new dampness beneath his hand and eased his weight into the saddle. His boot, searching for the sureness of the stirrup, touched the stallion's side. Dancer erupted, pawed the air, began climbing the chute and squealing in wild fury. The crashing blow of the horse's weight slammed first against one leg and then the other. He gripped the rope leads and tried to soothe him.

Dancer blew heavily into the frosty air and shook his head. He sat for a moment, hoping to wait out Dancer's panic. But the colt refused to calm, stomped his feet and butted his chest and forearms against the two-by-eight planks. He eased his right hand forward to slip the rope from the post, sat deep, pulled his feet across the heavy shoulders, jutted his pelvis and squared his shoulders over the horse's rump. The gate creaked open. Dancer, wary, waited for the trick in this offer of freedom. Seeing none, he bolted from the chute and dove against his stiffened front legs. David fought the leads, struggled to keep the fine-boned head from going to the ground. In a stormy yielding, the black reared, and he felt the awkward shift of weight rise above him and kicked to free himself from the falling fury.

A moment's descent and his back slapped hard against the earth. He looked up to see the saddle, a black mass above it pawing to gain a foothold in the air, slam across his right leg. He felt weight, but no pain, heard a faraway buzz, and sensed the awful dread of things changed forever. He lay on his back and stared helplessly as the flailing legs moved toward him, covered his face and waited, in a moment come too soon for fear, for the blow. Dancer grunted as the massive lungs convulsed. The black lay beside him, stunned and straining for air.

He craned his neck to see his leg. In the earth before his knee was the deep impression of the saddle horn and behind it the quarter-moon disc of the cantle. He stared in disbelief. His leg had been spared by the swell of the saddle.

Dancer rolled away from him, struggled to right himself, and in less than the second it took to shake free from his fear, he reached for the lead dangling from the three-ringer, missed and threw himself across the saddle just as Dancer found footing and air. A powerful thrust and the black was standing. He slid into the stirrups, took a firm grip on the one remaining lead and sat deep, prepared himself for what was to come.

Dancer trembled, shook like a dog coming out of water. He reached to recover the dangling lead, readied himself, in awe of the horse's weight and strength. Dancer appeared addled by the blow that had taken his wind, and stood perfectly still. He pulled the right lead, and the black responded to the request turning in an awkward spin to the right, then to the left. The horse remembered his cues and, after a few minutes, his gaits. The contest appeared to be over, but he withheld his praise. No words remained in him, and he was trembling too much to pat the quivering neck.

The two stood still and silent. He breathed deep and soothed the bristled mane, pulled the scattered tresses over the thin neck. "Now you know my will, boy."

\* \* \*

David spent every free moment with the colt, proud and pleased with him, but certain, too, that something had changed between them. Dancer came when whistled to, but came now in submission. If the horse had lost something in the contest, so had he. He'd come to depend on Dancer, to admire him and find joy in the affection that was offered or returned. Now there was only capitulation.

"Looks like he's learned who's boss. Long time in coming." Jesse stared at the pens as he stepped onto the porch. "See to it he doesn't forget. Respect's an easy thing to lose."

He nodded. The old man should know.

"It's God's order, boy. It's everywhere you look. One plant choking out another, one animal fearing another, all of them fearing man, and man fearing his betters."

He stood at the edge of the porch facing the lone cedar, his anger fanned by a south wind. The old man could never abide what wasn't in accordance with his perception of things, of one thing being subject to another, something always above, the other beneath. And what Jesse couldn't put into his order, he determined to be evil, contrary to nature. Contrary to God. An urgent fire burned within him to walk to the pens, throw the gate wide and free the stallion to roam the hills, return to Dancer his namelessness and will. But he couldn't bear to see him go. He drew hard from the coolness, stepped from the porch and scuffed to the gate to stare in silence at the dark eyes.

* * *

He gloried in the power beneath him. The horse had accepted the reins, made the transition from head to neck with ease. More importantly, he saw the colt's trust return. Dancer didn't wait now for a whistle but bounded to the gate at the first rattle of the door. When David worked in sight of the pens, the black nickered until he came with the brush or sugar or a soft word.

On days that Dancer worked especially well, the colt indulged himself, it seemed, after he had shown his cleverness and grace, in a greater play-fulness. David dared not wear his hat or leave his handkerchief exposed for fear of having it pilfered and carried off in thunder and dropped at the far end of the working pen.

David nudged Dancer toward two pink-eyed cows they'd separated from the herd. They'd been prowling cattle since early morning, had been at it for weeks. He grinned; Dancer had been born for this. The black already knew his job, dropped his head, pointed his ears toward the cattle, one ear twitching back to him. The horse waited for him to release the reins when he had centered on the cow to be taken. They were a team.

He squinted into the west. The sun was slipping low, a crimson mist rolling between the hills. The Summit Place had been the last purchase Jesse made before he was born and the biggest in the old man's life. Two sections of heavy loam and deep, mellow earth. Switch and Indian grasses

38

flowed in gentle swells, frothed in waves of white on purple heads; Little Bluestem cast a deep crimson shadow along the shallows and draws. He looked south in the direction of the house and lake though he could see neither. Miles of grass were broken only by the gilded shadows of yellowing locust groves and red and orange shinnery.

The old man must have been proud, seated atop whatever conquest he'd been riding at the time, to look over these hills at the swelling range, to sit horseback on the highest hill for miles around, his herd grass-fat and settled in the shallows. He must have loved being here, knowing he'd gained all this by sweat and persistence. And devotion. He felt the certainty of it in his gut. This was the old man's one real love. His throat contracted and his eyes filled. Jesse had lost so much.

He and Dancer pushed the two cows back to the pens, the miles taking the remaining fidget out of the horse. David leaned forward, patted the matted hair. "Won't be much longer, boy. We're almost there."

When they neared the pens, the cows balked, started to break, thought better of it when Dancer's head dropped, ready for the challenge. They turned and trotted, heads high and wary, through the gate. He rode quickly behind them pulling the gate with him as he came.

"We had a good day, boy. Real good day. Never would have guessed you'd take to this work like you have." He slipped from the saddle and gently lifted the bridle from Dancer's head, breathed deep and leaned against the wooden planks. The colt stared in quiet grace. He thought of the dove and Elise as he admired the black in the dimming light. "What is it that makes something beautiful, boy? You ought to know." He met the colt's stare. "I guess we all know it when we see it. Just none of us can say what it is. Has to have some measure, don't you think?"

Dancer nudged his hand. He made a loose fist and held it out to the black who gently lifted the fingers, nibbling with his lips, looking for hidden sugar lumps.

"Yeah, I suppose beauty is in the mouth of the beholder."

He turned and sauntered to the tack shed returning a minute later, his hands extended and full of sugar. He looked intently into the dark eyes and met a certainty that startled him. He had feared taking more from Dancer than he had a right to take, had worried over usurping the horse's freedom and will. In the end, they were surrendered, offered as a gift. And in the exchange, the colt had received something greater than he'd given. Dancer had become who he was born to be, had been unbridled from the dictates of the immediate and become something more than he could ever have been alone. By some exquisite harmony of design, some collision of destiny, the horse had surrendered his will in trust and gained a great truth.

But what was the light in those eyes? What was the truth Dancer saw? And could he, by some like surrender, gain something finer than the freedom to gather the objects of his most urgent needs?

# Chapter IV

## December 10, 1941

The distant thunder swelled within the morning chill. David slipped to the window of the tack shed, watched as Gus Hemner's cruiser surged above a plume of dust, the star on the door flaunting the morning brilliance between the pines. The Hudson strained to conquer the last knoll, halted and steadied beneath the bare elms. Sheriff Hemner dislodged himself from behind the wheel and trudged the remaining distance to the house.

Jesse sat leaning from his chair, poised at the edge of the porch. David's heart abandoned its steady gait, and he eased from the window to the doorway as the two carried on a pantomime that left the old man first shaking his head then holding it. Whatever Gus had come to deliver wasn't going to be avoided. He stepped from the dark and approached them at a reluctant pace.

"There's bad news, David." Gus was still puffing from his short walk. The big man paused and leaned against his right knee, his foot planted heavily at the top of the ramp. "The Japs attacked Pearl Harbor three days ago. We've declared war."

Prickly cold covered his head and spread quickly down his back. The chill settled in his bones.

Gus took off his Stetson and wiped the sweatband though the day was full of snap. "Nobody thought about you folks up here not knowing about it. Then this morning we got a telegram from Naomi Pendergraft. Your aunt?"

He nodded, felt his throat tighten.

"Seems she lost her boy, Robert. Went down on the USS Maryland. She asked that y'all be notified. I'm sorry, son."

He shuddered, looked at his feet, wondered what Robert had come to know before he died. *Robert.* "Thank you, Sheriff. We appreciate you coming."

Gus trundled back to the car; it still creaked in the morning chill.

He knew he should turn and face the old man. He hardly knew his cousin. The old man knew him little better. But Robert was Naomi's son, and for that reason, was special to Jesse. He stood looking after the Hudson until it was dust and memory, the scent of gasoline wasting into the hills. He kept his back to the old man, not wanting to see him cry, really cry this time.

"What do you want me to do?" He forced the words from his constricted throat.

"You go to her. Stay as long as she needs you."

"Why don't you let me see you there?" He spoke as gently as he knew how. "I'll come for you whenever you're ready."

"I'll not leave this place again. I'm telling you to go. Now, go!"

He pushed his hands deep in his pockets, felt the cold burrow deeper still. He was all the old man had to offer Naomi for her loss. But he wasn't enough. If Jesse had two sons, that still wouldn't have been sufficient.

Morgan could care for the cattle. It would cost them, but he couldn't begrudge having to give up a day or two, a week maybe. Naomi's loss was staggering. But what could he give her? He wasn't her Robert, was nothing like the toe-the-line ensign she'd written about in her letters. He scowled, felt the bile rise in his throat, reminded himself she might actually need him this time.

* * *

David was the last to exit the bus when it reached Grimsland. He scanned the boarding area, spotted Naomi standing wooden, eyes swollen. Her head took on the slightest quiver. She seemed charged, ready for battle. He moved solemnly, prepared himself to embrace her.

"David." She spoke before he reached her. Afraid he might mention Robert, maybe. "This is Timothy Turpin." Her hand fluttered toward a slight boy standing to her right. "He drove me here. Comes from a fine

42

Christian family. Parents very dear to me."

He nodded, offered a slight smile and turned back to Naomi. "I'm sorry." He bent toward her.

She grabbed his hand and shook it soundly. "We need to be going."

He sensed a sudden loss of control, remembered it as much as felt it. "I— I have to wait for my bag."

"Oh!" Naomi's hands twitched. "I can't be late for my meeting with the pastor." She ran a finger around her mouth and tapped her lips. "Timothy will take me then return for you." Her eyes shot away, returned. "A young woman from the church will be staying with us, David. She will be in the spare room. You will be in... the other room." She winced, something exploding behind her eyes. She visibly resisted, pulled herself back to the bob and steady hum of the crowd. "She's just a bit older than you. Not so much, really. I'm eager for you to meet her. She's very nice. And she's single." She smiled, tried at least.

The message was clear. It was time he took a wife. It had probably been an oversight on her part that she hadn't dealt with the matter before. The ghost of an old fire burned within his ribs. His life, taken as if it weren't his own. He went to work dousing the flames. She hadn't accepted her loss, had chosen to busy herself with his life to avoid her pain. It was nothing more than that.

* * *

The need for propriety relieved, the two blew across town, Timothy at the wheel. The rose cast of late afternoon softened the concrete and steel, some god of iron and smokestacks appeased, perhaps, by news of the war.

"Smoke?" The boy extended a pack of Luckys.

"No, thanks." David looked away.

"What do you think will happen now?"

He cringed at the strained depth of Timothy's voice. "Happen to what?"

"Think we'll get into it with the Germans, too?"

"I don't know." Whatever this kid's thoughts, the war was far from the cushioned seats of the Chrysler. Farther, apparently, than the boy imagined.

"Let's stop for a beer." Timothy shot him a sidelong glance. "Want to?"

"Sure. Be fine."

Timothy pulled into the gravel drive of a bar already crowded with the daylight shift of a steel fabrication plant, one of three David knew of that constituted Grimsland's claim to the industrial age. The heavy effluvium of stale cigarettes and cutting oil boiled from the open door. The place hummed with steady motion, the patrons, having brought the well-lubricated monotony of their work stations, filled the air with the residue of burned-out days.

He picked up fragments about the war and sensed a new exhilaration on the faces of those his age. Two men, late thirties, early forties maybe, sat near the bar, staring at the table. Neither spoke, but both wore the weight of something grave on their faces, something they were seeing for a second time.

He found a table in the direction of Timothy's nod. The boy marched off to pick up drinks; he seated himself and looked toward the front. Timothy had made it to the bar and was discussing something with the bartender, his gyrating hands mimicked in the mirror.

The man stood, his jaw set. Hair jutted from every limit of cloth stretched around his protruding abdomen, all held precariously intact by suspenders. The barman's head began to wag in determined rejection of the boy's pleas. Timothy was being turned down. Deemed too young to be there, he guessed. He rose, slipped around the chairs and stepped quietly behind him.

"You mean I'm old enough to fight for my country, but I'm not old enough to buy beer?"

"Whaddaya talking about?" The bartender looked as if he'd caught a foul odor.

"I signed up today."

"You ain't signed up for nothing, Turpin. Now get your butt outa here before I call your old man."

"Come on, Timothy. I'm really not in the mood for a beer right now." He put his hand on Timothy's shoulder.

"No, really!" Timothy grabbed the edge of the bar with both hands. "I signed up today. I'm leaving the end of next month."

The man looked from Timothy to him. "Okay, but if I find out you're lying, you won't drink in here no more."

Timothy straightened, looked at him, then the mirror, checked his collar and sniffed.

"There you go, hero." The bartender pushed a couple of headed mugs in their direction.

Timothy turned with the glasses and swaggered to the table.

He followed close behind, seated himself so that he could face the door, turned to Timothy and smiled. "Now what are you going to do when you run into Sam, there, on the first of February?"

Timothy swelled. "Sam who?"

He nodded toward the bartender. "I believe you've talked yourself into a corner."

"I am going to join. First thing tomorrow. Sam who?"

"Your bartender friend. Have you decided what branch you're going into?"

"Sure I have. Army Air Corps or maybe the Navy. You given any thought to enlisting?"

He looked around, wished he were somewhere else. "Not really. You going in as a private or just apply for a general's position right off?"

"I'm not too keen on your line, David."

He lifted his mug in mock salute then yielded to the boy's discomfort. "Look, why don't you wait until after the funeral to make up your mind about this enlistment business? Maybe the sight of a fresh corpse will make things a little clearer."

"There won't be a corpse. Robert was buried at Pearl." Timothy lowered his voice and stared. "You think I'm scared, don't you?"

"Anybody in his right mind would be scared. There's no shame in that."

"I think it's you that's scared, that's what."

"No question about it. Look, I didn't mean to step on your toes. There's just no sense in you putting yourself in harm's way over a couple of beers."

Timothy glared over the mug. "I buy beer here all a' time. He just didn't remember me."

He caught his stare. "He knew your name. Called you Turpin."

The boy turned away, studied the table for a moment. "I've thought this over. It's just something I have to do."

"Why do I have the feeling I'm talking to Tyrone Power in knee pants?"

The muscles in Timothy's jaw worked in the faint light. "You about finished that beer?"

He glanced at the mug, still near full. "Sure, whenever you're ready."

* * *

The drive to Naomi's was quiet. David tried small talk, asked about the fabrication plants, then Timothy's school. The latter subject seemed to deepen the boy's sulk. The car pulled into his Uncle Henry's drive, an opulent slab centering a concrete seashell fountain that had, by his reckoning, been dry since the Pleistocene. He reached for the door handle and Timothy touched his arm.

"Would you not mention what I said about enlisting? Naomi might say something— because of Robert and all, and my parents don't know that I—"

"Look, Timothy—"

"Tim, call me Tim."

"Okay, look Tim, if you think you have to go through with this, don't. I mean everybody has said things they wish they hadn't. This business with Japan may be over soon, and—"

"They're saying it could last thirty years."

"Fine, then you'll have plenty of time to get into it if that's what you want. If anybody from the bar asks, just tell them they checked your records and found out you were too young."

Timothy winced. "Just mind the hell your own business."

"Whatever you say." He raised one hand, grabbed his bag, slid across the red leather seats and let the door close behind him. When he turned to wave his thanks, the Chrysler had swept across the drive, the muted hum a slow wind moving through elms.

He approached the house, climbed the steps to the porch then stood before the door. He'd never been comfortable here, always the outsider, certain each word, each movement would be scrutinized. Even in Naomi's

46

absence, a sense of judgment visited the place.

The heavy door yielded to his grip; he stepped inside and pushed it closed behind him, moved through the entryway, glanced into Uncle Henry's study on the right and detected the faint betrayal of pipe smoke. He scuffed through the living room and opened the door of Robert's room, looked around. A mitt lay on the chest of drawers enfolding a baseball with signatures on it. A winning season, maybe. Memories unraveling now in the soft earth above Pearl Harbor. Uncle Henry's alarm clock rested beside the mitt. He smiled, remembered his uncle bringing it to the ranch when they came. The man was lost without a schedule.

He released his bag, stepped to the clock and wound it, listened, then pivoted in starched compliance, the place already imposing itself on him. He hung his suit on the back of a chair and wished for the order of his work, the comfort of his arms grown heavy with labor.

* * *

David raised the hood of Uncle Henry's Buick and checked the oil. As clean as it had been in the can. He cleaned the battery terminals with a little baking soda he'd taken from the kitchen and checked the radiator. The car had been his uncle's pride and joy, only a few months old when he died. Now Naomi refused to part with it though she didn't drive. He moved to the driver's seat, inserted the key. The car cranked slowly, fired and settled into an instant purr. He closed the door and eased the clutch. The Special rolled sweetly onto the drive, ready for the trip to the church in the morning.

Naomi sat at the end of a long table. Women scurried about setting plates and silverware, the air heavy with the smell of chicken frying in the kitchen. Four sailors in dress blues stood to the side of the crowd exchanging comments, their eyes occasionally catching one of the younger women and following for a moment before the presence of the place and occasion diverted them. Naomi was draped in black and wore an even blacker face. It was real. David tried to slip inside her pain, to know its height and depth so he wouldn't see the old man when he looked at her, the same set in her face, the hungry melancholy that pleaded to be seen.

"You must be David."

He turned to a young woman, square-shouldered with long blond hair. Willowy and tall, she had startling blue eyes that would have been enticing were it not for her disturbing smile. "Yeah, that's right." Her stare made him uncomfortable. He searched the air but found nothing else to say.

She giggled to fill the awkwardness. "I'm Delores. I've heard so much about you."

"About me?"

"I've been staying with your aunt, you know, and she thought, you know, that we should... get together."

"Oh, I see. Well, that's very kind of you to look after her. I'm sure she needs the company."

Delores made no reply, only tittered and stared. There was something comical in her presenting herself so openly, but he'd grown too uncomfortable to appreciate it. Despite her eyes and abundant cleavage, he found himself unable to respond to her. Two sailors in dress blues eyed the scene and didn't fail to see the humor in it. A little envious, he guessed.

"If you'll excuse me, I believe I'll speak with my aunt." He lurched across the room, edged between the parishioners to move ahead of the line forming to offer condolences.

"Aunt Naomi." He gripped her hands bunched loosely in her lap and felt them tighten beneath his.

"I see you've met Delores. She's a wonderful girl, David. You could certainly do worse."

"I'm sure she is."

"You'll be able to get better acquainted at dinner tonight."

The conversation needed some direction. "And how are you faring?"

"I'm struggling, David." Naomi quickly resumed the pose of grief and long-suffering. A long silence followed. "For a while I had thought that Robert, that Delores..." Naomi's voice broke and her eyes filled.

"Is there something I can get you?"

"Well, if you could have the pastor come, I would like to speak with him. Could you do that, David?"

"Sure." It was a relief to have a mission. He turned quickly, bumped into Delores.

"I'll find him for you." She offered an inapt smile, turned and trotted

48

off.

He wandered toward a group of men standing in the portico.

"Everything on the West Coast is sandbagged." A thin man sucked dryly on his pipe, surveyed the others, strained for sagacity. "They know more than they're telling. Just like Pearl."

"They've got machine guns around the White House," a younger man responded.

"It's Germany we've got to worry about. Japs are goners by themselves." It came from a small man, bent and agitated, white hair sprouting from his ears. An aging Walter Winchell.

The blackness gnawed at him. It was a thing beyond meaning or reason. He'd felt it before in the room with James and Elise as they listened to the radio, the cautious eloquence that spoke of war and death in Europe, that railed against the Nazi pirates in the Atlantic and the black hours of London's long night. And he'd sensed it standing in the conscription line in November, breathed it in, a constriction in his chest. Even then he'd come to know it as a dying man must become acquainted with the cancer within him. And now it had spread itself about him so that he could see it in the men's faces as they talked before the memorial of one of the first fallen. It was real.

"By God, those Nips have bit off more than they can chew this time. I give 'em three months. No more." Winchell again.

He turned away, looked at Naomi as a gray-haired man in black knelt before her, his hands compressing hers. Delores stood beside her. When she caught his eye, she smiled in a way that made her seem ghoulish. He turned back to the men.

"We ain't gonna stand by and just watch." Winchell stammered, working himself into a fury. "As far as I'm concerned, anybody won't fly our flag, that'll smile that yellow-dog smile and stab you in the back, shouldn't be allowed to live. They attacked our boys. Next thing they'll want to surrender and do it all over again. We oughtn't to stop 'til ever' one of 'em is dead."

David's heart was a rock. He knew it all at once as the little man cursed and Naomi and the pastor prayed. Something inside him was amiss. He had failed to slip inside Naomi's grief. Instead, he saw her straining to

49

hold to the old man's pain that wanted itself seen. Her son had died amid the screams of incinerating men, of sailors ripped and dismembered behind groaning steel doors, of boys having the air explode in their lungs beneath a thousand tons of water and steel. He might have screamed, too, her Robert, prayed to God to end the carnage and lift the precious, splattered lives above that incendiary sea. But his cousin had died in a sudden, watery grave. And now men talked of flags and dishonor as if honor were a thing and blood and bones were not. And Delores smiled in eager search, flashed her eyes that had, no doubt, inspired more than a few to longing.

He wished only to be with the black again, longed for what he knew was real, the rock and pines, yellow lights melting cool into the black of night and the lake. He would, at this moment, have been riding behind the cows, pushing them up from the sorghum stubble to the pasture behind the pens, stopping with them, letting the cows find their calves, watching the bouncing white heads of the newborns bawling and floundering in ignorant misdirection away from their mothers. Meaning grew within all that. And order. No mistaking the unreal for the real, symbol for fact, honor for sinew and bone. He stared at the crowd and resolved that animals were somehow wiser in their stupidity, more fortunate as dullards for only men killed and died for things that couldn't be seen or touched.

\* \* \*

"In the beginning was the Word." David closed his eyes, returned to the blanched steps and white-chipped doors, his thoughts set adrift on a holy breeze, the preacher's words weaving themselves between the thousand winged truths rising above the burning white. Or was that, too, a thing he so wanted to see that when he heard the steady cadence of the flow, the same eternal rhythm, he found in it a reflection of his hopes? But something sacred was in the flow. It was Word, and within the Word was Idea, the spark that burned in the mind of God, pure and holy, and wouldn't let him rest. And the Word just had to flow like music.

Only God couldn't be settled with that. His mind was a holy cauldron, white-hot and boiling, his Idea so pure it was a part of him. So he formed it into sinew and bone, and the Word was made flesh and dwelt among us, like the preacher said. Grew beautiful and pure, human, Word and Spirit. And the beasts of the field, and the birds of the air, and the black steaming

50

his desire into the shapeless gray dawn knew nothing of the Word for they could be satisfied. But man was born hungry for something more, something that made him discontent with only what he saw and tasted and felt.

And the Word came pure and holy. David took in the flow, determined, at least, that Idea must have been so hot it would turn to vapor if you looked away, that the first man that turned away lost it, but every man since has known that Idea existed, has had a piece of it pulling him inside, has known how it blistered in the Mind of God, had the very scent of it in his nostrils like the coming of rain on the hills. But with time and distance, it became vapor, idea twisted and curled and shapeless, floating thin and hardly seen at all. It was shadow that men took for Idea, held to as if it were Word.

The preacher's voice rained in a soft endurance, a music and a comfort in it, even for him. It came in the steady cadence of change and eternity. Every word blended into the symphony of things remembered or disclosed that coursed through his heart and over the congregation. The people sat listening to what was sure in the progression of spring and fall, in a constant and predictable flow of change.

He sat with Naomi on his left, Delores crowding into him from his right, sniffling in the proper rhythm of the eulogy, which, he was grateful, left no pause for her to giggle. She clutched his arm with her talons for all to see.

"Let not your heart be troubled." The organ died and the words picked up the measure of the seasons, the swelling green beneath the mulch, the insistence of the cicada's song. "Ye believe in God, believe also in me. In my Father's house are many mansions: if it were not so, I would have told you. I go to prepare a place for you. And if I go and prepare a place for you, I will come again, and receive you unto myself, that where I am, there ye may be also."

The church swelled so that he thought it wouldn't hold before the voice grew still and small, and sorrowing shoulders slumped as breath went out of the place.

The sailors presented Naomi with a flag. She kissed it, and the preacher began his final benediction. All was silent except for the wind whipping at the corners of the building.

Delores sat close, her hand bumping his leg as he piloted them home. David shifted, shrank from her touch. Her displays were annoying, seemed more avarice than affection. He stared ahead, squinted into the brightness, the expansive hood rippling with light and power. In the mirror, Aunt Naomi sat listening only to the scream in her heart. He looked at Delores, spoke against the steady murmur of the engine. "I appreciate your willingness to help Aunt Naomi, but I'll be here if she needs anything. Why don't you let me take you home? There's really no need for you to be troubled any further."

Delores leaned close, clutched his arm. "Why David, I don't think of this as trouble. I'm more than happy to do whatever I can for Naomi. And for you." She strained the words. "Don't you understand, David? It makes me happy to help." He turned, and she held him with her eyes, offered the slightest quiver of her lip.

"That's very kind of you, but I don't know if Aunt Naomi would want anyone staying in Robert's room just now."

"Oh, don't be silly. Of course she would want *you* to." Delores turned in her seat, her dress rising to mid-thigh, her leg sliding over his. "Naomi, you do want David to stay with us, don't you?"

Naomi's head rose from the dead, her eyes gray and vacant. "David? Stay? Yes, of course."

He felt his will being drained. She was intent on fitting him into her designs, and it was unthinkable that he wouldn't cooperate.

* * *

The three sat in silence at the dinner table. David knew for the first time Naomi's pain as she clutched the tablecloth and closed her eyes. Now, with no one watching, she grieved. Delores offered more fried chicken to assuage the pain and continued to try to light the room with her presence. But it was the rightful time for grieving, and he wished she would let it be.

He helped clear dishes and stepped onto the porch. The night had fallen cold and quiet around him. He tried, drawing on a memory no longer clear, to fill himself with nothingness, with the calm of a windless void, to know a contentment cut off from thought.

Headlights washed the porch as Turpin's Chrysler floated into the drive. He saw Tim's outline in the green glow of the dash, a cigarette dangling from his lips, saw him crush it before the door slammed shut.

He nodded at the boy's approach. "Tim."

Timothy stopped short. "Evenin', David."

The screen door squeaked behind him. "What're you two doing out here?"

David didn't turn or acknowledge Delores. She had been an intrusion even in her absence since it was certain she would come.

"I have some news." Timothy shifted on his feet, glanced back at the Chrysler, then at him. "My dad thought you ought to know. It happened this morning, during the service, I guess. Germany and Italy both declared war."

His stomach rolled and knotted.

"This evening Roosevelt announced a recip..." The word eluded the boy. "He declared war on them, too. We didn't figure y'all had the radio on."

Delores squeezed his arm, pressed her breasts against him. "Are you scared, David?"

"Not sure what I feel." He turned to Timothy. "Thanks for the news, Tim. Appreciate you coming over."

"Sure." Timothy shifted awkwardly. "You holding up okay, Delores? Must be a real tough time for you."

"It is, but—" She turned, squeezed his arm tighter. "David is my strength."

The words jolted him. He looked at her.

"He is? I thought with Robert going off—"

Her hand tensed on his arm. "You'd best run along, Tim. Your Dad will be worried."

Tim nodded and receded into the darkness. The Chrysler came to life, threw light beyond the house and backed from the drive. The evening hushed.

Delores remained silent for a while. "Do you think you'll be called up?"

"I don't know. I have a deferment now because of the ranch, but who knows?"

"Oh, David, I'm so frightened for you."

"You shouldn't be."

"And why not?"

He had no words for her, wanted to tell her she had no right to fear for him.

"Oh, David, I'm so frightened for you." She repeated it, demanding a response, he guessed. When he offered none, she put her arms around him and rested her head on his neck.

Backed against the railing of Naomi's porch, he arched his back to put a distance between them. "We really don't know each other, Delores."

She moved at his words, and he stepped stiffly down the steps, put the freshly painted railing between them.

"But I feel like I know you. I know everything about you." She leaned against the porch post and rested her hand on his chest.

He held her shoulders to keep her at bay. She looked hurt. He felt an old anger at himself. She was no less deserving of love than he. How was it that he couldn't hold her as he would have held Elise if she had reached out to him? His hands relaxed, grew gentler, caressing her shoulders, hoping he could remove the hurt. "You really don't know me."

"I know you graduated from the university— what, three years ago?"

He nodded. "Almost."

"And I know you've been on the farm with your father since then because he fell off a horse and was paralyzed from the waist down." She continued even when he looked away. "It was just a couple of months before you graduated, and you stayed and finished even though your father was hurt and in the hospital."

*Naomi.* He worked his jaws, choked back the irritation.

"And I know that you were always quiet and that you like books and music and airplanes." Delores beamed, seemed pleased to have remembered all the points she'd gathered.

"My father didn't fall off a horse. The horse fell on him. And... " He stopped, checked himself. "You don't really know *me*, Delores."

"Now, who do you think I've been talking about, silly?"

"You don't know what happened to me at the university, what happened inside me. You don't know what happened when my father was paralyzed. You don't know how I feel about the ranch or who I read, or—"

"Okay, I want to know those things, and I will. Just give us a little time." She seemed delighted. Something had been settled for her, graven in stone. She kissed him on the cheek and turned to go inside.

She had offered more than could be held and taken more than he had to give. Of course, he needed to believe it was some deficiency in her that made him recoil, something he could see but had no name for. But he suspected it was her hunger, a hunger he knew as well as she, and that was an injustice.

She was pathetic in her reaching out, and he withered from her touch. However he chided himself for it, he couldn't return what she offered. She was as deserving as Elise, he supposed, and certainly more needy. And that may have been what it was, after all. She had no claim on his affections except her need. But what better claim could she have? It was his only claim on Elise and James, perhaps his only bond with Dancer. It was an injustice that this hunger was an independent thing, that it could grow in the dark of our imaginings without being wanted or nurtured.

He was alone. He settled it once again. He had been born alone and would die alone, and nothing in between would change that. He filled himself with the old man's emptiness, drew it about him like a blanket and vowed without words in the shadow of a thought that if he couldn't be warmed, he would embrace the cold, would hold himself from shivering and learn to be content. It would be his strength, and he would never fear losing anything again.

# Chapter V

David pressed through the sea of green at the bus station, Delores bobbing in his wake. He turned to her at the boarding area and reached to shake her hand. She dabbed her eyes, threw her arms around him and smothered him with a kiss.

He pulled away, looked toward the bus. The other passengers had boarded. She took his face in her hands, constrained him to look at her and giggled. "If you don't promise to write, I won't let you go."

He pressed a smile to his face, covered her hands with his and moved them away, stepped back and glanced at the driver who seemed to be willing him to promise whatever she wanted. "Sure, I'll write sometime." He pushed against her grip, patted her shoulders, leaped for the step and breathed deep for the first time in days.

\* \* \*

The old man was silent after his return. David rid himself of the burden of his promise, wrote Naomi and enclosed a short note to Delores, told her again that he appreciated the support she was providing Naomi and wished her well.

The hills hadn't seen the first snow. Most of the cows were fat from grass still hiding tiny shafts of green beneath the crowns, but David increased the ration of milo and cotton seed. The fall-calving cows needed the protein, and the first springers would be calving in a little over a month. If winter turned hard, they'd need the extra flesh to breed back.

He rode the pastures, found the cows that looked closest to calving, watched for filling udders. In the next few weeks, he'd begin driving those that appeared ready to the pens. The old man could watch them, alert him to any problems when he came in.

It was a joy being with the black, feeling the thunder and grace beneath him tearing at the sand along the dry creek bed beyond the kaffir stubble. He checked cows, though that was mostly an excuse to be with Dancer, and headed down to Morgan's store to pick up mail and catch up on news of the war.

The ride was a pleasure that ended too quickly. Except for Dancer. The black hated the smell of the place, snorted and pranced when he pulled him up out front. David stood near for a few minutes, patted the lathered neck and rubbed his throatlatch. When the black quieted, he eased toward the door.

"Got something for you, boy." Morgan offered his picket grin, passed him a yellow Western Union envelope. "Come in last night. Ain't the first I've seen. Miller boy got his the other day."

He felt a weakness move into him, the hardness in his arms melting inside his coat sleeves. He hadn't been aware of dreading it. Not until now. He hesitated before opening the envelope, made a sudden vow to see Elise before he left, tell her of how she pulled him from his sleep at night, how she was the beauty in his mornings, her smile his music. Right or wrong. His hands shook as he tore the envelope.

TO: MR. DAVID DREMMER
AM COMING WITH AUNT THE TWENTY-THIRD XXX I MISS YOU
SO XXX PLEASE MEET BUS 8 PM BRIGHTON XXX SHOULD NOT
SPEND CHRISTMAS ALONE XXX
LOVE DELORES

It should have been good news. He should have felt relieved.

"Boy, if you want to sell that black before you go— I mean if you get called up or anything, I could give you your money back."

"He's not for sale."

"You sure? I mean—"

"I'm not going, and he wouldn't be for sale if I were." He stuffed the telegram into his pocket and pushed through the door.

57

He was still trembling when he took the reins, almost lost his balance when Dancer ripped the earth from beneath him. What would he tell Jesse? He'd never brought a girl home, had never even mentioned one.

\* \* \*

"Well, I suppose it's time for that." The old man let the telegram drop to his lap and peered above his glasses. "She'd make you a fine wife."

David clenched his fists, shoved them in his jacket pockets and turned to challenge the decree. "And what else has Aunt Naomi told you?"

The old man stared, his mouth drawn tight. "That you two really hit it off. Anything wrong with that? Or maybe there's something more to tell. Did you take advantage of that girl?"

His jaws twitched with restraint. "She's not a girl, I didn't take advantage of her, and we didn't hit it off."

"Then why is she coming here?"

"Because Aunt Naomi is bringing her. She's meddling where she shouldn't." His voice was as taut as new barbed wire.

The old man's face reddened. "Would you expect her to come alone after what she's been through, losing Henry and now Robert?"

He stood firm but regretted saying what he had, didn't want the fight he knew was coming. "I offered to take you there. More than once."

"She wants to come here. Is that asking too much?"

The words stoked the fire in his gut, the old man guilting him into bowing to her plans. "When she comes here to meddle, it is."

Jesse raised himself with his arms, shifted in his chair. "I won't have you speak that way about her in this house. I won't have it!"

David pushed the door wide, caught the scent of a storm on the wind.

\* \* \*

He hadn't seen Elise since before Pearl, had written only once. He held his breath at being so near her, afraid that all he felt, the intensity of his days and yearnings could somehow be seen, that she would find in his face the recklessness of his resolve.

"David!" She stood in the door, a dish towel in her hands, her eyes wide.

"Hello, Elise."

58

She turned and walked inside, leaned against the hutch to face him. "Oh, my gosh, David, isn't it awful? We all knew it was coming, but I just can't believe it."

"I know." He faltered, looked down then raised his eyes to meet hers. "You look great, Elise."

She pushed a lock of hair from her forehead with the back of her hand, held his stare for a moment. "Thanks." Her eyes seemed sad. The war, most likely. "You still have a deferment, don't you?"

"As far as I know. I hear they're reviewing them all the time. How's James?"

"Oh, he's busy. He's been going day and night since all this started. I don't know how he keeps it up." She paused, pursed her lips. "I was sorry to hear about your cousin."

"Thanks. My Aunt Naomi is coming for a visit. That's why I'm here. In town, I mean." Elise moved quickly. He followed her to the kitchen. "She's bringing a woman with her, someone she's been wanting me to meet."

She stopped, turned. "Oh? So are you excited?"

"Well, no. Actually, I've already met her at the memorial service. She's something of a clinging vine." He shrugged. "She sent me a telegram telling me she missed me and that she didn't think my father and I should be alone for Christmas." He grinned, shook his head. "She doesn't know it, but my father and I should never be alone."

Elise offered a feeble smile. "Sounds like more than just a meeting. Is there maybe something you're not telling? I've heard about these wartime romances." She turned to the table and wiped it with a damp cloth.

"To tell the truth, I'm a little worried about it. I'm afraid my Aunt may have convinced her I'm her destiny or something. She just won't take 'no' for an answer."

Elise stopped her work and stood erect. "So have you told her 'no'?"

"I've tried. Nicely, of course. She doesn't seem to believe me."

"You'd best say it so she understands, if you're sure you're not interested."

Something in her eyes… "Yeah, I'm sure."

It seemed hollow talking about Delores. He even felt a certain loyalty to her. For all their differences, she was the same as him. Neither had any hope of having what they wanted. It wasn't fair, but no effort, no force could have made him need Delores that way. Still he sought a justice for her. Maybe it was right that Elise would never be his. He wanted her with a hunger that had somehow forsaken sense, found sex too temporal a thing to contain it. He wished only what would be bright and good for her. Though he couldn't hide from what he knew himself to be, couldn't deny that he had wanted her for himself, he also wanted her to be happy with James, wanted them to be together always. And he wanted to be a part of them somehow.

"Say, I've got an idea." Elise offered her first real smile. "I hate to think about it, but none of us really know where we'll be soon, and wouldn't it be fun if we could have some friends over tonight— while you're here, I mean? We could make it a Christmas party."

"That'd be fine, Elise, but I have to meet the bus at eight. I borrowed Morgan's truck, and I need to get it back as soon as they come in."

"You mean you're not bringing the future Mrs. Dremmer for a visit?" She looked over her shoulder, smiled, but there was a question in her eyes. Or a fear. Or maybe just the war.

He looked away. "Don't even think it."

"This evening, then. I'll call Rad and Jenny. I haven't seen them in ages."

"Sounds like fun. I mean if it's not an imposition."

"It was my idea, Davey."

* * *

David held to the wheel of Morgan's truck, stared through the cold drizzle sticking to the windshield and pretended to concentrate on the road. The day had no connection to what he knew to be real, a link cut out of time. He examined it, hoped to find a meaning. But his thinking was a pretense, and he knew it, an attempt to hold back the river that would have taken him in the bright swirls of laughter and held the life from his lungs so that he couldn't cry out.

"And have you been busy, David?" Delores squeezed his arm, tried to draw him out.

How could he begin to explain his work to her? Even if he wanted to.

"Oh, just the usual. Feeding cattle, doctoring cows."

"Really? So you're your own veterinarian? Did you learn all that in college?"

He chuckled. "Hardly a vet. You see something often enough, you know what it is. Doesn't take much training. Besides, the vet's too far away to call for every little thing."

"Oh." He heard the disappointment in her voice. She'd failed again to make him more than he was. It was irritating. If he were satisfied with being so little, why was it she needed to make him more? Her hand relaxed on his arm, and the truck moved on through the cold rain. Delores turned to Naomi, asked something he couldn't hear, seemed content, for the moment, to leave him alone. His thoughts drifted into darkness. He looked out the window at a passing truck, returned his eyes to the road, his thoughts to what had happened.

The day was a tomb, full of treachery, holding in the pain and decay of his years, condensing it into one place in time, crushing him with its weight. He tried to hold himself from caring, tried to hold to the emptiness that would have been a buoy, but it betrayed him, too, and the memories flooded into the void.

He could have taken it, could have let them say what they imagined, accuse him of what they would, hold the blackest corner of his heart before the light. He could have taken all of it if only Elise hadn't entered in. But she'd directed it, laughed at his denials, took what he said with the darkest disbelief. He couldn't find sense or meaning in it, could only see her lips spit words at him, no less powerful for the hours that had passed, words that kept him from the sweet death of his thoughts.

He turned the truck onto the blacktop, cranked the wiper and pushed his hand against the glass to melt the freezing rain. It had been an illusion. There had been no unity between him and Elise, only his pernicious need of her. It was a thing he could not yet bear to look at though he had suspected it, had said it to himself a thousand times before today as if he knew it to be true. But he had never really believed it. She could think that he had set out to take something from Delores, take it only because Delores could be had, because he was "just another man" looking to slake his need.

"Oh, don't act so hurt, David." The heat had gone out of her words, but the slightest quiver remained in her voice. "You're just a man after all, aren't you? Always looking for it, not caring who you hurt. I mean, let's be honest. You have let this girl think she means something to you, haven't you? You've led her on just to get what you want."

"Of course not."

"Come on, David." James broke in, smiling, the voice of reason. "I mean I can't, and Rad can't say that we couldn't do the same thing under the right circumstances. I'm sure it must be lonely on that ranch of yours." There was laughter all around. He heard only hers. "You say you don't care for this girl. But she wouldn't be coming here if she didn't think there was some hope of marrying you. If she thinks that, it's either because you encouraged her to think it or you didn't correct her when she got the idea on her own. Isn't that so?"

He'd told them about Delores simply as a way of making conversation, of being a part of them again. He hadn't expected her reaction, or her leading the others in an assault. "That's not the way it was. I didn't encourage her to believe anything, and, if I didn't tell her plainly enough, it was because I didn't want to hurt her feelings."

"Whoo!" Elise expelled a bitter laugh. "The heartbreak kid. Women, hide your hearts!"

His thoughts tumbled in misdirection, took no shape that he could form into words.

"This is crazy!" He forced himself toward anger to keep her from seeing what he was really feeeling. He would deny her that, at least. "I've got to go." He pulled himself from the chair and charged for the door. Through the cloud he heard Elise laughing and James running behind him as he tried to close the door.

"David!" James called after him. "You're taking this way too personally, sport!"

It rained as sharp as needles. The jagged words cut into his soul, covered the road in icy judgment, the truck moving into night with a shiver.

* * *

The rain had turned to sleet. David pulled the blankets around him in the tack shed. It felt good to be with the smell of sweat and leather and

62

alfalfa. It was the smell of peace, an anchor to the earth, sure and solid, and he was away from Naomi and Delores who had seized the house and were trying to make it into something else.

"There's certainly a lot of work to be done here," Delores had said on their arrival. "You just wait. You won't recognize this place when we're through."

He had no desire not to recognize the place, but it was a comfort to be away from them and the old man glutting himself on their pity. He was glad for their plans as he'd been glad for the chore of driving Morgan's truck to the store and walking back in the cold drizzle.

He turned on his side, tried to find sleep, but the words returned and the image of Elise spitting her betrayal and laughing at his weakness. The sight of it grew above the still, and he felt the earth slip away as his thoughts took him into a deeper darkness.

When the sun came gray and thick through the cracks in the wall, he still hadn't slept. He knew there would be no peace today with Delores hovering over him and Naomi making plans for the old man to carry out. He grew angry with himself for being too weak to hold to the emptiness, but he had a plan. He would take the black to the far end of the Summit Place where he would graze him on a tether and rest on a creek bank. He filled the bucket with oats and pushed the door open.

The earth was covered in a white and silent dream, and he heard cows bawling in the pasture above the pens. There would be no rest today.

The black was playful, delighted with the newness of things, and he wished he could spend the day with him. Instead, he fed the mules, selected a team, hitched them to the wagon, and began filling it with the ground milo and cotton seed he'd left sacked in the barn. The mules fought the harnesses, disgruntled at having to work in the cold, but he whistled gently, and they fell into the complacency of their traces.

* * *

The sun slid beneath the wall of gray. Frigid air found force and moved across the frozen ground and burned against his face, filled his eyes with salty remembrance. It was the way with dreams, to start in a soft, white illusion and grow into a blistering certainty that would take your very breath if you let them. He unfolded the blanket he had taken from the tack shed, pulled it tight around him and stiffened against the cold.

* * *

David sat with the blanket pulled around him on the buckboard seat. Delores watched from the porch as the mules pulled the wagon into the yard. He felt her stare as he unhitched the team and threw three millet bundles over the fence for them and another to the black.

Dancer stared at the dark figure on the porch with a readiness that reminded him of the way the horse was before. Delores was silent until he reached the steps. "I was so worried about you." Her voice was soft and compelling.

"Why?"

She moved in close so that his clenched hand was forced against her. When he failed to release his fist, she pressed harder with her legs.

"It's so cold out here. How could you stand it all day?"

"Yeah, it is cold." He avoided her eyes. "Let's go inside."

She edged between him and the door. He moved to her left, but she didn't yield, stood firm looking beyond him across the crusted snow to where the black was poised and ready.

"That horse." Her brow was drawn.

He looked into her face, ready to look away if she caught his stare. "What about him?"

"I don't trust him."

He turned and looked at Dancer. "He doesn't trust you, either."

"Is he wild?"

"No, just cautious. He's been tricked before."

Her head jerked toward him, a suspicion in her eyes that seemed near anger. She had understood. He pushed against the door and stepped inside where Naomi and Jesse were drawn close around the table, speaking in quiet tones. Jesse drew his eyes tight and nodded to let Naomi know that whatever it was she had told him was theirs now, their shared and secret knowledge.

"I made breakfast for you this morning, David." Delores' voice was tender, vulnerable. She offered no hint of what had just passed between them. "When I went out to get you, you were gone."

"Had to get an early start, get that wagon loaded and out there before

64

the ground thawed. If it'd gone through the ice, the mules wouldn't have been able to pull it, at least while it was loaded."

"You have company, David. You should have thought about that." The old man looked to Naomi.

He made no response. His mind was beginning to wander, a young dog, frantic with the scent, hoping to pick up the telling odor of fear before his prey escaped. But the prey wouldn't escape. He was the prey, and though he knew the end of it, knew because his mind had been running the same trail all day without rest, he also knew he would follow it again.

It was, perhaps, because he might have reached the end of something. Whatever his need for Elise had been, whatever illusions he'd fostered, he'd also known her as a friend. She had been the one he turned to, and now she'd shown that she knew nothing of what was in him, nothing of what he told her or left unsaid. All that felt like betrayal, and he wondered what was lacking in him that left women so unsettled. Or was it simply the leaning of a woman's heart to wait out weakness, to bide her days until a man's soul was like a field she'd walked a thousand times, until she knew its rises and falls, its textures and smells, its shallows and rocks, until it held nothing new for her and she walked away in some scorching heat and took nothing from it but discontent? But he had trusted her; they were friends. He vowed again to hold to the emptiness and never again to hold anything so tightly.

"Something sure smells good. What are you treating us with, Naomi?" Jesse gushed honey-smooth and sweet as the women scuttled about the kitchen.

"Beef tenderloin." Delores spoke first. "Naomi told me you always had tenderloin on Christmas Eve when you were kids. She wrote Mr. Morgan before we came, and he brought it to us from the store this morning. Wasn't that nice of him? He's such a sweet man."

David wiped the smile from his face.

"Tenderloin. Oh, that sounds wonderful, dear. I'll bet you're hungry aren't you, David?" The old man stared, but he pretended not to notice.

"Smells good. Haven't had that in a long time."

"Well, welcome back." Delores showed her hurt.

"Pardon me?"

65

"You've been drifting away again. Is something bothering you, David?" She was the picture of concern drawing his arm tightly against her. It was blackmail, pure and simple, acting out in front of Naomi and Jesse what didn't exist.

"No." His tone was sharp, and Delores moved away, abused. He could feel the old man's stare but didn't turn to it.

After dinner David waited, listened to the old man's stories, smiled when spoken to. Though it wasn't late, he was overcome with heaviness and thought only of how to escape. Delores moved under his arm, seemed content and in control there. The old man was delighted with her, and Naomi had given up her picture of grief and suffering, but he'd had enough.

"If you'll excuse me, I believe I'll be off to bed. Morning came early. I'm afraid I'd be poor company even if I stayed. Ladies, it was an excellent meal. My favorite, by the way. I haven't eaten so well in... well, maybe ever. Thank you for all your hard work." He rose, grabbed his blankets and scooted out the door.

The tack shed was his center. It held the memory of the earth, warm and moist and eternal. He leveled the grass hay once more and spread the tarp over it, kicked off his boots and slid between the blankets, his mother's favorite quilt touching his face. He was exhausted. His mind had trotted in a frenzied fear of losing the scent, had run without rest, always knowing what the end of the chase would bring but following it all the same. What compulsion, what force condemned him to an endless running after loss? He yawned, felt the warmth grow around him, let his eyes close on the darkness. Tonight he would sleep, dream of Elise one last time and then be free to hold forever to the cold and windless void.

* * *

"David!"

He woke with a start, aware, somehow, she had called his name before.

"Are you awake?"

He cleared his throat. "Yeah. Yeah, sure. I'm awake."

"You left without getting your Christmas present. I wanted you to have it."

He could hear the tinkling of glass.

66

Delores giggled, moved before the light that pinched between the cracks in the walls. "I brought you a bottle of Scotch."

"Well, that was nice of you. Thanks."

She sat beside him. "Ooh! It's cold in here. Let me under your blanket."

He lifted the covers, and she knelt beside him, raised her dress so that one knee touched his hip, the other his side. She removed her coat and raised her hair with both hands, her form in clear relief before the shadow light oozing from the window. She leaned forward, her hair touching his face.

He edged away. "You'd best not stay too long. They might wake up and find you gone."

"They were both snoring. Besides, I'm not worried about it, are you?"

"Well, yeah, I am a little."

"Oh, David, don't you think they know how it is? They were young once."

"No. I don't think they know how it is."

"Silly. Now open the bottle and let's have a drink."

"Now?"

"Of course, now. You mean you won't share it with me after I brought it all this way?"

He'd never developed a taste for Scotch, and all he wanted now was sleep. "No, it's not that. It's just that I'm a little tired, you know."

"Oh, David. We'll be leaving tomorrow, and I haven't spent any time with you. I've missed you so much." He felt the coolness of her hand on his thigh.

"How could you miss me? I wasn't around long enough for you to get used to me being there."

"Sometimes it doesn't take time. You just know." She punched him in the ribs, pulled his arm over her neck and leaned back. "Now, how about some Scotch?"

"I can't."

"Why not?"

"Opening a bottle is a two-handed maneuver."

She lifted his arm and pushed it back in a pout. "There."

67

He patted her knee. "Come on, now."

The pout was over. He felt her hand, warmer now, move down his chest and rest across his loins. She pressed herself against him in request. He was found out, had no desire for her, and her entreaty was unequivocal. Turning away would have left her with no graceful way of retreat. He shouldn't have touched her. He knew that. She'd been too hungry for hope, too eager for some reciprocation, had left herself unalterably committed to her offering. She leaned toward him, kissed him. It was a long, unrestrained kiss, and she seemed unwilling for it to end.

"Delores?" He whispered, concealed with tenderness that it had been a lie, that the kiss was hollow. "This isn't right. Not between us. Not this way." He pushed gently to move her away, but she buried her head in his chest.

"Oh, David. You try so hard to be perfect. You can't earn your way to heaven. Just let yourself be human."

It wasn't heaven he'd been thinking of. He cradled her gently for long minutes, held her in the pretense of tenderness, weighed yielding to her desire, reaching inside for a passion that wasn't meant for her or telling her plainly he couldn't hold her, that he knew desire well, but not for her. That would be best, to tell her plainly and be done with it. But the minutes grew long, felt like hours, and he held her to his breast and sipped the Scotch. The burn began to quiet him, make him more content. Still, he couldn't tell her. She lifted her head and kissed him, and he reached inside to find a memory, rose to meet her burning supplication with his own.

"It's just not right." The words surfaced in a hushed eruption. He took her roughly, almost in anger, wanted her to turn and leave. But he knew she wouldn't. She'd waited this long, had come this far.

"That doesn't worry me." Her words were defiant. Then she softened. "The only thing that worries me— I mean, I could get pregnant."

Morning was close. She lay beside him breathing in the depth and rhythm of sleep, and he hated her for staying, hated her for pressing on him a desire that wasn't meant for her. He tried to move away, but she clung to him even in her sleep, so he waited out the blackness for her to wake. When he feared she wouldn't rouse, he touched her shoulder, and she moved on him again.

"No, listen." He spoke softly as if they could be heard. "You've got to go inside before they find you gone."

"No, I want to stay here. With you."

"You can't. Go inside, now. Please."

She was quiet, breathed without sound. The room grew pale as he waited for her response.

"What difference does it make if they know about us? They've got to find out sometime."

He stirred with a new fear. "Listen, Delores, what happened last night can't happen again. I'm just not ready for that."

Her shoulders heaved in quick tremors, and he hated himself for not telling her before.

"Why can't I ever have what I want?" Her voice was charged with something he thought he understood, an anger at the injustice of things.

"Just let's be friends, Delores."

"Oh, David, can we? I want us to always be this close."

She'd taken more than he offered, but he had no time. Naomi and the old man would be waking soon. He had to get her back into the house. "Please, Delores. Go inside before they find out."

"Oh, all right, but I still don't see what difference it makes." She struggled with her clothes beneath the blankets, rose in the heavy light, edged toward the door, lifted her dress showing her narrow form and pulled at her slip in the thick gray.

# Chapter VI

The chimera wouldn't fade into the distance though the sand boiled beneath the colt's hooves. Neither would it be dissuaded by the blows that left the earth trembling in his wake. It was everywhere, without shape or form.

David sensed again that Dancer had taken the threat as his own and was tearing at the earth to leave the specter in the sand and leaves. The fear the horse was trying to escape was cinched to his back and straddling his heart. But he felt no joy in their accord. Dread had taken him, too, so that he didn't think even to comfort the black, to still him, urge him to release what wasn't his to bear. Instead, he let Dancer run, shared with him the hope of leaving the truth behind, of making it haze into the distance until it was no longer real.

Four weeks. Four weeks and a day. And she said that she was sure, that she was never late, that there could be no mistake. How could that be?

Dancer stopped to heave in the gelid air, and he stroked the colt's neck. "Let it go, boy. You don't have to carry this." He leaned forward, wrapped his arms around the slender neck and slid from the saddle, his face buried in the wet silk, tears streaming down his cheeks. Dancer turned his head and nuzzled him, and his hand left even blacker streaks above the swells. The horse recoiled, blew a cloud into the frost and pinned his ears.

"It's all right, boy." His words were soft and low. "There's nothing out there."

But Dancer didn't ease, so he pulled the steaming muzzle to his chest. "It's okay, boy. It's in here. You've got nothing to be afraid of."

The black took the comfort of the steady beat, seemed to know the softness of the hand and voice as something he could trust. David pulled a rope from the saddle and tied it to an oak that held its weight like wisdom bending toward the water-smooth sand, looped the hemp into a makeshift halter and slipped the bridle over Dancer's ears, released the cinch and lifted the saddle from the horse's back. He walked to the edge of the sand, laid the load beneath the tree and sat on the tufts of grass that would be a creek bank come spring. Dancer followed, not recognizing that he was free to wander to the limits of the rope strung high in the tree.

"It's okay, boy. Go on and graze." He ascended the shifting bank. The air was sharp, and the memory shot through him, made him swear not to take the thing from his mind again, not even for a second, because when it returned, it was as if he were hearing it for the first time, hearing her say, as if there had been a contest and she had won, "David, I'm going to have a baby." There followed the same disbelief, the same icy scream in his gut, and she would repeat: "We're going to have a baby." He heard himself tell her that he didn't love her, as if in telling her that he would change the thing, correct the misunderstanding and the awful truth would go away.

It hadn't gone away, and when he told her he didn't know what to do, she'd said that there was only one thing to do, and he knew what it was. It was an incredible thing, and he couldn't bring himself to believe it. He wanted to stay forever beyond Morgan's, north of the houses and lake. Just him and Dancer.

But he would go back, couldn't do anything else. He had told the old man nothing when he left, only that he was going into the hills for a few days. But Jesse would find out, probably before his return. Naomi would see to that. Delores had told her everything. She simply couldn't bear it on her own any longer, she'd said, and took it to Naomi and their minister and the elders of the church, and they had all agreed there was but one thing to do. And, of course, he knew what that was.

He traced his steps again. If he could only return and change things. But the time for that had passed. That was four weeks ago. He had tallied it on the ride back from Morgan's store where he had found the telegram waiting and called Delores as he was instructed and ridden back in a blind stupor feeling the full weight of God's wrath.

He snapped a branch from an aging cottonwood. Dead, the bark flaking beneath his grip, a split along its length. He endured, for a moment, the rage of some early freeze splitting him in two, twisting him before a frigid wind. Why were some born to be loved by God and others pitted against him from the opening of their mothers' wombs? He dropped the branch, gray and sere against the sand, wiped his hands of it. That was the crux of it. His mother's womb, curdled with the hot black sin of her birth, the sin of not being chosen like Naomi or the old man. Naturally, he had to share in that blackness. He was only half Dremmer, not raised in the Separatist fullness of knowledge that gave them their certainty of place and conviction.

The hills were full, bursting with beauty even in their winter gray. He saw it as he had always seen it, but couldn't feel it except as something being torn away. He thought of the first day he mounted the black, the sudden and furious way the colt had pawed the air, yielded to his effort and fallen across his leg. There had been a certainty that all was lost, that things would never be the same. But the finality had only been delayed. He was now as crippled as he feared he would be then.

He thought of Elise, and his heart swelled with need for her, not to tell him what was not true or could never be, but to be the anchor she had always been. He needed to feel the tenderness that would have had him give his heart, to know that at least that would never change.

He sat, let the darkness fill him, winced as the thing came back, refused to turn, even in his thoughts, to the God who hated him. He had been pitted against the chosen from the moment he was conceived. And now God had his vengeance, and all the righteous could point to him and say, "See what happens when you go against the ways of the Almighty?"

Sand shifted beneath his boots. The near liquidness of things, always troubled, never sure. He moved beneath the tree, untied the quilt from behind the cantle and slid it under his arm, led Dancer to another tree where he could find more grass and tied him there. He moved on a bit, laid against the creek bank, drew the quilt around him and waited for the warmth to grow, but his thoughts refused to die. He lay awake, hearing Delores tell him they were going to have a baby, and there was only one thing for them to do. He heard it again and again until the tiredness and the cold became a mirror of the day. He shivered and tried to turn from the chill, to burrow himself into the sand, but the earth refused him, too.

He woke to coldness all around. The night was long and his thoughts grew sharp with honing. The slightest hope of gray leaked across the sky, and he could feel no difference between night and the gray waking except for Dancer stirring by the tree, so he held to that as if it were a promise. He lay in the cold and listened, was glad that there was life left in the world and that it was his Midnight Dancer.

His meandering prayer was directed everywhere and to no one and remained unanswered. Until dawn. Then, as the earth took form from the void, he thought it must have been just so on the first dawn when God looked down at his creation. And just as surely, he knew that he would do what was expected of him, but he would never make her a husband. He would enlist when he returned, marry her and pray to be sent where he wouldn't come back. The old man would have his place, and she could revel in the short glory of being a war widow, and Naomi would have fulfilled her plan. He wouldn't hope to come back from the war to live the lie he'd started, would resist even the thought of it.

Part of the bargain was even more painful. He vowed to hold nothing he loved from its will, went to Dancer and put his arms around his neck. His throat grew tight, and he couldn't hold the tears. The black nuzzled him in some misunderstanding hope of reward, and he loosed the halter, pulled the sack of oats he had brought from the tack shed and opened it in the crook of a fallen cottonwood. When Dancer had finished the oats, the horse stood not understanding that he was free.

"Go!" He strained the words from his throat. "Go on now. I've held you too long."

The black looked up the creek for a new trick, and back at him. Then, as suddenly as he had come into his life, the horse thundered away. He listened to the hoof beats fade into the leaden air. When all was still and he could breathe again, he coiled the rope, laced it to the saddle, dropped the bridle over the saddle horn and tied the quilt and saddle blanket to the cantle. The world was silent and empty, and the grass along the creek bank crumbled beneath his feet as he bent to shoulder his load. He moved away from the creek and trees and Dancer's hoof prints in the sand.

It was a long walk home, and the strength had gone out of his legs. He tottered with a heaviness beyond his years and remembered that he hadn't eaten. He searched the skyline, found the highest point and pressed upward. It was only a rounded knoll, but it was high enough to see the lake and the lay of the land, to find his place again and put an order to things.

From the hill he traced the very edge of the earth, coursed it with his eyes until it curved and fell away. The land was eternal, frightening in its beauty. It spread out in an ocean of hours that fed on a man's soul like blind plankton, unraveling his complexity cell by cell leaving no remembrance of his having been. But for now, at least, he was willing to be swallowed up.

His legs pushed through the Switch and Indian grasses, purple and waist high, the deepening red of Little Bluestem, his eyes set only on the lake to the south. Surely the hope of a hereafter would be too small a thing to send men pulsing after myths and poetry in an ocean of hours, hours to be endured with an altogether meaningless courage. But if there were more than the hills and the pine and the dark quiescence of the earth as it curved and fell away beneath the sky, if there were something beyond the edge, it was something that flowed naturally out of what he saw or allowed a perverted earth, running down and dying at the source, to flow naturally out of it. So whomever God might be, he must also have created a perverseness to destroy the wonders he had drawn from the void, twisted a wretchedness into the brain and heart of whatever slithering creature first pulled itself from the slime, knowing that all the wonders of his hand would wither and rot from the inside like a blighted locust grove.

\* \* \*

James eyed David across his desk. "It's an old question."

"Maybe so, but I've never asked it before."

"God didn't create evil, David. It's not a thing in itself just as cold is not a thing in itself. Cold is the absence of heat and evil is the absence of good. We're creatures of choice just as God is a spirit of choice. God's will is good, but we can certainly choose to do other than God's will. That, though it may not appear to be, is evil. Sometimes what you will is just the same as what God wills. Then there's no problem. You don't stand and shake your fist at the sky or at your insides either. Your problem is that you want something other than what God wants."

"You're saying that God wants me to do what Delores wants, to marry her?"

"No, I'm not saying that. You both made a choice, and you're both suffering the consequences. I can't tell you how to choose the lesser one. Part of the reason God didn't want you to take her to bed may have been so you wouldn't have to face this." James paused. "You know something about Jewish law."

David nodded though he knew little enough.

"You can't forget there are reasons those laws existed. Actions have outcomes. God's laws exist to help you avoid unpleasant ones. If God has prohibited something, rest assured that prohibition exists for your good. God exists, David, and he loves you and wants what's best for you."

"How can you believe that?"

"I can't."

"But you do."

"Yes."

"That's crap, James."

"No, it isn't. Faith isn't something that makes you accept what's irrational. It's a whole different way of knowing something."

He said nothing, looked away. Why was it so easy for some?

"That's something I can't explain to you. You wouldn't be satisfied with my explanation anyway. It's something I hope, I pray, you'll understand for yourself someday." James leaned back in his chair. "I can't give you faith, David. The fact is, you already have it. Just don't push it away. If you'll pray—"

"I couldn't do that."

"Why not?"

"I won't be a hypocrite, James. I won't cheapen myself by whispering into some empty attic."

"And you think it would be hypocritical to admit you don't know, that you would like to believe there's a God? You would, you know. That's why we're having this conversation. I'm suggesting to you that there's a way to know for yourself. With certainty." James appeared determined but calm. "If I can help you, David, I'll be around, but I won't fight with you.

75

It's pointless." He paused. "I'll tell Elise. You won't have to see her now if you'd rather not."

He closed the door to the rectory and wondered if he were walling something into the past that he might not be able to live without. He didn't know why he needed to talk to James. He already knew what he would do. Perhaps it was the finality he needed, to be settled on the thing, to say it to James so that it would be sealed, written in stone. Or maybe he needed to be angry and thought James would tell him what he already knew, and then he could be angry at James for the inevitability of it. But he was grateful to him for telling Elise. He would be spared that, at least.

* * *

The house smelled of loss and cedar. The old man stared at the fire, refused to turn even when the door closed. David hung his jacket on a kitchen chair and scooted it beneath the table.

"What are you going to do?" Jesse spoke without turning.

He shrugged. "What can I do? She's got me where she wants me."

"She get pregnant all by herself?"

He didn't answer, was too weak for anger. Besides, the old man was right. "I've joined the Army, taken the test. Hope to get into the Air Corps, maybe pilot training after basic. I'll be leaving the sixteenth of March."

"That's just over a month."

"Six weeks. And you don't have to worry about the place. Most of the cows will have calved by then. Probably be less than a month of feeding left. Morgan can help with that. He'll want to lease the place. It would be better for you to keep the cows and let him take care of them for a percentage of the calf crop. You could keep the best heifers. Keep the herd up." He paused, letting go of the place in the bargain. "But you work it out however you think best."

"What about the colt?" Jesse's voice was softer now.

His heart swelled, and his throat grew tight. He didn't want the old man to hear the sound of what was inside him so he choked the loss, the hunger for the eyes that were all depth and filled himself with emptiness.

He took a deep breath. "The black got away from me. He's running on the Summit Place, I guess."

The old man wheeled around. "You let him go, didn't you?"

76

He had no fight left. "Yeah, I let him go."

"Well, he came back."

He stared into the old man's face, the lips drawn tight in reproach, felt the shame he guessed the old man wanted him to feel.

Jesse stirred in his chair. "He's out by the tack shed waiting for you. I tried to let him into the pens, but he runs whenever I get close."

"How could he?" He worked to hold the quiver from his voice. "I left the gates up."

"On the Summit Place, too?"

He shook his head. "No, I didn't think he'd—"

"Must've followed the creek all the way to Morgan's and come up the road, then."

He pushed through the door and ran toward the tack shed. The black looked around the corner as if in hiding then stepped back. He stopped. If Dancer had come back, it would have to be on his terms. He waited as the horse plunged his head and pawed the ground.

"No. If you want to be here, you'll have to come to me. I won't take you."

Dancer stepped cautious, uncertain, seemed to weigh the choice, not wanting to give up what he knew of being free but holding to something in him, maybe, to the measure of his days by his comings and goings, the sport of pleasing him and the sweetness of the reward.

"So what have you been doing roaming those hills? Haven't you collected a herd of mares yet? Doing it isn't so easy as dreaming it, is it pretty boy?"

Dancer acknowledged the voice, lowered his head and breathed deep. David wished for a lump of sugar and turned to go to the tack shed to get some. The horse stepped forward, urged by a sudden fear, it seemed, of losing what he had come back for.

"It's all right, boy. I'll be back."

Dancer's ears were erect, his nostrils flared. He wondered if the horse truly feared losing him again or if he only feared the bridle. But it would never be clearer than it was. He'd come back.

\* \* \*

Delores stood in front of Naomi's fireplace wearing a white robe and a woman's scorn, and they both knew he would never be forgiven for what he'd said. It made no difference. She would marry him because that was what she'd planned. She hadn't foreseen his telling her he had no love for her. That wasn't part of her plan, David guessed, but she would bear the child and give it his name, and she would have as much of her plans as he allowed. Until she concocted a way to have the rest.

"You really hurt me." She spoke in a tone he hadn't heard before. The hurt was real. He slumped in the new weakness of his posture facing her as he would a winter morning.

When he made no response, she moved on. "When would you like to have the wedding?"

"Today."

Delores flinched, stared at him with fire in her eyes.

Something about her hurt, something deeper than rage reached him, and he relented. "As soon as possible then. I just have a few weeks. There's a lot to do. I've got to get back to the place."

"I can't just plan something like this overnight. There are a lot of people to call. My parents will—"

"No. The minister can marry us. You pick a few witnesses. Then we'll go back."

She stood cold as stone, and he wondered if she saw the distance between what she'd wanted and what he was. He couldn't help her. He would play his part, but if her designs had gone sour for her, they had never existed for him. He was grateful beyond words that Elise would never be bound to him by a desire she couldn't feel. A quiet softening grew in his chest. Maybe it was the same with God.

He spoke as gently as he dared. "Tomorrow then?"

"I told you I can't plan something like this overnight!" Her passivity was gone.

"It seems to me you planned it overnight once before. I'm going back tomorrow. I came here to marry you because I thought that was what I had to do. If you want to go back with me as my wife, you can. If you don't, that's fine with me."

He saw something drain from her face and a familiarity come into her expression. "Please, David." She moved away from the fire, stepped toward him, pressed her breasts against his arm and laid her hand on his chest. "Please, let's not say things we'll be sorry for later."

He would have turned to her in gentleness if he could, but he withered from her touch.

"Have you decided?" Naomi marched into the room, the permanence of insult and suffering etched into the lines of her face.

He nodded. "We'll be married tomorrow and leave tomorrow night. We want a private ceremony."

Naomi shook her head. "No, that won't do. Delores' family will have to drive up, and there will be a waiting period on the wedding license."

He'd lost and knew it. "When, then?"

Naomi turned to Delores. "What do you think, dear?"

She'd been listening. He was sure of it.

"I thought Valentine's Day would be nice. That would give me two weeks to invite friends and relatives, and I really need the time to get the church ready. There is one thing." Delores turned back to David. "My parents can't afford this. If it were under other circumstances we could wait, but the way things are, I'll have to rely on you to do what's right."

Naomi looked at him and nodded as if he were waiting for her approval.

He swallowed hard, thought only of escape. "I'll be back the fourteenth. I have to go."

"David!" Naomi's head shook in the rhythm of her rage. "How can you leave now? Delores needs you. You both need this time to get to know each other."

"She's gotten what she wanted." He spoke beneath their hearing, only needed it said. His voice grew. "I've got lots to do, too." He marched toward the door.

"Neither of us planned this, David." Delores' voice squeaked with rage. He didn't turn, but the words held him with a strength he had no power to escape.

* * *

Being on the bus offered less relief than he had hoped. What he had before him was always present. Then he reached Brighton. Through the bus windows, the campus seemed oddly dissimilar to his memories, smaller and less significant. Though his ticket would have taken him all the way to Morgan's Crossing, he stepped forward, and the driver left him at the entrance of the university. He had the most particular need to be there, to walk the same ways he had walked, to sit in the chapel where he sat with Elise and listened to James urge his heart from the keys.

He stepped across the dry grass creaking beneath his boots, opened the chapel door, and stared at the rows of empty pews. But he didn't climb the stairs to the choir loft. Instead, he stole to the front as in the presence of those who were asleep, and knelt before the altar. In the proper attitude of a supplicant, uncertain of what had drawn him, he waited for his thoughts to form words. There was silence, a holy hush about the place, and he didn't have breath enough to break it.

"God." The echo filled the emptiness with his need. His voice sounded weak and sick, and he couldn't bear to hear it. He rose and walked out. There should have been more. He had come to say something to God, but he could find no way to begin. He scraped across the frozen ground and through the gates, stood at the highway and waited for a ride.

* * *

The hills had almost lost their light when the truck stopped in front of Morgan's store. David thanked the driver. He'd been lucky to catch a ride before dark, luckier still to have found a truck going through Morgan's Crossing.

He hungered for the peace of the hills, the white silence of their winter grace. Sitting in the cab, he had filled his mind with them, longed for paths he had walked as a boy, for the comfort of the song of the wind in the pines. Now, at last, he was home.

The road beyond Morgan's store was a white ribbon, clean and flowing beneath the sky, but the rocks and pine called him away. The land was full, white and calm in its abundance. Still, he felt a keenness for something greater and more permanent than the hills, the same keenness that had drawn him to the chapel, an allure that had urged him to cling against all grasping to the hope of something beyond emptiness. It evaded his comprehension, for the less he had to put his hope in, the stronger it became.

Now, with all else lost, it called him to a new anticipation, a promise that seemed wholly out of order with all that had happened. The promise had moved him to kneel at the altar, but the hills seemed a more apt place to find what he was after. He stood beside the dry creek bed beneath the vacant canopy of a cottonwood, felt free of the constraints of the righteous and knelt in the snow. This time his thoughts found voice, and he prayed as a child—with the hope of being heard. His heart launched into darkness, seeking. He cried for all the loss, for truth, for certainty, for his mother. In the end he cried out for Elise, but also for himself, that the spirit of the hills and the rocks and pine, the cool yellow meltings of the cabin lights, the wild verbenas and the dove held out against the blood-red sky, would be taken with the magic behind the white-chipped doors, the black mystery of the eyes that were all depth and longing, gathered in one piece and held out to her as he could never do.

The night was clean, the air cold and pure. He rose and the snow creaked in untainted sharpness beneath his boots. He grasped at the faint luster of completeness, and though all before and all behind was loss, a promise grew from what he sensed but could not see. It was what he hungered for, and though it was not a thing he could form into a thought, he knew it had something to do with what James called faith.

# Chapter VII

Something had changed. David knew it that night in the snow and pines when strength came back into his legs, and he'd marveled at the joy of the climb and the fullness of his breath. Still, dread grew alongside it.

His days moved swiftly with labor, but evenings made way for thought. It took his breath to know that he would soon go to Grimsland, marry Delores and return with her to the ranch. And then, in a few more weeks, he'd leave again bound for some hellish place on earth where he would likely stay. While it comforted him to think he wouldn't be coming back to her, what he'd chosen knotted his gut. He thought of Robert, wondered about his last moments, the fire and fear. What kind of hell had men created for each other, and how much of it would he come to know? He even came to question if it might not be worse than the hell of never knowing a woman's love, of being yoked to someone he could hold no tenderness for, of having his life and will torn from him like a gelded horse in harness.

* * *

In four days he would board the bus to Grimsland. He thought of nothing else on his ride to Morgan's. The black could not be held for the fineness of the day, so he let him run down the creek bed almost a mile before turning back to the gravel road and pushing him toward the store. He tied Dancer and stepped inside.

Morgan grinned from behind the counter. "Damn, if you ain't the most popular feller I ever seen. You got another telegram."

David held his breath, wondered what else could be taken. He tore the envelope, the words severed so that he had to hold the pieces together to read it.

TO: MR. DAVID DREMMER
COME IMMEDIATELY XXX NEW DEVELOPMENTS REQUIRE YOUR ATTENTION XXX WILL BE EXPECTING YOU SOON XXX LOVE DELORES

He thought he had prepared himself for what had to be done, but her words opened a chink in the dark cover of his days, and for all his resistance, hope shone through. Perhaps she wasn't pregnant after all. He was ashamed for having been angry at God. It may have been that his prayers were heard, the horror he faced taken away. But he was wary, for as quickly as the hope had come, it could be erased. He tried to fill himself with emptiness, to hang onto it with all his renewed strength, but it wouldn't die.

Dancer seemed unable to make the house appear quickly enough. His neck frothed as he tore at the earth and barreled in air, passed his pen and ran to the tack shed without a single request. David removed the saddle, curried him and ran to the house. He told Jesse about the telegram, bathed and packed in minutes, heard the door shut behind him before he remembered the money. Maybe it was for nothing. Still, it couldn't be avoided. In the last few weeks, he had depleted the small reserve he kept. He stood, satchel in hand, wishing for a way around the humiliation of asking Jesse for it. He pushed through the door, felt the old man's stare but refused to meet it.

"What's wrong?" Jesse's voice rose from the darkness of his room.

"I'm afraid… I guess I'll have to have some money."

"How much?"

"I don't know. She asked me to pay for the wedding… if we have to go through with it."

Jesse was silent, and he could find no way of telling him the hope he'd found in her few words.

The old man wheeled into the kitchen. "Will a hundred dollars be enough?"

"I really don't think so."

Jesse wheeled about in the dark. He watched from the door as the old man pulled a metal box wrapped in a Navajo blanket from under his bed. His father had kept his valuables there for as long as he could remember. The old man didn't trust banks and vowed his assets and indebtedness would remain his own concern as long as he lived. But it was no secret that whatever was taken would be missed.

"I'll give you two hundred. Just be sure to bring back what you don't need. It may still be a hard winter."

He nodded, needed no reminder of that. It had been nothing but hard times since Jesse's fall. For two years the ranch had brought in almost no money. Then, last year, the calf crop had gone to pay off the debts for the two winter feedings before. And last fall, the maize had been poor. Even before, when he'd first returned to the hills, they could buy nothing. What they needed was bartered for or done without. Now the little money that had come in was being siphoned off because he had lived her desire as if it were his own and been caught in the lie.

He clenched his jaw, felt the bile rise in his throat. What money had gone out had been for him— first for his school, in the meeting of some promise Jesse had made to his mother, then for the black, and now this. The old man seemed to want nothing for himself except his Bible and meat in the salt barrel.

Jesse took out the bills, fumbled through them with the greatest deliberation. He stood behind the old man feeling the shame of what he was. He'd spawned so much grief in his short life. Jesse handed him a wad of bills. He shoved them in his pocket and turned quickly to avoid the eyes that had seen so much of his failure.

* * *

David couldn't catch his breath as he lumbered up the steps to Naomi's porch. He hoped with the most awful yearning to be free of Delores. It could have been that she had never been pregnant, and now that she had seen he would make her no husband, she might release him. His hands trembled with hope, and he could scarcely force them to the door. When he did, excited voices were set afire. Strange that Naomi would have company just now. Delores answered the door, smiling as widely as he had ever seen.

"Oh, David!" She threw her arms around his neck. "You came early."

"I got your—"

"I want you to meet my friends." She pulled him into the house, displaying him with the most peculiar delight. Three girls stood against the hearth. His heart fell. Green silk cuttings and scraps of white trim lay all around. They were fitting dresses. It was as if at each step of coming to know the unreality of what he had been drawn into, a deeper madness was exposed. Delores was planning a wedding. A costly one.

"I want to talk to you!" He hissed the words through his teeth. Delores turned away pretending she hadn't heard. He grabbed her wrist, willed to crush it.

"David!" She yelped so the others could hear. "You're hurting me."

He relaxed his grip. The blackness inside him seemed to have no end, and he had no way of knowing when it might emerge or what it might produce. He hated himself, but he hated Delores, too, and the endless humiliations she foisted on him.

He pulled her into his Uncle Henry's study, held his tongue until they were safely walled inside. "What the hell are you doing?"

Her eyes flashed in defiance. "We're planning a wedding. You left it all for me to do, so I don't see that you have a lot to complain about."

"Look, this isn't the social event of the year. You're pregnant. We're getting married because you and Naomi, your minister and the elders of your church decided it was the only thing for us to do. I told you I wanted a private ceremony."

"Oh, David, why are you treating me this way? All I ever did was let you make love to me. Are you always going to hold that against me, not saying 'no' to you? You know I could never refuse you."

"I didn't make love to you." It was out before he could check it.

Delores glared. Something opened inside him, the barest edge of pleasure at her contempt.

Her lips pursed white. "I guess it must be different for a man."

"Why did you call me here?"

"I can't do everything. All this will have to be paid for. You haven't done *anything*." Delores was crying Jesse's tearless cry. "You haven't selected your groomsmen, or bought your wedding suit. Was I supposed to do that, too?"

"No, you were supposed to have the minister and a couple of witnesses at the church next Saturday. That's all."

"You mean you'd deny me this, too? I've waited all my life for this, and now you're trying to take it away from me."

He planted his feet, refused to be moved by her display. "I guess this is the way you get what you want."

"I don't know what you're talking about."

"How am I going to pay for all this?"

She stared blankly, her mouth open. "You mean you don't have enough money?"

He waved his hand toward the other room. "For all that? Of course not."

"Can't you just sell some cows or something? Naomi will loan you some."

The muscles in his jaw ached. "There's no reaching you, is there? You just go on pretending things are the way you want and expecting others to fall in line. And do you know what? From what I've seen, most of the time they do."

Delores was wide-eyed. Nothing he said appeared to have touched her.

"Delores." He forced his voice to soften. "Do you ever just ask yourself why you want the things you want or why you do the things you do?"

She lowered her head for a moment. When she raised it, her eyes were wide with fury. "You piker! Do you think these get-ups are free? Don't you pretend you can see through me or figure me out like I was some kind of jigsaw puzzle!"

He felt the weakness move through him again. "Look, you've put me in a hell of a bind. I mean this thing is humiliating enough without you bring-ing the whole world in on it. I can't afford all this, I don't know anyone to be a groomsman here, and it's not the kind of wedding you make a public spectacle of."

Her face brightened. "Oh, David, is that all you're worried about? Tim will be a groomsman and my brother, Daniel, is here." She stopped, flat-tened her extended hands. "And we'll come up with another one. You can all go down today and be fitted for suits. It's not too late."

"You've got this all figured out, don't you?"

"Well, somebody had to."

"No, Delores. Nobody had to do all this."

* * *

Being with her made him desperate, and the ceremony and reception seemed without end. He was on display among a strange people and wanted only to be free of her and them in the bargain. The minister had told them he would say a few words, but when he spoke of the two becoming one flesh, David thought he wouldn't be able to bear it. He held his breath, fought the sudden urge to tell them all it was a fraud, that he was a fraud. The ceremony was a lie and neither the flowers nor the candles, the white robes nor the one hundred and fifty-dollar wedding dress could make it not a lie. When he had to repeat his vows, the words stuck in his throat like cotton. The minister repeated, stared them into him. At last he parroted the words that told what they had decided he should say. They were no more true than the rest of it. He put his mind to something else and said them.

It was the old man he thought of. He felt an awful tenderness for Jesse who'd paid dearly for all this. Delores had overspent his two hundred dollars by two hundred fifty more, half enough to buy a new Buick like Naomi's, and now if Jesse couldn't lease the place, he would have no money for planting in the spring or to pay a hand to put his crop in for him.

On the ride to the ranch, David closed himself from her. There was a wordless feud between them, and she moved next to him to break him down. He couldn't touch her, held tight to the wheel of Naomi's car.

The old man was sleeping when they arrived, but he lit the lamp, and they heard rustling for a long while in the other room.

"Well, well." Jesse smiled, looking in on them from his chair when he emerged. "Don't you look nice?"

"Thank you, Jesse. And isn't David a regular Joe Brooks in that suit?"

The old man smiled, nodded. "Yes, I don't believe I've ever seen him look so fine."

"I think he should wear a suit all the time, don't you?" Delores all but danced beside her new groom.

87

Jesse seemed at a loss. "Well, I don't know about that."

David forced a grin. "Wouldn't do to haul bundles in. We brought you some champagne and a piece of the cake."

"Well, thank you, thank you. I wouldn't care for the drink, though, and I believe I'll have the cake in the morning. I'll just say goodnight to you two."

"Goodnight, Jesse." Delores beamed.

"Goodnight." He spoke low, looked after Jesse pivoting gracelessly in the door. His heart boiled over for the old man wheeling in the dark. It would be an adjustment for him, too, having Delores here, though he would grow accustomed to her soon enough. Maybe it was his years, but Jesse seldom seemed ill at ease with anyone. That, and he had the Truth.

"Champagne?" He raised the bottle in a calculated warmth. Delores had had her hour. Now it was over, and he was sorry for her. He would treat her as well as he could, but he wouldn't be a husband to her. She would be a guest. When he left, she and the old man would make whatever life for themselves that suited them. He'd send what money he could.

"Champagne! Ooh, yes!" She moved close, but he slid away, went to search the cabinet for proper glasses. Finding two alike, he filled them to the top, almost emptying the bottle, and handed her the first.

"Planning on celebrating?" She giggled, put her hand on his shoulder.

"No."

"It's okay, now." She pressed herself against him, but he drew back and wouldn't look at her. "What's wrong? Bashful all of a sudden?"

He met her eyes. "Delores, I hope you're comfortable here. I know it's not much, but I'll do what I can to spruce it up before I leave. I'm sure Jesse will do what he can, too." He picked up the heavy quilt and tarpaulin and walked to the door.

"Where are you going?" She stared, her mouth wide.

"I'll sleep in the tack shed. I've got to get an early start tomorrow." He pointed toward his room. "You sleep there."

Outside the night was still and clear. He perched himself with the bedding under his arm at the edge of the porch and felt oddly at peace. Glass shattered, and he turned to see wetness seeping around the door sill. He lifted his glass and drank it down.

Dancer stood shining in the blackness, eyes alive with fire and anticipation.

He left the blankets at the door to the tack shed and went to him. "Won't be much longer." He soothed Dancer's winter coat and rested his head on the horse's neck. "But the next four weeks will be ours, pretty boy."

\* \* \*

The depot was frenzied. David searched the crowd and felt the loneliness of it. He'd phoned James and Elise, said goodbye, mentioned the departure time hoping they might come to see him off, but they hadn't. Tomorrow he would be at Fort Sill. A new struggle would begin, but it had to be better than living with the chill of Delores' disappointment.

The four weeks had brought a change in her that made him ache in sympathy at times. She had just begun to fight her expectations, and there would likely be many months of pain before she could rest without them. Living without hope would not come easy for her. It wasn't her way to accept things. Her desires were the only justice she knew. The only injustice was not having them met. But that was something he understood, too.

The world was spinning too fast. He was married. It was an ugly parody of a marriage, but he was bound by it all the same. And he was quite probably going to be a father. Delores, at least, was going to be a mother. He was about to leave for basic training and then the war. For the moment at least, that was a consolation. In light of it, all the other changes would be only what they were, words on pages of some form somewhere and no more real than they seemed now.

\* \* \*

"Greyhound passengers bound for Childress, Lawton-Fort Sill, and points east now boarding at gate three." The blare of the speakers rattled his insides. David gripped his bag and moved closer to the departure gate.

"David!" He turned to see Elise moving toward him. "I was afraid we missed you."

"I was afraid you had, too." He laughed, unable to conceal his delight.

"David, I know this isn't the time or the place. You're going to think I'm crazy, but I just had to tell you something."

He sighed. "I'm really glad you came."

"Remember when we used to tell each other our dreams? I know you're thinking, 'She's lost her mind,' but I had this dream last night and it was so— I don't know— it wasn't like any I've ever had, and I just had to tell you about it."

"So go ahead, crazy lady. Tell me about it."

James appeared behind her, smiled at David and rested his hand on Elise's shoulder.

"It's hard to explain what it was like, but it was beautiful. I was in the center of this meadow, and there were trees on four sides. I kept thinking it was like an amphitheater, only it was more beautiful than that. It was as if all this beauty had been put there just for me. It was so peaceful. There were these flowers all around, I don't know what they were."

David laughed. "Verbenas."

"What?"

"The flowers. They were wild verbenas. And Indian Blankets."

She returned his smile, her head at an odd tilt. "Anyway, I was going to pick some, but I stopped because everything was too perfect. I didn't want to spoil anything. Then this dove came down. It wasn't just a dove. It was, I don't know, so perfectly white. It started to coo— sing really, hovering right over me like it was painted there. I know it sounds crazy, but when it sang, it was the most beautiful music I'd ever heard. I didn't want it to end. I can't tell you how beautiful it was. I couldn't describe it in a hundred years, but I had to let you know. When I woke up, I was crying. I know this is crazy, but I couldn't let you leave without telling you."

"It isn't crazy at all. I'm really glad you shared it with me. More than you know."

The line in front of the entryway was gone. He turned away, fearing he might have missed his bus. "I have to go, now."

James extended his hand. "God bless, David."

"Thanks, James." He pulled his friend into him, then turned and kissed Elise lightly on the cheek. "Thank you for coming, for telling me that." He ran for the door, turned back for a last look. "I'll miss you both."

# Chapter VIII

## St. Petersburg, Florida, April 1942

Life with the old man never seemed so desperately male and incomplete. The sameness of the place, the drab uniformity of night and day, of land and sky had slipped inside him so that his heart took on the dull hum of machinery. David dragged his sleeve across his face, looked at the wetness as he ran, felt his heart race at the passage of days, shadows floating across an ocean of land leaving nothing of their having been but a gray wisp of memory.

Rain and sweat covered him in a woolen blanket, the thunder of boots on concrete drowning out thought. He'd started with his platoon in a tepid dampness at the Martha Washington, double-timing to the Savoy Hotel for evening mess. His feet sluiced in his boots, his fatigues spotted with sweat. Cumin and coconut drifted from the shops along the street, burned his nose, tempted him with promises of islands and sand. The drumming grew discordant, and he raised his eyes to see another platoon in wet fatigues huffing from the Savoy to the Martha Washington. He let his head drop, released a chuckle, convinced this "discipline" would be a finer thing if a man could be kept from thinking about it.

Fans stirred the heavy air above the chow lines. David shuffled, waited as a sharp-nosed private ladled beef and potatoes onto his tray. For all the homogeneity of the place, St. Petersburg was preferable to the mindless misery of Fort Sill. The delay after taking his aptitude tests had set his nerves on edge. Then he'd learned he wouldn't be sent to Fort Bliss as he'd been told. He'd completed basic there, in Oklahoma, a little more than a hundred miles from home, then been sent to the Primary Air Corps Gunnery school, the last gunnery school, he hoped, the Army would send him to.

He looked up from his tray, studied the young men in his platoon, curious at his affection for them. He was warmed by their laughter, had almost forgotten what it was to be young. But they had relinquished something for their ready humor; a price had been paid for their quickness and wit. He could find no word for it, though it had to do with choice and finality, with things that once done couldn't be undone. Something in these recruits denied that. In most of them, at least.

He glanced across the table, met the dark eyes of a soldier in his company about his age. The others called him Bear for his reaction to the banter when it grew caustic. Billington wore a quiet wisdom on his face but seemed to lack the words to ward off their assaults and resorted to rolling his back upwards from a slight stoop to stand erect and growl. The others in their company laughed at his deliberateness, but he was convinced that Bear understood something they didn't, had found a resolution for his loss.

* * *

David thirsted for more than the day had brought, rolled on the narrow mattress, tried not to shake the frame and stir the bunk beneath him. He remembered Dancer and the hills, the dove held out against the sky. And Elise.

In the weeks he'd been away, he'd begun to see something in their last meeting. A promise had been fulfilled. He'd given her what he held most dear, his yearning satisfied so that if he never knew love again, at least he was sure she had received what he most wanted her to have, and on that comfort he slept.

Delores' voice hissed dryly on the phone, "There's only one thing we can do, David, and you know what that is." His back cooled as he came upright in his bunk, and he smelled the sourness of his corded watch band as he drew it near his face. Four-thirty. He slipped quietly from the bunk, pulled the sheets and blanket up and stepped to his footlocker, just visible in the paltry light leaching from the latrine. He opened it, found the worn copy of *A Midsummer Night's Dream* he'd picked up at the bus station in Lawton and padded quietly across the concrete floor to the showers.

Delores was likely still asleep. He hoped she had some joy in her life, breathed it in a silent wish that surprised him. He sucked in a breath, still half anticipated waking and finding that these past few months had been a dream and that no baby was to be born to them. *The baby.* His breath left him. He dropped the slim book in the corner and moved beneath the shower, lathered his arms and back then rinsed again, stood beneath the steady stream a while longer hoping to quiet the memory of the voice on the phone.

He dried, at least for the moment, and perched himself on a commode just beneath a dim bulb, opened the narrow book and pulled out a pen and letter he'd started to the old man, reread his questions about Dancer, the weather, the condition of the cows. And Delores. What else? The nub of the pen whispered across the page as he pictured Lieutenant Baker strutting at inspection, his pomposity on display, the icy stares that were meant to intimidate. Baker was the sort of man Jesse would have found revolting. He could, at least, offer the solidarity of mutual disdain. Not that Delores wouldn't have sufficed by now.

The door to the barracks flew wide and the lights switched on; Sergeant Pruitt filled the darkness of the doorway. "Fall out! Get your asses in the air and your feet on the floor *now!*"

He slipped the letter inside the book and scuttled into the barracks, moved quickly to his bunk and tucked the corners of the blanket squarely beneath the mattress, turned to catch the sergeant's stare. He jerked straight.

"You drop that on the floor? Your mama ain't here. Who you think's gonna pick it up for you?"

He looked down, saw the narrow book sprawled, the letter and pen inside. "Sorry, Sergeant." He grabbed the book, closed it.

"Interesting book you got there, Dremmer?"

"What Sergeant?"

"Damn thing's got fairies on it. You a fairy, Dremmer?"

"No, Sergeant."

"This what college boys read?"

"Some of them, Sergeant."

"Fairy ones or ones with culture?" The sergeant turned, seemed to demand at least a snicker from the troops.

He could think of no answer.

The sergeant grinned, looked back. "If I was to read this, you think I'd get culture?"

"I don't know… that it would be necessary, Sergeant."

"You don't mind if I borrow it, do you Dremmer? I want to see what's in it that makes some puke hide out in the latrine to read it. Lots of fairy pictures in there?"

"No Sergeant, I—"

Pruitt snatched the book from his hand. "I'll get it back to you."

The day was still, even against their pace, and David's fatigues, damp from the earlier run to the Savoy for morning mess, grew wet. He climbed into a truck headed for target practice, rode to the far end of the base where an unused runway had been commandeered for mobile base, mobile target training. He thought only of the letter, felt the squeeze in his gut, hoped the sergeant found Lieutenant Baker as repugnant as he did. The truck made a pass, the instructor droning the procedure. He was first, stiffening against the trigger of the shotgun, wishing for the M-1 he had trained with in basic. He breathed deep, loosed half the air he'd taken in and held, waited for the release of the clay pigeon. The target appeared, and he squeezed the trigger, saw the shot scatter well behind the pigeon, pulled the barrel forward and squeezed again. The target reached the top of its arc and plummeted to the ground intact.

* * *

David moved forward, stood next to Bear at the front of two lines outside the colonel's hut. Cogliani, the librarian from Philadelphia, and Spiller, the big kid from Oklahoma, stood behind them, holding their apprehension in silence. Rumor had it they were about to receive their assignments. The threat loomed, silent and suffocating, that he wouldn't be given a chance at pilot training.

"Billington! Dremmer! Fall out!"

Lieutenant Baker stood at the door holding two folders. When he

94

turned, David nodded to Bear. "Guess this explains why we've been standing in the hot sun when we could have been sitting in the shade."

Bear nodded, his shoulders shaking.

The lieutenant barked into the darkness of the Quonset. "Billington, report to the colonel. Dremmer, follow me."

"Good luck," Bear whispered.

He grinned against the tightness in his gut. "Why would I need it?"

The lieutenant seated himself behind his desk and scanned the file. "At ease, Dremmer." He didn't look up. "Says here you're a college graduate."

"Yes, sir."

"A literature major? You read a lot of Shakespeare, Dremmer?"

His stomach clenched, and he felt a flush move into his ears and face. "Some, sir."

Baker shook his head. "Graduated with honors. Don't figure. You one of them idiot savoires or something?"

He stared at the wall, a fire igniting in his gut. "I don't know what you mean, sir."

The lieutenant gave him an icy stare and glanced at another form. "You scored pretty high on the tests you took at induction. Indicates officer potential. Looks like you're predicating on pilot training."

"I'm still hoping for that— Yes, sir."

"Your degree would mean no CTD. You could go straight into preflight." The lieutenant shuffled papers. David's heart soared. It was the reason he'd requested the Air Corps.

"However, you got some problems with your disciplinary record. You have anything to say about that?"

The lieutenant was winging it. He was sure of it. "I wasn't aware of any problems, sir."

"It's been my observation, Dremmer, that men who don't venerbate authority usually aren't qualified to exercise it." The lieutenant pegged the moment with the point of his pen and leaned back in his chair. "And just because you qualify for OCS or flight school on an aptitude test don't mean you're a shoe-in. It requires a nomination from a CO or personnel officer. That's me, Dremmer." Baker paused, stared. "You don't have that nomination. Do you know why you don't have that nomination,

95

Dremmer?"

"No, sir."

Baker stared. "You think you're too good to be here, Dremmer?"

"Not at all, sir. I volunteered."

"But you've done damn little to merit a nomination. Isn't that right?"

"If you say so, sir."

"Well, I do say so. What have you done to merit a nomination, Dremmer?"

"Sir, I'm not aware of any problems, sir."

"You're not aware of any problems, Private?"

"No, sir."

"Do you think it's normal to sneak into the latrine to read about fairies, Dremmer?"

"Sir, I—"

"You what? Were you doing something besides reading, moron?"

"Sir, I was—"

"You want to tell me something? You want to get something off your chest, Dremmer?" Baker grinned, waited only a second. "I guess not. You didn't answer my other question, either. So are you one of them idiot savoires? Because as far as I can see, you don't have the sense God gave a jackass." The lieutenant stood, walked around the desk, moved within inches of his face. Baker stared, his breath sour with stale coffee. "I'm an officer in the United States Army Air Corps, Dremmer. I worked for my commission. It wasn't give to me because my mama and daddy paid to get my pansy ass through college."

"No, sir."

"Your mama and daddy, are they normal, Dremmer?'

"Yes, sir." He pressed his lips together, willed to swallow.

"You must have been a disappointment, then, being an idiot savoire and all. Do you even know what that means, Dremmer?"

"I believe you mean idiot savant, sir."

"Is that right? Is that what I mean?" The lieutenant's nostrils flared, and vessels swelled above his collar. He jutted his chin, his chest heaving. "Dremmer, I'm recommending you for specialist-gunner training. You're going to Fort Myers." The lieutenant turned, walked behind his desk and looked over a roster. "You ship out the twentieth of May. Until then, you'd best spend all the time you can in the back of one of them trucks out there." Baker raised the file in front of him, started to open it then placed it back on his desk. "From what I read here, you have some major ineptitudes with moving bases and moving targets." He leaned forward with his palms resting on the table. "There's something you need to understand, Dremmer. If you wash out of gunnery school, you're going into the infantry. And you *will* wash out of gunnery school. But don't worry— they can use you in the Pacific. Pansies like you stop bullets just as good as real soldiers. You understand what I'm saying?"

"Yes, sir." He worked to keep the disappointment from showing on his face, didn't want Baker to have the satisfaction.

The lieutenant opened the folder, shoved something toward him. "Here's your little book. Dismissed!"

"Yes, sir!" He saluted, felt the roiling of his gut, waited for Baker's return salute, grabbed the book and stepped out the back of the hut. When the door closed, he splayed the pages, watched for the letter to drop. It wasn't there.

Bear was sitting in the shade waiting for him. "What'd he say?"

"The lieutenant and I didn't hit it off too well, Bear. Looks like I'm going to gunnery school."

"At's the berries." Bear seemed delighted.

He faced his friend. "Why?"

"You going to Fort Myers or Kingman?"

"Fort Myers."

"Me, too. Only I requested it. I take it you didn't."

"To tell the truth, I've always wanted to fly. This was my last chance. And I can't hit the broad side of a barn. Baker just set me up for a one-way ticket to the Pacific."

Bear scratched his chin. "You don't have nothing to worry about. Barns ain't strategic targets so far as I know, and nobody's flying 'em yet."

He met Billington's smirk. "You want me to have my driver take us to the gun club?"

"Might be a good idea. You ain't going to volunteer to be a target, now are you?"

He pushed the thought away that another hope had died. He really wanted to fly. One of those new P-38s maybe, or a P-47. But at least he and Bear would be together through gunnery school. That was something. "Make you a deal, Bear."

"Yeah, what's that?"

"If you teach me to shoot, I'll give you some pointers on handling officers."

* * *

David sat in ballistics class, sweat trickling down his collar. Fort Myers was hotter than St. Petersburg. Rains came every day, and he waited for them to cool the blistering concrete, but they only made the air thicker.

The first week was a whirlwind. He learned to identify the silhouettes of aircraft and estimated ranges. After the second week, he could recognize and give the approximate distance of every plane silhouetted. The fighters, the P-47s and the blunt-winged Messerschmitts, the playful looking Spitfires, the P-38s and the Stukas fascinated him. He wanted to crawl in one and take it up. His problem was guns.

The formation stood at ease as the instructor began his spiel. "What you're looking at here is an M1918 Browning Automatic Rifle. It's a thirty caliber, selective fire automatic weapon with a muzzle velocity of twenty-eight hundred feet per second. It has an effective firing range of fifteen hundred yards. This particular BAR has a thirty-round detachable box magazine and weighs sixteen pounds." The master sergeant grinned, held the gun high for the entire platoon to see. "Take a good look at it, because it's likely the last one you'll see for a while. It's a play toy compared to what you'll be shooting, but it will suffice for our demonstration. I need a volunteer." His eyes roamed the men in front of him. David glanced down.

The sergeant pointed. "You! Step forward!"

He rose and edged to the front of the group.

"You see that target, Private? The nearest one?"

He nodded, dried his hands on his fatigues. "Yes, Sergeant."

"I want you to cut that target in two from left to right."

He raised the gun, tried to concentrate, set the sights left of the paper.

"I want that target cut in two *now*, soldier, not next week!"

98

He squeezed, the recoil hammering his shoulder. The target was visible for only a moment before the ratcheting had him staring into open sky. He released the trigger, lowered his head and looked downrange. The target was intact with only three holes, two in the upper right corner.

"Soldier, that's the most pathetic display of incompetence in the use of an automatic weapon I have had the misfortune to witness! What made you think you could be a gunner?"

"Personnel officer convinced me, Sergeant."

The sergeant shook his head, explained the propensity of an automatic weapon to pull up. "Bullets flying off in space are no more effective than you sitting on your hands. To find the target, you have to counteract recoil." The sergeant stared into the faces of the men in front of him, grabbed a full magazine. "I need another volunteer. You!" He pointed at Bear.

Billington stepped forward and pulled the gun to his shoulder, seemed as at ease as a kid with a slingshot. The sergeant hollered for him to fire, and the hammering riveted David's gut. When the smoke cleared, the target was sliced diagonally, but from left to right.

The sergeant looked and nodded. "Not a bad first effort."

David's head still rang as they double-timed back to the trucks. Bear moved up beside him, began to speak in the rhythm of his labored breath. "You're just freezin'… up, College boy…. Make you a deal."

"Yeah? What's that?" He turned, watched Bear see-saw beside him.

"I'll teach you… to shoot if you… help me through… ballistics."

He shot Bear a grin. "Thought you were… a whiz at… ballistics."

Bear laughed, sweat rolling off his chin. "I am…. Just need an excuse… to teach you to shoot. You waste rounds like that… you'll drag the war on… another eighteen months. I figure it's my… patriotic duty. They put us on… the same ship… it'll qualify as… self-defense."

He and Bear on the same ship. The thought brought an instant ease. "You've got… a deal, Bear."

# Chapter IX

"Hey, Joe College, better get a move on. Truck just come through the gate."

"Right behind you, Bear." David stared into the mirror. The uniform, the gunner's wings, the Corporal's stripes. He stood erect and adjusted his tie, pleased with what he'd become, proud of the weight he carried and the clear symbol of it on his collar. He took a deep breath and placed his hat on his head. He was a gunner.

He looked a moment longer, fingered the written orders assigning him to a B-17. Fort Myers was part of his past. Forever, he hoped. Bear had been assigned the tail gunner's slot, and he'd been given the ball turret on the same ship. It was an unexpected positioning since he was too stocky and a bit tall for a belly gun. And it was a dreaded slot to fill. He couldn't help wondering if Lieutenant Baker had sent a special request.

Still he was thrilled with flying and had surprised himself in his air-to-air test by slamming the fourth highest count of markers into the tow sock. He'd waked early on the mornings of air-to-air practice drilled with adrenalin and ready for the gunner's seat in one of the AT-6s.

He gave himself a sharp salute in the mirror, grinned.

* * *

David woke to a blue dream. Islands of pine and tamarack emerged from an ocean of mist. For a moment he was flying, but the familiar rhythm of iron and rail, the easy sway that had rocked him for days, brought him back. He stared across miles of mountaintops, nothing between but cloud.

"Be in Spokane in a little over an hour."

He smiled, the voice comforting. "Don't you ever sleep, Bear?"

"When I need to. Be meeting the crew pretty soon. I'm going to get a shave and clean up."

He continued to stare out the window. "Beautiful, isn't it?"

"Like being woke up by the Almighty hisself."

\* \* \*

"I'm Captain James Dougan, your commander."

David looked across the line of faces, stood outside an assembly hut at Geiger Field. Home, at least for a while. He knew no one on his crew but Bear. It wouldn't be at all unlikely that he'd see the last of some of these guys. Or they of him. He shivered.

"I'm a Winslow, Arizona, boy." Dougan's eyes twinkled as he stared across the line of faces. "You probably all have a sad story to tell about how you got here, but since I'm in charge, you're going to hear mine. I was prepared to be the first P-40 Ace in the ETO. Even instructed on the little jewels for a time. Then the Air Corps decided in its infinite wisdom that it had enough P-40 pilots and scrapped my unit." Dougan shrugged. "Luck of the draw, I guess. So I was reassigned to 17s— Fortresses." He stopped, looked at his nervous crew, grinned. "Of course, you're my third crew. None of the first two survived training. Kept falling out the gunners' slots when I did Immelmann maneuvers."

David looked at the other gunners, saw a slack jaw or two and chuckled.

Dougan winked, leveled his hand toward the men beside him. "The flight crew has been together for a while. They've gotten used to me flying inverted, but you guys might consider tying yourselves in."

The captain asked the gunners to introduce themselves. Bear went first, he followed, then the two waist gunners, Crawford Aimes, also from Arizona, and George Lioni, a tall, good-looking kid from Pittsburgh. Lioni ended his speech with a bow and proffered his cap. "George Lioni. I look forward to getting to know you all better. And your sisters."

Dougan turned, pointed at a training bird across the tarmac. "We've been flying this fortress for a while, but we've gotten used to it with no guns on board. Don't be surprised if Sheen or Ream here takes umbrage at your racket and shoots back."

The other gunners laughed this time. David studied the engineer who seemed out of place among them. A dark, balding fellow, he stood with his left arm wrapped loosely across his chest and pinned beneath his right elbow, and sucked on his pipe.

"Speaking of the flight crew, guess you boys ought to know who's shooting at you." Dougan turned to the gangly engineer. "Sol, why don't you go first? Introduce yourself."

The tall lieutenant nodded, came dangerously close to smiling but managed to keep it in check. "Lieutenant Solomon Berkowitz. Engineer."

Lioni groaned behind him so that only the gunners could hear.

The bombardier was next in line but seemed hesitant to speak. Dougan opened his hand, pointed to the lean, baby-faced kid. "This laconic lad is indeed out of grammar school. In fact, he has a degree from Columbia. Majored in blond pursuit, I understand. Our bombardier, Sergeant Walter Sheen." Sheen's face reddened. He laughed and ducked.

A squat man with Asian features stood quickly as if called to attention, remained poker-faced. "Corporal Bill Ito. I'll be your navigator on this cruise around..." He looked at Dougan. "Where exactly are we, sir?"

The men laughed again. A tow-headed boy, heavy-jowled and wearing a massive grin stood from a squat. "Uh, Corporal Jerry Guy, at your service. Oh, I'm the radio operator."

Dougan turned to an angular, sandy-haired fellow, thin and handsome, a grin on his face. "This is my co-pilot, First Lieutenant Carl Ream."

\* \* \*

David woke to the scent of the Spokane River. Tamaracks and white fir mingled in the distance. Black pine jutted beyond. As the others slept, he slid from his bunk to watch the mountains, bristling green with life, emerge from the mist.

The crew was awakened a few minutes later when a jeep rolled up— an aide sounding wake-up. Morning chow, the corporal shouted, was at oh six thirty hours. Dougan, Ream, and Berkowitz were at the officer's mess and would join them for a briefing immediately after chow.

\* \* \*

102

Dougan checked a list he'd pulled from his pocket and paced the floor of the briefing room. For a long while, he seemed unaware of the crew. David shifted in his seat, wished he were in the pines or walking along the river, riding Dancer through some of the farms he'd spotted to the south. Ranches, he'd heard a local call them. Small stock farms really, but as green as anything he'd ever seen and dotted with livestock. Could likely carry more cattle on eighty acres than he could a section. And they were beautiful.

"All right." Whatever had held Dougan's attention seemed to have been resolved. "Today your real training begins." He stared at Berkowitz. "No more theory. No more exams." Then at Ream. "No more classrooms or AT-6s." He turned to the gunners. "No more riding in the backs of trucks and shooting clay pigeons, or firing BARs bolted to six tons of concrete. Today you'll begin doing what you'll be doing in combat, getting behind the guns you'll be firing." Finally, he held David's stare. "Under the same exposed conditions."

"Two things will be different from combat, men. First, no one will be shooting back. Second, the deflection you'll be dealing with won't hold a candle to what you'll deal with over there. But let me assure you, the habits you form now will serve you well when we are being fired upon. Form good ones. They may save your life and the lives of your crew."

The gunners huddled in the belly of the plane. When they reached altitude, Dougan ordered them to their stations. Lioni grinned from behind the right waist gun and reached for his throat mike as David struggled to spoon himself into the glass bubble.

"Better Cosmoline your ass, Dremmer. That's your only hope of getting in there."

He strained, grunted into the interphone. "They forgot to install a commode in this one. No ice box, either. Let's hope the rent's cheap."

Lioni laughed. "Won't need an ice box, and you're not allowed to relieve yourself on duty, Dremmer."

Nine hours. The drills were incessant, the questions fired over the interphone at each crew member. Dougan was nothing if not thorough. David remained in the glass bubble suspended above the earth almost half that time. He climbed out twice as they were drilled on ditching procedures, stayed out for a couple of hours as they rehearsed emergency landings. Later, after landing, he spent another hour climbing in and out, learning to keep his chute free of the oxygen lines and rest it behind his head. Just in case.

* * *

David lay on his bunk, tried to piece together the whirlwind of the past few months. From Geiger Field, they'd flown from base to base for specialized training. Within weeks, they'd been to so many bases they no longer received mail. That was somehow crucial. The threat they faced became clearer, drew them closer. They were family, would trust each other with their lives.

From Fort Seven Miles they boarded a troop train bound for Blythe, California. The Mojave was a miserable collection of baked clay hills and scalding sand. He thought it no loss to drill the sandstone and rock with hot lead in their air-to-ground runs. It was a land forsaken by everything but a few dust-laden junipers. But the crew was sharpening; he could see that. The air-to-ground firing split the bombing practices when the hundred-pounders were trained across the desert floor in a string of dust or salvoed so that the ship bucked from the sudden loss of tonnage. It was a game, and the crew had become a team leaving to each his job and looking back at the end of a run to see how well they'd worked together. And their pride was an open book but for him.

He knew he was an enigma to the others, though he'd never intended to be. When they spoke of their girlfriends and families, and Lioni of his conquests, he remained silent. For all of Bear's monologues about his wife and baby girl, he never spoke of Delores except to say that they had recently married.

He received a telegram in August telling him she had borne him a son and named him Isaac. He said nothing to anyone, but he had kept the date in the back of his mind and was sparked with hope that the baby had arrived three weeks and a few days early.

The telegram said there were no complications. That was fine. Now she had someone who needed her. He hoped she was making a good life for herself. And Isaac.

* * *

Bear eased to the corner of the barracks, sat on his bunk and sliced the letter open with his penknife, careful not to touch the contents. It was heavy, likely held a picture or two of Babs or little Irene. He smiled at the thought, and tipped the envelope. The scalloped edge of a photograph sifted from inside. He reached as delicately as his cracked and stubby fingers would allow to pull it free, traced the edge of the faces, saw the fiery red of his daughter's hair hidden within the gray, looked into Babs' eyes.

"It won't be long now, Honey." The whisper overflowed from his swelling heart, and he touched the letter to his nose, hoping for a hint of her. A breath, a scent. He read each line, listened for her voice hidden in the words, tried to picture little Irene walking with her fingers wrapped around Babs'.

There'd been a rumor floating around that they might be sent home for Christmas. He'd tell her when he wrote tonight. He brought the letter to his nose again, looked around, suddenly aware he might be seen.

Dremmer lay on his bunk directly across and lifted a book to cover his face. He wouldn't say nothin'. Be more apt to apologize for intruding than to make a joke of it. It was the others he watched for.

He started through the letter again but couldn't take his mind from Dremmer. College Boy was married, had said as much, though it was clear it wasn't much of a marriage. He wrote his father sometimes, but never his wife. And she never wrote him. Then a few months back, he got a telegram. Whatever was in it hit him hard, though Dremmer didn't say nothin'. He'd seen it in his friend's face for days, wondered if Delores might have left him. Then when word come down that they might get home for Christmas, he'd asked Dremmer if he was looking forward to it. The look on the man's face. He stumbled around, said something about seeing her and her baby, and for sure his father. Then he started talking about his horse. But he'd caught it, knew Joe College had said more than he intended. "Her baby" was what he said.

Whatever Dremmer carried, he seemed shamed by it. Bear fought the urge to tell him there was hope, that his life wasn't sealed up for good or bad at twenty-four. He wanted him to know that whatever had come be-

105

tween him and his wife could be dealt with. But Dremmer never gave him the chance to say it, wouldn't talk about her. Wouldn't talk about home at all. Always turned the questions back to him and Babs and Irene. Seemed happy enough for him to have a wife and child he loved. Said so— like there was no hope of that for him, like something he'd done had ruled that out.

* * *

The crew was clustered around the door talking about being home for Christmas. David wandered to the opposite side of the barracks. He wanted to see James and Elise— needed to see Jesse, to offer him something to complete what had been between them. He simply had no way to go about it. There would be only a few more legs of their training before they received their orders, and his prayer that night kneeling in the snow pressed heavily on him. It wasn't an easy thing to think of death, but it was little easier to think of going back to Delores.

The thought of the child still sent a shiver down his spine, and he clung to the hope that the lie he'd lived hadn't caused another creature to be born into the hot, black sin of his blood, hadn't brought upon the earth a spirit filled with the desire to know mysteries that wouldn't be revealed and or to seek a justice he would never find.

But Delores knew about injustice, too. For all her plotting, she was no different than he. She'd sought no more than her dream demanded, and he had offered her nothing for it but contempt. He wished he'd been gentler. Most of all, he wished he'd stood up to her. It would have been the kindest thing.

"We gonna make it home to the wives for Christmas, Dremmer?" Bear broke the monotony of the howling wind and the sharp insistence of his thoughts. It was the second time he'd asked. Bear sensed something, probably wanted to help, but there was nothing he could do. Nothing anyone could do.

"I don't know, Bear. I'd sure like to see my father. There's something I want to tell him."

Bear sat up in his bunk. "Yeah, what's that?"

"Just that I'd like for him to be the one to see to my horse is all."

"You ain't plannin' on coming back?"

Lieutenant Berkowitz stepped in. Everyone rose, saluted.

Berkowitz returned the salute, waved the formality away. "As you were. Where's the duty roster?"

Corporal Guy ran to the corner to retrieve it from the nail it was hung on.

David shrugged, turned back to Bear. "Well, you never know, do you?"

"You have to be the most morbid SOB I ever met." Lioni had moved behind him when Berkowitz came in. He turned to face the perfect smile.

Crawford Aimes sidled close. "Morbid? Oh, you've never met my sister. You wanted to meet our sisters, right?" David shot him a look. There had been, for some time, a discernable tension growing between the two. "She's a nun. Just what you need."

"Yeah? Any dirty habits?" Lioni winked.

Aimes shook his head. "You know, Lioni, sometimes I think you're fighting your own war, a one-man crusade to make the world safe for hedonism."

"That's the pitch! They teach you troglodytes about hedonism in Arizona?"

"No, I learned it in Jesuit school. Something to spice up confession, you know."

"Why don't I go home with you, meet your sister. The two of us could go to confession afterwards. That ought to spice things up."

Crawford's neck grew crimson. David looked at Bear, saw the gentle knowing in his eyes.

Berkowitz found a folding chair, drew it beneath him, sat, crossed his legs and brought his pipe to his mouth. "I'm reminded of a story my rabbi often tells."

"Your rabbi, Lieutenant?" Lioni stepped to the side, made a face behind the lieutenant's back.

"That's right. The story is about a king who slept with the wife of one of his best officers. She was a dish, and as the king began to wear a path from his back porch to hers, she became quite expectant. The king's army was at war with some band of Huns or other so the king calls the husband home, ostensibly to gather intelligence on the war. The fact was, he assumed the officer's libido would be faithful to crown and nature and cover

107

his royal misstep. Unfortunately, the officer was so keen on the war and the privation of his troops, he refused to sleep with his wife and requested to be sent back to the front."

He glanced at Bear again, was surprised to see him smiling.

"Well, this wily king saw an opportunity in that and had the man placed in harm's way. As soon as the king received word of the officer's demise, the dish was free to join the royal entourage, and all seemed well. For a while. Then one day a reporter from *The Daily Herald* came for a royal press conference."

Berkowitz paused, sucked on his pipe, made a quick scan of the faces gathered around.

"The reporter stays for drinks and begins telling the king a story. Seems a rich man was receiving guests and needed a lamb for lunch. He didn't want to choose from his own flock, so he picks a lamb belonging to the local poor man who had but one and, being lonely, was inordinately attached to the little woolly. Now the rich man, on being refused on his offer to buy the priceless pet, proceeded to take it from the man's arms and quickly convert her into a feast fit for a king."

He spied Lioni, his mouth wide, looking incredulously at the others. Aimes stood to his right, red-faced but listening.

"The king immediately demanded that the man be brought to justice."

Berkowitz stopped, relit his pipe. "To the king's chagrin, the reporter told him that he, the king, was that man and that he had killed an innocent and taken his wife."

The room grew uncomfortably still. Only Bear seemed to know what Berkowitz was up to. The lieutenant stared directly at Lioni and Aimes. "Now, you boys need to discuss this matter further before it endangers all our lives."

Crawford nodded. "Yes, sir."

Lioni raised his hands. "Okay, so what gives, Aimes?"

Aimes stared out the barracks window and swallowed hard. "My girl is what. When I left, we were talking about getting married." He faltered, seemed to be fighting for his voice. "Now she writes and tells me she's seeing this guy I know. Thinks he's a lady killer, you know— like you, Lioni." Aimes stared at the other waist gunner. "He's got the sex drive of a billy goat and the scruples to match."

Lioni laughed. "Hey, I read you. I didn't know." He reached across the bunk to put his hand on Aimes' shoulder.

"No!" Aimes faced him, the veins in his neck bulging. "You think you can flash that Wop smile and slap a back or two and make everything okay. But you never think about anybody else, so long as you can get togged to the bricks couple times a week and sweet-talk some skirt into the sack. Like in Spokane. She was engaged to a sailor, right?"

"Sure, but she could have said 'no.'" Lioni seemed to have lost his footing.

"Yeah, she could've. But she was lonely and scared, and you knew just what to say to make her feel better about it. For a while. She still engaged to her sailor?"

"Hey, I don't know. I haven't kept up—"

"But she wrote you, didn't she?"

"Sure, a few times, but—"

"But life goes on, right?"

"As a matter of fact, it does, Aimes. Hey, I'm not too keen on taking the heat for what happened to you. I'm not the one stole your sheba."

"But you're no different. You're just like the one that did."

"So I'm a monk until you get over this girl of yours?"

"Yeah, I think that would be all right. A good start, anyways." Aimes was animated. "And I think we need to help you live up to your vows."

David was silent, surprised at his need to demand of Lioni all that Aimes required.

Bear looked at the floor but said nothing.

"How about you, Lieutenant?" Aimes turned to Berkowitz. "Do you think we need to help Lioni live up to his promises?"

Berkowitz smiled, pulled the pipe from his mouth. "You know, I do see your point. And vows hastily taken are often forgotten. He may very well need us to help keep him on the straight and narrow and in his own bunk at night. Not to mention making matins and vespers."

Aimes turned his back on Lioni and smiled at the others.

"Hey, you guys are jazzing me, right? There's no way I can sit in these barracks every night of the week. I can't do it." Lioni looked around, his eyes wide.

"Sure you can, Lioni." David surprised himself. "We'll help you. That's what friends are for."

Bear eased forward, rested a restraining hand on his shoulder, looked at Lioni. "You know, what you've been doing ain't right." His friend turned and looked at him. "Fact is, we can't make you do what's right. But we can protect Aimes here from you rubbing salt in his wounds. We don't have to listen to your stories no more." Bear squatted, scratched on the concrete with his finger. "You're right about one thing, though. What happened to Aimes wasn't your fault."

Bear turned. "Aimes, your girl ran around on you of her own free will. She betrayed you. Whether she meant to hurt you or not, it was her choice, too. Maybe you're puttin' more on Lioni here than he deserves."

Aimes dropped his head. "Yeah, could be. Maybe so."

The silence grew into discomfort. Finally, Lioni looked at Aimes. "You're really gone on this girl, aren't you?"

David waited, but Crawford made no sound or motion.

"That's tough, buddy. I'm sorry." Lioni extended his hand.

"It's okay." Aimes spoke just above a whisper and reached for Lioni's hand.

# Chapter X

## December 1942

Winter pressed hard against the hills. Jesse sat in his chair before the window, glanced occasionally at Delores as she worked at the sink. The wind had picked up a blistering, white quickness and spun around the lone cedar and into the pen where Dancer stood with his head low, facing the gray wood of the barn.

"It's been a while since I've seen a storm the likes of this."

She offered no response, so he turned back to the window. The dark silhouettes of mules' heads bobbed above the drifts for minutes before Morgan appeared in the buckboard, his hat pulled down and a scarf wrapped around his ears. The mules were pulling hard to move so slow. Snow had to be getting deep.

Delores wrung her dish rag and draped it over the faucet. "Just the time for David to be off God-knows-where playing soldier."

He had seen her anger grow in the months she'd been with him in the hills. There was an insolence, too, since she'd come back from Brighton with Isaac, as if she'd drawn a line with him on one side and her and the baby on the other. Save for the excitement she showed when Morgan came around, she seemed intent on sulking, letting him know he was a nuisance and keeping him away from the child.

The mules pulled the wagon in front of the house. Morgan dropped into the snow and waded to the door. Jesse could see from the window that the team was gaunt and tired. It set a fire inside him. For all of David's lack of understanding, he would never let an animal go hungry or be worked down. Especially in the cold.

Morgan pushed through the door and bellowed in the force of his ample wind. "Hey there, girl. Whatcha' got for a tired, wayfarin' stranger to eat?"

"Shhh! You silly! You'll wake Isaac." The words were a protest, but Delores gleamed with delight. He'd seen it before. That and the looks between them. A worrisome thing, and not just because of David. It was clear before the boy left that it was no real marriage, but for her to be moved by the hunger in her loins... He shook his head. It could surely be said that the boy drove her to it. Still, for her to show her need for a man, this man, so openly...

He wheeled himself toward his room. He might not be able to change such things, but he would not, by God, be a witness to them. He reached to close the door behind him.

"Jesse, where are you going? Your dinner is almost ready."

"Not hungry." He turned to see her standing before the door red-faced, her mouth gaping wide.

She threw his tin plate against the table. It clanged and rolled onto the floor. "I've been slaving for two hours fixing your dinner and now you're not hungry?"

He closed the door, sealed them from his sight though not his hearing. Something else they didn't understand, always speaking behind his back as if his useless legs somehow kept him from understanding their words.

"Hey, girl, don't let him get to you. He's just an old man."

*Just an old man.* He could imagine Morgan baring his teeth, drawing her in.

"Oh, Morgan. It's so good to have a friend like you. Sometimes I get so lonely here I think I'm gonna die."

The baby began to cry. Probably awakened by her throwing his plate around.

"Here, Baby Boo! Here now." Delores cooed in her embarrassing way. Morgan laughed. He could hear it through the door and above the wind howling at the corners of the house.

Morgan shuffled before he spoke. "I'd better go unhitch the team."

"You don't have to go. He'll go back to sleep in just a minute, won't you, Baby Boo?" He knew the look she was giving him, had seen it often

112

enough.

"I'll be back, girl. You can count on that."

He picked up his letter to David, resumed his scratching even before he heard the door slam. It was an unnatural thing to put his thoughts on paper, not raising and lowering his voice or showing with his face more than the words could tell. He wrote of the snow, early and terrific, of how Morgan had been tending the stock and of how David would not have liked seeing the mules so thin. Cattle, too, he'd wager. But he wrote nothing of the horse, of how he stood at the far end of the pen not taking his feed until Morgan left. He held his thoughts in spite of David's letters always being filled with questions about the black. But he couldn't write what he had seen because it was not a thing he yet believed.

Over fifty years he'd worked with horses and never seen one bound to a man as a dog might be. Seen plenty of smart ones, sure enough, but the black had lost his spirit and learning after the boy left. Grazing all summer close to the house, staying near the barn and tack shed and cedar, Dancer would let no man close. When Morgan penned the horse for winter, he'd choked him down at the end of a rope. He feared Dancer might have outlawed from that, for any horse, once broke, should have led when the rope was around his neck.

\* \* \*

December 10, Blythe, California

David sat on the steps of the barracks. The desert was still, and the sun burned red against the coming chill of night, a powerless shadow behind the potency of day. The sand burned back an airless light paling the moon and empty sky like a molten bed of phosphorous that wouldn't cease to burn for all the flesh it consumed. The place was possessed with a slow gluttony that couldn't be appeased, and he couldn't take his mind from the scorched flesh and twisted limbs within the fire claps that would soon be erupting beneath them.

Bear rested his heavy paw on his shoulder. "What's got you so quiet tonight, Joe College?"

"Just thinking."

"When d'you get commissioned?"

He smiled, felt the pleasure quickly fade. "Bear, do you ever think about what we're going to be doing? I mean about the people we'll be bombing— what they're really like? I don't mean the SS or the Jew-haters, but people like you and me that are just doing what they think they have to do. Simple people. You ever think of that?"

"Yeah, I think about it. 'Course I don't think of myself as simple— you, maybe. But I think about the SS and the Jew-haters, too. I feel sorry for them."

"You do?" He looked at Bear, the waning sun forming a corona about his friend.

Bear nodded, scuffed the powdered earth. "Yeah, I do."

He shook his head. "Seems to me they have it coming."

"We all got it coming, Dremmer. But there's a justice after all this they're not ready for."

"Wish I could believe that. Sometimes I almost do."

"Justice ain't all there is, you know. It's not the last thing. Doesn't have to be, leastwise."

"No? What is?" He raised his eyebrows, dubious.

"Mercy or an amends bigger than any of us can carry."

He stirred and looked away, didn't like dealing in conjectures. "Do you think it will bother you when it comes time to fire at them? Watch the bombs drop?"

"I s'pose it will." Bear nodded into the desert and pursed his lips.

He followed his friend's stare. The night had begun its luminous burn beyond the rows of barracks.

Bear cleared his throat. "It would bother me more, though, not to try to stop them, just to let them keep torturing and murdering those that don't deserve it. Not a very tolerable thing either way."

"No, it isn't."

"Know what I do?" Bear seemed less relaxed, shifted his feet. "I pray for 'em."

"And when they tell you to shoot them, you'll shoot them."

Bear nodded. "Yeah, I will."

"You think praying for them will make them any less dead?"

"It might. Leastwise, it'll give them a chance not to die."

There was something disturbing and unacceptable in what he said. It sounded too much like what one might believe when there was nothing left. But it haunted him into the night, not letting him go until he thought that even if it were a thing he told himself to bring sleep, it might not be so foolish, so he prayed for those who might die by his new skills. And for himself and Bear.

David awoke to more practice bombings and air-to-ground passes, was then ordered into Bear's station in the tail. It felt odd for the targets to be in fixed positions, always in the slipstream. In the afternoon, he took a waist gunner's slot before being sent back to the belly gun. He was glad for the cramped feel of the harness, his knees numb and pressing against the Plexiglass, the quickness of the hydraulics as he spun about. It was a feel he knew. The guns were where they should have been, and it made him secure as in the eye of a hurricane, as he had felt with the cantle of Jesse's saddle scooped beneath him.

The crew's orders awaited them when they returned to base. They were to report for advanced training in Pueblo in sixteen days and were free to be home with their families until then. There was general pandemonium, but for him.

He hadn't seen the child. Not even a picture. Except for those moments when he woke at night and couldn't look away, his being a father to her baby didn't seem real. Seeing the baby, he might not ever force it from his mind. Isaac, a testament in flesh to his lying touch and spineless relenting to her need, a life coming from him with needs all its own that might never be met. And he was to blame for the hurt of it, for all that came from the subterfuge of taking on her desire. All so he might be spared telling her the truth.

\* \* \*

The train ride was interminable. David rolled in the berth, tried to get comfortable. He would see Elise and James soon. That would be a real reunion. His heart grew hungry in the night as the train rocked over the desert and into the mesas, and, finally before the sun rose, into the white-capped bloom of the mountains. Elise had been given the peace and spirit of the hills, the black-eyed mystery of the colt, and the beauty of the dove in all its startling purity. She had known his "Für Elise," had seen it was for her.

He thought of Jesse. It would be good to see him this time, to put things right. And the black who would be in his winter coat now, dull and heavy. But the eyes would be the same, the black depths as drawing as night, and the certainty between them.

But, of course, Delores would be there. And Isaac. His stomach knotted.

It was the afternoon of the second day, and the sun was burning low when the train ground to a stop above Brighton. The housetops and streets were covered in white, and David looked again; he could not help looking to see his Aunt Sarah's house though she had been widowed and moved on eight years before. He listened for the chapel bells, but they were too far away. He would have liked hearing their steady peal, the tintinnabulations.

It was warm, and the snow melted in steady plops from the roofs. He could scarcely restrain himself as the baggage was being unloaded. He would see Elise today. He would hear the soft shucking of James' voice like fresh roasting ears snapping from the stalks and smell the sweetness of his pipe. He lugged his duffle toward the campus, his excitement advancing toward fear. He wanted to turn back and let his heart stop pounding, catch his breath, but he pushed on. His shoes soaked through, but he scarcely noticed. His words were frozen in his throat when he reached their door, and he feared he would be unable to speak.

\* \* \*

"David!" Elise stood, her arms drawn tight about her as though she were chilled. "We certainly never expected to see you. Why didn't you tell us you were coming?"

"Sorry. I was a little short of notice myself."

"Well, come in."

He couldn't keep his mind from the dream or his eyes from her. She'd known the beauty of his gift. The thought thrilled him.

"James is out on a call. It's Bill and Gladys' son— I don't think you knew them. Billy was killed in the Pacific. They were notified yesterday."

He was suddenly out of place. His joy at seeing her seemed somehow

116

wrong. "Oh, I'm sorry. Have there been many?"

"This is the second, and I pray it's the last. Would you like some coffee?"

"Sure. Gosh, Elise, it's good to see you. I've missed you two."

"Well, it's nice to see you, too, David. James should be here soon. I'm sorry he wasn't here to meet you."

The distance in her voice was unmistakable. As much as he'd feared it happening in his long months on the ranch, it hadn't occurred to him that the war would drive a wedge where Jesse's place hadn't. And she had known his gift. That should have brought them closer. He'd lived so near them in his absence. They had been what he knew of home. He wanted to hold her, let her feel in his embrace that he had missed her. Instead, they talked with the caution and civility of strangers. He rose and walked to the cabinet where she was filling the pot with fresh coffee.

"I never had the chance to tell you how much I appreciated you coming to the station to see me off." He reached to put his hand to her shoulder. She jerked away, a furious lack of faith in her eyes. There had been nothing in his touch. She turned again, still carrying the edge of caution on her face,

He took the coffee when it was offered, but heard little of what she said. The hours they had spent together, all they had shared. Could she have forgotten that?

"So tell me about the Air Corps, David." She was straining now, draining her words into the quiet death of his sunken dream, a perfunctory flow of the give and take of strangers. Before him the meat, salted and bloodless, clung in white fragility to the bones of dead men on the bottoms of a dozen reefs and harbors. There among them was his hope and all within that had made him think he belonged. He had no home, had no center but a dizzying wind.

"David, are you listening? You seem distracted."

"I'm sorry, Elise. I have a lot on my mind. I really should be going. Please tell James I said hello, would you?"

"He'll certainly be sorry he missed you. Maybe you can stop again before you leave."

"Sure, maybe so. Guess I'll be seeing you."

"Do take care, David."

She stood as she had when he came, her arms encircling her as he slipped through the door. That was the way he remembered her on the walk to the bus station. It crossed his mind not to go home, to get on board and go wherever he chose. But where would he go?

He'd failed to hold to the emptiness. It was a hard thing knowing only the vacant rattle of his insides, but it would spare him much if he could hold only to that and not want for more. He had needed Elise these past months, needed someone to belong to. But she had shown him he was only someone she knew and had been kind to; if she had ever been bound to him, she wasn't now.

The gift now seemed something other than it had before. She had known it, held it as her own. That had been too clear. She had been given what he wanted her to have, but it had been a farewell gift, and he couldn't return for what was no longer his.

He sat in the depot hoping for Elise to come in and say that it had been a mistake, that she had misunderstood his touch, that they would be family again. Elise and James and David. But she didn't come, and he boarded the bus that would drop him off at Morgan's Crossing.

# Chapter XI

Melting snow filled the creek, tried to cover the memory of hooves slicing black and quick before the moon. The sun was high and the road soft
and yielding beneath his shoes. David shivered, pulled his coat close, remembered warmths he'd known and wondered why they'd slipped away.
But it would be good to see the old man and Dancer again. He had them, at
least. And this time he would leave Jesse with something of himself.

The house appeared beyond the lone cedar and bare elms, and he
lengthened his stride, reached the fence and looked to the pens. Empty. No
sign of Dancer. A chill ran up his spine.

Snow covered the porch in the corner where the overhang hid the sun.
He edged to the door, knocked, stood breathless. The door swung wide,
and Delores stood fixed in the threshold, the brightness of her smile dissolving in an instant.

"Hello, Delores."

She was silent for a moment, made no move in his direction. He was
grateful. "Come in, David."

He stepped inside, and she closed the door behind him. He was lost in
the sudden gloom, cut off from the brightness of the sun and snow, sensing
the presence of the old man.

"Well, I'll be. David, you're home!" He could just make out Jesse's
silhouette against the obscurity and stepped toward the familiar voice. His
leg held, and his shoe hooked against something unseen. He stumbled and
fell headlong across the floor.

"You idiot! Are you trying to kill him?" A bassinet leaned against the
wall, and David lay on a rumpled rug he'd never seen before. The baby

began to cry, and Delores rushed to pick him up. "You're just like Jesse! Both of you need to get out of here until I find a safe place for my baby!"

"I… I'm sorry. I couldn't see. It's so dark and I…"

Delores glared, Isaac's crying little more than intermittent whimpers now. "Get out and let me straighten this room." She marched to the windows and yanked back new drapes, deep green and flowing to the floor.

David straightened his coat, looked at Jesse. "Come on, Dad. Maybe we should go."

* * *

Jesse stared at his son, his chest grew tight and his vision blurred. It had been years since the boy had called him "Dad."

"Well, well, well," he said when they were safely on the porch. "I sure never expected to see you this Christmas. When do you have to go back?"

"Got to be in Pueblo the twenty-eighth. That will give me almost two weeks." The boy waited, looked away. "You doing okay here? With her, I mean?"

Jesse nodded, decided not to linger. "Pueblo. Well, that's not so far, is it? Not like Washington or California. How long will you be there?"

"I don't know. Not long, I'm sure."

The boy wasn't satisfied with his answer. He was like his mother that way. He breathed deep, looked away. He'd said what he had to say.

"Where's Dancer? I noticed he wasn't in the pen when I came up."

Well, there it was. The question was sure to rise, but he hadn't expected to be answering it now. "He's gone. Morgan had some trouble with him. Tried to rope him. The fool horse ran clean through the corral. Morgan patched it, but I'm afraid the colt's ruint. He's been no account at all since you left."

"Trouble, huh?" The boy looked away. "What'd he need him for?"

He never could read the boy when he got like this. "He's running with the cows. Losing some weight, I reckon. Don't even come up when they're fed. Been there a week, ten days." David wouldn't take to what had to be done. Still no use in mincing words. "Morgan figures he ought to be cut. I reckon he's right. Won't be able to handle him otherwise."

"Like hell! If Morgan hadn't tried to choke him down, he wouldn't have broken out."

Jesse squared his shoulders and squinted into the brightness. "Now that's not it. I'm telling you, that horse is outlawed. You can't handle him any other way." The boy never could see the proper way of doing things, had always fought things being as they were.

David turned to go back into the house.

"She won't take to you going in there."

The boy walked on as if he hadn't heard. He wheeled his chair about, vowed to hold the pleasure of David defying her to himself. The woman took on more than was due her.

* * *

David pulled his clothes from the trunk where Delores had put them. It was her room now. He felt her stare but didn't turn, stepped instead into Jesse's room to change. He passed the bassinet on the way, felt both the dread and lure of it. He'd bide his time. The child was hers.

He changed and was out, past Jesse sitting in his chair, headed for the upper pasture without a word. The door to the tack shed waved dumbly in the breeze, the hinges pulling from the frame. Morgan had left it open, most likely. He'd have to fix it before leaving. The sugar tin was as he'd left it, the bridle and hackamore. Jesse's saddle was covered in dust and splattered from rain that had blown through the open door. A good oiling would bring it around. He closed the door and propped it with a two-by-four, headed toward the upper pasture along the trail that Morgan had made with the buckboard and mules, straight up the side of the hill and sure to wash at the first heavy rain. He shook his head. How could some people spend their lives working the land and not learn to care for it?

His steps were strong and sure, and he breathed in the lightness of the day, glided across the snow and soft earth. He climbed to the ridge north of the barn and looked across the upper pasture. Dancer stood high and alone above an outcrop of rocks a quarter-mile away.

His heart pounded in his chest. He angled first to one side, then the other, avoided a direct approach and whistled, not sure the wind would carry the sound. The horse turned, pitched his nose in the air to catch a scent. David slowed, took in the sight. His friend stood with his neck outstretched, ears erect, his body tense and alert. He knew the rippling swells of strength and quickness even without seeing them. He whistled again in his old way and the horse flinched. It was as if the black had more power than he could quite contain, was at once fragile and explosive.

"Hey, pretty boy." He breathed the words into the wind, hoping Dancer could hear enough of his voice to know it. He slowed his pace, waited.

"Hey boy, it's me. I hear they want to cut you, pretty boy. We'll see what we can do about that, won't we, Dancer? Yes, sir. We'll come up with another plan. That's for sure." He took a few more steps, stood within fifty yards. Less than fifty yards. Dancer pawed the earth and jabbed the air with his nose.

"You just take it easy now, pretty boy. I won't let them do that to you. No, sir. Now, just sit tight, Ol' Dancer."

He'd halved the distance. Dancer pricked his ears and flared his nostrils, ready to bolt. He reached inside his pocket for sugar, slowly raised his hand to the air so that the horse would catch the scent. The black leaned forward but didn't move.

"It's been a long time since you had a taste of sugar, hasn't it? But you remember. You've just forgotten how to trust, haven't you?"

He shuffled to the side as if he were going to walk away. Dancer took a tentative step. Then another. Delight welled in his chest, a flame catching dry tinder. He spoke softly and Dancer took a few more steps, waited for assurance that it was he offering sugar.

"Step up, now. I've got two pockets full. You can trust me. We're still friends." The black made a cautious approach. "Yeah. That's right."

At last the horse sniffed his hand and jerked back, licked his lips and reached to take the offering. He stepped slowly toward the outcropping, eased back on a rock and let Dancer come to him and take the sugar one lump at a time. When he finally turned to walk away, Dancer followed with all the ease and confidence the horse had ever shown. After a few steps, he stopped and let the horse nibble at his fingers. He stroked the black's neck, scratched along his back and under his chin. Dancer breathed deep and nuzzled back as he always had. He put his arms around the slender neck, felt the comforting weight of Dancer's head as it came to rest on him.

"I've missed you, boy." The words were choked, his throat tight as Dancer squeezed against his shoulder.

* * *

Delores stood at the kitchen window rinsing out Isaac's bib. She watched as David sauntered in from the pasture behind the pens, the horse following like a stray dog. She wrung the bib, a fire growing in her breast. She'd seen David come from the tack shed earlier, his pockets full of sugar and knew this would happen, hated him for the way he loved that animal, and not because she wanted his love, either. She was beyond that. There'd been a time, and not so long ago, when she needed his desire, but he'd failed her. He'd never once just done what the situation called for, never just took on what she needed. He'd been no man at all. Still wasn't.

And he hadn't so much as looked at Isaac. Not that she wanted him to. He had no part in her baby and never would, however small or great the blood they shared. Still, if he had been any kind of man, he would have gone to him, shown some concern.

But he'd be gone again in a few days. If he returned, he'd be surprised at how little he had to come back to.

* * *

Jesse watched the pair coming in from the pasture and shook his head. Dancer followed even without a halter. He wouldn't have believed it if he hadn't seen it. He gripped the push rings and wheeled around. David closed the gate behind the horse, fed him, more than was needed by his estimation, and brushed him free of mud. Dancer stayed at the oats, turned and nuzzled the boy's hand a few times. It was as if David had never gone.

The boy stowed the brush in the bucket and headed for the tack shed. Jesse rolled his chair back and stared beyond the fence. A minute later, David emerged from the shed and ambled toward the house. The boy stopped at the porch to pull off his muddy boots. He stared at the lone cedar, heard the boy mumble something.

"What was that?"

"I said, 'Outlawed, my ass.'"

The door slammed shut. Jesse shook his head. A laugh rose from somewhere deep, and he didn't try to hold it in.

* * *

David heard drawers sliding, the snap of a sheet in Delores' room. He

123

moved a chair next to the bassinet and watched the baby sleep. It wasn't as he'd feared. There was nothing revealing in the tiny face that would take his hope. Nor was there anything to nourish it. He sat for minutes staring at the intricacy and innocence. The child was like other children, small and fragile. Except that Isaac might be his. It was an immense weight. The baby had done nothing to deserve being born into this. He touched the tiny hand, felt Isaac squeeze his finger as he slept. His heart grew tender, and a prayer formed beyond his will, more uncertainty than hope, that the child would not seek what could not be found or be cursed with the black sin of his blood.

* * *

Delores stood watching behind the door as David sat beside the bassinet. She grew full with fear at something words couldn't hold. The baby needed her as he needed no one else. She had borne him, nursed him, cared for him without a husband, and she didn't want this man coming in now to take his love as if he were a father to him. Isaac was hers, and David would have no part of him.

The baby stirred and she went quickly as if he needed tending.

* * *

The three sat in silence. David hurried to pick up the dishes, but Delores took them from him and carried them to the sink. The old man, caught up in reverie or perhaps forgetting why the silence was so deep, began to tell the story of a mule he'd broke. It was when he was young, he said, and his legs could run forever. He could breathe deep the clover mornings and the scythe would sing all day at his behest and not grow heavy.

This mule, the old man said, had been ruint by the fella who owned her, and she was strong and full of the devil. Couldn't be trusted, and if you weren't watching she'd kick, try to break your leg or bust your head. He grew peaceful at the telling, remembered the story and settled back against the chair.

The man who owned her, Jesse said, had let her loose after she'd kicked him so when he got her, she couldn't be put in harness for she knew what it was to win the fight. So what he did, he said and showed with his hands, was he put a rope on her hind leg and brought it up over her withers and tied it to her opposite front leg. If she tried to kick, she'd trip herself. He did it every morning— first tied her legs, then put her in harness and hitched her to the plow. At the end of the summer, he took her back to the man who owned her and told him she was broke sure enough. Well, the man rode by a few days later, and stopped to talk so he up and asks about his mare mule. Yup, the man says, she's broke mighty fine and works mighty fine, but what he can't help wondering is why she raises her hind leg every time you hitch her to a plow.

He laughed. It was the best telling of the story he could remember.

Jesse grinned, shook his head. "Mule must have looked like a dog after a fresh wheel."

Even Delores smiled.

* * *

David woke to the sound of Morgan's truck and slipped out from under his mother's quilt in the tack shed. Through the crack in the door, he watched as Morgan stepped toward the house and stared over his shoulder at Dancer in the working pen. Delores and Jesse would tell of how he came to be there. He was glad of that, for now he wouldn't have to face the picket grin and the look that told him he had the heart of an old woman. He pulled his jacket tight against the morning chill and caught the fragrance of her soap. She'd washed even his scent from the place, and he was warmed by the comfort of her scorn.

He stepped from the tack shed and smiled when he spotted Dancer waiting. The black nickered low and throaty, and he knew the horse was glad that it was him coming with oats and alfalfa and the smell of sugar. He put the feed out, and while Dancer ate, he curried and brushed until some of the silk came back into his blackness. When the grain was gone, Dancer nuzzled back in his old way.

It would be noticed if he didn't go inside, so he left Dancer, climbed the fence and stepped through what was left of the snow, the sweet, rich smell of the earth rising about the place like a promise of spring. When he reached the porch, he pulled his boots off so as not to anger Delores and stepped through the door in sock feet.

There was a flurry as Morgan pushed Delores away in a sudden panic and spun toward the door. Delores staggered, caught her balance and straightened.

He closed the door and fought the delight that threatened to surface on his face. "Sorry. I didn't mean to interrupt. I should have knocked."

"You wasn't interruptin' nothin'." Morgan's voice was high. "It ain't like we was—"

He raised his hand and headed toward the coffee pot. It wouldn't do to smile.

"I was seeing to Morgan's cut!" Delores put her hands to her hips and jutted her chin.

He blinked. "Oh, yeah?" He looked at the gash on Morgan's cheek. "That looks nasty, all right. What happened?"

"Oh, just a branch. Mules took the buckboard right under a tree yesterday." Morgan stood gray-faced, fingering the brim of his hat.

"Delores, isn't there some iodine in the cabinet above the sink?" He displayed all the solicitude he could muster, was almost sorry for the cut.

"Isn't Jesse up?" David turned to Delores scurrying to the cabinet.

"No, he's been sleeping late." She was moving every bottle, frenzied in her search.

He turned a chair around and sat with his arms resting on the top rail. "Morgan, how's business?"

"Been purty good. As good as it can be with the rationing and all. Some things actually been pickin' up with the war. Not that I like it. I mean, I know it's been pretty rough."

"Has for some. I haven't suffered anything worse than blisters, myself. Anyway, we're glad to be of service."

"Well, I think I've had my share of KP, if anyone is interested." Delores' voice rattled, her hands busy scrubbing a clean cabinet.

He shook his head She was still struggling with the injustice of things. "Well, you know what they say, Delores: 'War is hell.'"

Morgan chuckled, then caught Delores' scowl. She stared a threat into him, and he looked away.

He stood, swallowed his coffee and cleared his throat. "Well, if you two will excuse me, I think I'll have myself a little ride."

"You ain't gonna try to board that crazy black, are you?" Morgan was smiling, hoping he would find his revenge quickly from the looks of it.

"No, Morgan, I'm going to *do* it. So long as you stay out of sight and smell of him, he'll be fine." His jaws rippled, and he turned away, startled by the quickness of his anger.

Dancer hadn't been saddled in almost a year, and Morgan's rope wouldn't make the horse apt to take the leadings of the bit with grace. His stomach fluttered and his palms were wet. Truth be told, he was nowhere near as sure of what would happen as he let on.

He took the bridle and saddle to the pen. Dancer was wary but let himself be caught. David waited, tried to steady his breath, stroked and soothed in all the ways that might bring back what was once familiar. The horse calmed, and he eased the saddle over the narrow withers, cinched it only half tight, spoke soft and still, leaned against the rail and waited for Dancer to ease, then turned to see a narrow sliver of darkness at the edge of the front door.

He slid to the side of the black and cinched the saddle tight, hung his weight from the saddle horn so that Dancer would remember the feel. The horse stood, a river, black and fierce, scarcely held within its banks. He comforted, his hand patting and pressing the hot, black neck as a mother would hold a baby to her breast, then pulled himself into the saddle and took the slack from the reins.

"Easy, pretty boy. Easy now." Both were still, each waiting out the other.

"Dancer, just ease on out." David nudged him and the horse took a tentative step and then another. "Good boy!" He stroked the damp neck. Dancer breathed deep, moved into a quivering trot around the edge of the pen, recalled in seconds his gaits and cues, worked as if it had been the day before that they'd rehearsed them. He pulled the horse close to the gate, slipped the rope from the gate post and let it swing wide. Dancer thundered from the pen, and he gripped the saddle horn, his heart free in flight.

He spent the next ten days riding the hills, lying atop a sage-covered knoll as Dancer grazed or bringing in cows that hadn't been tended, the both of them remembering the games of their days together. Dancer nickered in his stallion way, calling him from his sleep in the mornings, and when he was fed, they slipped into the hills.

David stood before the fence thinking of the trip to Pueblo in the morning. The old man wheeled out to him and began to speak of the fineness of the day and the beauty of the horse. He knew there was more.

"You happy with the way Morgan is seeing to things?" He rubbed Dancer, watched Jesse from the corner of his eye.

"You've seen how things are. It's what we've got." The old man shifted. "I suppose you've seen them together."

He felt ashamed, found out. "You were awake the other morning?"

"I was awake. And on a few mornings besides that."

He didn't know what to say. "I guess you can't blame her. She needs someone."

"Then be a husband to her. Don't you see it's your duty?"

"I can't." He shook his head. "I can't be with her, Dad."

Jesse stopped, stared. "And what about your son?"

He met the old man's gaze. "You really think he's my son?"

"Can't you look at him and see that?"

"No, I can't. And it's obvious she doesn't want me that close."

"That's some excuse."

"No excuses. I think he may not be my son. What's more, she doesn't want me to be a father to him."

Jesse shook his head. "It's you that doesn't want it."

"No, I don't, though that's no fault of Isaac's." He remembered the touch, the innocent sleep, a hurt for the child swelling in his breast.

The old man slipped into the silence where his comfort lay, and he knew he had failed his father once again. Still, nothing could be done about it.

"There's another thing." Jesse began again, a hushed pain in his voice. "She's spoken a couple of times about us moving."

"If she wants to move, she's free to go." He held out the barest hope she might.

"No, that's not what she has in mind. She wants me to sell the place to Morgan and move with her to Naomi's."

A fire rose, roared through him, and he knotted the lead rope in his hands. "This is *your* place. It's taken two lifetimes and part of mine to build it. It's all you ever wanted. How many times did you tell me that a man builds a business for himself, but he builds a ranch for those that follow? He does it for his children and their children, so they can know the life he knew, only better." He dropped the rope, stared at Jesse. "It's what you said. Land is a sacred trust. You can't let them get away with this!"

The old man stared at his legs. "It's not that I want to."

"Nobody can make you sell. You don't owe anything to anyone." He looked away, stared at the lone cedar. Rage kindled, was starting to blaze, at what they were taking from the old man. And from him.

"It's not that easy. I'm crippled. One day I was young; the next day I was old."

He clenched his teeth. "She's got Naomi trying to talk you into this!"

"You leave Naomi out of this! She only wants what's best for me."

"She wants as big a piece of this place as she can wrangle away from Delores. Those two will take the gold fillings from your teeth and let you eat mush if you let them!"

"Don't you ever talk about Naomi that way! Ever!" The old man was white-faced, turned to wheel away, but not before he saw something. There was in Jesse's turning a shadow of doubt in Naomi's claim to truth, and perhaps in her heart being wholly devoted to him.

He fought to still his anger. "Wait. Listen just a minute. I have something to ask you, and it's got nothing to do with Aunt Naomi."

The old man was silent, but kept his back to him.

"I want you to take care of Dancer while I'm gone." He waited, sought for words. "And if I don't come back, I want you to see to it that he's taken care of. Don't let him go to someone that will cut him or take his spirit. And don't let Morgan touch him."

Jesse was quiet, his face bent toward the ground, motionless for seconds. Finally, the old man raised his head, brushed his eyes roughly with his sleeve, offered a slight nod, and began pushing himself toward the house.

"You'll take care of him, then?" He waited, needed an answer.

Jesse stopped but refused to turn. "I will."

129

# Chapter XII

## Pueblo, Colorado, January 1943

David stood beside the barracks, watched the sea of light drain from the land. For three days they'd been hammered by a blizzard, grounded by winds that lifted long columns from the desert floor. The desiccated snow blew for miles until what settled in a frozen rut or caught in a remaining clump of grass was more brown than white. At night, the cold winds wailed so that he couldn't discern storm from wolf.

He stared across the mesas, beyond the sparse grass and yucca, watched the light dwindle to a coral haze. Cold rose from the earth, and coyotes howled alone again and pure. In the day he seldom saw them. They blended into the land where they couldn't hide, ran as suckling pups torn from their mothers' teats by the fever of the chase, ran until their legs bent from the weight of their years or the air grew too scant to fuel their need for freedom.

A few were caught in the burning iron of a hunter's trap, and some, refusing to wait for the quicker peace of the trapper's gun, ripped meat from captured paw. And when they reached bone, white and chalky cold, they tore it socket and sinew from the searing jaws.

He leaned against the Quonset, propped his heel on the corrugated metal, wondered if in ripping bone from iron there might have been a moment when they came to see that what was done could not be changed, that they had lost their free and silent lope across the land. He shivered, pulled his jacket close. What inklings labored within their hearts and compelled them to cling so tenaciously to life?

He laced his boots and set off into the encroaching gloom, his pace too quick for wisdom's solace but scarcely enough to content his heart. He ran until the lights over his shoulder dimmed to pinpoints, searched the night hoping to find something beyond the emptiness and fought the fear that the search was in vain. The night grew silent, the howls ebbing into darkness. Still he ran, hearing only the pounding of his feet against the frozen earth, his heart surging in his ears. He was wet with sweat, his lungs hungering for the sweetness of the cold, and he stopped, aching for an answer.

But the question was bigger than any choice he'd made, bigger than anything he'd done or known. It was something every man before had faced alone and every man after would confront without appeal. This was his time. He stood against the night, sucked in the frigid air, determined to embrace whatever the truth might be.

* * *

The briefing ended abruptly. Dougan ordered the crew to saddle up. David rose with the others and stepped silently from the Quonset, then waited in the cold for the jeep. When it came, they piled on, and he claimed his spot on the back.

The captain scooted in beside him, rested a hand on his shoulder and shouted above the whine. "Dremmer?"

"Yes, sir?"

"I want you to walk through preflight with me."

He stared, nodded. "Yes, sir."

The jeep bounded across the frozen tarmac and began winding down seconds before the brakes squealed. Dougan waited until the others jumped off, then slid to the concrete. "I've heard you say more than once that you'd like to fly one of these things. That being the case, you're going to have to know what keeps this hunk of aluminum in the air."

"Absolutely, sir. But won't I be a threat to your job?"

Dougan laughed. "I'll take my chances." He pointed to the ailerons, reviewed the basics of lift and drag, quizzed him on the controls as they swept past the flaps, asked him stall and landing speed.

"Ninety-five and ninety respectively, sir. No load, of course."

Dougan scurried to the ladder. "So what else do you think you should know?"

He put his heart on the line. "Maybe how to fly it, sir?"

Dougan stared over his shoulder. "You really want to know?"

"Yes, sir, I do."

"Dremmer, you're good at this stuff, and the men look up to you. You'd have made a good commander. I don't know why you didn't opt for OCS and pilot training." He paused, looked toward the paling horizon. "None of my business, I suppose." The captain took a deep breath. "Tell you what. If you'll make your way to the cockpit when our objectives are met, we'll start flight school."

"Yes, sir. Thank you, sir." He felt his pulse through his gripped hands.

"Oh, and Dremmer, I'd like you and Billington and Ito to take the sergeant's test before we leave here. You interested?"

He grinned. "Yes, sir. Of course." He grabbed the lip of the open escape hatch and pulled himself into the plane.


## Selfridge Field, Michigan, February 1943

David bounced in the turbulence, braced himself against the fuselage. Pyote and Blythe and Pueblo and Salina were only weeks behind. Now the land was a frozen wedge in his heart that severed him from the past. The turret, when he was ordered into it, was an ice crystal, and though the glycol kept it clear so that he could sweep the skies as if panning for a Messerschmitt or Focke-Wulf, his gloves froze to the banding where he steadied himself, and he left patches of polished leather all around.

He rose, crouched between the fore bulkheads and settled behind the catbird seat. Dougan circled the field, collecting his chicks, worked at a join-up with an element of six.

The captain panned the left side, watched the other planes bobbing and shuffling to stay inside the lead. "Lieutenant Mathews, maintain your bank at thirty degrees. You're about to slide into a sucked position."

He leaned forward, saw almost nothing and settled back to listen. Within minutes the chill began to creep through the wool and leather. It didn't warm now even when the plane dropped to the tree tops.

Something else bothered him about the place. He could see now, as he had in Pueblo when he looked into the endless nothing of the desert, that emptiness was more than something he felt or saw. It was the mirror of a man, a wide and searing chasm.

He scanned the windscreen. Nothing stretched everywhere and forever, what he'd been searching for and running from. It was why he'd looked into the emptiness of night, why he'd bathed himself in the wind beneath a sightless moon and gone away seeking more. The night was full of nothing, and he knew it as the reflection of his own soul.

Still it had no home in him, and he wondered about the prayer and the dream Elise had known as her own. There must have been something beyond the emptiness to supply her with his heart and spirit, to present her with the magic that had been trapped inside him.

\* \* \*

David ambled toward the others gathered around the coffee pot in the corner of the briefing hut. They stood for long minutes waiting for Dougan's return.

Berkowitz appeared at the door. "Time to saddle up, cowboys. The captain will meet us at the plane."

He followed the others into the bitter air and tramped to the jeep, looked beyond the edge of the cleared tarmac, stared into the insipid white and hungered for his land of promise. It was his war, this battle between hope and emptiness, and he would fight it filled either with peace or homesickness.

He stopped suddenly, bent beneath the plane, gathering his gear. The thought so took him that he almost shouted. If his soul were an empty plain, vacant and cold with a wind that blew from nowhere to nowhere, why was it such a hard thing to look into? Why, when he looked at nothingness, did he have to look away or grow sick with longing for something else? If this were his home, he should have been filled with the peace that came at the end of a long journey. Instead, it brought a heartache. And if his turning away were only a thing he'd been taught to do, then he should be able to come to accept it. But he could never come to look at nothingness and not know hunger. He was made for more.

\* \* \*

"Your Brownings are to be reassembled in six minutes. Lieutenant Berkowitz will be inspecting your work." Dougan's voice cracked over the

133

interphone, the plane bobbing and weaving in the heavy air. David went to work, his hands sliding the bolt in place, the blindfold superfluous in the dark belly.

He and the other gunners had spent three hours in the classroom that morning calculating ranges. The first hour aloft, they'd cleared stoppages and worked to harmonize their sights. The activity was a relief that kept him from the darkness of his thoughts. But with nightfall, the ache that had no name would return. He knew the war he fought was real, that if his days were nothing when they passed, then death was not a thing to dread for it already was. It was from everlasting to everlasting and all the days a man might know, all he built or grew was a shallow effort to escape the void.

But if his heart had been created for a land of promise, if he hungered for more because he was created for more... The thought of his discovery charged him again, and he drew hope toward him like a lover.

The crackle of Dougan's voice broke through his wall of thoughts. "Dremmer, I need you forward."

He ascended from his tomb, slipped deftly through the dark. In seconds he was between the bulkheads, his interphone plugged into the auxiliary jack, waiting for Dougan's word.

The captain began without turning, drilled him on the controls, every switch on the pedestal. He took him through the preflight checklist, the engine starts, the run-ups, asked him at every point what to do next and why.

They reached altitude, leveled off. "Okay, Dremmer. I've got a problem for you. You ready?" It was a game, Dougan coming up with a tight spot for him to work through.

"Ready, sir."

The captain looked over his right shoulder, grinned. "You're well into your descent, preparing for landing. You're at twenty-five hundred feet and lose power. What do you do?"

"I bring my throttles up, set mixtures to rich then check my needle-ball and see if I'm off level."

"You're experiencing some yaw, left wing is dropping."

"Left engine, then. I confirm it— dead foot, dead engine. I bring it up with aileron, step on the ball to bring my left a little above level."

"How much above level?"

"No more than five degrees, sir."

Dougan glanced at his left engines. "Go on."

"I check the tachs."

Dougan nodded. "Number two is reading only a couple hundred rpm."

"It's windmilling. At twenty-five hundred feet, my gear will still be up, and I wouldn't have lowered my flaps, right, sir?"

"You're asking?"

"No, sir. My gear is up and there are no flaps."

"Correct. Keep going."

"I begin feathering procedure on two, set prop to low rpm, cut off fuel, feather the prop and shut off number two boost pump."

"Then what?"

"I'm in a go-around sir?"

"No, you're low on fuel. The control tower has you cleared for landing."

"Then as soon as I'm in position, I begin my downwind approach."

The captain nodded. "Okay. You're in position. Now, how do you get down?"

"I lower my landing gear on downwind, but limit my flaps to one notch and keep my airspeed above a hundred and ten until I have landing assured."

Dougan grinned. "Felt smooth to me. How about you, Lieutenant Ream?"

Bangor, Maine, March 2, 1943

David's legs were numb from crouching behind the cockpit. The plane nosed into the clouds that covered the ground with deceit. Dougan's voice buzzed through the headphones.

"Air control reports hazardous runway conditions. Heavy rains, possible mud on runway. Landing is at our discretion. Option to return to Selfridge Field. How say ye, men?"

The captain didn't have to offer them a choice, but one by one the crew called off.

"Bangor, it is." Dougan seemed pleased with the vote. "Heavy cloud cover. We'll drop her down and give her a try."

The crew had grown impatient. He felt it. They were ready, wanted to be done with it. Bangor was to be their last stop stateside, then Newfoundland and the trip over.

"Over there. Over there. Oh, the Yanks are coming, the Yanks are coming..." Ito broke in, unable to restrain himself. He shook his head, laughed.

"Sure glad we're not going to the Pacific. Think I've heard all of Tokyo Rose I can stand." Lioni, sounding testy again.

"Guy, tune in a weather report." The captain, tense. "See if maybe we can go for a swim when we get down."

"If we end up swimming, I think it means we missed Maine, sir." Ito again, unable to contain the jokes.

Dougan grunted. "Well, considering our navigator, that's a possibility."

He could see only white beyond the plane, could just make out the wing tips and tail the last time he'd ventured back to the gunners' slots.

"Looks like pea soup to me, sir." It was Bear, his voice revealing some concern.

Dougan came back immediately. "Too white. Any of you boys know what chowder tastes like?"

Sheen chimed in. "Could be it, sir. It's tasteless enough."

The captain turned into his base approach, David watching over his shoulder. Dougan had added altitude and distance, probably because of the lack of visibility. The captain turned into the final leg. "Sure hope there's a runway down there."

David crouched, stared through the windscreen. They broke through the clouds. Runway lights appeared from nowhere rising fast. His stomach knotted.

Dougan hit the alarm, slapped the throat mike. "Emergency landing positions!"

The tail of the plane fell as if it had been dropped from chains and the engines roared and shook him to the bone. They quieted momentarily as he shot across the catwalk, chute in hand, dove behind the aft bulkheads and pulled himself behind Berkowitz and Guy, his chute behind his head.

Lioni and Aimes sucked up along the opposite side, their chutes dividing them. He heard the flaps still droning, glanced to his left. Ito and Sheen hadn't made it. Dougan was fighting, trying to pull them skyward.

The wheels slapped water. The runway was covered. Had to be. They slowed. Something yielded, and the plane pitched, felt as if it were nosing into the earth. His back slammed into Guy's legs, then the bulkhead. A blur flew forward. *Bear.*

Air exploded from his lungs, and he felt the hard momentum of the ship move round so that he was pinned against the bulkhead. Something snapped beneath him, and he slammed into the fuselage. The plane shifted and slid, seemed not to break its speed. Another blow. The plane scraped, shuddered and they lay helpless and still.

He pulled himself to his knees, drew hard for air and tried to shake himself free of the haze. He peered forward, goaded by a half-formed thought of escaping the creaking wreckage and the smell of fuel, scrambled for the escape hatch, pulled the emergency cord, kicked it free but checked the urge to jump. He slipped to the side to let the others through. Ito and Sheen shot across the catwalk, lunged for the open hole. He looked around, spotted Bear lying face down at the bottom of the bomb bay, stepped down and grabbed his jacket.

"Bear, you okay?" His friend was heavy, as frameless as a sack of sand. He strained, slid his arms around Bear's chest, heaved him backwards, climbed with his heels dragging his friend to the open hatch. Guy and Berkowitz appeared in the imprecise light, reaching, pulling. He grabbed the flight suit and lifted. The shapeless form slid through the hole like flotsam blurring into the gray uniformity of sea. He heaved through and jumped, hit the mud-covered concrete and crawled blindly beneath a wing, stumbled in a dizzied run through the mud and reached the rest of the crew. He turned, stared in disbelief.

Number four engine lay a few hundred yards down the runway. Water covered the concrete, and beneath the water, nearly an inch of mud.

An ambulance slid to a stop. David ran to Berkowitz and Guy who were still supporting Bear. His friend was standing now, wobbly but conscious.

He leaned forward, shouted above the rain. "You okay, Bear?"

Bear rubbed his head and squinted. "Guess so. Took a pretty good lick."

The remainder of the crew stood silent, staring at the mangled fortress. The rain let up a bit, and he looked beyond the ship to see sheared landing gear not fifty yards shy of the runway. The captain had almost made it.

Berkowitz put a hand on Dougan's shoulder, water running from his cap as he leaned toward him. "Thanks, Cap."

"For what? Too cold to swim here. We might as well have gone back to Selfridge."

"Thanks for pulling the nose up like that. You saved our tails." Bear didn't let it pass.

"He's right." Ream chimed in, having a shot at dissuading the guilt the captain might be taking on. "Altimeter was off, and we all elected to come in."

Dougan shook his head, his chin low to keep the rain from his face. "We had to be six or eight hundred feet lower than it read. I tried to pull her up. Don't know what made me come in so high and wide. At least, I thought I was high. Just instinct. Or something."

"Everybody okay?" A young corporal strutted from the ambulance, addressed Lioni and Aimes.

"Everyone's alive, Corporal." Dougan shifted, frowned from the back of the assembly.

"How you boys like our training program?" The corporal squinted at the two gunners.

"Corporal, weren't you taught to salute an officer?" Dougan stood white-faced and rigid.

The boy snapped to attention. "Yes, sir!" He saluted in the perfect pose, a soldier.

David blinked at the incessant rain. There was something familiar about the boy, even from a distance. He waded closer.

"Timothy?"

The corporal pivoted as if to another reprimand. "Yes, sir!"

"It's me, Tim. David Dremmer. So you made it in, did you?"

"Uh, yeah, I did." The boy pivoted, seemed embarrassed, returned to the ambulance without another word.

He shrugged. "Well, it's good to see you, too."

The crew piled in, left Timothy alone on the front seat. Dougan, Ream, and Berkowitz ambled back to a jeep that had followed the ambulance.

The infirmary was stark white, empty even of medical equipment. David stared, looked at Bear sprawled on the gurney, his hand shielding his eyes from the light. A young medic filled the doorway, began turning away even before he spoke. "You will all be held here overnight. Procedure." He took a step into the hallway.

"Where will we go from here?" Ito, voicing the fear they all held that they might be split and reassigned.

The medic shrugged, then seemed to respond to something in their faces. "Just a guess, but you guys will probably be assigned a new plane after the investigation."

# Chapter XIII

She glistened in the early light, ice-crystal lace sparkling on her skin and wings. David stared for minutes, walked around her. The factory-fresh B-17G had been flown in from Washington state the night before. The crew had only just been told she was theirs, had scurried the half mile from mess just to look at her. He strained against the reflection in the windscreen, couldn't see the catbird seat.

A jeep whined behind him, and he turned to see Dougan crawling out, lips pulled tight, his face drawn. David moved quickly toward the rest of the crew.

The captain faced them. "Men, we're required to put in another fifty hours of flight time on the new ship before leaving for Gander Lake. Then we can fly either with stops in Greenland and Iceland to refuel or go straight to Prestwick. If we choose to fly straight across, we'll risk running short of fuel if we drift off course or run into weather." He stopped, looked at the crew. No one spoke. "If we fly through Greenland and Iceland, we risk hazardous landings. Both runways are apt to be icy."

Ito scuffed the tarmac, dropped his head. "Sir, did everything turn out all right? I mean with the investigation?"

Dougan was silent for a moment, his face softening. "Everything's fine, Ito. The seal was broken on the altimeter. Our high and wide approach saved our tails— even if it wasn't by the book." He caught the captain's stare, returned his smile. "I assumed you knew, boys. We're still a crew... all the way to England."

No one spoke, but he felt a weight lift from his shoulders.

Dougan looked at the plane. "She's a beauty, isn't she?" He grinned, let the clipboard fall to his side. "No need to be in a hurry about deciding our course. Newfoundland's soon enough. Oh, and before you disperse, I need to see Ito, Dremmer, and Billington. Pronto."

Bear caught his glance, shrugged and looked away. The others ambled off, Guy and Sheen looking back.

"Sir, if there's a problem, I can assure you Dremmer is responsible."

Dougan stared at Ito, crossed his arms, his face angular and stern. "All right, this is for all three of you. We'll be here for at least two more weeks. Before we ship out, I want you guys to bring your uniforms up to spec."

Bear caught him with a glance, seemed concerned.

"The thing is, there's a PX here. Got to be someone there that can sew sergeants' stripes on for you." The captain paused, smiled. "If not, sew them on yourselves."

* * *

David lay on his bunk. He'd finished a novel set in Mexico, a less than memorable story of a revolutionary that strongly resembled Pancho Villa. The brief passages describing the dust and heat did little to warm the barracks. He'd done push-ups and chinned himself until he thought sleep would come, but it hadn't. He lay on his stomach, watched Bear reading his Bible in the corner bunk.

Nothingness wasn't his home. He knew that now. But he hadn't been able to give himself to hope as Bear had. He prayed, certainly, but it wasn't like Bear prayed, as if he knew he was heard and had some pull with whomever might be listening. His prayers were more a stay against the cold, undirected and unsure. Bear's were—

"Sergeant Dremmer, you asleep?"

He rolled over, a bit confounded by the title. Tim stood fingering his hat. He extended his hand. "A little joe'd, is all. So you heard."

The boy nodded. "Just thought I'd come and offer my congratulations."

"Well, that's fine. Glad you did." He sat up, motioned for Tim to sit on the bunk opposite him, leaned back against the metal frame.

The boy seemed ill at ease. "Guess you'll be shipping out soon."

"Couple weeks if the weather breaks."

The corporal was quiet, seemed all too fascinated with the floor. "So how are you and— I mean, is Delores doing okay?"

"So far as I know." Something was up.

"I was really glad you two got together. I mean, it was so quick for her and all."

He grinned, tried to cover his embarrassment. "Yeah, well, it was pretty quick for me, too."

Tim looked up then dropped his head. "No, I mean quick after Robert. I... Well, we all thought they'd get married after he was home the last time."

"Is that right?" David slid to the edge of his bunk, tried to hold Tim's stare.

The boy looked away. "Well, yeah. Guess it was quite a shock for her, him going back and being killed right away, then, well, you know."

"No, I don't." But he wanted to. He wanted to know everything, wanted the boy to spit out whatever it was he had to say.

"Well, hey, if this is a touchy subject..."

"No, no, it's not. Not at all. I just didn't know Robert had been home before he was killed." He tried to read the boy's face. Did Tim know what he was telling him?

"Oh, sure. Yeah, he'd been home on a two-week pass. He and Delores were, well, you know. They were just always together."

Another quick glance. He knew. He tried to squelch the urgency from his voice. "Is that right? Well, how long was it after he went back that he was killed?"

"Not long. Two weeks, maybe. What surprised everybody, it wasn't long after the funeral that Delores started saying you two were getting hitched. I mean, don't get me wrong— we were all glad she could bounce back and everything, but..."

"Yeah." He was lost in thought. This could explain so much. "Yeah, that was a good thing, I guess."

"Well, hey, David, I've got to scoot. On duty, you know." Tim averted his stare.

"Absolutely. I understand." He rose, shook his hand. "Thanks for coming by. It did me good. You don't know."

"Maybe I do." Timothy smiled, held David's stare for a moment. "Well, hey, you take care over there, will ya'?"

He nodded. "Sure thing. Do your part to make Maine safe for democracy."

He lay back on the bunk stunned. Robert. Two weeks, four from the beginning of his leave. Could it be? And Naomi's insistence on their being together. Could Delores have known? Not enough time for that. But she could have suspected, could have been late. And by Christmas, she would have been more confident. If she told Naomi... The spark of hope incited a firestorm.

* * *

The weather cleared, and the flights began. Dougan summoned David to the cockpit before the engines were started.

"No need for you to be getting sack time while I'm working, Dremmer. Might as well get some tutoring. Can't beat the price."

"You're a born salesman, sir."

"You think so? Could I interest you in signing up for a second tour?"

"While I'm sober, sir?"

He went through the familiar checklist, remembered to turn on the generators and set the gyro when the captain intentionally skipped them. Ream repeated the procedures, went through the motions, nodded.

The engines were started and run-up, the brakes and trim tabs set. The tailwheel was locked and the propellers shook the earth. They broke free, surged into the morning chill.

"What do we do first?" Dougan snapped.

"Retract the gear."

"And now?"

"Continue to altitude and retract the flaps. Reduce power. Check wheels, left and right."

"Good." Dougan grunted then grew sullen through the long ascent. David crouched behind him, waited for a question. None came. The insistent possibilities Tim had planted began to worm their way to the front of his mind.

"Okay." Dougan broke the heavy rattle of the cockpit, his hand on the throat mike. "I've asked Lieutenant Ream to give you his seat for a while. Knowing the controls is one thing. Feeling them, something else entirely."

He looked at Ream. The lieutenant winked, slid out of the seat and slapped him on the shoulder leaning into his ear. "Keep her steady, Dremmer. I need the sleep."

"Do my best, sir."

Dougan began as soon as they reached altitude. "All right, Dremmer. I want you to initiate a right turn. Ninety degrees."

David turned the wheel, dropped the right wing and watched the turn and bank indicator. The plane seemed not to respond. He pressed gingerly on the right rudder.

"Step on the rudder, Dremmer."

He pressed harder, met more resistance. The plane came about slowly.

"She's not going to fall out of the sky, Dremmer. Stand on that rudder."

He pushed hard, edged the wheel to the right.

"Watch your airspeed. Why is your airspeed dropping, Sergeant?" Dougan waited.

He rehearsed his actions, frowned at the controls.

"What's your stall speed, Dremmer?"

"One-o-two clean and loaded, sir."

"And what's your airspeed, now?"

"One sixty-five."

"Are we loaded?"

"No, sir."

"And what's your rpm?"

"Twenty-three hundred, sir."

"So are you anywhere close to a stall?"

"No, sir."

"Then why did you increase your throttles?"

"To up my airspeed, sir. You said—"

"You have us in a climb. What's your altitude?"

"Ninety-six hundred feet."

"You get us any higher, we'll have to go on oxygen. Drop that nose a hair, and you'll get your speed back."

"Yes, sir." He released his breath, glanced at the captain. "I didn't know I'd done that."

Dougan laughed. "When you pressed the rudder, you pulled the yoke back. Relax, Dremmer. It'll come."

It did. By the second week, David had gained a sense of the balance of it all. Ream slipped out of his seat, spoke into his ear. "Commendable of you to provide me with all this sack time, Dremmer, but today I'd like to sleep lying down if it's all the same to you."

He offered him a thumbs-up. "Let me know when you're ready to roll over, sir."

Dougan was patient, encouraging. "Today, I want you to bring us in, Dremmer."

His hands tightened on the yoke. "You mean *land* it, sir?"

"Just get us to the runway. I'll ground handle it. You've taken us through downwind and the turn to base. Today, I want you to take us all the way through final. When we're ready to touch down, I'll take the plane."

"Yes, sir." He swallowed, tried to steady his voice.

Dougan laughed. "My grandmother could fly this thing straight and level. You want to fly it, you're going to have to bring it in."

He nodded, smiled above the trepidation.

"Relax, Dremmer. I'm here. I won't let you have it any longer than you can handle." Dougan turned away, radioed in, set the altimeter and addressed the crew. "We've got a new pilot, boys. Say your prayers and hang on tight." He wiped the smile from his face. "You better hope neither of us messes up, Dremmer. We set them on their ears, they'll be suing your widow for everything you have."

He glanced to his left. "You trying to make me feel sorry for them, sir?"

Dougan chuckled, faced the control panel. "We're approaching from downwind. Pick your path."

David nodded and began the checklist. "Booster pumps."

"On." Dougan took the co-pilot role, let him usher them through the procedure.

"Mixture controls."

"Rich."

"Intercooler."

The checklist continued as the speed and altitude dropped. David made

145

for two pencil lines crossing a white sheet, a third off to the right.

Dougan pointed. "That's where we're going, Dremmer. Can you get us there?"

"Absolutely, sir. Which side we using?"

"Preferably the side with the wheels on it."

He laughed, loosened his grip on the yoke.

"Now, shift your boosters and back your rpms to two thousand to begin your descent. Keep the second runway in sight and find a point about a half mile to the left side. You want to be at a thousand, twelve-hundred feet when you begin the downwind leg."

"Yes, sir." David stared, hoped his jitters weren't visible.

"I'm here, Sergeant."

He nodded, picked the path. At twenty-five hundred feet he dropped the left wing, pushed the left rudder and brought them parallel to the field. Closer to the ground, the response to the controls seemed exaggerated, but he'd anticipated it this time.

"What's your airspeed, Sergeant?"

"One thirty-five, sir."

"Manifold pressure?"

"Nineteen inches."

"Good. Now begin reducing your speed."

"Flaps, sir?"

Dougan waited. "Not yet. You have time. Now what's your altitude?"

"Two thousand feet."

"Airspeed?"

"One-thirty."

"What do I do now, Dremmer?"

"Extend flaps to one quarter." He saw it. The procedure had to be routine— too much going on to sort it all out.

"Extend flaps to one half, sir?"

"Was that a question, Sergeant?"

"No, sir. Extend flaps to one half. Altitude?" He resumed the PIC role.

"Thirteen hundred feet."

"Airspeed?"

"One-twenty. You're good, Dremmer. Watch for the end of the runway

146

over your shoulder. Remember what I told you."

"When I'm at forty-five degrees to the end, bring her abeam."

"That's it."

"Bringing her abeam, sir." He stood on the rudder and felt the earth shift on its axis.

The base approach was quick. He watched until they were perpendicular to the runway. "Bringing her about again, sir."

They came about, a second perfect ninety, the runway less than a mile in front of them.

Dougan laughed, seemed as delighted with his achievement as he would have been his own. "Airspeed?"

"One-o-five."

"Altitude?"

"Three hundred feet." David waited, held his tongue for long seconds, continued the descent until the runway was right outside the windscreen. "Landing assured, sir. We're... "

Dougan chuckled. "You ready for me to take the aircraft, Sergeant?"

"You have the aircraft, sir." He spat the words.

"I have the aircraft, Sergeant." Dougan winked, grinned.

The plane shifted slightly and they were on the ground, taxiing smoothly down the field. He breathed deep, turned and looked at the captain.

"Good approach, Sergeant."

"Thank you, sir." He leaned back in the seat, released his breath and grinned.

* * *

Gandor Lake, Newfoundland, March 14, 1943

David lay awake, drawn by a longing, ancient and inexplicable. He dressed, slipped into the bitter consistency of darkness, stood in the cold waiting for the summit to find substance within the void and breathed the ancient air. Beyond the narrow inlet to the south, a new world was taking shape within the gray mist. Peaks appeared jutting skyward, lengthening, filling, an unseen hand forming them before his eyes. Finally, light erupted in crystal shards slicing through the gray, burst in the dazzling brilliance of a new sun.

He was mesmerized, took care to tuck the awe deep inside where it

147

couldn't be stolen by the gloom. He stood a few minutes longer, wanted not to miss a moment, turned to find Bear staring. He stood exposed but felt no shame. Bear seemed to understand the war he'd been drawn into even more than he. He had no country for his soul, no land of his belonging where he could rest his rushing thoughts and draw strength, but there was comfort in knowing Bear had found such a place.

"Best get to chow, College Boy. Looks like the weather's broke. Likely have a long ride ahead of us." Bear smiled, slipped back through the barracks door.

He started up the side of the rugged hill. Jeeps began to roll and lights appeared around the base, floated within the lifting gray. The ground crews were checking out planes. It was on. Fighters rolled from hangers to be coursed to Greenland. Medium-range bombers began to pop and moan as flight crews started their engines, began topping tanks. He straightened, breathed in the chill. If the weather held, they'd be in Scotland by nightfall.

He pulled his jacket close and headed for mess. Stories had been told for days of B-17s being led directly into Germany or Austria or running out of fuel and going down at sea. The Germans, the fighter jockeys said, had developed an instrument that could draw a compass off course. The flight to Prestwick would take almost eleven hours. They could carry enough fuel for an eleven-hour forty-minute flight.

He pushed the thoughts away, stood at the coffee pot until the crews began filing in. Ito was the first of his bunch to show. He nodded and smiled when Bill saw him. The two moved toward the north end of a long table, a group of fighter jockeys at the other end.

A young pilot, blond and sallow, looked their direction. "Hey, I heard about you guys. You're the ones that ditched the ship in Bangor."

Ito winked. "Yep. Going for purple hearts and an early discharge." He stuffed his mouth with eggs. "What do you think, Dremmer? Those English girls all they say?"

"I'll tell you, Bill, I don't think anything is all they say it is."

"How'd you get so cynical, Dremmer?"

He shrugged. "Riotous living. A dissipation to the soul."

Ito laughed. "I've seen your riotous living. Chin-ups and push-ups till noon. Running after lunch, then a long book in the evening. And lots of sack time. Snoring in cadence, now that's your idea of depravity."

He grinned. "But didn't you ever wonder what made me so tired?"

The engines droned beyond hearing, and David came to feel it as an unknowable part of himself like the rhythm of his heart. Only ocean and the steady pulse for an hour after Dougan's call to saddle up.

The interphone cracked. "Dremmer. I need you up front."

"Yes, sir." He unplugged his headset and moved through the bulkheads, stooped immediately behind the seats. Ream rose, slipped quickly past him without a word.

Dougan pointed at Ream's seat, tapped the headset.

David plugged in, pressed the throat mike. "Sir?"

"Montezuma's revenge. Ream tried to eat half the hog this morning. Hadn't had ham in a while."

"You guys had ham, sir?"

Dougan smiled.

He was quiet for a moment. "Didn't think Montezuma got this far north. Must have had one of Ito's ancestors for a navigator."

Ito cackled into the interphone. "I heard that, Dremmer. I'll remember you when the gods of navigation demand a sacrifice to take us home."

Dougan grinned. "You need the stick time, Dremmer. This is autopilot territory, but it won't hurt you to stay tuned up."

The solid green of the sea rolled before them until it curved and fell away, was broken only by the occasional patch of white. David caressed the throttles, wrapped his hands around the yoke. The white beneath them grew. He stared, consumed by the vastness until all was blanched to nothing save an occasional wisp of blue.

Dougan raised his finger, moved them slightly off course. "You have the aircraft, Sergeant."

He turned, saw the captain wink, felt the subtle resistance of the yoke.

After a few minutes Dougan turned away, looked into the expansive white. Finally, he spoke. "Dremmer, let Sol have your seat."

"Yes, sir." The words rolled in slow reluctance.

"I want you to take mine."

"Sir?"

Dougan ignored him, pushed the mike to his throat. "Sol, you feeling okay?"

"Fine as frog's hair."

"That wasn't kosher ham we had this morning?"

Berkowitz chuckled. "Afraid not. I stuck with the lox."

"Good. I think the ham was tainted. I'm headed in the same direction as Lieutenant Ream." Dougan rose, struggled around the seat.

He turned to look. The captain's face was pasty white.

"You two stay in contact with Ito until one of us makes it back. That understood?"

"Yes, sir."

The coast of Scotland jutted sharp and green into the crimson sky. David checked his watch: nine hours, forty-seven minutes. Dougan had made a pallet with the blankets between the bulkheads but wore his headset, had been quiet for the last hour.

He compared his watch with the ETA and glanced back. "Feeling better, sir?"

"Some."

"How about Lieutenant Ream? Will he be able to take his seat?"

"I'll take my seat, Sergeant. Lieutenant Ream has decided that Erik the Red is more vindictive than Montezuma."

Ream appeared above the captain, leaned on the bulkhead.

"Still among the living, Lieutenant?" Dougan pantomimed and grinned.

Ream's face was pale, but his smile unwavering as Berkowitz handed over his headset.

The lieutenant pushed the throat mike. "Man comes from the aft not in total nakedness, but trailing streams of glory."

Dougan chuckled. "I was pretty sure that was toilet paper we were trailing."

Ream shrugged. "If you guys have it under control, I believe I'll go lie down."

"We've got it, Lieutenant. Lie down before you fall down."

Ream handed the headset back to Berkowitz and slid into the dark belly.

Dougan pushed himself against the bulkhead. "The man's a genius. Give him access to a relief tube, a hydraulic funnel, a can of water tucked in a heated suit, and he'll build a flushable toilet, though not an altogether comfortable one."

David switched to autopilot, and they maneuvered around the cockpit. He took Ream's seat while Dougan reassumed the PIC position. Berkowitz returned to his roost.

Dougan chatted with Guy then touched his mike. "Radar contact has been made. We're on course. Prestwick reports fair and partly cloudy, fifty-one degrees. Tea and scones tonight, boys."

He went through the checklist as they nosed into the clouds covering them in the sightless gray. When they emerged, they were flying straight and level with the field visible in the distance, the hills rolling and green.

# Chapter XIV

## August 17, 1943

David rolled over in his bunk, tried to turn away from the apparitions rising in the dark. He drew his pillow over his head but couldn't escape them. The missions were taking them into Germany now, and every mile had been stained with blood. Not that he hadn't spilled any. He'd been credited with two kills. The real numbers were uncertain. He'd seen any number of the Führer's boys go down in flames as he'd fired at them, but others had been firing, too. No way of knowing who really brought them down. That hadn't bothered him as he'd feared it would. It was kill or be killed. More than that, every one he brought down meant one less out there bringing his friends down. And he'd lost plenty.

The forts were what kept him from his sleep, seeing them wallow in the air, sucked into the earth in a spin no one could escape. Forty-six of the hundred and twelve originally assigned to the group. And he'd seen far too few parachutes.

He'd learned a secret, though, one he couldn't tell because they'd think him daft, as the Limeys were prone to say. He'd found a way to avoid being killed. He was sorry for those that didn't know, but still and all, it was the only way he'd survived, and it wouldn't be right to ask him to give it up. Anyway, it wasn't that he couldn't be killed. He could. It was just that he was harder to kill than most.

The trick was simple, at least what he could explain of it. When he heard the steady drone of the engines, everything slowed. He shut off feeling and thinking of himself as being separate from the plane, thought only of what he was about. He let go of his fear and quit being himself for a few hours, until they were home and the fire and panic were behind them. In those hours, his body became a machine, his hands and eyes working on their own. Only lately, he hadn't been able to turn off not being him, and he slipped away even in the barracks or in the chow line.

He pulled the pillow from his head, heard the whine of the jeep, the squeal of brakes. His stomach knotted. The door swung open. Lights scalded his eyes, burned against the darkness inside. "Rise and shine! Briefing at oh four hundred hours!"

He threw off his sheet and eased from his bunk, careful not to make eye contact with his crew as he made for the latrine. The oh three thirty wake-up was a dead giveaway. This was a deep one, maybe *the* deep one they'd all been hearing about. The expectation hung in the air, held tongues mute. The crew prepared with rote efficiency, exited the barracks without a backward glance and walked together through the silence and dark fog.

"It's the big one for sure." Bear's voice, a breathless whisper.

David stopped, stared. He'd never heard fear in his friend's voice before. "You all right, Bear?"

Bear stared straight ahead. "Yeah, I'm fine. We'll be fine."

He took a chair next to him and settled in below the quiet murmur of the briefing room.

Every eye in the place fastened on Colonel Blake as he strode to the front and pulled down a map that included the whole of Germany. The room grew deathly still.

"Men, your targets for today are Regensburg and Schweinfurt. You will deploy in three divisible waves. Each wave will have both British and US escorts for twenty minutes into France. From that point on, you're on your own."

He clenched his fists to still the trembling, couldn't detect a breath in the room. The buttons on Blake's shirt clicked against his pointer. "At a predetermined point known to your pilots and navigators, the waves will split. Designated squadrons will continue on to the Messerschmitt factory in Regensburg—" The end of the pointer smacked against the map.

The Messerschmitt factory would be heavily defended. He glanced at

Bear. The muscles in his jaw tightened, and he tried to choke down the bile.

"The remaining squadrons will fly south to Schweinfurt." The pointer smacked against the map again. "Your target there will be a ball bearing factory."

A series of slides came up showing the separate buildings and the relative value of each, as well as civilian targets to be avoided in the area. He scanned the room, saw Sheen scratching notes for the IP, the initial point of release.

"The squadrons will be deployed as follows: In the first wave…" Blake droned on, gave groups and altitudes. He held his breath.

"In the second wave, the 534th will fly as high squadron of the low group."

He released the air trapped in his lungs. They would at least be coming home tonight, not flying to North Africa with the Regensburg group. If they survived.

The colonel closed the folder, squared his shoulders and stared across the room. "If you aren't crippled and aren't required to make excessive evasive maneuvers, you will have ample fuel to make it home. For those that don't make it back across the Channel, Air-Sea Rescue will be waiting for you with fighter support." Blake hesitated, searched the ceiling. "Men, if we were to lose every ship that goes out today, it could still shorten the war by eighteen months and save a million lives at the invasion." There was a crack in the colonel's voice. When he looked back, his eyes were glistening. "Some of you won't make it back. It's not inconceivable that most of you won't. But do everything in your power to come back. *Don't give up.*"

The colonel paused. "May God be with you. Good shooting and good bombing."

"And goodbye!" A wiseacre in the back discharged his secret terror. No one laughed.

Blake left the podium, his head down. The room grew deathly still. The gravity of what they were entering made it difficult for him to move. They weren't expected to return. But he'd likely come back, if anyone did. He swallowed hard against the curdling in his gut, looked around him, sorry for the others, wished they knew his trick.

The intelligence officer's footsteps echoed through the hut, as if the men filling the chairs were already ghosts and lacked the substance to absorb the sound. A throat cleared, and he looked to the front.

"By our estimates, this armada is likely to incur six hundred single-engine fighters, four hundred twin-engine fighters and dive bombers, and eleven hundred anti-aircraft guns between the coast of France and Schweinfurt." The captain had a heavy Boston clip, read from his notes, refused to look them in the eyes. "This mission has been scrubbed three times due to weather. German intelligence will know our plans. You can count on that, men.

"They don't think you can make it in this deep, but they will be waiting for you just in case. You will encounter the heaviest flak in the target areas where eighty-eights have been brought in on flatcars."

David's head pounded. Sweat rolled down his chest. He was ready for the engines to roar, reach their steady drone so that he could slip outside himself. He'd learned his trick on his fourth mission when Me-109s and Fw-190s came from all directions, singling out their ship. He downed a 190, put a lot of lead into several others. They came under attack from as many as three 190s at a time. That's when he slipped away. When he did, his hands took over. Pinning one, he somehow knew when the others were sweeping for their approach, and he swung around just in time. It became suddenly clear— with his guns firing, he was invincible. Their ship returned riddled with holes but not a scratch on the crew. They dubbed her *The Swiss Cheese*.

The intelligence officer was droning on about their responsibilities if taken prisoner. He tried to picture what it might have been like at home. The last letter he received from the old man said Delores was now insisting that he sell the place so they could move in with Naomi. He knew what that meant to Jesse— and to him, though he wondered now if he would ever see the hills again. He'd been caught in a trap, mostly of his own making, had chewed bone from sinew, gnawed away his easy lope across the wide land.

Delores and Jesse and the hills had become a dream he once lived. He hadn't meant for that to happen. He thought often of the black, sometimes

155

of Elise— not really as she was, but as he would have her be. She could be any way he wanted now.

The briefing was over. The others laughed in their fear as they scuffed toward their planes. He couldn't hear the jokes for the hammering in his ears and fought back the impulse to vomit, drew deep from the morning air and climbed through the escape hatch to wait in the belly until they were in formation. He prayed in the way he had of praying, not asking for anything, his faith as insubstantial as the fog, with only the slightest hope of being heard.

They crouched together in the dark belly, but no one spoke. He tried to think only of his breathing, each breath an assurance he was still alive. A jeep whined outside the gunners' slots, and he heard some kid hollering they were still socked in, the fog too heavy to risk formation of an armada this size. Ito, Guy, and Bear crawled from the plane and lay on the tarmac.

After twenty minutes, he joined them, closed his eyes, feigned sleep to avoid conversation. He resumed counting his breaths, couldn't bear looking at his crew, hearing them, thinking what might be coming.

On breath three hundred seventy-one, a second jeep wound down, squealed to a halt. He opened his eyes.

"Your squadron is still grounded, sir. The ships going to Regensburg are taking off so they can land in daylight. Good luck to you, sir."

He watched the corporal salute Dougan then closed his eyes, heard the jeep start and drive on. His stomach tightened, and his hands grew cold. The group would be split, each wing facing the concentrated wrath of the German eighty-eights. If they didn't take off soon, the German fighters would have time to refuel between missions and come after them in force.

He looked in all directions as he crawled into the turret, above and below into the Channel. It was almost ten hundred hours before the fog lifted. Fortresses broke the gray as far as he could see. The engines droned and filled him with their constancy, and he ceased to think or fear.

A few minutes inside France, the bandits hit. Fw-190s circled, menacing, wasps in swarms of four, but out of range until closing for a strike.

Anti-aircraft barrages began over Belgium, the heaviest flak north of Liège. He saw a fortress lift and shoot flames and smoke before it bellied over in a death spiral like a huge fish rolling into the sea, watched as long as he could bear but saw no parachutes. Another group of Me-109s picked them up and the formation wavered and broke; a few crippled ships dropped back. He spun to see another fortress swarmed by 109s drop its wing and tumble through the brutal cold.

* * *

They'd been in the air over five hours, the flak stilling for a while.

"Huns in the sun!" Sheen blasted into the interphone. Yellow noses were everywhere. David's hands and eyes flashed beyond thought or will. His body shook with the violent ratcheting. The barrels grew hot, and his hands knew to wait, catch the fighters evading the other ships. A 190 dropped its wing and dipped around another fortress. When it did, it exposed its silver belly, and he brought it down. Excitement threatened to take him, but he settled back into not being there, couldn't let himself come back just yet.

The formation steadied, and he knew they were near the IP, the Schweinfurt factory. The bomb bays opened and the plane lurched as if loosed from its moorings. A flood of bombs peppered the glittering sky. The group ahead began a slow turn, was almost out of sight, and the skies grew black with flak. *The Cheese* hurled and cracked against the solid walls of fire until he thought they would break apart. *Lil Bo Peep* to their left took a direct hit. The explosion shook him loose from his guns and hammered him against the frozen turret. He turned to see *Bo Peep* twisting wingless toward oblivion.

The Focke-Wulfs and 109s returned, fewer now and divided, but flying with a vengeance, taking more chances than before. Two singled out *The Cheese* flying squadron leader. They were just out of range then circled above and dived, tracers coming right at him as the plane came into view.

"My guns are burned! Oh, God! My barrels are fried!" It was Lioni, his voice frail.

From nowhere, flecks of light appeared, pops as copper pierced the aluminum skin. He swung around but couldn't find a second bandit.

"Lioni! Up and out of there! Lioni!" Dougan, shouting above the frenzy.

The silence on the interphone swept over David like a frigid wind. Another barrage lit up as the top and nose guns blasted away. On his right, a 190 corkscrewed leaving a thick, black cloud. It was pure poetry watching it being sucked into the earth.

"We're hit! Ream!" Dougan shouted into the interphone. "Somebody check on Ream. I can't see." A moment's silence, then: "Dremmer, get up here!"

He drove the guns to the bottom lock and turned the power off, released his safety strap and struggled with the lid. When the hatch broke free, he threw his arms into the belly, pushed free of the turret, rose weakly, and plugged in his oxygen bottle. There was screaming above a frigid wind that stung like acid against his wet face.

He grabbed the bottle and spun to see Aimes, covered in blood and cradling Lioni who was ground almost in two, his bowels steaming against the frozen catwalk.

He leaned toward Aimes, screamed. "You all right, Aimes?"

"Help Lioni, Dremmer! You gotta help him!"

"I can't help him, Aimes. Neither can you. I got to get up front." He hesitated for a moment, stared. Aimes held his friend's lifeless head and rocked. He shoved in close so Aimes could hear. "Put a blanket on him, Crawford. There's nothing you can do." He patted the boy's face, kissed his head and then Lioni's.

He scrambled past Guy who hung weak and panting into his mask, holding to his gun. Freezing vomit covered the floor. He dove into the cockpit, looked to his left. Dougan had one hand to his face trying to stanch the blood that ran onto his flak jacket. The captain's mouth was moving, and he was writhing in pain. The other hand held the wheel. Plexiglas was shattered on the right side, and the cockpit roared with a bitter wind. Berkowitz shouted readings, struggled to pull Ream, limp as a rag, from his seat. David grabbed Ream's jacket and yanked. The lieutenant's arm flopped above his head, his chest gaping wide exposing bone and organ.

Berkowitz pulled David close, placed his mouth against his ear. "I gotta get in his seat."

He gathered as large a piece of Ream's flight suit as he could hold and pulled. The body toppled backward. Berkowitz found a hand-hold and dragged the co-pilot toward the bomb bay.

He looked at Sol. The blood on the lieutenant hadn't all come from Ream. His left hand was mangled, his index finger dangling. He grabbed him around the wrist and spoke into his throat mike.

"Sheen, get the first aid kit up here!"

Berkowitz pointed at Ream's headset and motioned for David to put it on.

"Dremmer, where the hell are you?" The captain, his voice filled with panic.

"Taking care of Berkowitz, sir. He's injured."

"Get up here! Now! I can't see to even put us on autopilot!"

Sheen appeared in the passageway. David pointed to Berkowitz's hand and scrambled over the top of the seat, plugged in. "I'm taking Ream's seat, sir." He slid onto a pool of blood specked with white and frozen against the canvas.

"Tell me where we are." Dougan rocked his head from side to side.

"We're flying straight and level, sir. Berkowitz got the last fighter. None in sight."

"Yeah, well, he sure as hell got us, too! And that wasn't the last, Sergeant, and we both know it. You gotta' tell me everything and tell me straight or we don't have a prayer."

"No fighters, sir, but we're dropping out of formation. Buzzards could show up any time."

"What's our altitude?"

"Twenty-one thousand feet."

"We've dropped a thousand feet. What's our airspeed?"

"One eighty-five."

"We've lost speed, too. Check the manifold pressures."

David studied the gauges. "Number three, sir. It's only eleven inches."

"Check it out. Any smoke?"

"No smoke, Captain, but the nacelle's shot up."

"Got a hole in the induction, most likely. Losing boost. Keep watching the oil and manifold pressures. Ah, God!"

"You can't see at all, sir?"

"Out of my left eye, but I can't keep it open. Either got 'em full of

159

Plexiglas or Ream's insides." Dougan cursed, held his head. "How's the oil pressure?"

"Normal, sir."

From the corner of his eye, he saw the captain tugging at his eyelid, raising his chin for a quick peek and gritting his teeth in pain. Blood dribbled from cuts on his forehead and his closed right eye.

"Sir, I can follow the others. You get help. Ito can take care of you."

"Ito stays where he is. Guy, bring that syringe and morphine up here."

David broke in. "Sir, I know you need morphine, but I can't get us back without you."

Dougan shook his head. "I've gotta have something. He can give me half the syringe, but I can't keep this eye open."

He fought for breath. "Sir, I can get us back, but not if you're not clear enough to help me. Please."

Dougan dropped his head.

His gut clenched. Was the captain out? He pushed the throat mike. "Check on the—"

Dougan raised his chin. "All right, Dremmer. I'm giving you my seat. Sol takes Ream's seat. I'll stay with you on the interphone."

He scanned the contrails. The formation had closed. Their group was well beyond them now. He inspected the gauges, kept an eye on the altimeter and manifold pressures. Nothing seemed to be changing. Guy pushed the syringe into Dougan's arm beneath his jacket.

"Should I increase throttle on number three, sir?"

Dougan was slow in answering. "Having to fight the rudder much?"

"I trimmed it out."

"That's good." He paused. "No, leave the throttles where they are. Fuel's enough of a problem already."

"Yes, sir."

Their group was starting the slow sweep to the south. He followed the contrails above them. There'd been no more buzzards. Likely flak ahead. If they could make it back to Belgium, Guy might be able to call in some little friends.

"Dremmer, think you can get us back into formation and keep us

160

there?"

He fought within himself, wanted to answer "yes"' but knew better. "Sir, if number three holds out and we can keep up, sure. But if we run into engine problems, or if we have to drop out again with buzzards all around us…"

Dougan's voice erupted on the interphone. "Ito, you have the route of our directed return if we lose sight of the others?"

"Yes, sir."

There went his hope for fighter support. If they fell too far behind—

"Dremmer, if Ito can get us around the gun emplacements, we just might be able to make it back."

"How's that, sir?"

"We follow the others, but fly below radar, skim the treetops. We'll get down to denser air, help that number three engine keep up."

His stomach tightened another notch.

"You can do it, Sergeant. I'll be here."

The interphone was silent. They were waiting for him to respond. "Sir, you're wanting Ito to follow the directed return, right?"

"Yeah."

"I have an idea." He bit his lip, tasted an ice crystal on his stubbled beard.

"Let's hear it."

"We head straight for Ridgewell from here, run as close to a parallel course to the formation as possible except we ignore the sweep and rally. We keep our speed up the best we can, let the difference in miles make up for our loss of speed. Even if we're spotted, the corridor between us could keep the buzzards away. We might not be worth coming after. We stay behind on the same path, we'll draw them like a ten-day-old carcass."

Dougan thought for a moment. "It just might work."

Ito broke in. "Sir, we could save maybe fifty miles by going straight back from here. We'll have to maneuver around the guns at Liège, then Brussels and Ghent, losing fifteen, twenty miles, but the Channel will be narrower. Cut our time over water."

"Thirty-five miles give or take. Not much of a gain."

"It is if we're swimming, sir."

"Duly noted, Ito. Dremmer, take us home. Shift the blowers, drop her to two hundred feet. We shouldn't be far from the beginning of the second wave when they come out of the sweep. Ito, figure out where we'll be in relation to the second group when we reach the coast."

He dipped the right wing toward the green hills below. "Sir, what rate of descent do you want?"

"Twelve hundred feet a minute. That would put us on deck in just over fifteen minutes." Dougan moaned. "Might as well be shooting firecrackers and waving flags up here."

Ito stuttered, started again. "Sir, these calculations aren't precise, but assuming their speed is constant, we should be hitting the coast close to the end of the third wave."

"Good. Be some other stragglers off to our left drawing fire."

"Forty miles south, if we're on course, sir."

"Close enough, Ito. Don't want to make it too easy for them."


They reached a thousand feet and David raised the nose and slowed the descent, the treetops blurring beneath them.

"What's your altitude, Sergeant?"

"Shows eight hundred feet now, sir."

"Take her down, Dremmer. We're way too visible up here."

He pushed against the yoke with wet hands, forced himself to release the stranglehold on the wheel.

"What's that?" Berkowitz pointed off their right wing as they topped a ridge.

"Buzzards?" Dougan shouted into the intercom.

"No, sir, a town." Berkowitz stared.

He held them straight and level, thought of all that might be required to keep them flying below radar.

"Should be Darmstadt." Ito, his words coming in short bursts.

"Should be or is, Ito?" Dougan's face was white beneath the streaming blood.

"Sir, I've never been there. Lioni's probably chased some skirt…" The words froze on the interphone. No one spoke. "Sorry, sir." Ito waited, apparently shaken with the sudden apprehension. He began again.

"Dremmer, course heading will be two-two-seven all the way to Wiesbaden. We'll do a side step there, try to avoid being picked up by artillery."

The plane roared through the valley, hugged the hilltops and drifted lower over the open fields. The land was rocky, the hills irregular, and he was tempted to nose her up.

"What's your altitude, Dremmer?" Dougan, reading his mind again.

"Sir, the altimeter shows just over two hundred feet, but it looks more like twenty."

"How about it, Sol? We close enough to deliver their mail?"

"I believe they could sign for it if we slowed down, sir."

Dougan drew hard for air. "All right. How's number three holding up?"

"Readings are the same," Berkowitz said. "Still eleven inches manifold pressure, oil pressure normal. Heat could be moving a little. Not sure."

"Should have come up some at this altitude. Keep watching, Sol."

He stared at the horizon, afraid to blink. The plane responded quickly to elevator pressure. At this altitude, every inch was discernable. He feared having to make a sudden turn, didn't want to scrape a wing. Broken lines of hedges blurred beneath them. He fixed his eyes on the horizon, communicated every knoll, every tall tree to the elevators, slid over them.

"Approaching Wiesbaden. Prepare for course correction." Ito wouldn't have offered such an accommodation to Dougan, and he knew it. It didn't matter. Ito could coach him all he wanted so long as he got them home.

"Rüsselsheim is to your left up ahead." Ito led him slowly.

He turned his head. "All right, I see it."

"When you're parallel, correct your course setting to two-five-nine."

He looked to find a point of reference. "Two-five-nine. Got it."

"Call it out. I'll time us."

The rocks jutted up to meet them. He drew even with a steeple in Rüsselsheim. "Course heading two-five-nine." He yanked the wheel and stepped on the rudder. "Now."

"Roger."

The land was rough. Pockets of air jolted them as they skimmed the tops of trees and barns. A road ran on their right near parallel. He scanned the horizon, saw a hill to the west covered with trees that hid the point of intersection. He hoisted the nose, the oaks dissolving beneath them into a

163

green haze. They cleared the hill. A convoy of trucks loaded with ordinance appeared on the side of the road in front of them. Wehrmacht uniforms scattered in all directions.

"Holy…" His words ended with his breath.

"What is it?" Dougan hollered into the interphone.

"Wehrmacht, sir. A convoy."

"We're spotted, then. Ito, how far to our next course correction?"

"About four minutes, sir."

"Good. We should be out of sight by then."

He interrupted. "Should be before that. Terrain's pretty rough, sir."

"If there's a chance we can be seen making a course change, don't make it. Is that clear? Not until we're out of sight. We don't want them knowing our heading."

"Yes, sir."

"Ito, if we continued on this course, where would we go?"

"Headed straight for Cologne, Cap."

"All right. So long as we're in their line of sight, we'll hold this course. All they know is what they see. Your unborn children's lives depend on where they think we're going. You boys pray all the smart Nazis are on furlough today. Bear, holler when you lose sight of them."

"Yes, sir, Cap."

"Dremmer, can you get us any lower?"

"Not without leaving tracks, sir."

Sol broke in. "Number three head temp is crawling up. Still in the normal range, but climbing."

"What about oil pressure?" Dougan seemed less anxious.

"May be dropping a little. Hard to say."

"That convoy's out of sight even from the hilltops." Bear, from the tail.

"How long to course correction, Ito?" Dougan's words seemed slower.

"Forty seconds, sir."

"What's our heading going to be?" He didn't wait to be coached.

"One-six-seven."

He lifted the nose, hoping to give them a few extra feet of altitude for the turn.

"Don't take us too high, Dremmer."

164

The captain's words were slower. He was sure, now. "No sir. Just trying to miss the chuck-holes."

"Make course correction to one-six-seven now, Dremmer." Ito, cool and precise.

He swung *The Cheese* left, stood on the rudder and brought her about. They trailed a valley for several miles then roared skyward to crest a line of hills covered in pine. He could just make out an assemblage of buildings sprawling across a hillside and onto the valley below. Wiesbaden.

The third course correction returned them to the line that would take them home. The land smoothed, and he dropped below two hundred feet, skimmed pastures and topped the sparse trees.

Sol broke in. "Sir, oil pressure on number three just dipped. Still in normal."

"We've... got an oil leak. It drops below normal, I want you to begin feathering procedures. Got it?"

"Yes, sir." David squirmed in the seat, his flight suit wet with sweat, hot wind ripping through the cockpit.

"And what will you do then, Dremmer?" Dougan's words were slurred.

"Try to trim out the power loss. Keep her low until we're well into the Channel. Increase the throttle on number four." He looked over his shoulder. "Still in a lot of pain, sir?"

"Not so much, Dremmer. Not so much. You'll need to transfer fuel from three to four after you feather."

David observed a few farmers crossing the Rheinland, continued to fly along roads. He saw no military vehicles. Aimes, Bear, and Sheen hadn't spotted any fighters, Bear insisting it was because they were afraid to fly that low. Aimes had been slow to respond.

"Whatsa' oil pressure doing, Sol?" Dougan stirred from a stupor.

"Continues to drop, but slowly. We might make it without having to feather."

"That'd be good. Dremmer, you ready for your first landing?"

"Sir, I've been waiting for that question since I sat down here. You know I'm not. I've never ground handled this thing."

"You remember orientation flights... first got to Ridgewell. You

165

brought us all the way in lotsa…"

"Sir?"

Berkowitz looked over his shoulder. "He's out."

His heart pounded above the roar of the engines. He worked his hands, forced them to ease their grip on the wheel.

"Prepare for course change." Ito again, his voice steady now, readying him to bypass Brussels.

"What will it be, Bill?"

"Two-five-seven. Should see Tienen right side in a couple minutes."

"That going to be the turning point?"

"Yup. When you're parallel. Lots of activity in that area. Don't want to turn too soon."

Over Belgium the farms grew smaller, hedgerows closer together. Plane trees reached to pluck them from the air; heat radiated from the blistering wind.

He squirmed in the catbird seat. "Gotta get these clothes off. Afraid I'll pass out."

"We're losing oil pressure." Berkowitz shouted. "Needle's bobbing."

"Sir?" He waited for Dougan to respond.

Sol's eyes grew wide. "He's still out, Dremmer. It's up to us."

"We'll feather number three. That thing blows, shrapnel could bring us down."

"You gotta make course corrections to two-five-seven. Now, Dremmer." Ito, demanding this time.

"Making course corrections to two-five-seven." He paused. "Now."

The turn was sloppy, but he corrected, heaved against the rudder, brought them back on course. He strained against the elevators, drug the nose into place and looked at Berkowitz. "Increase throttle on one, two, and four to twenty-two inches manifold pressure."

"Why?" Sol stared, shaken.

"Got to have some altitude if we want to stay in the air. Still have oil circulating to three?"

"It's bobbing."

"Should have a few seconds, then."

"Throttles increased on one, two, and four. Manifold pressures twenty-three inches." Sol's voice wavered.

He eased the yoke and the plane climbed. "Prepare to feather three." He tried to appear confident. Ito and Berkowitz were near breaking. Had to keep them focused. When the altimeter passed three-fifty, he leveled off. "Throttle back number three."

"Throttle back," Sol repeated.

"Booster pump off." He continued the procedure, the plane sliding sideways through the air as he pressed the rudder. The altimeter slipped to two-fifty.

"Booster pump off." The lieutenant appeared to have regained his composure.

"Turn prop to low."

The ignition, generators, and fuel valves were switched off. He battled against the crab to maintain the heading. "All right, Lieutenant, ease back on number one. Tell me if manifold pressure gets below eighteen inches."

Sol backed the throttle, and the pressure against the rudder eased. When it caught the level of trim, he raised his hand. "Hold it there. What's the manifold pressure?"

"Twenty inches."

"Good. That's manageable. We'll leave it there." He breathed deep, wiped sweat from his face, and glanced at the altimeter. Two hundred feet. He turned to Sol. "Sir, we'd better get whatever fuel is left on three transferred."

"I'm on it!" Sheen shouted over the interphone.

He made another course correction west of Aarschot, turned to head for Brugge and the Channel. Twice they spotted German artillery emplacements, the last several kilometers north of Wetteren. A hush had fallen on the crew. They were close, but not too close to be brought down. Guy worked feverishly to contact Ridgewell.

"Bandits! Yellow noses! Six o'clock high and closing." Bear was breathless.

"I'm on my gun!" Berkowitz piled over the top of the seat.

"Guy!" He shouted into the interphone. "Get us some help. Have to be some little friends close."

Running was out of the question. The 109s had twice their speed with all the fort's engines working at peak, and now the airspeed indicator was showing under one seventy-five.

He needed information. "Bear, tell me when they're closing in for the kill. Wait till they start to open up."

"What are you thinking? You going to outmaneuver them in this bus?" Berkowitz was on the edge. Sounded like he might lose it.

"Once." David shot back. "That's all I can hope for."

"Yeah, what then?"

"I don't know. You have another idea?"

"Drop your wheels, maybe?"

"Lieutenant Berkowitz— Sol?" He turned in his seat, locked gazes with the engineer, spoke against the screaming wind. "You've got the least chance of any of us if we do that, sir."

"First one's closing, closing. He's firing!" Bear roared over the interphone. Berkowitz scrambled for his guns.

He heard Bear's guns open up; cases began to spray from Sol's guns behind him. He yanked the wheel hard, stood on the rudder. A second later the fighter blew past his right wing and began a climbing loop.

"Help is on the way." Guy's voice, an octave higher.

Heat rushed through his breast, burst from this throat. "Where's the other one? Keep your eyes peeled!"

Bear gasped into the throat mike, short of breath. "Don't know. Must've held back."

"I've lost them both!" Berkowitz hollered.

"What the hell is happening? Where are they?" Sheen entered the fray.

"Sheen, look below." David fought for air, leaned back in the seat. They were headed straight down a line of artillery. Wehrmacht troops stood gawking, some running for cover.

"Stay on this line till they shoot us down with cap guns, Dremmer. Those buzzards ain't gonna strafe us now." Bear was laughing, his words exultant.

"Where's our help? We need them now!" The reprieve brought hope and with it fear. It would be short at best.

Guy struggled to catch his breath. "Don't know. They said they was close."

168

The end of the line of artillery came into view, and David pushed the throttles forward, pulled back on the yoke and put *The Cheese* in a climb. The plane was in an instant crab, the left wing jutting ahead and he backed off number one.

"What the... What are you...?" Sheen, his voice filled with panic.

"Leave him be!" Bear shouting from the back. "He's done good so far."

They sailed above the artillery. He banked the plane in as tight a turn as it would take.

"What are you doing, Dremmer?" Sol shouted from behind David's shoulder.

He fought the irritation of the burr in his gut. "Have a seat, sir. I need you here right now."

"You taking us back over that artillery?" The lieutenant seemed on the edge of panic.

"Worked once. Maybe it'll work till our little friends show up."

"You gotta be..."

The climb had cost them speed, and the turn was laboriously slow. His eyes darted between the flurry of activity beneath them to the skies above, waiting for the 109s to reappear. Two dots appeared flying toward him in an intersecting path. But how had they gotten so far west? He pushed the throat mike. "Bogeys, two o'clock high!"

There was nothing he could do but complete his turn and race them back to the line of artillery. *The Cheese* seemed to weigh an extra fifty tons. She lumbered and swayed and continued to slow through the turn.

They were now at four hundred feet and David pitched the nose toward the ground in hopes of picking up speed and beating the two bandits back to the safety of their own troops. The fighters were closing fast. He fixed his eyes on the first eighty-eight in the line. There was nothing he could do about the approaching fighters.

"They're friendlies!" Sheen was laughing. "P-47s here to pick us up."

"Make contact, Guy." He lifted the nose and turned them away from the enemy guns. "Tell them we want to go home."

# Chapter XV

David sat at the controls, watched the coastline emerge on the horizon, a P-47 at each wingtip. The water below capped in white undulations snaking from side to side as far as he could see. He'd limited their rate of climb hoping to conserve their dwindling fuel, left them skimming the channel at fifteen hundred feet.

"Should be at just over three thousand feet when we begin our descent." Ito, responding to his request for maximum altitude at the current rate of climb. That would leave the crew only a few minutes at parachute altitude. Pretty much as he'd figured.

The interphone grew ghostly still. He ached for a quip, one remark from Lioni, a single blistering comeback from Ream, wished someone would break the silence. But the hush wasn't born solely from their loss. The crew was scared. No one knew how they were going to land *The Cheese*. Except him— and he didn't know how to break it to the others.

Guy's twang rattled through his headset. "Ridgewell's made contact. Colonel Blake wants to talk to the captain."

He looked across the cockpit, met Sol's stare.

Berkowitz nodded. "I'll speak with him, Corporal." He waited for the patch. "Lieutenant Berkowitz here, Colonel. The captain is unconscious."

"I understand you're piloting the plane, Lieutenant."

"No, sir. I'm second seat. Sergeant Dremmer is flying the plane, sir."

"Sergeant Dremmer? Is he…"

Sol glanced at him, looked away. "He's had some training, sir. By far the most qualified to be in command at the moment."

"I see." Blake paused, came back a moment later. "Men, how are you planning to bring your plane in?"

Sol looked him in the eyes, a rising sea of dread behind them.

He pressed the throat mike. "Sir, this is Sergeant Dremmer. We'll have to bring her in on her belly."

Blake cleared his throat. "Sergeant, I know you've been through quite an ordeal, but we need that plane. If you belly land, there's a great likelihood she'll never see service again."

He grew rigid, steadied his voice. "Sir, I understand the critical need for planes. But I have seven lives on board besides my own. If I attempt to ground handle *The Cheese* and fail, the loss could be worse. Much worse."

"You've done a bang-up job so far, son."

"Thank you, sir, but that doesn't mean we can land her. I've never ground handled this plane or any other. Neither has Lieutenant Berkowitz. Sir, we wouldn't have a snowball's chance once we touched down." The silence echoed in his headset.

"I understand, Sergeant. I wasn't fully aware of your situation. We'll have the north runway cleared for you."

"Thank you, sir. If it's all right, we'll take the grass outside the runway, keep things cleared of... keep things clear so the other ships can land. Less chance of a situation, sir." *Fire.* He couldn't let the others hear it, though they knew the chances as well as he.

More silence. "Under the circumstances, Sergeant, I believe that's best. Good luck to you."

The radio went dead. He looked at Sol. "Should we ask them if they want to bail when we reach altitude, Lieutenant?"

Berkowitz nodded, stared at the approaching shoreline. "Boys, you have the option of bailing out. We'll be at altitude shortly. Thing is, we won't be there long before we have to begin our descent. If you choose to jump, you'll need to prepare now."

Sol's hand scarcely moved from the throat mike.

"I'm staying. Dremmer's brought us in plenty of times before." Bear, in the belly now.

He shook his head. "Only to the runway, Bear."

"That's all you got to do this time. We've seen them come in on their bellies. It's doable."

Guy was close behind. "I ain't jumping."

"I'm staying." Sheen, from below.

Ito broke in. "No way I'm chancing it alone. Not with my face. Some farmer'll think the Japs have attacked."

He waved his thanks to the P-47s, watched them break away as the space beneath them turned a deep green. "What about you, Aimes? Need to make your mind up pretty quick."

"I'll stay here with Lioni."

He looked at Berkowitz, let his question show on his face, felt the full weight of their stake. "You've got some time, but you guys might start making it back to emergency landing positions. Guy, you might stay with that radio a while longer."

* * *

Fortresses swarmed above Ridgewell, those on the ground edging between the hangers. David guessed half had landed, revised his estimate when he remembered the number that wouldn't return. The others held, and he slid beneath the circling pack.

*The Cheese* was graceless without the number three engine, but he positioned her for a dogleg approach. He and Sol thought it best to spare the crews above them any wait. Seconds counted now, every tick of the clock a measure of fuel.

He approached the field at one-thirty, let the runway slide behind his shoulder, turned, lined himself at forty-five degrees. The ground rose fast and Sol extended the flaps to full. He shot a quick glance at the airspeed indicator. One-fifteen. He missed the drag of landing gear, turned hard to left for final, stepped on the rudder and pulled the nose up, hoping the additional pitch would slow them, soften the landing. He eased her toward the grass.

"Step on the ball, Dremmer!" Sol was shouting, his good hand gripping the pedestal.

"She'll be level." He was calm, knew this part by rote.

*The Cheese* touched down aft, the nose flopping like a beached whale. Grass and dirt shot over the Plexiglas and into the cockpit. The aluminum belly thudded and wailed, and he fought to keep from being torn loose from the pedestal, Sol working to cut the ignition and fuel. They slid sideways for what seemed minutes before grinding to a halt. Dust cleared and an ambulance skidded between them and the runway.

David climbed from his seat, scrambled for the captain, grabbed his feet as Sol lifted his head. He dropped from the hatch, reached to grab the captain. Two corporals with a gurney pushed him aside. He turned, watched as Bear dropped from the rear and ran for the ambulance.

* * *

Morning came before sleep. David slipped from his bunk, rolled his boots inside his pants and crept to the door to sit and stare into the blackness. Stars shone as he raised his head. In the dark, all seemed normal. Lioni's empty bunk was hidden in obscurity, as was Ream's, he guessed, over in the officer's quarters.

He slid his pants and boots on outside the barracks and sauntered in the direction of the ammo dump, shuffled aimlessly for a while then picked up his pace. Within minutes his feet were pounding against the tarmac, his fists driving into the morning calm. Ream was dead. Lioni, too. They were no more. Or were they? He broke into a sprint, pushed himself into blackness, reached until he had no more. Still he drove his legs, came to the end of the runway, ran on until there wasn't enough air in East Anglia to feed his lungs. He collapsed onto the grass, tears streaming down his face, convulsing in heavy sobs. He lay for a minute, the heavy rhythm of his lungs forcing him back onto his elbows, fighting the lure of the earth to sink forever into its bosom. His breathing slowed and he relented, yielded to the draw. Ream and Lioni were dead. He closed his eyes, let the truth settle deep, shook with sobs until he ached. His head grew heavy, and he let go of the fight, breathed deep and surrendered to the inevitability of the dark.

* * *

"Hey, you Sergeant Dremmer?"

David roused from a dreamless sleep, rose on one elbow, grass prickling against his bare arm. He worked to make sense of the question.

"You Sergeant Dremmer?" It was an MP, baton in hand, standing wide as if David posed some sort of threat.

"Yeah, I'm Dremmer."

The MP slapped his left hand with the baton. "You're wanted at the infirmary at oh nine-thirty."

"Who wants me there?"

"Colonel Blake is who. You drunk, Sergeant?"

"Sober as a judge. What's he want with me?"

"Beats me. Your crew's been looking for you. S'posed to be at a captain's bed at oh nine-thirty."

"Dougan? What time is it now?"

"Oh eight-twenty."

"You give me a lift back to my barracks?"

"Guess that'd be all right."

The shower failed to wake him, and Aimes brought him a cup of coffee as he dressed. David downed it in a few swallows and left for the infirmary. Sweat formed beneath his collar and dribbled down his chest, made damp spots on his uniform.

He stepped inside the infirmary. Disinfectant burned his nose. Two rows of beds ran parallel down the center with another butted against each side of the Quonset. Berkowitz was standing at the far end, cap in hand at the foot of the raised mattress. He shuffled close, made out the captain's head wrapped in bandages.

He dropped his chin, announced his presence. "How you feeling, sir?"

"Dremmer, huh? Is he late, Sol?"

Berkowitz pushed his sleeve above his bandages, winked at David. "Right on time, sir."

"An officer should be punctual." Dougan offered a slight smile. "Sol, you see the colonel, yet?"

Berkowitz glanced toward the door. "Not here yet, sir."

Dougan grinned. "Well, forget what I said, Dremmer."

"Always do, sir. What's the word on your eyes?"

"Left one's going to be fine. Take a few days is all. Jury's still out on the right. Said it was full of Plexiglas. Doc says there's likely to be scar tissue, maybe worse."

"You'll be flying us around Europe in no time, Cap. You ought to know, though, we've decided we'd rather stay in England on our next

174

trip." David tried to sound cheery, turned to Sol. "How's your hand, Lieutenant Berkowitz?"

"It'll be okay. Snapped the index finger so I'll have to wear a brace on it for a while. Looked worse than it was."

"For the record, I won't be flying you on any sightseeing excursions, Dremmer." Dougan's voice took on a surly tone. "Or anywhere else for that matter."

"Sir?"

"I've recommended you for flight school. You'll be shipping out as soon as your orders come through."

*Bear.* Trepidation crept in, and his throat tightened. "I don't understand, sir."

"The Air Corps needs good pilots. You're a natural. I had you pegged first time you sat in my seat. Before that, really. This was coming anyway, but we've gotten word of a big push for pilots. You've done your job here, Dremmer. By the time you get back, the war could be over."

"Sir, I don't know what to say. It's just, I don't like leaving my crew."

Dougan bit his lower lip, released it. "Dremmer, none of us knows if we'll make it. I'm giving you a chance. Take it."

"Sir, it's not that I don't want flight school. I do, but..."

"We'll miss you, Lieutenant, but it'll do the boys good knowing someone made it out alive. Give them something to hope for. And Lieutenant?"

David looked at Berkowitz.

"Not me, Lieutenant. You." Sol laughed.

Dougan twisted his mouth. "Oh, I forgot to mention that part. That's what Colonel Blake is coming to see you about. He thought it might be a good idea for you to go to flight school as a second lieutenant. Naturally, I concurred."

"I'm grateful, sir, but..."

"Look, Dremmer. Your reluctance to take a pat on the back won't bring Ream or Lioni back."

*Reading my mind again.* "My gunning that bad, sir?"

Dougan rolled his head, grinned. "You've done a good job on that belly gun, but you've done a better one up front. You're a pilot, Dremmer. You're the only one doesn't know it."

"Thank you, sir. Will it hurt your feelings if I show up here in a P-38?"

"You can fly with me anytime, Dremmer. Kite and washing machine motor if you want."

A low murmur swept across the infirmary. Footsteps echoed behind them. David turned to see the colonel, snapped to attention, offered his sharpest salute.

Blake caught his eye, returned the salute. "Good to see you, Dremmer. And all in one piece. Had no idea we had untapped talent available. I'd have put it to better use."

He returned the smile. "Thank you, sir."

Blake extended an envelope. "By the powers vested in me." He chuckled, reached for his hand. "Congratulations, Second Lieutenant Dremmer. You realize how unique a field promotion is here?"

"I haven't heard of it before, sir."

"This event happened to coincide with a request for pilots. Couldn't think of a better candidate." Blake paused, caught his eye. "For the record, Lieutenant, you made the right call yesterday. Your crew's alive and *The Cheese* will be serviceable in a few days. Damn fine job."

"Not all of them, sir."

A dark question formed on Blake's brow. "What's that?"

"Not all my crew is alive, sir."

"I know that, son." The colonel's face took on the gray of the infirmary. "I regret it deeply."

"I know you do, sir. So do I."

The colonel's eyes lost their luster, his face sallow. He looked toward the door. David lifted his hand in a perfect salute. Berkowitz followed suit. Blake returned it, held the position long enough to make him uncomfortable then turned and walked slowly toward the door.

Dougan shifted uneasily on his bed. "Lieutenant, it's procedure that you move into the officers' quarters. Be you and Sol. Could have some privacy."

"Thank you, sir, but I think I'll spend what time I have left with the crew." He shifted, looked at Sol. "No offense intended, sir."

Berkowitz chuckled. "None taken, Dremmer."

# Chapter XVI

David stood in the barracks door, stared into the distance and fought to reconcile what he saw with what he knew. The land was plain and unpretentious, the soil deep, heavy clay rich with loam and soaked by frequent rains. The shallow hills were green, most left free of the plow.

Cattle grazed on a hillside above a fertile bottom freshly tilled and ready for winter wheat. Too peaceful a place for men to be drawing a final breath. But the soil, he was sure, had been blackened by the blood of the young.

Sheen and Guy shouted behind him, pushing away what had happened, dressing for a celebration at Land's End. Aimes and Ito stood mute. His stomach soured at the idea of a party, and the promotion only made things worse. He'd come here expecting to die. Ream and Lioni had taken what should have been his, and he'd been given a commission. He couldn't look at the others, especially Aimes.

A hand gripped his shoulder as heavy and unyielding as the knot in his gut. He held himself from moving though the warmth shamed him. "Dremmer, you know what happened to Lioni and Ream wasn't your fault." Bear, seeing to the heart of things. "You earned that commission."

"I don't think so, Bear. Should've been me they carried off that plane yesterday."

"That right? How you figure it?"

He stared beyond the tarmac into the green hills. "Something is missing in me, Bear. I have this weakness. Always been there."

Bear turned, ambled toward his bunk, motioned for him to follow. "You can go to Land's End later. They'll be there for hours." His friend sat on his bunk, leaned against the wall, and pinned him with his stare. "What kind of weakness?"

He hesitated. The vacancy inside was beyond any meaning words could carry. "I don't know what it is to be right. To be sure. I'm not like you or Dougan or..."

"Or who?" Bear held his stare, wouldn't let him loose.

He relented, looked away. "My father."

"And what do you think it'd take to make you sure you were right? Like your father."

"I don't know. I don't think I can ever be that sure."

"You probably can't." Bear leaned forward, his eyes insistent. "How can you know you're right if you don't believe there *is* a right, Dremmer? Or that what's right can change? Or that you have to figure it out?"

That much had become clear. He wanted more. "You familiar with a passage that starts out, 'In the beginning was the Word?'"

Bear picked it up. "'And the Word was with God and the Word was God.' That the one you talking about?"

The cottonwood stirred above him, lifted a magic in the breeze. "Yeah, that's it. It says something, too, about the Word being made flesh and dwelling among us." He grew uncomfortable, looked toward the door. "I thought once it might be true."

Bear leaned back. "Do you understand it?"

He nodded. "It's talking about Christ."

"Sure it is. But do you understand how it all come about?"

"No, of course not." The conversation was disturbing. He shuffled, grew impatient, wanted to escape and didn't know why.

"Well, I don't either, Dremmer, but I know it's true." Bear's face brightened, seemed pleased with something. "Tell you what, Lieutenant. You figure out why you one time thought it might be true, and we'll talk some more." His friend waited, dropped his chin. "So if you're wantin' to go, go ahead. I'm gonna take a nap. I'll be here whenever you're ready"

He nodded, swallowed the urge to tell Bear he was afraid of flight school because it would mean not having him there. He turned, hesitated, then edged toward the door, and let it swing shut behind him.

The group had wandered ahead, was almost out of hearing range. "Hey,

Sheen." The others stopped, too. "I'm not gonna make it this time. You guys go on."

"You sure? This is your celebration, Lieutenant."

"Yeah, well, word is the war has cut beer production to dangerously low levels. It's my patriotic duty to conserve what's left."

"Suit yourself, Dremmer... uh, Lieutenant. If you change your mind, we'll be the ones in the back with the brunettes hanging all over us." Guy shook with silent laughter.

"Blonds, Lieutenant." Sheen wagged his head, countermanded.

Guy shrugged. "Few of each, I guess."

He watched them amble away, cross the pivot pads scuffling like kids. They *were* kids. He wasn't much more than a kid, himself. Just felt like it. He looked back at the barracks, trudged toward the landing field.


The concrete burned its refusal through his soles. David pushed on, determined not to feel it. His actions had been rewarded. He should have been reveling in the approval of everyone from God on down, but he was alone, couldn't remember being more on his own. Except maybe the day he got married.

He walked, paid little attention to where he went, circled the base, sauntered along the fence where calves, fat and ready for weaning, grazed alongside their mothers. He glanced at his watch. Nineteen hundred hours. Some habitual fear pushed him toward the mess hall.

Airmen stood crowded around the rosters. His gaze slid down the list. A mission had been scheduled for the next morning and two crews from the 534th were slated. No chance his crew would be on it, and he wouldn't be going if they were.

He shivered, stared at the board. The fact was, they could fly off and not come back, and he wouldn't be with them. A sudden spasm drove the air from his lungs. Aimes, Billington, Guy, Sheen, Ito, and Berkowitz had been put in with part of another crew, some shot up bunch, most likely. The names weren't familiar. Replacements, then. New belly gunner, too.

He slipped through the flyers gathered around and headed for the barracks. Bear had to know. And the others. He'd have to jerk them out of Land's End before they got too drunk.

He found Bear in his bunk dozing, his Bible beside him. The words came tumbling out, his fear mounting with the telling.

Bear groaned. "Give me my boots, would you Dremmer? Uh, Lieutenant."

"Cut it out, Bear." He slid them across the concrete. "I'm going to Land's End. I'll meet you there."

"You weren't with them?" His friend's voice rose in expectation.

"I had a question to answer. Had to give it some thought."

Bear's face softened. "And what did you come up with, Lieutenant? What made you think those words might be true?"

He stared at his friend. "It's something anyone should know, Bear."

Bear finished tying his boots and met his stare. "Well, yeah, if they've heard it. But how can that be, Lieutenant?"

"You're wanting me to say it's faith."

Bear leaned back and drew a boot across his knee. "You're guilty, aren't you, Dremmer?"

He nodded, laughed. "I guess so. What's the charge?"

Bear withheld his smile. "You're mad, and you're scared, and you know you're guilty. Things aren't the way they should be. They're not right. You're scared because you know you're not right, either, and you might be called to account." He stopped, searched the shadows. "Dremmer, you'll have to make the choice for yourself. If you choose right, the fear you wake up with every morning will go away. You own up to what you are and what's right and take forgiveness when it's offered, the guilt will go, too."

He stared into the dying light. "How do I know what to choose, Bear?"

"You know the answer to that. It won't do no good for me to tell you till you're ready to stop fightin' it." Bear stood and looked at his friend. "We'd better get them boys out of there and sobered up."

* * *

The jukebox was turned low. Benny Goodman's clarinet softened the heat and wailed a mournful lament. Guy stared into space while Aimes studied the bubbles in his mug.

"Change your mind, Dremmer? Lieutenant Dremmer, I mean." Sheen toddled from the latrine tugging at his zipper.

"No." He slid into a chair. "They've got the schedule up. Looks like you guys are going out tomorrow."

Aimes' head shot up. "Tomorrow? Dougan back?"

"No, they've made up a crew. Got you riding with somebody I never heard of. Name of Massing. Replacement, I guess."

Guy looked away, worked his jaw.

Aimes stared through a child's eyes. "I can't do it, Dremmer. Lioni and Ream are gone. Dougan out... and you. I can't do it."

"Look, Aimes, they're not sending you guys on anything hairy. Not after yesterday."

"It was just yesterday?" Sheen stared in the direction of the jukebox.

He looked past Sheen, saw Ito sitting at a table by himself. "What's with Bill?"

Guy shrugged, flopped his head to the side. "Don't know. Hasn't said two words since we got here. Just sulked off by hisself."

He nodded. "You guys better get back to the barracks. Be waking us up at oh five thirty."

"So it's not Schweinfurt, then?" Aimes stared, needing some assurance he couldn't offer.

He shrugged. "Of course not."

"You won't fly with us?" Aimes, pleading now.

He looked away, the knot cinching beneath his belt. "They've got a replacement slated for the belly gun, Crawford."

The barracks were quiet. David lifted his head, sure he heard muffled sobs in the corner. He closed his eyes, fought back tears, dozed off after midnight, woke when he heard the jeep making rounds and slid his feet to the edge of his bunk.

The door swung open and the lights came on. "Rise and shine! Chow at oh six hundred. Briefing at oh six-thirty. Give them hell today, boys."

He sat on the edge of his bunk and watched the others come to life. Bear looked somewhat rested, but he was the only one. Guy was in a daze and Sheen scratched himself, eyes closed as Ito wandered toward the latrine. Aimes lay in bed, his arms wrapped around a pillow, his knees tucked against his chest.

He scraped across the floor, felt the coolness of the concrete. "You okay, Aimes?"

"No, I'm not okay. I can't do it, Dremmer." Aimes wrapped himself around the pillow, shook.

"Sure you can, buddy. This will be one more down, and we're due an easy one."

"What's this 'we' business, Second Lieutenant Dremmer? You going with us?"

He drew hard for air. "Aimes, would it really help if I did?"

Aimes nodded, his eyes wide. "Yeah, it would. It'd help, Dremmer. Will you go?"

"I don't know if that's even possible." He stared at the thin hands trembling against the pillow. "But I'll try."

"Dremmer." Bear's heavy paw rested on his shoulder. "You don't need to do this. There's no reason."

"Our butts, Bear! That's reason enough, don't you think?" Crawford rose to his feet still clutching his pillow.

Bear fixed his eyes on the boy. "You think having Dremmer on that belly gun will make any difference if we get shot down?"

"I don't know, but can the new guy bring us in if something happens up front?"

* * *

David negotiated the exchange. He breathed deep, couldn't account for the relief he felt.

The briefing was short. The mission would be soft. They were to bomb the Gilze-Rijen Airfield in Holland. The number of enemy aircraft was anticipated to be low, but some flack was expected over Belgium. He nodded, guessed he might have seen some of the Wehrmacht responsible for sending it up, would likely recognize them at a couple hundred feet.

A mountainous man with lieutenant's bars, his dark hair spilling from beneath his cap, swaggered into the briefing. His belt pulled taut over his heavy paunch, he surveyed the crowd, paused for a moment before sitting down, seemed to invite the eyes resting on him.

David turned to Bear. "Fresh out of flight school. Shows all over him. Here to single-handedly bring this war to a forthright conclusion."

182

"Yeah, figure that's Massing? Don't look like he'll need our help. What say we take the day off?"

David stepped out of the briefing hut, gathered with what was left of his crew and waited as Massing made his way over, planted his feet wide and stared.

"Men, I don't know what you're used to, but I hold to tight military discipline. On board, I'm the man at the top. Everything goes through me. That understood?"

The crew looked first at Massing then at each other. No one spoke.

"Do you understand the rules of the game, men?" Massing demanded a response.

Berkowitz stepped forward, cleared his throat. "Is this to be a temporary arrangement or is it supposed to be permanent, sir?"

"I know it'll last until we get back, Lieutenant... what is it? Beer-ko-vitz?"

"First Lieutenant Sol Berkowitz, sir."

"Beer-ko-vitz, we may be the same rank, but I'm commander of the aircraft. Is that understood?"

"Yes, sir, I simply inquired as to the length of this arrangement."

"Could be today or could be till the Little Corporal mortgages the Chancellery. I really can't say."

"Sir." David choked back bile. "We don't know which plane we've been assigned."

"Who are you?"

"Serg... Second Lieutenant David Dremmer, sir. Ball turret gunner."

"Belly gunner? A lieutenant? Ever'body on this crew a lieutenant?"

"Just be flying with you, today, sir. Shipping out soon."

Massing looked at him as if he were examining an oozing sore. "Our bird is at your old pivot area, a little battle-scarred, but airworthy. Brought her here from Prestwick myself." He stopped, looked him over one more time. "Lieutenant Jim McKay will fill the right seat. Be here shortly."

David trailed the crew to the pivot pad. Massing talked the whole way, mentioned twice his class had been in awe of him. No one offered comment. The new waist gunner dashed over, blue eyes darting, curly, blond hair escaping his leather cap. A kid. Looked like Sheen's younger brother. The boy introduced himself as Milton Hyde. He shook Sheen's hand and Bear's as they sauntered toward the pad. Then he reached Aimes.

"I don't want to shake your hand! I don't want to know your name! I just want you to do your job. Don't let nothing get past you. I'm right gunner— you're left. That's it. You capeesh that shit all right?" Aimes spun around, headed for their pivot pad.

Assembly was quick and painless in spite of Massing's heavy hand on the controls. They wobbled into position before reaching the Channel. David crawled into the turret, tied in and ran it around to get the feel.

It was a simple, straightforward mission in two waves. The morning was clear and the skies bright. The approach to the IP was to be direct at twenty-one thousand feet with a wide sweep over Belgium planned for return.

Ito offered only what Massing demanded, left the interphone quiet and the crew tense.

* * *

The coast was beautiful. Cerulean water extended to a bright, silver ribbon of coastline. The land, a deep green, lay in tiny rectangles, a vibrant patchwork of color.

"Time to IP thirty-four minutes, sir." Ito, his voice subdued.

Massing groaned. They'd still seen no fighters. David watched the skies, ran the gun from lock to lock.

When they reached the airfield, the load was salvoed, and they began the sweep to Belgium. He watched the skies, waited. Things were eerily quiet.

They flew toward Brussels, intersecting the path he'd flown only two days before, turned and merged with a near-identical course. At altitude, the land looked gentler, the countryside less encumbered, but he knew it was a lie. The hills below were crawling with Wehrmacht, and it would only get worse as they approached the coast.

He rotated the turret forward, saw the horizon grow dark.

"Flak, boys. They're sighting in." There was a quiver in Sol's voice.

"Lieutenant Beer-ko-vitz." Massing boomed into the interphone. "Report all sightings to me. I'll inform the crew as I deem necessary."

Berkowitz made no response.

Light flashed below, sent shrapnel bouncing off the turret. Oily gray lines crossed their belly and flanks. David straightened, scanned the skies. No fighter would willingly follow. The sky was thick and gray, the guns homing in on their altitude.

They flew on, the air dense with metal. Flak burst just above them, the explosion slamming them against the limits of the wings. He took a deep breath, hadn't fired his guns, had no defense against this. He shook, had failed to slip outside himself.

The group banked in a final arc that would point them toward Ridgewell. Light burst to his left, and the plane heaved in a violent shudder, was in an instant spiral. He slammed against the turret bands, pinned by the force of the spin, looked to the left wing and saw only gray sky beyond the number one engine, the prop twisted and still.

The fort again slammed against a wall of air and somehow leveled. He could move again.

Massing throttled the number two and four engines, whined them into a violent crab. The plane rattled as if the two remaining engines were coming apart, and he pictured the ship dropping from the sky like an aluminum ball.

"Hang on!" McKay, his voice high and excited. "We'll try to get to the Channel. Gunners, heads up. We've got buzzards."

The bandits appeared in his sights at three o'clock. Fire spewed above him. Hyde's guns. Me-109s and 190s swarmed from high and wide. He fought for vision, prayed for his hands to know what to do. The 109s were baiting them, drawing fire, passing above and below, staying out of range. He swung about, saw them separate and disappear over the fuselage, the 190s out of sight, likely stacking for a frontal assault.

A 109 appeared behind them, lifted. Bear crippled it, forced it to drop back. Three more stayed out of range. Massing nursed the ship, headed unflinching toward the Channel. The fighters held back. Minutes drained away. They lost altitude. He looked for water but saw only patchwork green hiding Wehrmacht artillery. A 190 from somewhere high made a pass, showered them with lead. Massing tried to pull away, but the plane listed eerily as if they were sliding off the top of an icy hill.

"We can't hold her. Bail out! Now!" McKay's voice had reached a squeal.

"Ignore that order. I didn't order that!" Massing, bellowing into the interphone.

"Everybody out!" Sol screamed above the roar.

The bandits circled, climbed. The others would have no chance if there were no return fire. David followed the first 109, let it begin its lazy loop, opened the turret door and scrambled into the dark belly. He grabbed his parachute, slid his legs back in the bubble, tried to drop. The chute held him. He kicked up, pushed the chute behind his head and slid around his gun, free of the retainer belt. He pushed the cord to his head set, tried to force it into the interphone jack. His fingers shook beyond use. The plug bumped against metal, dropped. He pulled it back, tried again.

A deafening flash set the air around them ablaze, and he slammed against the turret, blinked, forced his thoughts to clear. They'd reached lower squadron altitude, were picking up the remainder of the eighty-eight barrage, likely the last before the shore guns.

He looked up around the left wing. The fighters were high at two o'clock, skirting the flak, forming two lines and starting a double stack, preparing to nose around for the kill. They'd passed the limits of the big boys. Yellow noses peeled toward them, grew monstrous, filled his sights. He waited, breathed, gave a quick burst, and the first broke off.

"Dremmer! Get out! I'll stay with it till I see your chute!" Bear, screaming into the interphone. He drove the turret around. Five parachutes floated a mile or more behind. He pushed the door, scrambled out, jumped to his feet above the gaping bomb bay, his chute pressed to his chest. He clawed at the snaps, his fingers numb with fear. The cold wind ripped at his face. Bear's fifties tapped armor somewhere beneath them.

He jumped, forgot to count, the breath sucked from him by the blistering wind, and pulled the ripcord. The chute snapped full, jerked him skyward.

He looked back. Sheen, stumbled from the bomb bay, somersaulting beneath the plane. The rear escape hatch flew outward. Bear. He breathed, started a count, saw his friend's chute billow brightly. A flash somewhere above. He jerked. Sheen, the silk snapping, shot past him, a piece of cat-walk from the bomb bay tangled in his shroud lines. The boy climbed, frantic to free them. He closed his eyes, tried to pray, but an urgency beyond reason constrained him to look again. The catwalk broke free and the silk unfurled, but a panel had been torn in the struggle. Sheen slowed but continued to fall away.

He looked skyward, strained to see Bear in the brightness. Above the speck surrounded by white that marked his friend's position in the universe, a brilliant blaze filled the blue and sent the nose and wings of the fortress surging into the cold.

From behind the flames, a specter filled him with fresh terror. A 190 nosed directly toward him, and he thought in a senseless joke to himself, "Who's afraid of the Focke-Wulf?" Bullets sliced the silk canopy— tiny, ripping pops. His body writhed in the seconds before the peace came, his hip and back sizzling with a peculiar heat. He drew hard for air as a chill moved through him and covered him with a quiet darkness.

<u>August 22, 1943</u>

Jesse looked beyond the pines and saw the place as it had been the day he took it over from his father. Little was there then save the land itself. All that had grown out of it since had emerged by the slow contrivance of necessity. He could look now at a swale or flat and remember why he came to form it so. And he remembered more than the hard-bought change to the place or the needs behind them. He remembered the sweet ease of his breath when he was wet with sweat and the stride he took across it when he was lean and strong. The hunger to see a thing done that kept him from his sleep at night stirred in him again, and the wonder that a man could own a thing as hallowed as land. He thought of how he first set out to cross fence the place, not solely because he needed separate pastures, but because he wanted to put his hands into the warm, moist bosom of the earth, to know its textures and smells so that if he came to need a spot of sandy loam to put in melons, he would know just where it lay, or if he wanted clay to seal his tanks, he could rein the mules and buckboard to the place and get it.

And the joy of having built the pens the way he had so that at weaning time the calves would be protected from the north wind and wouldn't bawl themselves into pneumonia. Each pen and alleyway he'd fashioned after a need so that, having been caught in want, he wouldn't be found lacking again. He thought back at the fine horses he'd been astride and called his own and worked each day, rain or shine, and come to know like some men would a woman. He pictured them grazing where the sorghum now grew.

It frightened him to think of leaving, but he'd grown sick of contending with her about it. He would refuse, even now, because it wasn't his way to yield to such bedevilment, but Naomi had said it would be best, had told him they would visit every day. There was promise in that. He was amazed, looking back, for he'd never agreed to sell. When he said he'd consider it, Delores took it for as good as done. Still, he refused to overlook his promise to the boy.

She couldn't hold to a thing like that, a man feeling the way David did about that animal. But he wouldn't sell the horse. Told her so. She'd turned her back on him then. If it weren't for fear of David coming home, he suspected the horse might already be gone. Though he wouldn't say it, he held to the hope, even now, that the boy would come back in time to put a stop to it all.

Morgan's truck clattered up the hill. He was supposed to bring more papers, a lease-purchase agreement that both were to sign. He'd insisted on that, at least, so that if the boy returned or Morgan missed a payment, he'd have some recourse. Delores had boxed a load for the two of them, Morgan and her, to take to Grimsland. The day had a stillness to it. A fine day, too, if it weren't so full of loss. The black stood in the working pen staring. Beyond the pens, cows grew fat on ample grass. The heavy spring rains had put the pasture ahead, and they'd kept their flesh all summer. Jesse yielded to the inevitability of it, the heat and stillness taking all his fight. It wouldn't be long now. He'd be going home.

He turned and wheeled toward the house where Morgan stood, hat in hand, looking at Delores. Something wasn't right. It wasn't his way to look into peoples' faces to know their minds. That was the boy's way. If he wanted a thing known, he spoke it plainly and expected others to do the same. But he saw something now in Morgan and Delores as they stood on the porch and wouldn't look at him, so he made up his mind to go on past

188

without a word. What went on between them was no concern of his, her already making plans to come back to check on things from time to time. He knew exactly what it was she'd be coming back for.

Delores stepped in front of him, held out a yellow envelope. "Jesse, we have a telegram." She turned away and braced herself against the porch. He sank in his chair, felt the earth spin beneath him, had feared such a thing in the dark so many nights. He hated her for what he knew was in her heart. It's why she'd turned from him, so he wouldn't see what she wanted hidden.

He gritted his teeth. "I can't see the print. You read it."

It was a lie. He'd wager she knew it, too. But she took it up, put a quiver in her voice, even now, he reckoned, fitting it into her plans that David wasn't coming home.

TO: DELORES FAYE DREMMER:
I REGRET TO INFORM YOU THAT THE COMMANDING GENERAL EUROPEAN AREA REPORTS YOUR HUSBAND SECOND LIEUTENANT DAVID B. DREMMER MISSING IN ACTION SINCE AUGUST 19 1943 XXX FURTHER DETAILS OR OTHER INFORMATION OF HIS STATUS ARE RECEIVED YOU WILL BE NOTIFIED PROMPTLY.
ULIO THE ADJUTANT GENERAL

Jesse turned inside himself. Living was such a small thing to hope for when you'd spent your life watching the earth yield her bounty year after year then turn her fecundity over to death. After a while it seemed that what lived and what died was a shallow thing, and so you bent yourself to think of it that way, one thing living and another dying but the succession going on. Most of the time, it was enough to live without answers. Then, when you thought you'd bent yourself to the ways of the Almighty, you found you'd held to one thing more than all others, and it was taken from you, and you were broken by its passing. That's how you knew you'd failed.

He nodded into the hush and creeping darkness of the room. After the fall, he'd pleaded for God to strike down with a mighty hand the arrangement of things. He'd abjured God to take from the pitiless hand of nature the right to take and to leave, had begged him to overrule as he'd done before. But that wasn't his way. The Almighty had let him be broken before quieting him with tenderness. When he touched him, Jesse was sorry for his anger, but even then, even in his willingness to live without his legs, a part of his anger remained, and he'd vowed to never again let anything close that God could take or allow to be taken and do nothing about. And now the anger he'd thought mended was rising again.

Delores and Morgan had gone on, left him sitting by the empty tinderbox, alone with a silent God. He prayed, tried to force his anger down, but it wouldn't be constrained. He raised himself on his arms and looked above the ceiling joists.

"Why?" He screamed it into the dark, tears streaming down his face. "Why do you sit by and let the wicked undo everything around them? Why do you watch as they bring this senseless Hell on others? And why did you let my boy be taken before I could set things right?"

He'd not demanded justice since he was young with eager limbs like David's. God had been silent then, too. He fell back in his chair and watched the shadows grow long on the wall.

# Chapter XVII

The music flowed, a cool sleep-falling magic in the breeze. The strained silk timbre of a trumpet narrowed to a point of light, became a single star within a dark cover and held pure and licorice-smooth. Around the single star, tiny specks appeared, voices crowding the trumpet with their distant grace, saintly and sure. And somewhere beyond the blue-black curtain and the light, a clapboard church overflowed in gentle certainty.

Something wouldn't let him be taken in the breeze, pulled him loosely across the ground. David opened his eyes to the shapeless edge of color and motion, turned from the unsteady force and coughed. His mouth and nose brimmed with the metallic taste of blood.

"Dremmer, you've got to help me. I can't drag you no more."

He strained to make words of his thought, but the earth spun beneath him into blackness.

"Dremmer, listen to me. You've got to help. Fight to stay awake. I'm hurt, too. My leg's busted; so's my arm. Krauts'll be here soon. Just help me get you across that road over there, and we'll rest. What do you say?"

"Let me go, Bear." The words were more breath than sound.

"No! If you want to die, do it later. They find you here, they'll know I'm here, too."

He fought to clear the haze, to open his eyes into the blazing light. He moved his right arm to Bear, tried to lift himself with his left. His legs had grown heavy, foreign, as if they were no longer his.

"Sorry, Bear. Can't."

"All right. We'll rest a minute, but I ain't leavin' you."

He surrendered to the silken blackness, the sweet smells of the earth, sod and fresh-mown hay. And music. *Blues in the Night.* The trumpet climbed to a silver clarity, exploded in the August sun and plummeted like a fortress falling wingless from the sky. And a voice, grinding out the hollowness inside him, drained into a suffocating heat. The smell of hay grew heavy, and he fought for breath, for light and clarity, but found neither.

* * *

Bear struggled to scatter the graying edges of timothy hay over David's limp body so he couldn't be spotted by a passing patrol. In another hour, the upturned green of the disrupted hay would be wilted and undetectable. Dremmer would be safe there. Unless they had dogs. But he'd done what he could for now.

He clenched his jaw, shoved himself erect. His ankle throbbed, swelling inside his boot. If he didn't remove it soon, it would cut off the blood completely, but he'd have to make it to the trees first.

Prayers emerged on heavy grunts. He pushed through the weighty growth where the mower hadn't cut, sensed a giving under his weight that shouldn't have been there. He stopped, squinted from the pain and looked toward heaven.

A sound, distant and mechanical, rose on a cloud of dust in the west. A column of vehicles, likely German reconnaissance looking for whatever was left of their plane. The fighter pilots would have reported parachutes going down. He swallowed, fought for calm, was still two hundred yards from the road. No way to retreat to the hay. He had to cross the road before the convoy reached him.

His ankle pulsed with pain, his leg and hip ablaze. The sound widened, a menacing growth that crowded itself into his awareness until there was nothing else. His lungs burned and his left leg ached from the weight. Trucks downshifted to make the grade of the hill to the west, the road still seventy, eighty yards away. No way to make it over the low fence and across before they cleared the hill. He pushed himself forward, strained against certainty that time had run out.

The earth opened before him. An irrigation ditch, apparently unused for some time, timothy grass growing to its edge, radiated a fetid stench. He held his breath, jumped in. His right leg pounded into his hip, and he felt a nauseous heat sweep over him. Swirling darkness threatened. The pain began to subside, and the sweat on his face bore a fresh chill.

Above his head the first truck passed. A second downshifted and shook the earth. His arms and back were half immersed in mire and stagnant water. A third truck passed, but a fourth backfired and slowed, coasted past him a short way. He heard the excited shouts of German boys, green, no doubt, and hungry for their first blood. The brakes squealed, and the crunching of gravel beneath tires gave way to the cacophony of troops. Children. With rifles.

A tailgate slammed. Boots struck heavily against rock and resonated within the walls of his chest. Shouts, confounding and excited. A dog whined, anxious for the game, yelped as a leash unsnapped. He heard it sniffing to catch a hint of fear.

David, a quarter mile away. *Oh, God, don't let the wind blow from that direction!* Boys whispered from somewhere near the truck, likely letting the dog have air free of their scent. The dog barked, broke its pace and ran. Bear held his breath, prayed amid a flurry of rifle clatter. Bolts were charged, voices full of breath and excitement. He closed his eyes, prepared himself for what he would see when he opened them again. If he did.

The noise moved away. He waited, tried to quiet the thunder in his chest. The dog had the scent of something, was running away from him, away from Dremmer. Boots thundered after it. Someone growled an order, and the barking stopped. A man spoke French in the direction of the trees. Non-military. A farmer, maybe. David would understand the words if he was here.

A German hollered, seemed to be demanding something. The Belgian pleaded, the interpreter grinding out the responses in a monotone. He listened as the troops boarded the truck, their rifles butting against metal and wood. There'd been no shots. The farmer arrested, most likely. The truck started and pulled away.

Bear waited, seized with a new fear. If the man was hidden in the trees, he'd witnessed the parachute drop, his hiding David. Everything. If he broke—

Rocks ground beneath boots. He caught his breath. The Germans had left troops behind. Or maybe it was the Belgian. The steps drew closer, deliberate, stopped some distance from where he lay, stagnant water seeping through his flight suit.

A soft whistle. He strained to hear. *Yankee Doodle*. A trap?

A shadow, too long and distorted to be helpful, moved across the far side of the ditch. He watched until the shaded form stood above him. A splash. He jerked, slowly wiped mud from his face and looked down. A bottle of wine lay half submerged. A duller splat, and an apple emerged from the mire.

"Tonight! Eight o'clock. Across road." The words were whispered but emphatic.

Bear drank the fetid air, offered thanks. The walls of the ditch looked to be eight to ten feet high, the earth a fine silt. It would be slick, difficult to climb especially with a fouled-up ankle and busted arm. He needed to get to clear ground, ditch the boot.

A peculiar deadness spread from his hip down. He tensed and tried to raise himself on his fist. His hand sank deep into the mire, his right leg refusing to move. He pulled it slowly beneath him, forced his back against the wall and edged up until his hand was free, began digging hollows behind him to take the weight off his good leg. He rested a moment, dug a higher handhold to pull himself around to face the wall. A stabbing pain shot from the center of his back into his right hip. He eased his weight from the offended leg. His vision blurred, and he was covered in an instant sweat. What he needed was a rope, not a bottle of wine.

* * *

David floated, carried on a deafening hum, across a wide and lifeless plain filled with nothing forever. A trumpet riff blew over in a cloud, vanished, left the wide land blanketed in thirst. He'd been thirsty all his life—born to a creation void of drink yet eternally thirsty. A paradox, primal and eternal. In a land void of water, a man thirsts for what is not. Where did the need come from?

He woke to the dark heat of his tomb, the cloying sweetness all about. He coveted the clarity of his dream, waited, forced himself up on one arm. Light broke as through a thatched roof. Cool prickled his face, a brief freshness before he fell back, descended again into the suffocating darkness.

Bear edged to the opposite side of the irrigation ditch, the incline more gentle, and inched his way to the top. He dragged himself across the road and up the side of a hill under the shade of the trees. He unlaced his right boot and tried to take it off. His head spun, and the world tilted on its edge. He folded his jacket beneath the right ankle and lay back helpless, began to pray in the full assurance that he was heard. It brought a wholeness, deep and certain. He uncorked the wine, splashed a little in his mouth. It tasted sour, perhaps worse than nothing at all so he spilled a little onto the apple, bit deep and remembered pleasures he'd known. His wife and daughter. The sweet contentment of hearing their breathing in the night, free and secure. He missed them. Still, there was a completeness to it all, even if he never saw them again. The time lived with them had been a gift. It was a good thing to have held them, to have known their love. A man could live longer and have less.

The quiet settled deep. He closed his eyes and felt the leaf-filtered light dry his skin. It was good to be at peace with God. But David, always struggling with something his friend had no name for, though he knew what it was. He began to pray from someplace deep, beyond thought or words, pouring out a hurt and longing that weren't his. He'd known this prayer before, the shouldering of someone else's pain, hurting from the heart of God that flowed through his.

The words ceased, and he opened his eyes, looked around. The sun was failing, the day losing its strength and taking on a pallor in the west. Light littered silver-edged against the leaves and soft as cotton where it fell to the earth. He looked at his foot supported by his flight jacket and jolted. His sock, exposed by the unlaced boot top, was scarlet and wet. He knew he'd twisted his ankle when he hit, but this was worse. Had he taken some flak maybe? He wanted to move it, but feared the effort. Whatever was wrong, he had to keep a clear head.

The sun lowered, streaked the sky red and gold. He checked his watch. Just past eighteen hundred hours. Be dark soon. Engines hummed in the distance. He held his breath hoping for the familiar drone of fortresses, the comfort in their being overhead. The purr grew louder and more distinct. Pitches changed, sharp and quick. Trucks, likely the same convoy as before. They ran through gears, labored against the hills. He stared at the road, just visible between the leaves, his apprehension growing like early light. There was no place to go, and his ankle pinned him to the earth as sure as any chain. The trucks rose over the hill to the east, their half covered lights flickering through the trees, gears whining into evening. The first passed, men and rifles silhouetted against the dimming sky. The second and third followed close behind. The fourth dropped back, slowed then regained its place behind the others.

The road dulled. He dug his escape kit from its compartment in his flight suit, pulled out a book of matches, lit one and checked his watch. Nineteen hundred twenty hours. The seconds drained, the shadows birthing a thousand speculations. He pushed the thoughts away, closed his eyes and prayed into the night. Peace came, and he rested for a bit, rose then lit another match. Twenty hundred thirty-six hours. Still nothing on the road. A stallion squealed in the distance, and it struck him as odd that life should go on as if nothing had changed.

\* \* \*

David rode the wind flowing sweet and light as music. Dancer squealed his stallion squeal. *Body and Soul.* Coleman Hawkins. He'd never seen before how the sweet-flowing pleasure of that tenor sax and the smooth and certain cadence of Dancer's gait were the same. Dancer had never been more beautiful, more powerful and flowing. He held to the mane in the cool dark, was carried along body and soul.

\* \* \*

Bear waited, prayed that if David were still alive, there might be a way to save him. He prayed for all the things he'd imagined might go wrong and the many more he hadn't. Then he heard it, held his breath and listened to be sure. The rhythmic clink of bicycle chains growing more distinct. At least two riders, maybe three. The road burned back a pale memory of the day, the moon filling the emptiness of night. The sound stopped and someone whistled *Yankee Doodle*. Bear answered the whistle, finished the stanza, waited. He heard nothing, began again. Twigs snapped and branches stirred, rubbed roughly against canvas. In a moment the air was silent, and the tune began again. He whistled softly, finished the verse.

Three figures moved into the half-light above him, shadows without faces.

"Who are you?" The words floated within his stifled breath.

"Yankee Doodle, we come to take you home. You okay."

Bear looked into the shadowed face, hoped for something familiar. "I've got a friend out there in the field."

"Yes, yes, I see. Can you walk?"

"I don't know. My leg's awful fouled up."

The shorter one lifted Bear to him. "Hold to me!" They held him, one on each side, and carried him so he could lift his right foot. Even suspended, it was painful. Something was wrong. His head was light and his stomach clenched. He convulsed, pushed himself away from his rescuers, felt his throat release the apple and the sour taste of wine.

"You no good. We take you quick. Don't go out. You can sit on bicyclette?"

Bear nodded, lay suspended on his elbows, waiting for the coolness to leave his face. He rolled over in the moonlight and looked at his unlaced boot top, saw the barest edge of white glistening beneath the blood and torn skin.

"What about my buddy? He can't ride."

"Don't to worry. We take him."

\* \* \*

David was lifted into an abrupt cool, an intrusion into the thirsty place that tore him from the sugared scent of fresh-mown death. He frowned, wished only to return to the peace, to embrace the dark until he no longer felt it, to drown in his thirst and not know he was thirsty and hollow. His emptiness was a consolation, his want an enemy he no longer wished to fight.

There were voices hushed in the blackness. "Est-ce qu'il est morte?" Someone asking after him? Am I dead?

"Pour... la plupart." The words rose from a distant place, and he breathed them out.

"Parlez-vous français?"

"Oui, un petit peu."

"Parlez vous français?" A distant voice, familiar. He tried to shake the heaviness, but something loomed, frightening and unfinished. A French exam he hadn't studied for. He wasn't ready, couldn't stay awake. Then the familiar instructions: "Récitez, s'il vous plait."

"Je m'appelle David Dremmer. Je suis... étudiant de français le quatrème semestre." The words fell from his lips with a familiar ease, the giving of his name and semester. Laughter rose, muffled and far away, but he was too tired to make sense of it.

* * *

Bear watched two figures move quickly before the moon. They carried a blanket between them, a formless mass sagging toward the ground. Heaviness welled inside him and air refused to pass his throat. It wasn't that David's life was of more value than the others who had gone so quickly, but his going seemed a greater loss. Such a puzzle, so childlike and profound, capable of understanding but so confused, never knowing what it was to be at peace with God.

"Dèpêchez vous! Nous allons." The nearest man hollered to the others, anxious, turned to him. "Vite! Quickly, take away your clothes."

"I can't." Bear strained breathlessly. "My ankle. The bone's plumb through. My boot's got to stay on."

The man moved swiftly, unfastened Bear's belt, lifted his leg from the knee and slid the suit leg over his boot. "Now, you finish."

Bear strained to lift his other leg while a dark figure slipped the flight suit over his boots. The man worked feverishly with a canvas roll, his hair light, floating in the air above a receding chin. When the canvas was untied, his rescuer pulled out a pair of dirty trousers, a shirt and cap, smelling of sweat and earth. Inside the clothes was a small, worn shovel. He handed Bear the clothes.

"Put on! If we meet the Bosch and cannot hide, your name is Michel. You will answer only to this name. If they ask to you, you say this name only. If you say, say only the French."

"I don't know no French."

"Perhaps they not also. You say: 'Je ne parle pas allemande.' Can you say this, that you don't to speak German?"

"I don't think so."

"Then you are drunk. Make to sleep. If they wake you, you sound like to talk the French. This you understand?"

"Oui."

"Only to sound like. But your friend speaks the French, yes?"

"My friend? Is he alive?"

"Now, yes." The Belgian glanced at the other dark figures. "These will take you to bicyclette. You ride with me. Remember, you are drunk. Your name is Michel. I am Gaston. Charles has brandy. You drink, but not too much. You still must think."

"I thought the shovel was…" Bear looked in the direction of the blanket holding David.

"For your clothes. We will get them later. If we are stop before…" He struggled with the words, showed with his hands that the two groups were to separate. "We say you hurt on fall from wagon because of drunk. Your friend fall on— how do you say?— on pitchfork, yes?"

"Sure, okay."

The two men carried him through the trees, his weight suspended between them. He held his foot, hoping to stay the nausea and pain. David lay on the blanket suspended between the two bicycles, the work shirt they had placed around him blood-soaked and his face ash gray.

Bear looked into the big man's face, pale in the moonlight. "Will he make it?"

"Charles has not much English," Gaston said. "Your friend has not enough, how do you say, no 'tension arterielle,' not enough blood. He has drink water. This much I know."

"Do you have any water left?"

"A little." Gaston handed him a bottle wrapped in burlap. He drank it quickly.

"And this." Gaston pushed the other bottle toward him. "You must drink. Smell from this."

Bear raised the bottle, shivered. "How can you drink this stuff?"

"Is good brandy. You not to like?"

"Not used to it, I guess."

"No too much. You smell drunk, only."

He took another swallow and poured some on the front of his shirt.

Gaston pointed down the road to the west. "We go this way. These will hide your friend. If he live, they bring tomorrow. If he die, he go in ditch.

Not this one." Gaston pointed up the road toward other irrigation ditches. "No one know we are here."

"Were you… you left the apple?"

"Yes, and the wine."

"Thank you. I owe you my life."

"Yes, okay. Maybe I owe you life before war is end. Quiet now. Lean to me so as you drunk." He circled his hand in the air. "The Bosch could be… anywhere."

Bear was quiet for a moment feeling the hurried pulse of Gaston's effort against the pedals. Rocks popped and skidded from beneath the tires, the brandy loosening his neck, softening his fear.

He leaned against Gaston's shoulder. "My friend's name is David. I don't want him to die with no one knowing his name."

"Many die with no name, Yankee Doodle." Gaston panted, pushed against the grade. "Also, he is not yet dead."

# Chapter XVIII

## August 21, 1943

A sallow glow floated on kerosene fumes as David's eyes slid closed on the shadows. Dreams took root, sprouted amid men speaking French in a hay field. No, not dreams, memories. Partisans with a blanket, cradling him in a hammock— suffocating, and him too tired to roll away from the parched wool.

He opened his eyes. The girl moved in and out of lamp light, her smile lighting the gloom. He breathed in the scent of her dark hair, honeysuckle sweet as she offered him a drink. Water dripped from his chin, exploded like glass on his chest. She spoke again and disappeared.

He fought to keep his eyes wide, strained against the spinning, wished for something to hold on to. Always that wish. A pick handle leaned against the shelf he lay on. He slid his arm dryly across his chest, stopped to catch his breath, dropped his hand around the shaft, and gave himself to the darkness.

Something stirred beyond his sight. He tightened his grip on the handle, lifted and strained against the edge of darkness. It inched backward into the yellow glow. He let go, wholly spent, could only watch the light bend around the edges of the dark. The handle slid slowly from his grip, and his eyes closed against his will.

* * *

David clasped the pick handle, had submitted to the darkness only for a moment. How long had it been? Hours? Days? The girl had come with water, spoken something secret to his heart. How many times? He looked around the edge of a tarp hanging in front of his bed. Ashen light pulsed through a small window at the top of a wall. A kerosene lantern hissed in a sconce swallowing the gray. He rolled his head, slid his gaze around the room. Two wine barrels butted against the bunk near his feet, one atop the other, hiding him from the meager light. Another window most likely. A third barrel lay perpendicular, enclosing his makeshift bed. Between the barrels, he saw a fourth just around the edge of the tarp in the leg of the L-shaped room, twenty-five, thirty feet away.

"So, our French student is awake." The soft, liquid syllables brought an instant thrill. The girl from his dreams. She slid the tarp back, her skin as smooth as honey in the lantern glow. Brown hair, flowing like silk, fell in slow curls over her shoulders, her eyes electric blue. He held her stare, found the answer to a question he hadn't known to ask, his heart quieting to a stone surety as a blush spread across her face. She looked away, broke the spell. "You pushed against the tarp yesterday. Did you want to see out? We can slide it back only when the lamp is in the window or when it is dark so no one can see in."

"You my guardian angel?" The thickness of his voice surprised him.

She laughed, seemed delighted. "You look too much alive to see angels, I think."

"You're with the Resistance?"

She moved inside the covering of the tarp, lifted the lantern from the floor, took him into her circle of light. "You thought Gestapo, perhaps? Is that why you've been holding on to the pick handle?"

He returned her smile. Tried.

"I am Nicole."

"David." He cleared his throat. "Very thirsty. Could I please…"

"More water? Yes, of course." She turned to leave, looked back, her eyes bright and full. She quenched the lamp and pushed the hanging tarp wide.

When she'd gone, he stared at a second tarp covering him, lifted his knees until it yielded. First his left leg, then his right. The specter of his limbs withering beneath him— only his fear, then. Still, the effort of moving was extraordinary.

He rolled his head to the side. Three men sat at a table, smoke curling above their heads, dressed in work clothes. They spoke in hushed French. One faced him, a mountain of a man with thick, black hair and mustache and piercing blue eyes. Another sat with his back to him, squat and sturdy, dark hair sprinkled with white curling in confusion at his neck. He gestured, leaned over the table. The third sat with his head in his hands, his face covered.

Footfalls sounded on wooden steps. The three men looked toward the near wall. Nicole turned from the stairs holding two cups, one steaming, moved with the steady grace of someone accustomed to being admired. "I brought you water and broth. Can you manage both?"

"Think so. Thank you." David drank the water, warm this time. It tasted good, cleared the fog. "Bear, my friend. Is he here?" Something about Bear had troubled his sleep.

She nodded. "He's resting. In quite a lot of pain. We're taking care of him."

The mountain rose from his chair, scraped across the floor. Words, French, ratcheted from his lips, struck familiar chords, the meaning inchoate and slow to surface. The man shrugged, walked his fingers in an awkward pantomime and pointed. "You. Yes, sure."

"Thank you. I hope so." He hesitated, chanced his rusty French. "Merci, beaucoup. Je m'appelle David Dremmer. Comment vous appellez-vous?"

"Charles." The big man spat his name as if it were an oath.

"Merci, Charles." He thought for a moment. "Mon comrade…" His French was worse than rusty.

"Il dort." Sleeping.

"Est-il…"

"Il est blessé. Comprenez-vous blessé?" He was wounded. That much he'd guessed. Charles slapped his ankle, shook his head. "Sa jambé et son bras."

His leg and arm. He nodded his thanks.

Charles stood for a moment, glanced at Nicole, turned toward the others.

Nicole extended the broth. "This, too. You need it."

He held the tin cup with both hands and raised it to his face, the task immense. She rose, smiled, and turned toward the stairs.

He watched her go, marveled that he should know such loss at her leaving. Pain grew between his shoulders, extended into his legs, his back burdened and dull. The men mumbled, rose from their table next to the wall.

He examined the heavy timbers supporting the trusses, the stone and concrete. A wine cellar, probably beneath a sizable building, the air musty and cool. A few bottles lay covered in dust in racks along the wall. Boxes were stacked beneath the shelf his pallet was perched on, the barrels tapped and bunged. He watched as Nicole and the men knelt in the corner, praying in some ancient rhythm. The older spoke in what sounded like Hebrew; the three responded in French. When they finished, he heard Bear's diminished but emphatic "Amen."

She came for the cup, turned. "I am happy you are awake. Our discussions were becoming one-sided, though you do talk in your sleep. Did you know this?"

He smiled, wished for words. "And what have I told you?"

"Ah, that I shall take to my grave." She grinned, a slight pinch forming at the top of her nose, slipped around the tarp, and followed the men up the stairs.

He smiled, hoped he hadn't admitted how taken he was with her.


"Bear, you awake?" He waited a long while for an answer then surrendered again to the darkness.

He woke to light pouring through the window. It slithered around the edges of the tarp, pulled closer while he slept, and ushered him into an encircling presence of pain. He ached from cold and sweat, his nausea so intense he feared moving. The room blackened as a shadow moved before the window.

"Charles?" He hissed the words through clenched teeth.

"No, it is Albert. I am your fellow inmate. How are you feeling?" The tarp moved back, and the older of the three men from morning prayers stared down at him.

"I think I'm going to vomit."

"You must try not to. You are still dehydrated. Can you take more wa-

204

ter?"

"Too sick. You a doctor?" He closed his throat behind the words.

Albert chuckled. "I am a Jew. We have an instinct for suffering."

"What do your instincts tell you about me? Will I walk?"

"I believe so. The bullet damaged some muscle in your back. The tissue trauma has undoubtedly produced—" Albert stared, appeared to be searching for words— "perhaps intravascular debris. Your kidneys must now dispose of it. Until they do, you will likely remain quite ill."

David sucked a quick breath, held it. "Sick, yeah."

"You were fortunate that it was a shallow wound. It traversed your lower back. The right side, only. If the pain becomes too great, we will give you morphine from your escape kit. There isn't much, so you mustn't ask unless it is necessary. I'm afraid your compatriot, Sergeant Billington, will require more."

He jerked a quick nod.

"Now, I must move out of sight of the window." Albert reached to pull the tarp in place. "If you can take water, call me."

"Thank you."

"Call quietly, though. We must take no chances." Albert ducked to slide beneath the tarp, a shadow without substance or sound.

"Wait."

Albert straightened, lifted his grizzling brows. "Yes?"

"What were you praying for this morning? My buddy?"

The stubby man pulled the tarp back in place. "Yes, for Sergeant Billington and for deliverance from our enemies, for guidance, for your healing..."

He fought for breath, pushed the nausea away. "He's taking his sweet time, isn't he?"

Albert chuckled. "It's his to take. You are too impatient, my young friend. Suffering is your finest opportunity. How you accept it is the measure of your faith."

"Have no faith."

"Of course you do. And you have a will. You can choose to act heroically and make your sufferings an injustice, or you can become an animal and merely survive. Learn to suffer well, and you will have accomplished something."

"I'm not Jewish. I have no instinct for that sort of thing."

"Ah, that is what I mean. You are smiling. Good."

"Are you a rabbi, Albert?" He studied Albert's round, handsome face. The dark eyes twinkled, and gray curled from broad temples and deep-lobed ears.

"Is my wisdom so obvious? I shall make an effort to better conceal it."

"Remind me of someone, that's all." David chopped his words, swallowed.

Albert bent closer. "A rabbi?"

"A clergyman."

"You must rest. Take water when you can. And no, my young friend, I am not a rabbi, but if you think I should, I shall consider changing vocations."

When sleep came, it came indelicately. The shadows of the cellar filled the spaces of his dreams until he was captured, caught up in a vision of Dancer, rippling black, running across the hill above the house where Delores and her child and Jesse choked in silence. The black stopped, stood powerful and contained where the outcropping of rocks jutted against the evening sun. Nicole slipped from behind him, silent as a secret wish. Dancer shielded her, poised and wary. Both stared. She smiled, laid her head against the black silk of the horse's neck. "He's beautiful, David. Thank you for sharing him with me."

His breath caught in his throat. There was movement, a graceful passing before the light, and he knew it was her. The nausea had subsided. As soon as she left, he would ask Rabbi Albert for water. He liked the sound of it. Rabbi Albert. Not old, but full of an old man's wisdom or lunacy, whichever it was, suffering his way to—

The corner of the tarp lifted. "You're awake then."

"Yes."

Her smile insinuated a goodness that he wanted to believe in as he wanted breath. "You've slept a long while. I was concerned. Would you like some water or broth?"

He returned her smile, wished his heart less tainted. "Sure, when you have the time. The rabbi tells me I should drink."

206

Her smile faded. "Albert is concerned only with your health. He is afraid you are toxic, and he is not a rabbi."

"I know. I'm only joking. I like the rabbi."

Her face softened. "Yes, he is wonderful. He has suffered much, that one."

"We talked about suffering."

She moved close, let the tarp fall back in place, stilled it with her hand. "You found an expert, I'm afraid."

He nodded.

She stood silent, her eyes soft but insistent, as if she were waiting for something to become clear, appraising him, maybe. "I will be back shortly with broth and water."

The tarp dropped loosely, swung for a moment. He straightened, tried to find comfort on the rough bedding, combed his hair with his fingers, eager for her return yet fearing it.

What had she been trying to decide? He was lost in her presence, had been since he first woke to her. He marveled at the sculpture of her face, the delicacy of her nose, her sweetness.

The quick shuffle of her feet echoed from the stairs. He drew a breath and combed through his hair again. The tarp lifted, and she slipped quietly into his dark sanctum, the light on the far wall revealing the tray and two steaming mugs, her face dispelling more darkness than the lantern.

"These will help you heal. Albert believes your kidneys are perhaps functioning more normally. We shall soon know."

He squirmed, felt the deadness in his back. His kidney function wasn't something he wished to discuss with her. He took a sip and put down the first mug. "What were you trying to decide before you left?"

She flinched, shook her head. The light was muffled and gray, but he was sure. "I don't know what you mean."

"You looked at me as if you were trying to make up your mind about something. What did you decide?"

She dropped her chin, pursed her lips. He hadn't been wrong. "It's just that I need to tell you things. Things that could be dangerous."

He took another sip of broth. "I see. So why would you?"

"For now, I'll just say because I want you to know. But I must be certain."

"I owe you my life. All of you. I won't betray you."

She stared, nodded. "You think not, I'm sure, but the Bosch have ways." She lowered her stare. "It is about who we are. About what we do. And why."

An odd discomfort moved in. "You were telling me about Albert."

Her eyes softened. She waited. "He was at the University of Munich, a professor of physics. He was well respected, but being Jewish, things went badly for him." Again she waited, silent, sitting so that she could face him without turning.

He smiled. "So you've decided I can be trusted?"

She took a breath, smiled. "And I was his student." She looked down then back, seemed to be waiting for a reaction.

He nodded. "I see."

"He had a wife he loved very much. And a daughter. After Kristallnacht, the Brownshirts began destroying Jewish businesses, homes, synagogues." She straightened. "He persuaded his wife to take their daughter and visit her sister in London. He stayed and continued his work at the university. Until the Gestapo came."

When she looked away, he saw a glistening in the corner of her eye. "People were being rounded up from all about. Everything was chaotic. When he was left alone, he simply walked out of the building. He worked his way north and left the country on a Norwegian freighter, afraid to contact his wife since the Gestapo might intercept the telegram. When he finally arrived in London, he went to his wife's sister's home, but his wife and daughter had received a telegram the day he escaped saying he was gravely ill and that they were to return home straightaway. He stayed in England only long enough to have documents forged then went back to Germany and spent weeks looking for them. He couldn't make contact with friends or neighbors for fear of being turned in. Eventually, he had to leave without them. Now he is left to imagine their fate."

She raised her eyes, held his stare. "Whatever that might be, he will see them again. If not here, then in heaven."

"So much loss." He looked away then back. "The rabbi believes in heaven, then?"

"Why do you ask?" Her expression was unreadable.

"I was curious about your beliefs. You're Jewish, aren't you? This morning you were all—"

"Praying together." She finished. "Christian. We're all Christian."

"All but Albert?"

"We're all Christian. Albert is Jewish and Christian. Did you find it offensive for us to pray together?"

"Of course not."

Nicole blushed. "Perhaps I assumed too much."

"And I wasn't trying to pry."

She smiled again. "Drink your water. Albert has been having me boil it for you." Her eyes brightened, and she flashed a playful grin. "He fears you might get dysentery."

"So I'm at your mercy. Did you boil it?"

Her laugh was delicate, tiny bells in the still air. "Perhaps. Try it and see."

He drained the cup. "Rabbi Albert would be impressed with my Stoicism, don't you think?" He waited. "How's my buddy? Still sleeping?"

"We had to give him morphine. But he is sleeping again, yes." She looked away. "You don't seem much the Stoic to me."

He grinned. "Another doubter. Will he be all right?"

"If we can get you both to England, yes. His arm will be fine, but his leg is not good, I think. Albert says it is not a simple fracture." She produced another cup. "He also says you should drink more water."

"Do all rabbis practice medicine in Belgium?"

Her face brightened. "You are joking, yes?"

A frisson ran down his spine. "Should I label my jokes for my Belgian friends?"

"Albert is German, not Belgian. And Charles is French. But for me and Gaston, perhaps you should label them, yes."

More information. "Then you and Charles aren't married?"

"Now you're assuming. You forget we are at war."

He worked to hold the delight from his face. "I didn't forget. You're united only in philosophy, then."

"United in philosophy, yes, though I think philosophy would not be

209

reason enough for us to do what we do. This country is my home. We risk our lives for each other and for people like Albert. It is a matter of conviction. You are feeling stronger, I think."

"I am, thank you." What he felt was exhilaration. She was captivating.

"Suppose I bring you more broth, then, and a little bread?"

She walked away, stopped, stood for a moment at the foot of the stairs, looked back. It meant something, her standing there. He held the moment, memorized it, took it as a promise.

She returned minutes later with a saucer, a piece of black bread and another tin of broth, began speaking before she reached the tarp. "In a few days, when you are stronger, we will begin work on your French. It may be necessary for you to become a Frenchman for a while."

"From a prince to a frog."

She laughed. "That, I believe, would require a kiss."

"Is that out of the question?"

Nicole shook her head. "It would be ill-advised."

He took the bread, noted the flush on her cheeks. "I was only joking. Where did you learn English?"

"Some in school. And at university, of course. I worked at the office of the British Consulate in Antwerp for a while." She stared beyond the tarp. "I haven't seen Antwerp since the Bosch came."

He sipped the broth, his gut clenching at the disclosure. But he desperately wanted her to stay. "You had to leave?"

"Oh, yes, my association with the British made it necessary."

He nibbled at the bread, wondered what she'd done. "Charles seemed upset this morning before he left. Is he angry at our being here?"

"He is frightened only. If you were found, it would go badly for us."

"We'll leave soon, then. As soon as we can. Please tell Charles I said so." He avoided her eyes. "What would happen to you if we were found here?"

She shrugged. "We would be shot. Or hanged. The Bosch are fond of hangings."

His blood chilled. "We'll leave right away, then." He handed her the broth, tried to raise himself on his fist, grew instantly incensed at his weakness.

Nicole placed her hand on his shoulder. "You can go nowhere. Either of you. You would be caught, and you might tell them where we are. You will stay."

"We wouldn't tell them anything, and I don't know where we are."

"You don't know what you might say." She extended the cup of broth. "Here."

He took the cup but couldn't meet her eyes. "I don't want to put you in danger."

"It was our choice. There was nothing you could do to prevent it." Nicole rose, caressed his arm lightly. "Now rest." She slid behind the tarp, pulled it further than before.

* * *

It was night before he had to ask Albert for a urinal. When he did, the urine appeared to be mostly blood.

"You should be grateful you are so well." Albert said. "Drink more water."

"How's Bear?"

"Sergeant Billington? Perhaps a little better. Tomorrow, you will go over to see him, nu? For now, you must drink water."

David drank and rested through the last hours of darkness and woke to morning prayers, the tarp pulled back, the lamp shining into his face from the sconce in the window. The four of them were in the corner. Even kneeling, Charles towered above the others.

Nicole wore her beauty with reverence, a shawl covering the darkness of her hair, her lips full and crimson in the kerosene glow. Albert spoke, half chanted, his back to him. The third man remained quiet, his face haunted by an intensity much like Charles'. He waited for Bear's affirmation. None came.

"Well, my impatient young friend, are our prayers having good effect?" Albert spoke into the gray, his head projecting around the edge of the tarp.

David nodded. "The good care isn't hurting, either." He watched as Charles and the other man shuffled up the stairs. "On their way to work?"

"To the fields, yes."

"Charles' companion seems concerned about something."

"Ah, Gaston. Now he could teach you something about suffering. The Bosch took his wife and daughter six months ago. He changed his name and escaped. He's not heard from them since. Suspected Jewish sympathizers. A terrible crime, nu?" Albert shook his head.

"This morning I will change your bandages, and you will show us how you appear standing. Then you will begin your French lessons. Charles is having work passes made as you and I are soon to become French laborers here for bridge construction on our way back to Paris. There we will be given new identities for our excursion to England, God willing. We will leave in a few weeks, and you will have to be able to walk and talk like a Frenchman. Do you think you can do this?"

"I'll try. But what about Bear? Won't he be going with us?"

"He will be traveling with an older woman, also French. He is to be her deaf-mute son. In England you will be reunited, yes?" Albert patted his shoulder.

"Why are you doing this, Albert?" He studied his benefactor's face, the drawn brow, the lines around his eyes. "If we're captured, I know it would go badly for you." The shadow light of early morning pressed a fear into him, a black cloud too heavy for breath.

Albert shrugged, offered a slight smile. "You are of no use to your Air Corps here, are you? I want you to go back and help stop this insanity. You can yet, perhaps, be a part of destroying the Nazis' ability to make it continue."

"That's not the only reason."

"Perhaps not, but it is reason enough. Now roll over, lie face down, loosen your belt, and we'll change those bandages. I will see if Nicole has an egg she can fry for you this morning. A real American breakfast, nu?"

He grunted at the effort. "Where is the food coming from, Albert? Does she have enough to share?"

"Nicole and Charles have a food allowance, and Charles steals his own potatoes and brings them from the field. And he captures squabs. Ah, the squabs!"

He turned his head, saw Albert's hands raised toward the ceiling.

"But should I complain if the Almighty blesses us with pigeons and potatoes? God forbid. Not even when Charles has to steal the fruit of his own labor. Gaston has also an allowance and lives in the flat above Charles and Nicole."

"Charles and Nicole are married?"

"Legally, yes. A little charade for the Bosch. You are fond of Nicole, nu?"

"Sure. She's very kind."

"And beautiful." There was disapproval in Albert's voice.

"Yes, she is."

"And you shall be gone in a few weeks. A couple of months at most. And if you survive and make it to England, and if Nicole is not found and hanged, you shall still likely never see her again. Be cautious not to make bonds that will cause you to act unwisely."

His blood rose. "Why shouldn't I see her again? Don't you have faith? This war could end someday, Rabbi."

"Perhaps in Europe it will end. At least for a while. But who is really fighting here, Lieutenant?"

He frowned, offered an answer he sensed Albert would find lacking. "Germany and most of what's left of the world."

"This war is between those God calls his own, their allies, and those who hate him. It may move from one place to another and from one generation to the next, but it will not end." Albert was silent for a moment then patted his shoulder. "However, you are concerned with Nicole. And for the two of you, for a while, this war could end. If it does, and if you should both by some miracle survive, how will you find her? Do you think she uses her real name? You must be careful what you share, how much you know of each other."

He hadn't thought— an alias was a necessary thing. Still, not to know her name... And he wasn't the one sharing.

Albert lifted the dressing from his back. "This looks dreadful. Still, it's healing, I believe. No evidence of infection. Is it very painful?"

"No, I have some pain beneath my shoulders and in my legs, but nothing in my back— not on my right side. I'm not sure if it's numb, or if I've lost feeling from not having moved."

"Do you feel this?" Albert touched a needle to both David's feet.

"Yes. Yes."

"Can you raise your feet? Go ahead, bend your legs at the knee."

He raised first one leg then the other. Something was amiss with the right.

"All right. Now keep your legs straight, and raise them at the hip." Albert's voice grew heavy with concern.

His left leg rose, but his right leg floundered, ignored his request.

"No pain?" Albert asked.

"Just under my shoulder blades." The knot tightened. "Why can't I raise my leg?"

"I don't know. And there is no pain..."

He fought to keep the rising panic from his voice. "What kind of rabbi are you?"

"Feet to the floor. We'll see if you can still jitterbug."

"Thanks all the same, Rabbi." His voice wavered.

"I dance quite well, my young friend. Don't tell me you're anti-Semitic."

Albert pulled him to his feet, let him stand alone. "All right, very carefully, step toward me." The rabbi stood in front, his hands out.

His right leg felt unstable. He raised his left foot, tried to push forward and almost fell. He lifted it without problem then steadied quickly, whispered through lips as cold as death. "I can't. I don't seem to be able to."

Albert motioned for him to sit. He lowered himself to the makeshift bed, fell awkwardly when halfway down. His heart raced. It wasn't possible that he would be crippled. He looked at Albert. "I don't understand."

"It appears muscles in the right gluteus group aren't working, though the hamstring seems fine." Albert shrugged. "It is possible you have nerve damage, though it is also possible that it is only swelling."

"Qu'est-ce qu'on fait ici?" Nicole whispered around the edge of the tarp.

Albert nodded toward him. David stood, embarrassed, carrying a new shame, tightening the belt in the heavy trousers. "He's having some difficulty walking. It appears at least one group of muscles is affected."

"What do I do?" He found it hard to breathe. It was more than he could take in. Death was expected, but to end up like Jesse...

"Let me give it some thought, see if perhaps Gaston can find some literature on the subject. That may be difficult, of course." Albert moved to the edge of the tarp, turned back. "Nicole, I suspect your presence might bring more comfort than mine."

Albert was wrong. She was the last person he wanted to see him now. He fell back inside himself, tried to imagine life without the joy of his strength and quickness. He brooded for a moment then hauled himself to the edge of his sleeping pad, pushed up with his left leg.

Nicole reached out to him. "David, perhaps you shouldn't do this now."

He tried to smile. "It's all right. I have to know." He tightened the muscles in his left leg, felt the hardness in his thigh and buttock, then grabbed his right leg and forced the muscles taut beneath his hand. The quadriceps were firm, just like the other leg, but when he touched his right buttock, he felt only the soft weight of useless flesh.

"Oh, my God." The words were only breath. He dropped back against the canvas.

Nicole slipped outside the tarp, spoke in hushed tones. He made no sense of the words, could only hear the cracking of twigs and fallen branches beneath his feet as he had run into the pines, remembered the hardness of his limbs, the burning hunger of his lungs.

The tarp moved at the foot of his bed. "Dremmer, listen to me. When we get to England, we'll take you to see a doctor. Think of that. This could be your ticket home."

He turned, saw Bear standing, holding the boards above his bed, his friend's leg lifted from the floor like an injured bird. He pulled himself to his feet, years older than when he'd awakened, and leaned forward. A convulsion rose from somewhere deep, and he threw his arms around Bear. For a moment he was a child and release came, pure and uncontrolled.

"Hey, cowboy." David dried his face on his sleeve.

Bear chuckled. "Not much of a cowboy. What kind of cowboy rides without his bandana? Looks like you could use one."

"How you feeling? Pain better today?" He avoided Bear's eyes.

Bear shook his head. "Not near as bad."

Albert moved back under the tarp, Nicole at his side.

215

He smiled. "I'm no good as a silent sufferer, Rabbi. I tried, but—"

The rabbi shrugged. "We can't all be Jewish, I suppose."

"How are you going to get rid of me now? I'll never pass as a construction worker."

"Now you're an injured construction worker with good reason to be returning to France."

Bear moved in close, looked at Albert. "It'll never wash. Can't you figure out a way for us to go back together?"

Albert raised his hands. "And this will 'wash,' as you say? Two injured construction workers, one a deaf-mute, the other speaking only rudimentary French who just happens to have a bullet hole in his back in Belgium in the middle of the war?"

"It might be best to come up with an entirely new identity for David, don't you think?" Nicole twisted her hands, spoke in short breaths. "If he had been injured in a bridge rebuilding, the Bosch would have taken him on military transports. Perhaps he should stay."

Albert glanced her way. "We'll leave that to the committee. They will have to prepare the documents in any case. Charles will notify them."

Everything was wrong. He'd been summoned to give his life, his youth, because some madman had twisted the world with his beliefs, become drunk with power and certainty. The insane indirection of it all, the burning terror that could not end until all were dead or destroyed, the lunacy of one people turned against all others, stoking the fire against the cold conviction of their superiority. Sheep, following the dictates of the peculiar insanity to which they'd sworn allegiance, unwilling to call a halt until no one could. The war was a cancer, as were the abstractions that bore it. David looked around the room, his eyes coming to rest on Nicole. She was what mattered. And Bear and Albert.

He stared into the musty light. The others, save Nicole, wandered off.

"David, you should rest. You must build your strength." Her voice washed over him as soothing as warm water.

"I suppose." He met her gaze, knew what it was he wanted most and dared not hope for.

She rubbed her arms. "I am sorry, David. Perhaps this won't last."

The sound of her liquid consonants made him ache. "I'm really very grateful for all you've done. All of you."

"I know. I'll get you breakfast now. For Bear also, yes?"

"Thank you." He reached to touch her hand, caught himself.

Bear moved across the floor, holding to what he could, worked his way back to them, his leg suspended. "Dremmer..." His wise friend began some comfort, his voice heavy.

He raised a hand, couldn't bear the words. So far as they knew, they were the only two alive in their crew. His loss was insignificant. He had no right to be consumed with it.

"All the others, Bear. How many chutes did you see?" He was tired of asking the questions of himself, wanted to hear Bear's answers.

"I for sure saw five. Then me and you and Sheen. Massing and McKay were the only ones I know couldn't have made it out. Maybe the others did. Even Sheen could have made it. Likely busted up, but he could've made it."

The answers were the same as his. He'd wanted more to hope for. "I was thinking about Lioni this morning. A royal pain, but God, I wish he were here. And Ream."

"Yeah. And Berkowitz. D'you know his wife left him?"

His face went slack. "How'd you know that?"

"Come to me a few weeks back." Bear looked away. "Had to talk to somebody."

He looked down, his mouth dry. With all that had happened, it seemed the worst news. "I didn't know. Never would have guessed." He shook his head. "Even if he made it..."

Bear nodded. "Maybe they didn't find him."

# Chapter XIX

Nicole's thin soles whispered across the concrete, brought an ache to David's heart. A yellow glow curled warmly at the edges of the tarp where she stood silent, waiting. A word, a hint of need and she would have lifted the barrier, turned his canvas cell into a sanctum, her presence a continuation of his dreams. He coveted the right to whisper her name, but two things were inescapable. His crippling had diminished him, and even if he were whole, his relenting to Delores' demands a lifetime ago had taken what little he might have had to offer. He held his breath, denied himself her presence and lay in silence until she left.

Dawn had seeped through the seams of the tarp before the men shuffled down the stairs. Chairs scraped against the floor as their shadows circled before the lamp, low murmurs preceding their prayers. Albert called in Hebrew, and Nicole's fluid French mingled with the men's in response. David closed his eyes, committed the music of it to his heart. They finished the doxology and shuffled toward the steps. He ached for her closeness, the sound of her laughter, stared at his legs beneath the tarp, detesting his weakness.

The light from the window reached the stairs. She came again, moved the tarp, the brightness of her face taking his breath away.

"David, you must eat. I brought some bread and squab." Her goodness seemed instinctive, her kindness like Bear's, wise and full.

"I thought you wouldn't come back." The words were out before he knew to stop them.

"So, you are hungry?" She feigned exasperation, but the corners of her mouth lifted.

He laughed. "Just missing your threats. You haven't warned me today how bad it's going to be with you as my schoolmaster."

She leaned forward, almost touched him. "I'm going to make you sweat." She pulled a notepad and pen from behind her, waved them in his face. "No more warnings. Today you become a Frenchman."

He allowed a smile, chewed the squab, worked to hide the depth of his delight. She began with French phrases, asked directions, had him ask them of her. He tried but couldn't concentrate, her presence a reminder of what he needed most and could no longer hope for.

She closed her notepad, looked at him. "David, are you listening?"

"I'm sorry, Nicole." He let the words attenuate into the filtered gray. "I expected dying, but not this."

"And if your life were all you had, if there were nothing you were willing to sacrifice even your legs for, what would it then be worth?"

He looked back, sank into the depths of her eyes, wondered if there might be a passion that would never fade. He clenched his fists, forced the thoughts away. "And what have I sacrificed for? Some abstraction that puts a lump in the great throat of Europe or America?"

"If you have sacrificed for that, then you are a fool. You have sacrificed for Albert, and tens of thousands like him; for Charles and Gaston and Gaston's family. For your wife—"

"No, not..."

"All right, then. For me and thousands like me so that we would not have to live under tyranny and torture."

"There is no one like you. And you're enough." His vow was mostly breath, more thought than words.

The fire in her eyes dwindled. "Just as we are willing to give our lives, if need be, for you."

He pushed upright, met her head on. "And when some other madman comes along, replaces this one, what will we have sacrificed for then?"

"For the years and lives between. For the hope that such a thing won't happen. And what does it matter, David? We can die only once. If our lives are willingly spent then what more can we lose?"

"But we won't *be* anymore. What will we have gained?" He stirred, looked away. The thought of her dying for *any* cause was a greater injustice than he could bear. "How is it that you can give all that is required of you and not be angry at the unfairness of it, and I can't?" He stared into the brilliant blue of her eyes.

She cleared her throat. "Friend. I want the word for friend."

His hesitation was momentary. "Âme, mon âme."

She smiled, rested her arms on her lap. "The word is ami. Votre âme is your soul."

"Yeah." He nodded and met her smile, wondered if she guessed it hadn't been a mistake. "My soul, yeah. Le grand peut-être, oui?"

"The big maybe? Not for me." She relaxed, settled back. "It is for me the second greatest certainty."

"And the first?"

"That Someone above all this is quite conscious of me, that he loves me." She was quiet for a moment. "Do you believe this also?"

He searched her eyes, wanted desperately to please her. "In the field after we were shot down, when I was drifting in and out, I had the most overwhelming sense of being more than what I'd known. It seemed that if all I knew of myself ceased to be, what I really am would continue. I was more than all I'd done. I was who I was whether my body lived or died. Does that make sense?"

"Yes. Have you never also had an awareness of God?"

"No, and I'm not sure I could believe it if I had." He looked around the tarp into the dark corner of the cellar.

"I think you could not then believe otherwise. Nevertheless, I have not experienced this awareness of my spirit, if that is what you meant, and I believe in it. My faith is more than a conclusion I have reached. It comes from the outside in."

His heart sprang in recognition. "A wholly different way of knowing something."

Her eyes went wide. "That's it precisely."

He caught her gaze and smiled. "A friend told me that once. I guess I don't have any faith."

"Or perhaps you've invested it in the wrong things."

He shrugged, hid his heart with a smile. "I had a prayer answered once."

"Perhaps you should try another."

He laughed, and her eyes lifted.

She straightened, seemed to recapture something. "You have difficulties ahead of you, and I don't wish for you to be caught up in thoughts of your loss."

"Ami. The word was 'ami,' friend, not to be confused with mon âme, mon ami."

Albert appeared at the edge of the tarp. "How is our young Frenchman progressing?"

Nicole looked up and blushed. Something in her face brought a quiver to his gut. "I'm afraid we're dealing with issues weightier than learning French, Albert."

"Having long ago answered each question of significance, I could perhaps enlighten you so that you might consider such banalities as saving our tushes, yes? Now what problems have you discerned in our orderly universe, Lieutenant?"

He shrugged. "For one, men have this affinity for abstractions. They create systems based on them— commit the most horrendous crimes to support them." He paused, looked at Albert. "I think maybe they're not worth defending."

Albert put a hand to his grizzled chin. "So it is the abstractions that have led us to this?" The professor looked at him, his cheeks lifting. "I think not, my young friend." Albert moved his hand to his chest. "It is what is here. It is the hunger to control, to have another do our bidding. It is pride, and it is a tumor that grows in the heart of every man. Including yours."

A frisson ran up his spine, and he drew in the dense air. He thought of Jesse, what had come between them, of Lieutenant Baker in gunnery school. He released his breath, loosened his grip on the edge of the shelf.

Albert studied his face, laid a comforting hand on his shoulder. "So easily I resolve the mysteries of the universe. Now, learn your French."

\* \* \*

David walked from his bed to Bear's then back in a step-swing cadence, chinned himself in the corner, did push ups with his feet elevated from a wine rack, lifted and curled potato sacks to bring the hardness back to his arms and shoulders then bathed in the corner where Albert left buckets of water each morning for him and Bear.

He moved back toward the window, pulled the tarp aside and fell on his improvised bed. The door squeaked at the top of the stairs and Nicole's feet murmured on the steps. A moment later she slipped around the corner of the tarp.

"Albert said to have you stand. He says your exercises are fine if you want to go to the Olympics, but you must also encourage the nerves to work in your back. And he thinks standing will perhaps reduce the swelling." She stood above him, her hands extended.

He couldn't resist the pleasure of her touch, took her hands, rose and faced her. "I was thinking about what you told me about Antwerp— how you loved it. And your affiliation with the British. It must have been difficult leaving."

She shrugged. "Yes, I loved my work at the Consulate. Some of it, at least. Still, I was one of many working there who had to go into hiding. The Germans would have executed us without question. MI5 ordered the Resistance to find a place for me. They put me here with Charles, where I could be of some use." She stopped, pulled her hair away from her face. "This is a better life. Antwerp had grown so dark." Her voice faltered. "But I worry about my aunt. She doesn't know whether I am alive. Nor I, her."

He lifted his hand to her cheek, let it rest against her cool, smooth skin, and battled the need to draw her close, put his arms around her, shield her from anything that might hurt her again. She pressed her face against his hand, smiled the saddest smile he'd ever seen.

"This craziness will end someday. I swear it will. And when it does..." He held his breath, stopped before his words betrayed him.

He moved away, leaned against his bed and told her of growing up with the old man after his mother died, the gentle peace of the hills, the holy hush that came when they were covered in snow. He talked of his university days, the warm afternoons in the chapel. Of Elise. He needed for her to know.

"Do you still love her?" She spoke with the respect one reserves for the dead.

He smiled, the answer clear now. "No. I haven't in a long time, I guess. I've just needed someone to wish for. Of course, there's Dancer. I think I miss him more than anything else of home." He held her stare. "All things of beauty share something. They're like gifts to a hollow world."

Her eyes glistened. "A gift without a Giver?"

He met her smile, could almost believe when he looked at her.

She leaned back against the barrel. "Tell me about your wife."

He'd been waiting for it, took a deep breath. "We were hardly husband and wife. I never loved her. We married because," he stopped but refused to look away, "because she was pregnant. We'd been married only a few weeks when I left, but it was long enough for her to learn to despise me." He shrugged, held her gaze. "Her hatred was a freeing thing."

Nicole nodded, offered a sad smile. "Your marriage is somewhat like mine, though I'm quite fond of Charles."

"And you have no plans to make yours permanent?"

"Our marriage was only to establish our identities. It is curious; your marriage was a deception to each other, your family, your friends. Ours is a deception only for our enemies, but both have had such consequences." She looked away.

"Mine wasn't so much a deception as a weakness. I couldn't stand up to her."

She rested her hand on his arm. "It was easier for you to let her believe what was not true than to tell her plainly?"

He shook his head. "Not exactly."

Bear scuffed beyond the tarp, still struggling to walk with a plank under his arm. He coughed, appeared to be letting them know he was near.

"Want to join us, Bear? Nicole will tutor you. You could write Babs a love letter in French. Be really romantic."

The tarp moved back. Bear's sweaty face appeared, a dollop of black hair across his forehead. "She didn't complain about the ones I was writing. She might, though, if she had to find somebody to read it to her. And I'm not so sure the Krauts wouldn't get suspicious if I hobbled down to the post office in my flight suit and mailed a letter to Texas."

Nicole looked up at Bear, smiled gently. "David was about to explain to me why he couldn't tell Delores he wouldn't marry her."

The room grew silent. David rolled his shoulders against the weight of it, looked at his friend in apology.

"I believe I'll keep on working with this crutch. Need to be able to move better than what I'm doing." Bear stepped back. The tarp dropped and swung.

He fixed his eyes on her. "Why did you do that?"

"I didn't mean to be unkind, but we might not have much time." She touched his hand, withdrew. "You didn't want to tell me why you couldn't say no to Delores. I think I should know, don't you?"

"She was pregnant. I owed her."

"You owed her what? A hope that would never be fulfilled? Has your misery made her happy?"

He looked away, stared into the stillness. "Maybe it's different here. It was what was expected of me. I knew I couldn't give her what she wanted, but I thought I could maybe make her more respectable."

Nicole leaned toward him, gently pulled his face toward her. "And would allowing her to be a war widow make her respectable?"

He melted at her touch. "Sure it would."

"And what do you think she wanted from you?"

"I thought she wanted me to love her, but…"

"You don't think so now?"

"I think she wanted someone to give her a better life. Anyone."

She smiled, seemed satisfied with something. "And what do you want? Now, I mean."

He stared at the concrete, couldn't tell her all he'd wished for but dared not presume. "You said I should pray for something else, remember? Well, I have, and I do. I want to know what you and Bear know. I want to know when I'm right. I need to know what's true."

She smiled, leaned into him, kissed him softly. "Then you shall. That I promise."

A truck rumbled along the street and the windowpane rattled a weak response. The warmth of her lips remained even as she lifted the tarp and slipped away.

* * *

224

David took a bite of egg, listened as Albert told of his mother's raisin cakes and his father's architectural firm, closed following the Great War when government contracts were denied Jews. He marveled as Albert's eyes glistened when he spoke of the university, his work at Göttingen, the voice emerging from a holy hush.

"It was where I met my Angela. So beautiful and wise. I was working under Max Born. A genius. When he was given the chair of the department at Göttingen, he drew everyone passionate about atomic physics there. Including Werner Heisenberg.

"Our work was of the utmost gravity." Albert shook his head, chuckled. "We examined the very mind of God— the composition of his universe. We looked at the nuts and bolts he used in its construction. And do you know what we learned?" The professor paused, a ploy designed, he guessed, to draw students in, prepare them for some great truth.

He smiled, imagined how effective it must have been. "We learned the most basic components of the universe are more unreliable than we could in any way sort out. Our observations were inherently flawed and always would be. The building blocks changed shapes before our eyes."

Albert's passion delighted him. "It must have been humbling."

"Yes." Albert's stubby finger jutted toward the rafters. "It was humbling in the grandest sense. It proved that men could never gain all truth. Not through the senses, not through mathematics, not through science. In the end, man must operate by faith. It is inevitable. The only choice is what he places his faith in."

His delight withered. He looked down, stabbed the last bite of egg. Albert had told him too much, revealed his past, his identity, even his wife's name, precisely what he'd warned him not to do. And somehow he was sure it hadn't been proffered without intent.

He shifted, taut at his suspicion. "When you grew up, were you a practicing Jew, Albert, or Christian?" He spoke softly, worked with the unsettling implications.

Albert smiled. "Jewish, observing all 613 obligations of the law, respecting righteous Gentiles, of course, but very devout. Angela was Jewish also, though she didn't grow up observant. Her father, Otto Grossman, was also an architect and also denied work after the war." Albert's hands bounced above his lap. "It gave us one more thing in common."

David looked at Nicole, waited for an explanation. She smiled, glanced quickly at the professor. "Albert tried for an American university, you know, a research position, teaching, anything to get his family out of Germany. He was rejected when they learned he was religious."

He looked back, felt strangely embarrassed. "I'm sorry."

"Germany isn't unique in its dealings with religionists." Albert stood. "I'm afraid your universities are much the same. But I will leave that discussion for another time. Now you must continue. And do work in a bit of French, yes?"

Nicole shared another meaningful glance with the rabbi before he pulled the tarp back. He stilled the swaying canvas before walking to the stairs.

David took a sip of what the Belgians were given for coffee, especially strong and heavy with the cream Charles had been bringing home. His appreciation soured with his suspicions, and he wondered how far they might go in breaking their own rules.

"So tell me about *your* family."

She smiled, made small circles with her cup on the surface of the shelf. "My father was a carpenter, a wonderful man. Loving, always ready with a kiss or a joke. I never doubted he loved my sister, but his love for me was special. We spent hours together. What time he had, he gave me. I felt..." She shook her head, proud. Ashamed too, he guessed, at being the favored child. "I felt he lived for me, that there was nothing he wouldn't do for me."

He nodded his encouragement.

"He wanted me to go into medicine, become a physician. But I discovered mathematics, the music of the spheres." She blushed. "I found it intriguing. We rose early on Sundays. It was our special time. I shared with him the mysteries I'd discovered in my studies." She laughed. "What I'd learned was always such a profound surprise to him. I was twelve, you see, thirteen when he died. I was telling him nothing he didn't know. It was being with me that he wanted. Like you, now."

She seized him with her gaze, conceded she had his heart. "One morning my aunt came into my room. I was startled, still asleep. I seldom saw her and didn't recall that she was coming for a visit. Then I remembered. My mother and I were supposed to spend the day in Antwerp. There'd been no talk of my aunt visiting." She stopped, wiped tears from her eyes. "My aunt took my hand and told me that while I slept my mama and papa had been in a boating accident. They were celebrating Mama's birthday, had a few drinks and took a small boat out on a pond near our home. My mother lost her hat, leaned over to pick it up and tipped the boat." She stopped, sucked in a breath. "She couldn't swim. My father died trying to save her.

"My aunt and uncle opened their doors to me, but I never again felt that I was the center of someone's world." She put her hands in her lap, clasped them. "Until now."

The deep darkness in her face drew him in. The words he'd held back tumbled beyond his will to hold them in. "I listen for you on the stairs. I memorize your words, your voice, your smile, the feel of your breath. I rehearse everything I know about you until it's covered in sleep, and then I dream of you. When I wake, I think of you, and when I see you, it takes my breath away."

She clamped her teeth over her lower lip, looked away. "It is the same for me."

He had to stop it, could see in her face that she knew it, too. "You were telling me about your father."

She nodded, wiped tears from her cheeks. "Yes, he left provision for my sister and me. She went to a music conservatory, married a year later, and I eventually went to the University of Munich to study mathematics."

The pieces were falling into place. "Where you were Albert's student."

She nodded, smiled. "Schwabing was full of writers, poets, freethinkers. And Nazis. It was an exciting time but for the Reich. Somehow we managed to block that out of our lives. But the Reich was jealous for anyone or anything it didn't control. Several friends became active in the Underground. Some joined the Communist Party— a foolish thing. They were executed or sent to prison camps. Or just disappeared in the night. My best friend, Élodie Devillier, left, too. She had grown incautious, and…" Her face grew pale, her eyes liquid.

He touched her cheek, ached to hold her. But he couldn't. He withdrew his hand, and life drained from his fingers. "Your friend, Élodie, was French?"

"Belgian, like me. Now she's in Germany, I believe." Her voice broke, tears cresting at her eyelids.

He moved close, reached to put his arms around her as he'd wanted to do for weeks.

Albert bounded down the stairs, began talking even before reaching the bottom. "I'm sorry to interrupt, Nicole, but I have some important news."

Nicole released his hand she'd held to her cheek. He slid back, settled on his pallet.

Albert dragged another chair behind the tarp, pulled the canvas behind him. "It has occurred to me that you should know something about interrogations. It is my hope, of course, that you won't need this information.

"Military interrogations, especially Luftwaffe, can be humane. They will make every effort to trick you into giving information, but they seldom abuse prisoners, especially fellow flyers." He looked up. "If you should be apprehended by the Gestapo, God forbid, request a Luftwaffe interrogator. The Gestapo, even though you are out of their jurisdiction, can be quite brutal. I am not saying that they will honor your request, but they will know you are aware of their jurisdictional limits." He stopped, waited. "For precisely this reason, the committee has changed plans."

From the corner of his eye, he saw Nicole flinch.

"You will not change your identity. You will leave wearing what is left of your flight uniforms and continue to wear them until we are ready to execute our plan to get you over the Channel. Should that fail or should the Bosch learn you are in the area, you will fall back on the original plan to be French workers and make your way to the coast. You will be expected to find suitable clothing on your own. Our contact will supply you with names and addresses."

His heart hammered against his ribs.

Albert paused, searched the air. "It also appears I won't be going with you."

A hot coal ignited in his gut. No one had the right to keep Albert from a chance at life. He turned to Nicole. "Who is this committee?"

The two compatriots shared a glance. Albert nodded, and Nicole spoke.

"We are directed by WIM, the Dutch Underground. They, in turn, receive directives from British MI5. It is highly organized, our operations quite military."

He held is silence, tried to squelch the need to know what they weren't saying.

Nicole looked at Albert. "Shouldn't he know about Heinrich?"

Albert rubbed his grizzled chin. "I suppose it could prove helpful. Leutnant Heinrich Schneider, Luftwaffe. As a flyer downed in this district, you would be under his jurisdiction. If you should fall into his hands, you would, I am sure, be treated fairly. However, he is quite intelligent. Should you meet him, tell him nothing. Especially about anyone here." Albert's gaze strayed again to Nicole, returned.

"There is another. Gerhardt Schmidt, Hauptmann, Gestapo, known by the locals for his attention to their young sons. He has an immoderate interest in their political leanings, finds especially the good-looking boys suspect of holding anti-Reich sentiments. Questions them for hours behind closed doors. Few are ever seen again." He shrugged. "One can only guess."

David sucked in air, swallowed against the bile rising in his throat.

Darkness shadowed Nicole's face, colored her words. "And Blik?"

Albert nodded, turned to David. "We have a rather notorious intelligence officer, this one Wehrmacht. Leutnant Karl Blik is quite adept at getting into the pocketbooks of Belgian citizens. He ferrets out those who are thought to have hidden possessions— valuable art, jewelry, especially gold. He extorts them, finds them guilty of espionage and sends them to work camps. He is rumored to have built up a substantial cache in Switzerland."

David shrugged. "All my valuables are out of the country at the moment."

"I think not." Albert looked from him to Nicole. "Be careful not to put yourselves in a compromising situation. I know I haven't heeded my own dictum. I've said more than—"

"You've said far too much." He glared at Albert. "You've named places, professions, names. And you've said none of it in front of Bear. There has to be a reason."

Nicole dropped her head. "Perhaps we've been unwise."

"I don't believe that." He stared. "You're both too smart for it to be a mistake."

Albert nodded, raised his chin. "You are right. It was unfair. We simply wanted a chance to prepare you."

"Prepare me for what?" He smelled betrayal, should have known no woman could feel for him what he felt for her. "And what are all the looks about?"

"We'd like to ask a favor of you. It's personal, and we wanted you to know how important it is. That's why we told you what we did." Albert didn't flinch.

"Go ahead." His heart pounded.

"Nicole has an aunt, very dear to her—"

"Yes, she told me."

"We want you to have her notified, tell her that Nicole is alive. MI5 has it within their resources to find her and report back to us if she is well. And to get word to her of Nicole."

He nodded, felt the fool for his suspicions, though they hadn't yet died. Not all of them.

"You didn't have to put anyone in danger to have asked that." He looked at Nicole. "You know I would have done anything you asked. Anything."

She nodded, her blue eyes pooling. "We wanted you to understand how important it is. And there's more."

"Okay." His gut clenched.

"Do you remember that I told you we would also die for you if need be?"

The words stung. "I remember."

"Rest assured, we would. Albert's admonitions were to me, to encourage me not to endanger myself. I chose to ignore his words, to tell you everything, though I didn't quite."

Albert leaned forward, rested his elbows on his knees. "David, has anything we told you put you in danger? Anything? No one has deceived you. Not here. It is we who have been put at risk." He waited, searched the ceiling, seemed to settle something, inclined his head toward him. "My name is Dr. Gerhardt Stein. My wife's name, as I told you, is Angela." Albert paused, breathed deep. "Nicole's aunt's name is Claudette Lebec. I'd prefer you not ask Nicole her full name. Is that agreeable?"

He nodded, looked at his boots, breathed deep as the weight lifted from his shoulders.

# Chapter XX

## October 1943

A yellow incandescence sizzled from the window. After a silent meal of squab and potatoes, Nicole left with tears in her eyes. He hadn't seen her for hours. David rocked against the wall, pressed his hands between his knees and watched the burning shaft move inexorably toward the shelf that had been his bed, now the resting place for empty wine racks.

Albert sat silent beneath the window. The orders had come from WIM; the rabbi was to accompany him and Bear to the rendezvous point where they would meet their contact and be shuttled to the Channel then boated across with other downed airmen. If apprehended, the WIM operative said, Albert's presence would give the Germans an excuse to execute them all as spies. After contact was made, Albert was to return.

David stared into the darkness that had already swallowed the stairs. Albert had drilled him and Bear with possible interrogation questions for two days. They'd created a scenario of their survival since being shot down. The plan was to insist on giving only names, ranks, and serial numbers. However, if the interrogations turned nasty, they would have their stories honed to perfection so that they wouldn't have to think.

"One more time, please." Albert turned toward David, spoke for the first time since morning. "It's been a month and a half since your plane went down. Where have you been all this time?"

It had been a lifetime, and the thought of leaving Nicole left him empty and sick. "I was unconscious after being shot. The sergeant said I'd been

232

waking up to drink water. First thing I remember was waking in a grove of trees. My parachute was gone, and my flak jacket was tied around me. The morning after I woke up, Sergeant Billington brought eggs and some milk in a can. He'd gotten them from a nearby farm. We stayed there a few days, I guess, until the bleeding stopped. Then we started moving at night. We thought we were headed toward the Channel, but we were moving only in the dark, had no compass, so we got lost." The words no longer had meaning.

"Where did you hide? What did you eat?" Albert assumed the gruffness of an intelligence officer.

"In trees, twice in irrigation ditches when we heard dogs. We'd get in the water and move slow, a couple hundred yards, maybe, lean against each other and take turns sleeping. We stayed in a barn, a small dairy a couple of times. We were almost caught when the farmer came in before daylight. We'd just settled in." A board overhead creaked. Nicole? He stopped.

"How did you avoid being seen?" Albert leaned back as if in a swivel chair, his hands laced where an officer's belly would have been.

He made a face. "We hid in a manure pile."

Albert raised his chin in a pompous pout. "And weren't you sickened by this?"

"Nah. After flying over Der Faderland, it was a relief."

Bear chuckled, but it seemed strained. Albert rolled his hands in the air. "Let us return to the scenario. Now why were you not sickened by the smell?"

"Our stomachs were empty. It had probably been two days since we'd eaten. Later, we cleaned ourselves up as best we could in a creek then Sergeant Billington went back to the same barn and got milk that had been left out to cool. Took out a little from several cans so that it wouldn't be missed."

"And could you show us this farm? Having spent so much time there, you would surely recognize it." Albert's eyes pinched to tiny slits.

"I don't know. I don't think—"

"No!" Albert's slab of a hand collided with the table. "Better to let them suspect you than to know you are lying. You traveled at night. You hid by day. You were lost. You have no idea which direction that farm was, how far, or what it looked like in daylight."

"I understand." He looked at Bear, the pounding in his ears covering all else in the room. What if they were caught? Would he give his rescuers away? Would he, if they put him before a firing squad or wired him to a magneto, tell them even of Nicole? And Albert, or suffering Gaston, or Charles?

"Vos papiers, s'il vous plait." Albert's voice was monotone, preparing him for Plan B should the Nazis learn two airmen were in the area.

"Oui. Elle est ici— quelque part. Ah, ici." David took an imaginary travel permit from his pocket.

"Et votre identification?"

"Elle est ici." He pretended to rummage through his papers in Albert's hand. "Oui, celle ci."

Albert nodded, courteous. "Ah, pardonnez-moi. Vous pouvez passer."

"Merci." He reached for the nonexistent papers.

"No!" Albert's face paled. "This Bosch has detained you, harassed you. This could be— who knows?— perhaps the third time today. While you cannot openly defy him, you certainly are not cordial to him. Do not thank him. Say nothing."

"Oui, je comprend." He swallowed, wanted to tell Albert that he knew better, that his thoughts were with Nicole, that he needed desperately to tell her—

"Good. We have perhaps an hour." Albert rose, shuffled across the floor. "Sergeant Billington, where were you when your compatriot was in the trees after the crash?"

"Well, at first, looking for him. When I found him and cut him loose, I buried his chute and drug him up into the drainage ditch. There was Krauts—Germans all over the place. The dogs couldn't smell us in the stagnant water. Anyhow, the D-bars from our escape kits kept us alive for a coupla' days, but the lieutenant was awful thirsty. I crawled to a stream a few times, got him water in a can. He'd lost a lot of blood. Third or fourth day, after it got dark, I drug Lieutenant Dremmer up into the trees. Then I got to looking for something else to eat. I found a henhouse— couldn't have been too far from where we was. Couldn't hardly walk. They'd set out some milk to cool, so I got a little tin can full and a few eggs and brought them back for us. I mixed the eggs up with the milk and we drank it. The next night, I went back to where I'd buried our chutes and got our escape kits. My leg was hurtin' somethin' fierce. I needed the morphine."

"Who set your arm for you?" Albert barked, attempting to get Bear off track.

"Set it myself first thing. Grabbed ahold of a tree limb and pulled on it. Tied the splints on with my boot laces." Bear appeared unruffled.

"Good." Albert pulled another chair from beneath the table and sat. "Where I will take you tonight, five or six kilometers from here, there will be an open field and a small stream lined with plane trees. Beyond that lies a walled causeway, semi-circular, on the opposite end of the field. A pond lies between. The road atop the stone wall goes all the way through town. If something should happen to me, if we are in sight of it, go along the base of the wall until you find the edge of a handkerchief protruding from it. At that point, the stones will be loose. Take the handkerchief with you so the Bosch don't find it. Remove some of the smaller stones in the wall so you can see through. The ones above are mortared. Across the road is a building with the sign 'Vetements: Par Profession Parlent.' Beside the front door are stairs leading to the cellar. Your contact will be waiting for you there. But this is important— if you are seen or followed, do not under any circumstances lead the Bosch to that shop. Do you understand?"

David nodded, measured his voice. "Why you, Albert? Surely Charles or Gaston would be safer. They know the area—"

"Yes, and if either were caught, it would not only be his life, but the lives of everyone here, including Nicole's. It would be difficult to connect me with anyone. If the three of us should be caught before we separate, you know what to tell them."

David clenched his hands, answered first. "We met in an abandoned building two days ago. You said you had been hiding there for some time. Since you knew the countryside, we decided to try to escape together."

Albert nodded, braced the chair against the wall and stared into the paling light.

He held the tremble from his voice. "But if we tell them that—"

"It makes no difference. I would prefer they not deliberate before killing me." Albert's words were flat, betrayed nothing.

The half-light turned to blackness. He leaned against the wall, listened to the muttered prayers filling the room with fear. A world away, Jesse was likely whispering his certainty into the gray, too.

If he were to try, could he pray? He was hungry to, but it was as Albert had said. His anger wouldn't allow him to fall to his knees as he had knelt in the snow that night.

He sought for what it was he needed to say, looked into the emptiness of a dark corner, his head erect, not bowed, the cries of burning children filling him, the hot terror of a bullet ripping across his back, the anguish of his youth torn from him in less than a second. He lifted the image of a fortress wallowing like some great whale, the torment of those God's hidden hand had failed, wished for a voice to release the accusations. Instead, he uttered a petition against a more persistent dread. "Please, God, please don't let me fail them."

The door above the stairs creaked open. A thin band of light cut sharply in recurring right angles before Nicole's silhouette appeared. She descended the steps, the quick and easy grace now gone.

Every muscle ached from a sudden chill. It wasn't the specter of death that took his breath. Nicole was his fear as she stood in sharp relief, a bright certainty at the bottom of the stairs. A promise. She was beauty and peace and a future, and he loved her beyond words. Never had he had so much to lose.

She spoke with Albert first, kissed him, turned to Bear, offered a hug, whispered something and moved to him. Her eyes were warm, brimming with quiet certainty.

He reached into his pocket. "I... this is for you. It's nothing of what I wanted to say. It's so little, but it's all..." Words failed him. He handed Nicole a scrap of paper. "The labor of a sleepless night. A poem. Not much for all you mean to me."

She took his hand, led him away from the others. "I cannot keep this. But I shall commit it to my heart, carry it there always." Tears slipped down her cheeks. "There is something I must say to you. A confession."

He nodded, covered his ache, wanted to stay, take his chances with her.

"When you learned that you were unable to walk, that you would have to stay a while longer, I was overjoyed. I couldn't bear for you to leave. I still can't. I'm sorry. It's not that I wanted you not to walk. I wanted you to stay with me, to need me. I prayed for you to stay— I never meant..."

He rubbed his chest, felt the emptiness growing. "You got your wish. I need you, Nicole. Whatever your name is." He tried to laugh, failed.

"'My name is Nicole and will be even after this is over."

"I'll pray for that every day, every minute." He enfolded her in his arms, immersed himself in the gentle strength of her heart, memorized the hardened slope of her back, the narrowness of her waist, the sweetness of her hair and neck. He kissed her cheek, her neck, felt the warmth of her breasts as she pulled him close and whispered for no one but her. "Some things have to last forever. It would be unjust for them not to."

She moved away, looked into his eyes. "There is justice, David. We will be..." Tears came, stopped her voice, streamed down her cheeks. "I want you to know why I told you all I did. The whole reason. I needed for you to know me, who I really am. I wanted you to know everything, though I failed. We may not meet again in this life, but I pray God in his mercy will allow us to meet again in eternity, mon âme. We can have so much more there."

"I pray he will." He paused, waited for his breath. "Your last name. What should I look for? After this is over, I mean."

"I really shouldn't..."

"How about Dremmer? I won't forget that."

She wiped her cheeks. "Yes." A smile trembled on her lips. "I'll keep the name until you find me."

Bear rested his hand on his shoulder. "Time to saddle up, cowboy."

He pulled her close, felt a tremor in the tautness of her body. He kissed her cheek, allowed himself to linger at her lips, to know her goodness, taste the sweetness that couldn't be his. He released her, turned and forced himself into the darkness.

* * *

They climbed through the roof so that they wouldn't be seen leaving the house. The ladder wasn't a struggle. David's arms were easily strong enough to hoist him from one rung to the next, never losing sight of Albert. He was grateful for that, though he feared for Bear. So long as his

237

ankle was tightly wrapped, Bear's leg was considerably more useful than his, but his friend had only one arm to pull himself up with. He looked back.

Bear sucked hard from the blackness. "Go on. I'll keep up."

The air was pure and clean. They moved silently between the shadows and the moon. David swung his leg forward, hurried as best he could without the thrust of his right hip. His lungs burned, and he grew wet with sweat. They reached a wider road. Beyond it, he deciphered pale slopes, the shallows and hedges of farmland. Clouds moved quickly across the moon, the sky charged and boiling. Albert paused and they rested in the shadow of a wooden bridge, their labored breath the only sound.

Ancient timbers spread above their heads, massive, mortised and tenoned with absolute precision. It seemed laughable that men had spent so much care and labor on what could be destroyed with the slightest convulsion of a hand. He took in the cool, black air, stared at the ancient wood and stone and heard the rhythmed crack of boots against rock maybe a hundred yards up the road. German infantry. They marched, their heavy-heeled flamboyance like children hollering in the dark. He held his breath.

"Let's go!" Albert's words emerged on frozen breath when the heel clacks dulled. They slipped along a shallow, slithered on elbows and knees when the shadows failed them. They reached a grove of plane trees. A pond nestled on the far side, small and smooth as glass. David stared through leafy branches at the reflection, the thin luminescent ribbon of the stone-walled roadway on the opposite side.

A wavering drone, mechanical and threatening, grew in the distance. It sounded like farm tractors, only louder, more metallic. Tracks. Without a word they dropped to their bellies in the cool grass at the perimeter of trees, lay hidden from the road by swollen tree roots. David scanned the gray edge of night along the wall, shivered.

"Big boys." His whisper carried the chill. "Up there." He pointed to the skyline above the wall where a massive black projection edged across the gray.

"What is it?" Albert asked.

Bear looked at him. "Eighty-eights."

"What?" Albert seemed stunned. Likely nothing in his plans allowed for this.

"Bell ringers. Flak guns." Panic pushed the words from David's gut. "They must have the whole damned Kraut artillery up there."

"Perhaps you frightened them with your— what did you call them?— your deep penetrations." Sweat shone on Albert's face.

"We did more than scare them. They're moving coastal emplacements, getting ready for something big."

He looked at Bear. "They taking them deep or moving them up the coast? Headed back to Germany, you think? Wish we could let them know across the Channel." He couldn't keep down the hope that surfaced like thistles in maize. He feared trusting it, but it lingered. If there were an invasion, if Germany fell, he would see her again. Soon.

"What do we do now?" He stared at Albert's face shimmering in the half-light. "Should we go back?"

"No. It would be dangerous for the others. There is an alternate plan. Just over there is a well." Albert pointed to a stone and mortar sphere maybe a quarter-mile up the hill from where they lay. The wall he'd told them about looked to be another hundred yards beyond that.

Albert nodded toward the structure. "It is quite wide at the top. Five, perhaps six meters down is a ledge where the well narrows. Stay there until I come for you. If I cannot come back, follow the same plan tomorrow night. Your contact will supply you with information."

He nodded. One by one, his fears materialized in the murky gray. Being separated from Albert and Bear shown among the brightest.

"I will stay here until you are out of sight. Lock the crank and let yourself down the rope." Albert's words were short, carried on a shallow breath.

David hesitated. "I don't know what to say, how to thank you."

"All is well. Now go."

"Shalom, Albert."

"Next year in Jerusalem, my young friend."

The words hung in the air, the end of something. The hill was interminable with nothing but grass to hide them between the line of trees and the well. Bear reached it first, leaned back against the rocks on the side away from the road. He slithered in behind, twisted, felt dust sticking to the sweat on his face, running down his neck in streams. He stood without catching his breath, looped a section of the rope over the handle of the crank, then tied it to the base.

He turned to Bear. "All right. Loop this under your arms, and I'll let you down."

Bear shook his head. "You first."

"No. I've got two good arms. I can do this."

Bear looped the rope around his back, held to both ends with his good hand. David braced against the stone and watched his friend roll over the edge. There was a jolt, but he held tight, yielded the rope slowly, hand over hand, Bear disappearing into the abyss. The hemp jerked and slackened. His friend was free.

The road above was empty, the artillery quiet. Crouched behind the stone structure, he heard a distant drumming of boots against stone, secured the crank and clung to the wooden frame. He pulled the rope close, ready to drop into the well. A loud crack carried on the empty air like gunfire, a branch breaking somewhere in the trees. He turned to see German troops, shadows in the lighter gray, rushing toward the water.

Albert rose, peeled his shirt, his white undershirt glaring in the moonlight, his arms spread wide, the white flesh glowing soft and still, his head back. Senseless, insane, a perfect target.

Two guns blasted, the yellow muzzle flashes burning into the dark like fireflies. Albert was pinned for a moment against the gray, the muted flesh a twisting crucifix. David dropped below the ledge and shimmied down the rope.

"They shot Albert, Bear! He stepped on a branch— just stood up, took his shirt off and spread his arms. They couldn't miss. My God, they just shot him! He's bleeding out pale as linen on that hill."

"Probably drew their fire on purpose so they wouldn't see us. Don't make it for nothing, Dremmer. Pipe down so nobody hears you."

"Why Albert, Bear?" His whisper was coarse with pain, muted in their stone grave.

"There's two of us and one of him. That's likely how he looked at it. It was his choice." Bear's voice was husky, breaking, carrying more than his words. "We've got to go on, Dremmer, put it out of our heads. I hate it,

240

too, but what can we do?"

He let his head fall back against the cool, damp stone. "Wait in this hole for another Nazi bullet, I guess."

The artillery started again, shook the earth, continued until the dark yielded to gray, then pink, and finally to white above them. The ledge was little more than a foot wide, and he ached from immobility.

"Bear, the artillery's stopped."

"Yeah. Probably camouflage it during the day. Be moving again to-night most likely."

"Somewhere, maybe, but not here. The Big Boys are past us. The last half hour was just Deuce and a Halfs and a few staff cars. Listen, we'll need rest before night." David lifted his leg, touched Bear's knee with his foot. "If you want to lie down, I'll keep my legs on the ledge in front of you, keep you from falling."

Bear's flight suit rustled against the stones. David took his boots off, placed them on the ledge beside him, pressed his feet against Bear's arm draped protectively across his chest. Within minutes, he heard the ca-denced breath of sleep and tried to hold his mind from Albert pinned against the night by rifle fire. He thought of Nicole, her absence haunting and raw, quickly conjured Dancer, the peace of the hills, the horse steam-ing his impatience into the morning cool, pictured him tearing at the earth in the long working pen. Or, if Jesse had him on pasture, he might be standing at the outcrop of rocks, proud and sure.

It didn't work. Nicole's face re-emerged, the image of her kneeling in the wine cellar praying for them, Charles and Gaston marking the passage from black to gray with broken cigarette butts, Albert's funeral pyre rising within the boundaries of a coffee ring.

A sound, frightening and familiar, the cadenced crack of rocks beneath shoes. The rhythm was indefinite, grew closer until a shadow swelled within the brilliant sphere above them. He shook Bear with his foot, leaned as close as he could, heard the dry rubbing of the crank and saw the bucket grow large. "Someone above!"

He jerked his left leg back, extended his body from the ledge, his right leg straining to hold his weight. The bucket passed without touching him.

He hung precariously, his trembling right leg suspending him against the palms of his hands.

Finally, the bucket splashed into the water below. The rope hung loose, inches from his face. Two women speaking Flemish, talking about the Bosch, most likely. He shook violently with a cold ache, his leg threatening to let go.

*His leg.* He was holding himself with his right leg. The muscles quivered, threatened collapse, but held.

"Bear!" His whisper was sharp against the stone. "Push me back!"

An invisible might moved him against the rock ledge. The crank began its rub. The bucket bounced, splashed against the cool rock wall.

His leg had held. He was young again. He would run. The bucket tugged against his left heel extended into the abyss, tipped, splashed, and swung away. The women chattered, laughed, filled their buckets and crunched across the gravel, their voices fading into light. The morning grew silent.

"Bear." The word echoed within the sepulcher. "My leg held me up."

"That's swell, Dremmer. Sounds like our prayers got answered."

He wondered in silence, struggled to believe that it might be true.

The sun climbed higher, the light reaching deeper into the well until it caught the edge of Bear's sleeve, his cheek, the tip of his nose. David looked into the pale luminescence of the eyes that seemed to never blink. Some great light reflected from them. For a moment, he wasn't sure if he were looking into his friend's face or a projection of something else, someone maybe. What was behind Bear's peace? It seemed impossible that he could be held so certain by smoke and myth. He whispered into the silence, his words weak and full of doubt.

"Bear, I'm gonna walk. I'm gonna run. What do you think of that?"

"I think you oughta be grateful."

"You telling me this was a miracle?" It was a ruse, his denial, a shield against the deceit and disappointment that might be hidden within his growing hope.

"Are you telling me it wasn't?" Bear's voice, steady and sure.

"Can't be, Bear. Albert died out there. He deserved to have his prayers answered, not me."

"This ain't about deserving. And what makes you think his prayers weren't answered? He's likely with his family, now. Ain't that what he wanted?" Bear's words were quiet, filled with peace.

The weight of the dark hours compressed within their exchange, a gentle need wormed its way into his heart. To whom could he say, 'Thank you"? For Albert's sacrifice. For Nicole's love. For Bear. His leg, his youth. He'd heard men cry out to God over the interphone, had seen them bow their heads after briefings, had cried out himself in sudden panic. That was understandable. But to be given a gift and to have no one to thank? He bent his head in the darkness, closed his eyes and searched for a starting place. Tears washed down his dirt-streaked face. Tears for Albert— his pain, his sacrifice mixed within the brine of an all-sufficient surrender, an ocean of guilt, and loss. And joy.

An aging cottonwood stirred within a holy breath, voices lifting praises beneath it. Words long confined rose through rusty restraints within his breast. In the beginning was the Word and the Word was with God and the Word was God. And the Word came not to condemn those floundering in darkness and failure, but to rupture night itself, to remove the impenetrable barrier that kept him from unity with Holiness and Light. The Word who had created all things, who had been made flesh to dwell among those inhabiting their own ruin and stench, had invaded the darkness of his failure, was offering him consolation and peace, was tendering communion.

The certainty resounded, and the words returned. Light shone in the darkness of a bright sky, the true Light which came into the world, and him not comprehending but surrendering. A surety welled as nothing he had imagined. He was known, fully known and loved. He could have been no safer in a concrete bunker a world away from the war than he was in that well, Nazi troops all around. He was safe not because there was no danger but because nothing he could endure was of consequence in light of the Presence that surrounded him, knew him, loved him.

He remembered the dove, the day it appeared, lived it as though it were the first time. He'd seen nothing of what it had been sent to reveal. Yes, he was riddled with the blackness of a world gone mad. It was within him, but it had been hopeless only because he'd embraced the dark, held it up for light, refused to be forgiven. He closed his eyes, chose, in that holy hush of anthems growing in his breast, to know the Love being offered, to eschew all things he'd taken for light, to prize nothing more than the Word that had relentlessly pursued and held him. A fullness burst, flowed from deep within, and he joined a cloud of witnesses, whispered *Praise Jesus* into the forming darkness of day and let his heart join theirs.

His head fell back against the stone. He wanted nothing to break the sanctity of the moment, but he couldn't hold what had happened.

"Bear." The whisper seemed a violation.

"What's happening with you over there? You praising Jesus?"

"I prayed, Bear. I…" Tears stopped his revelation.

Bear's hand, warm and solid, molded around his shoulder. A melody softer than morning grew within the narrow tomb. Then words, scarcely audible. "Oh what a foretaste of glory divine! Heir of salvation, purchase of God, born of his Spirit, washed in his blood."

\* \* \*

The sun moved up the shaft, reached high up on the stone and wood. In late afternoon, a man came alone, filled his buckets, grunted, left without a word, his heavy-heeled gracelessness worsened by his load. David listened, ached from immobility, shaken but at peace.

"When it's good and dark, we'll go."

He started at Bear's words, had grown content in the stillness. Didn't answer.

"No use waiting for the Krauts to start another parade." Bear began tying his boots.

He stirred, heard the faintest crack of rock beneath a shoe. Someone small and alone. He looked up. Had they heard? The bucket began its descent, the crank pitting wood to wood. Light had grown more steady, the dying of the day reaching the darkness of their grave.

The pail reached water, began its ascent. Bear stirred, his hand slow and indistinct, pulling his leg onto the ledge. The rope caught his arm, rigid between the rough splints. The bucket tipped, splashed, swung in the dense air.

A shadow dimmed the light above. David hugged the wall, looked up. A young girl stared down, her face almost hidden, their eyes meeting. She emitted a raspy catch of fear, jerked out of sight, pulled the bucket splashing water over him. She ran, scattering gravel as she went.

He looked at Bear. "She left the bucket on top. We've got no way out."

"Be somebody come along."

The dread lay dormant in the gray. He pressed his hands against the stone to stop them from shaking. It wasn't right that they should be captured now, not with all that had happened, with such a price paid for their escape and such a sureness found. There'd be no justice in that. He'd been frightened all his life, had spent his youth in an awful dread of some new catastrophe. He leaned back, considered what had happened in their grave, decided no injustice could stand in light of it. Not even Albert's. "Then we wait."

Bear sucked deep. "For something besides a Nazi bullet, I hope."

Light slid off the stones at the top of the shaft. The sky turned cerulean, then pink, then red. Had it been a dream? No. He was more awake than he'd ever been. Just as surely as his leg had held, he had known the Presence.

The circle above turned an insipid gray. What did it mean to have his leg back only to be stuck in a well with no way out? It wouldn't end like this. Couldn't. He wasn't alone. He knew that, though it was certain they couldn't spend another day without food or rest.

A faint sound rose, the crisp cadence of rocks yielding to shoes. Light, timid. Probably a woman. A shadow dimmed the red sky above.

"David? Are you there?"

His throat contracted on the words. "Nicole? My God, what are you doing here? Someone will see you! Get out of here. Please!"

"Nazis are nightcrawlers. They are still below ground." Her voice wavered. "I had to know that you were safe."

"We are, but Albert... he's gone. I'm so sorry!"

"We heard this morning. No one knows who he is." She stifled a sob. "Who he was. Well, there is someone, but there's nothing to be done about him now." She was silent for long seconds before she spoke again, the words choked and full. "You must leave here tonight. The same plans as before. I'm letting the rope down to you. Margaux was frightened. She is one of us, but so young, you see. She didn't know what to do when she saw you. She told us she left the bucket on top."

"Nicole, you've got to be careful. Get as far away from here as you can." The lowering bucket blocked her face for a moment.

"I will. I had to be sure." There was a crack in her voice.

The bucket passed him. He could see the light reflecting in her eyes. Those eyes…

"God bless you both." She turned, her hair lifting in the crimson flow of twilight.

He had to tell her, couldn't wait out the war without her knowing. "Wait. Nicole, something happened to me."

"What?"

He wished he could see her face, touch her. "I'm different now. I *know*."

She laughed, delighted. "Oh, David, I didn't doubt, mon âme. I'm so happy."

"Je t'aime, mon âme. Please be safe. Now go, and take my heart with you."

They waited for the red to turn to black and for Nicole to be home before they emerged into the night. Bear nudged him. "You first. You'll have to pull me up with the crank. I'll never climb the rope."

David uncoiled, pulled his boots on, tied the laces off short. He found the rope and pulled, testing his arms, grabbed tightly and swung into the center of the void. In the moment before the rope caught, he gave himself to something he couldn't control or understand.

He moved deftly, straining, throwing off in a sudden frenzy the ache of the long hours, grabbed handfuls of light. When he reached the top, he tried to pull himself up slowly, peer over the stone edge across the field and up the wall, but the wall was damp, and his hands threatened to give way. He moved blind and quick, threw his right leg over the ledge and with it carried his whole body in one swift motion against the loose gravel. He lay still for seconds before opening his eyes, lifted his face from the loose rocks, scanned the skyline for guards or guns. He saw nothing, rose to his knees and looked toward the pond, and, above it, the other half of the stone wall. Albert's sacrifice had been the last thing he'd seen outside.

The air was warm and still, the sky clear, cleaner than he remembered. But he felt a distance, too. He was a stranger, no longer a part of it. The world was all around him, more real somehow. Life was more precious, but he'd never been less held by it.

He stood uncertain, his legs shaking and taut, took a step, his first. Not perfect, but he walked. He gave a quick jerk on the rope to signal Bear, wouldn't use the crank. The dry rasp of the wooden axle would carry on the night like tracer rounds. The rope grew heavy, then released. David slid his knees beneath him, braced against the rock tower. A sudden jerk pulled him toward the well, but he was strong, young again, and he held fast.

# Chapter XXI

David watched the bloodied flow stem across the sky. Branches yielded their crepuscular brilliance to the unformed darkness. The only sound was his steadied breath and Bear's beside him as they lay in the contorted shadow of the tomb that had held them.

He caught his friend's eye and nodded toward the deeper darkness of the wall. Bear crawled to the edge of the shadow, rose and hobbled across the clearing, eased low against the causeway. David scanned the breadth of the wall, couldn't discern man from rock and looked to the road above. Nothing moved. He sprang to his feet. His leg was weak, but in seconds he was at Bear's side.

Bear leaned close, placed his arms around him and squeezed. "I'm proud for what happened in there."

"So am I, Bear." His eyes were wide, seeing the world for the first time. "When we were training, flying over Michigan, the cold— you remember?"

"Yeah, I remember."

"Well, I kept having this thought looking down. It was like all the ice and snow was a picture of who I was. I couldn't get away from it. I just knew that if there were nothing more than this life, then that should have been enough for me. If nothing was all I was born to, it was all I should need or hope for. So why was I hungry for something more?"

"And now?"

"Now I know why. My need was like a homing instinct. Something inside me couldn't rest."

"Until you let him find you." Bear spoke with quiet confidence.

"Something like that, yeah. I guess I stopped resisting."

He felt Bear's heavy paw grip his arm. Tears filled his eyes again, and he wanted to tell his friend about the dove held against the sky and the chorus of worshipers behind the white-chipped doors breathing *Praise Jesus* into a cottonwood breeze, but he couldn't. He took a deep breath and released it before he tried to speak again.

"Any sign of the handkerchief?" He strained to keep his voice flat.

"Haven't spotted it. Could you see me against the wall?"

"Just a shadow."

Bear pointed west, his arm a darkness within a lesser shade. "We'll move that way, keep low. If we don't find it, we can turn back." He stopped. "That okay with you, Lieutenant?"

David chuckled. "It was my idea, wasn't it, Sergeant?"

Bear snorted. "Figured those bars would start working on you sooner or later."

The road above curved in a wide, level arc for over half a mile, the wall glowing beneath the paling moon, undulating at the bottom so that it was of varying heights. Bear moved out, scuttled along the base.

David stepped behind him, leaned close, pointed above. About eight feet from the base, a small, white corner of a handkerchief, less than two inches long, protruded from between the rocks. "I can't reach it. Climb on my shoulders."

He leaned against the wall, his leg trembling while Bear climbed his back and shoulders, pulled stones from the wall and looked through the hole, then passed the handkerchief down.

"Just buildings. Don't see nothing else."

He stuffed the handkerchief into the top left pocket of his flight suit and heaved as Bear pulled himself over the wall. His friend squatted, turned, offered his good arm. He grabbed hold and shot up to the roadway. The two crouched, scanned the buildings across the road, narrow slabs of blue stone stacked upright side by side. Guild houses. He pointed to a narrow entrance on the opposite side, a stairway leading down, but couldn't read the sign. "Let's try that one."

He sprinted across the road, reached the stone stairs, stepped down, crouched and turned to wait as Bear hobbled in beside him. They knelt facing the road.

"See anything?"

"No, but—"

"Halt! Remain as you are!" The heavily accented growl rose from behind them.

He jerked about. A rifle barrel collided with his cheek, and his teeth were instantly ablaze, his eyes filling with tears.

"Move off of stairs, put hands to your heads and lie flat!"

He looked at Bear, rose and stepped onto the roadway. His legs were kicked from beneath him, and he lay trembling in the pale light of the street, bricks pressed against his throbbing cheek. Troops filed out of the cellar behind and from stairways up and down the street.

"Overrr!" David turned as Bear flopped awkwardly protecting his ankle and arm, staring at his captors. A Wehrmacht feldwebel, years past his rank, growled something to a boy in uniform. A rifle muzzle pressed against his head.

"Luft gangsters!" The old sergeant spat the words. David stared into the well-fleshed face, saw the German smile before lifting his boot and dropping it heavily into his crotch. He doubled over, turned on his side, his stomach heaving against the emptiness.

"You shall answer questions for us, and perhaps you shall live."

His fear was covered with pain and nausea. Flotsam from training films surfaced. The Germans had thousands of bits of information. Even the most insignificant could be a link that completed a chain.

He opened his eyes to see the sergeant standing above Bear. An instant prayer formed in his throat. "Oh, God, not—"

The feldwebel's boot slammed into the wrapped ankle, and Bear emitted a groan into the dark.

"God help us!"

The old sergeant turned. "Do you think God can help you now, young criminal?" The portly German put his hands together, whispered in a mock prayer. "You are *mine* now. You should pray to *me*." The feldwebel shouted at the young gefreiter who moved behind him and began yanking at David's flight suit, trying to lift him.

"Okay." He pulled his legs beneath him and rose on shaky legs.

"Silence!" Saliva exploded at the old sergeant's command. Another boy soldier pulled Bear to his feet. "You vill tell me who you vas to meet at handkerchief." He pulled his Walther from his holster, jabbed it against his forehead, turned to Bear. "You vill tell me *now*."

Bear's blanched visage glistened, his mouth open, drawing air in a silent plea. "We was— "

"No, Bear!"

The sergeant bared his teeth, spun on him in threat.

"Don't tell the bastard anything!" The gun jammed against his head. Ghostly lightning blazed behind his eyes. Beyond the black barrel of the Walther, a stout finger quivered against the trigger. He looked into the gelid eyes, and the finger spasmed in a moment of awful certainty before the firing pin clicked.

He felt the hot release of urine against his legs and slumped, his heart pounding in his ears then turned to see Bear's blanched face writhing in a silent scream.

"Bear, it's okay." The words were breath. He strained to give them voice. "Wasn't your fault."

The feldwebel edged closer. "You are ready to die, young criminal? Then why do you piss yourself?" He slid the magazine into his pistol and turned to the boys gathered around him, snarled something in German. They laughed.

Across the wide arc of roadway, an engine screamed, lights glowing through slitted covers, no stronger than a candle as they rounded the curve. The feldwebel barked orders, and the gefreiter holding the gun to his head motioned for him to stand. He rolled over on his hands and knees, worked to steady his breath. The staff car skidded to a halt a few feet away. A young officer, dark hair, light blue Luftwaffe uniform, stepped from the back seat. There were heel clicks, a perfunctory "Heil Hitler!"

"Just as I told you, Herr Leutnant." The old feldwebel began before the young officer had completed his salute.

"Yes, Mesche. I am aware of your brilliance. You knew the handkerchief—"

"Herr Leutnant, I have not yet completed my interrogation of the prisoners. Please do not discuss—"

"Nor will you!" The officer switched to German, pointed at him weaving as he stared at them, then to Bear's extended leg and began to question the boy holding the gun. The gefreiter's eyes went first to the feldwebel, then to the leutnant. The young officer demanded something, and the boy began to stutter. The leutnant raised his chin, issued an order, and the old sergeant began a whining protest.

The leutnant lowered his head, stared. "Nein!"

Two boys rushed to lift Bear, two more to help him to the command car. The leutnant seated him to his left and Bear to his right, an obvious lapse in protocol. Something even an American would notice. The car started, and he steadied himself as they sped away.

*The handkerchief.* He edged his right fist, loosely bunched, toward his left pocket.

"Keep your hands where I can see them, Lieutenant. I will not hesitate to shoot you." The leutnant didn't turn his head, spoke in cool tones.

"Not allowed to smoke?" David strained to sound as unperturbed as the German. A quiver betrayed him.

"Have one of mine." The leutnant extended a pack of Turkish cigarettes.

He took one, held it inexpertly in his lips as the officer lit it. The first drag elicited a cough, and the leutnant laughed.

"Stronger than I'm used to." He worked to redirect the conversation. "Your English is perfect. Where'd you learn it?"

"My English is American. I spent my summers in New York City as a boy." The leutnant paused. "I didn't like it. So, how did you men find flying?"

It sounded like a trap. "Always preferred cruise ships, myself."

The leutnant snorted. "This seems a strange time to be on holiday."

He stirred, a bit lightheaded from the cigarette. "Huns don't take fall holidays?"

"Taking a fall holiday, are we? Inside the German Reich, a country at war with your own? I believe that makes you spies. You will be shot if you choose that story."

"I didn't say we were on holiday." He looked straight ahead.

Bear looked at the German, his face pellucid in the dim light. "Shame you left New York. You'd a fit right in."

"You'll find your derision unappreciated in the Reich, Sergeant."

David snorted. "I thought we were in Belgium." He had almost died, was scared enough to piss himself. Still, he'd been willing to go through with it. Somehow that made him powerful.

"As you know, Lieutenant, this is now part of the German Reich."

He shrugged. "Seems like these boundaries change every day. This time next year, it'll likely be central Russia."

A gloved hand rammed against his throat. "Listen, my smart, young spy. You shall die while trying to escape if you don't watch your mouth."

He caught his breath. "The name's Dremmer, David. Second Lieutenant. Serial number 0 636 215."

"I trust you shall tell me much more than that." There was something more than threat in the leutnant's voice. It sounded like sympathy.

* * *

Nicole ran her hand across the rough tarp folded and stacked on the shelf. A wine rack rested where David's head had been. Nothing suggested his having been there but the empty place in her heart. What was it about him? His eyes, his smile, deferential and, she had to admit, adoring. Such a contradiction. So full of heart. And anger. She turned her eyes toward heaven, not imploring this time but reminding, silently keeping him before a God who loved him more than she. It was her place of solace, and she remained there as a child at her mother's breast, no longer in need but restful.

The pressure grew within her breast, and she wrapped her arms around her shoulders. Yesterday, when the neighbor told her that a man had been shot during the night, something in her died. She'd thought it was David. Then the woman said it was a Jew. Not a local, just an escaping Jew that had not made it to the Channel. No one knew where he'd come from— Holland, Poland, perhaps even Germany. In any case, he'd not made it. She'd tried to talk normally, to breathe, to believe it wasn't Gerhardt, but she'd known.

Tears pooled. Somehow she had smiled, walked away and cried until there were no more tears, until her fears for David and Bear overcame her grief. Until she was moved to act— at any cost. And, of course, David had confirmed that it was Gerhardt. Now she was drained by the certainty of it.

Perhaps he was reunited with his family.

She unfolded the paper David had given her— should have destroyed it yesterday. It was a dangerous thing keeping it, but she couldn't let it go. Not yet. She opened it again, ran her fingers across the page, felt the slight impression of the pencil, read it though she knew the words, their flow and cadence, even the lilt of his voice as he would have recited it.

*Day of the Dove.* The poem was filled with wisdom, a prescience more beautiful and bright than any she'd imagined he had seen, though he knew now. Somehow she knew his heart had opened— had never doubted it would. The words flowed full of light and promise as if he wrote of more than he had yet comprehended, as if he had caught sight of something far beyond grasping and held it out to her, his one moment of truth and beauty, his glimpse of the eternal held within sweaty hands, within a child's heart to be shared with no one else. She pressed the words to her breast and swayed in the fading light.

His mistrust had hurt, though she had sensed it growing. The agreement between her and Albert— Gerhardt. A smile trembled, died. She had so quickly grown accustomed to the new name. What had they expected? Her ruse was absurd. She'd known David's heart, knew he would do whatever she asked. There had been no need to inveigle him. Of course he would think he was being used. What else could he think? In truth, she'd wanted him to know everything about her. Gerhardt only went along because of his affection for her, she supposed.

She drew the paper across her face, caressed her cheek. She'd risked her life going to the well to be sure he hadn't died or been taken prisoner. But it was worth it. Now David knew she loved him as she had wanted him to know every hope, every dream, every mistake, though she'd come short of revealing all of those. She hadn't told him of falling in love with Gerhardt— Professor Stein. Or of Heinrich's obsession with her.

The university was such a sheltered place. Dear Gerhardt had been unaware of her ardor. Until they used it to destroy him. But Heinrich knew— Herr Schneider in his blue uniform and bluer eyes knew every time a man looked at her, every man whose gaze she'd met.

But what had possessed him to do what he did? To go so far? Leaving the university, taking her best friend with him. It was such a strange retaliation. And dear, sweet Élodie, in love with him from her first days at university. The blue-eyed monster, she'd called him. Everyone knew. But being her friend sealed Élodie's fate. As if her not loving him was something that demanded a price be paid. But why Élodie? And now he had Gerhardt's blood on his hands, a man who loved him like a son.

She shivered, pulled her arms about her. She would have spurned the blue-eyed Herr Schneider even if she hadn't felt the way she did about Professor Stein. She breathed deep the languid air. So many mistakes. And such consequences. Perhaps Heinrich had grown to love Élodie, wasn't mistreating her. One could only hope.

* * *

David had no idea what might be important, took in everything he could. The office was near the center of a long hall, an outer office between it and the hallway. The building appeared to have been a warehouse with offices above the first floor, a desolate place, absent of pictures or credentials to break the gray. Two potted plants squatted in the corner behind the door, obtrusive in the sparseness of the windowless room. Potted plants in a room with no windows. He grunted. Must have been moved in and out on a regular basis. A large wooden desk sat in the center of the room with two chairs, the first covered in burlap. The leutnant's clerk had insisted on it before letting him sit in it with his wet flight suit. The second, a leather swivel chair behind the leutnant's desk, was empty.

It would have been comforting having the desk between them, something to mitigate the leutnant's stare, but the German stood immediately to his right, chin resting in his hand as though observing a specimen under a microscope.

The leutnant began pacing again. David breathed, surveyed his captor— commandingly tall and handsome, athletic. A soccer player, maybe, his dark hair unmilitarily long. A point of pride, most likely. His appearance took effort. Blue eyes, high cheek bones, a strong Aryan jaw, the man had probably played hero in the fantasies of more than a few fräuleins.

He swallowed, stared up at the leutnant who had stopped pacing to tower above him again. He slipped his hands beneath him, dried them on the burlap, and reflected on his experience in the well. He knew Truth, knew it to be personal and real. The most profound power a man could hold. He straightened in his chair.

"Lieutenant, I think it only fair to warn you that other members of your crew were captured. They told us a great deal about your mission." The leutnant began as if he were his last friend on earth, faced him, removed his glove and extended his hand. "Forgive me. I should have introduced myself earlier. I'm Leutnant Schneider."

*Schneider.* The one Nicole called by his first name. What was it? He extended his hand. "No apology necessary, Lieutenant. I considered your hand on my throat ample introduction."

Schneider ignored the sarcasm. "It's leutnant, Lieutenant. I will, of course, weigh what you tell me against what your fellow crew members have said. If all your information is correct, I will notify the Red Cross, you will not be charged as a spy, and they will notify your family that you are alive. You will receive humane treatment as a prisoner of war as well as Red Cross parcels when they are made available."

"How very kind of you."

Schneider's lips tightened. "We are not an uncivilized people, Lieutenant."

He held his tongue, looked at the German, saw something. The leutnant doubted the righteousness of his cause. The thought sprang from nowhere, free of uncertainty.

Schneider's face grew hard at his silence. "If you refuse to cooperate, however, I will have to ask you to remove your clothes. Which will it be, Lieutenant?"

His heart pounded. He couldn't betray the others. Somehow, some way, he had to keep them from finding the handkerchief. He rose, returned the leutnant's smirk. Humiliation wasn't lethal.

"So be it, Lieutenant. You may remain in your shorts. Everything else you will hang on the chair."

He stood, thought with each motion, prayed for an opportunity to avert the dreaded discovery.

"Herr Leutnant." The young clerk appeared at the door, anxious , distracted for a moment by his undressing. Something about the clerk didn't fit. His demeanor, his uniform, some strange combination of quirks. The little man jabbered, his stare wandering toward him as he draped his flight suit over the back of the chair. He took it in, turned away as Schneider's eyes narrowed with irritation. The leutnant moved back to his desk, took a deep breath, slipped his fingers around the phone, and hesitated before lifting it from the cradle.

"Jawohl." His tone was military, terse. "Heil Hitler." Schneider flushed. "Ja, ja, Ich verstehe das aber es ist meine Untersuchung!" His face turned a deeper red. "Jawohl!" The phone slammed down. The leutnant stepped toward the door, pushed the clerk ahead of him into the outer office and spoke over his shoulder. "I shall return in a few minutes, Lieutenant. Carry on." The door slammed shut behind them.

David shoved his hand into the top left pocket of his flight suit, squeezed the handkerchief into a tight ball, returned the suit to the chair. He glanced around the room, scrambled to the corner and spread the handkerchief around the base of the larger potted plant. He dug to one side of the roots, scraped a hole large enough to cover the handkerchief and leave a few inches of fill. Voices penetrated the door to the outer office. He folded the handkerchief around the detritus collected at the base of the pot, stuffed it in the hole, covered it, then hurried back to the chair and wiped his hands on his sock. The door swung open.

Schneider entered followed by a young, blond leutnant, Wehrmacht, and an aide. Schneider pointed to the pile of clothes, rattled something brusque in German. The Wehrmacht leutnant and gefreiter began rifling through the escape kit. Schneider watched, his lips curving upward in a perfect pose.

"I see you have a package of Chesterfields, Lieutenant."

His gut tightened. "Sure I do."

"Where is your lighter?"

He shrugged, fought to control his breath. "I used matches."

Schneider's hands bounced fingertip to fingertip. "But your cigarettes are unopened. They were still in your escape kit." The leutnant smiled. "Interesting. You had a fresh packet of cigarettes in your escape kit and didn't bother to retrieve it."

"Ran out of matches."

"And yet you were attempting to recover them from your pocket on the way here, putting yourself at some peril."

257

"I guess that's why they call it a bad habit, Herr Leutnant." He forced down the bile in his throat.

Schneider pulled his hands behind him, muttered something to the blond leutnant who immediately fingered through the empty left pocket of his drying flight suit.

The leutnant turned back to Schneider, shook his head. "Nein."

Schneider stared darkly. "Lieutenant Dremmer, while my assistants continue their work, please tell me what you did on your crew."

The Wehrmacht leutnant glowered at Schneider's back. So Blondie spoke English. Could be that Herr Blue Eyes was under scrutiny himself. It would add up. The phone call had put the leutnant on edge. Now Blondie shows up. The Wehrmacht just might be demanding to be a part of the investigation— or a share in his carcass. David pivoted, glanced at Blondie.

"When were you..." Schneider stopped. "What in the name of God happened to you?"

He turned back, smiled. "The scratch on my back, you mean? One of your Luftwaffe boys decided to strafe me in parachute. Rather indelicate behavior for such civilized people, don't you think?"

Schneider straightened. "How did you survive? You must have needed attention."

"My buddy, Sergeant Billington, took care of me."

"And you received no outside help?"

He snorted. "Not a very friendly place to be shot down, Herr Leutnant."

"Come now, Lieutenant. You survived— how long— over six weeks without help? Just the two of you?"

His mouth went dry. The Kraut even knew when they were shot down. He said nothing, refused to acknowledge the date.

Schneider took it up again. "This survival all alone, this was after your cruise, am I to suppose?"

He nodded. "All alone. Just the two of us."

"What did you eat?"

He wanted to tell Herr Leutnant the story they'd prepared, get on with it, but held back. If he offered it too quickly, the German would know it was prepared. "Name's Dremmer, David. Second Lieutenant. Serial number 0 636 215."

"We were having such a lovely conversation, Lieutenant. What on earth frightened you?"

He stared into the pale blue of Schneider's eyes, swore to himself the Kraut would have to work for everything he got. Even the lies.

Schneider broke the stare, asked Blondie something in German. The Wehrmacht leutnant rummaged through the escape kit and shrugged.

"You have no D-bars in your kit. What else did you eat?"

He remained mute.

"It's quite unfortunate that your navigator didn't survive his initial interview. Some interrogations can be quite grueling. Now, what bomb group were you with?"

His fingernails cut into his palms, the blood surging through his temples. "How do you know who our navigator was?"

"Navigators wear wings, do they not? His name was Japanese. Ito was it?"

His blood turned cold, and his legs went weak.

"I see I was right. What did you think of our buzz bombs in England? Were they sufficiently devastating to impress you?"

*Nazi bastard!* "I don't remember any buzz bombs. Unless... Were they the things that kept exploding in the air?"

"So you were stationed in England. Where exactly?"

"Of course I was, as was every other airman you've likely harassed."

"What were the names of your crew members?"

"Leutnant Schneider, you're a soldier, same as me. If you were in my position, would you betray your friends, your country?" He fought to keep his mind from Ito.

"I think, Lieutenant, that it is time for you to consider yourself. Do you want to live?"

"Probably as much as this guy you murdered. Tito was it?"

Schneider's face flushed. "I murdered no one. That was... a Wehrmacht investigation. A very unnecessary loss."

The frail officer stared hard in Schneider's direction. The feud appeared to run deep. Something about Blondie invited contempt. Slight of build, almost effeminate, his hands were sinuous and knotted. Strong enough to strangle the life from anything that failed to resist him. The Wehrmacht leutnant's chin was weak, his blue eyes diluted, near gray. Still, within the spheres was a dark malice, something unrestrained. He held back a shiver. The tension between the leutnants was palpable. A weakness, maybe an exploitable one. Iffy, but it was all he had.

Schneider leaned back in his chair, seemed to relax. "Lieutenant, it is to your advantage to be identified as American military. In order to do that, we will need to know your bomb group and squadron. Otherwise, we will be forced to assume you are a spy and have you shot."

"Hmm. You know my fellow crew members, but you don't know if I'm American military? Doesn't speak well for Aryan logic, does it?" Was the power he felt from having faced death, or was it something else? He caught a quick flash from the corner of his eye. His jaw cracked, and he was hurled to the floor. Blondie moved over him in a blur ready to strike again, a leather-covered rod in his hand.

"So you speak English." He spat the words wrapped within a short breath speckled with blood. "You here checking up on Herr Schneider?"

Schneider covered his smile, looked at Blondie. "Perhaps it would be best if you allow me to conduct this investigation, after all." English. Herr Blue Eyes wanted to humiliate. Blondie remained silent, his face an anvil. Schneider's eyes caught his, and, for a moment, they were allies.

He crawled back into the chair. His jaw throbbed and his ears rang, but it hadn't been for nothing.

"What happened to your Mae West, Lieutenant? Don't fliers normally wear them?" Schneider resumed his questioning as if nothing had happened.

He thought for a moment, decided to remain silent.

"Come now, Lieutenant. What possible military significance could that have?"

"If I'd been wearing one, I probably would have buried it."

"I see." Schneider smiled. "And where might you bury it had you been wearing one?"

"In the dirt." He fought to still the anger rising with the pain in his jaw.

"Of course." Schneider's eyes locked onto his. Blondie stood, arms crossed, glaring. Schneider picked up a paper from his desk and turned to leave, looked at Blondie as if in afterthought. "I'll call you when I resume. In the meantime, please get the American lieutenant a cup of coffee, will you Leutnant von Felder?"

Leutnant von Felder. It would pay to remember that. Blondie caught the door before it closed, slipped behind Schneider. He sat quietly looking at the empty room, shivered, turned gently to the comfort of his experience in the well. Even here it had power. He feared, felt pain, but nothing was as disquieting as before.

Von Felder reentered the room carrying two cups of coffee, sat the first in front of him, then looked away as if he had nowhere else to put it.

He smiled. "No cream and sugar, Herr von Felder?"

The leutnant's face reddened. "For a man facing execution, you display a good deal of cheek."

Blondie's voice was as colorless as his skin, paled, he guessed, by some inner lack. He smiled. "My profile you mean? Left side's my best."

"Why is it all Americans think themselves comedians?"

"When in Rome..."

Von Felder wrinkled his brow.

"We blend in with our surroundings. When we're surrounded by clowns, we act—" Blondie swung the club, set the side of his head ablaze. He found his feet this time, was ready to lunge but stopped at the sight of the leutnant's Walther.

"What's going on here, Herr leutnant?" Schneider spoke from the doorway, his feet wide.

"Your spy insists on insulting the Reich, Leutnant Schneider." Von Felder's voice trembled. Schneider turned to David.

"He was admiring my cheeks. I can't have that. Besides, what would you do if someone served you coffee that tasted like this?"

Schnieder looked from one to the other, focused on von Felder. "What happened to his head? Why is he bleeding?"

"Your arrogant luft gangster made—"

"That is correct, Herr Leutnant. He is *my* prisoner. Any further interference in my interrogation, and you shall be reported to *your* superiors. Do you understand?"

"Quite." Von Felder's face twisted. "But remember, my superiors are also yours."

"Aussteigt!" Schneider erupted, his hand aimed at the door. It balled into a fist and pushed against his desk. The door closed and Schneider rubbed his face, took a deep breath. After a few seconds he turned. "Now, Lieutenant, what is your complaint with our coffee?"

"It's no wonder you people are so mean. Look what it did to that amiable friend of yours. Hitler drink a lot of this stuff?"

Schneider's eyes burned a withering stare. "We have some problems with your escape kit, Lieutenant. We are very familiar with escape kits, what your government provides, what should be in them. Yours seems to be missing a few items."

He projected disinterest, tried to remember what Albert and Nicole had taken.

"We know you should have five passport pictures ready for use by the Underground. You have only three. What happened to the other two?"

"How should I know?" He stared blankly, his throat constricting and his head and jaw pulsing with pain. "Maybe they shorted me. I never thought to check."

"Come now. I expected more creativity than that."

He straightened, his heart still pounding in his ears. "All right, then. I used them to acquire passports for my cruise, my summer holiday."

Schneider dipped his chin. "Ah, of course."

"Herr Leutnant, you're not as familiar with the American military as you think. If you were, you'd know that seldom are things issued of the correct size or quantity."

"Yes, yes, I'm familiar with all that. Snafus, you call them?" Schneider's hand went up, brought an end to it. He walked around the room, stopped at the far wall, pivoted on his heels. "Lieutenant, do you know how many escapees are intercepted trying to make it to the Channel every day?"

"No idea."

"Many. And most are airmen— British, Canadian, American, shot down while bombing the innocent people of the Reich. Some, however, are spies— French, Austrian. But did you know all claim to be airmen? Even the spies. And do you know why?"

He shrugged. "Hopes of glory? Dreams of a real cup of coffee?"

Schneider wagged his finger. "They prefer humane treatment in a military stalag to being shot or hanged. Thus, we have a dilemma. Are you merely a good actor pretending to be an American airman, or are you, in fact, an American airman? My opinion is that you are who you say you are. Leutnant von Felder believes otherwise. So you see, I must have proof."

"Which means you need to know group numbers, commanding officers' names, crews, strength, and the day and hour of the invasion, right?" A slow rage was eroding his control.

Schneider pulled his chair out, sat down. "Those would be quite helpful, yes. Does Eisenhower confide in you a great deal?" He rolled his head as if he were addressing an errant child. "Lieutenant, I'm not asking you to divulge military secrets. I doubt that you know any. I'm not asking you for any more than I can read in the *Stars and Stripes.*"

The leutnant pushed his chair back, pulled his top desk drawer. He extracted a copy of *Stars and Stripes* and began to read. "'BOLING AIR GROUP BOOSTS KILL TOTAL TO 326. AN EIGHTH AIR FORCE BASE: Col. James A. Boling's Raiders, second-highest scoring group in the ETO downed a confirmed nine aircraft on August 18th. Boling's group was the first pursuit/escort group in the European theatre to "kill" more than eight enemy aircraft in one day.'" Schneider looked up. "An exaggeration, I'm sure. Shall I continue reading?"

He shook his head. "No, thanks. Just have von Felder bring me the paper with my morning coffee."

"It goes on to mention three of the aces in his group by name. So, you see, all you have to do is give me enough information to sufficiently prove you are who you say you are, and your name will be turned in to the Red Cross, your relatives will be notified that you are alive, and you will be placed in a stalag. Oh," he raised a finger, offered an afterthought, "and we must have the location and identities of your Underground contacts."

"You have an exceptionally short memory, Herr Leutnant. We had no contact with the Underground. We were alone the entire time. Didn't even meet any of the fine citizens of Belgium up close. Saw a couple of farmers putting out milk to cool, but they never saw us."

"So you're saying you stole milk?" Schneider raised his brows.

"I don't know if I'm saying that or not. Do you shoot milk thieves?"

Schneider laughed. "I suppose one could say that was a theft from the Reich, but perhaps we can overlook it this time." He stiffened slightly, returned to work. "Why don't you just tell me the name and number of your plane and the day you were shot down? That way we can verify it with the wreckages on the ground, you will have provided some evidence of who you are, and we will be on our way to proving you a member of the Air Corps."

"Is that a legitimate question?" David steeled himself, fought the temptation to ease under Schneider's amiability.

"Of course. If it were a military secret, would it be written on the side of the plane?"

"Then the answer is, 'Because it is against my orders and outside the requirements of the Geneva Convention.' I have been instructed to give you only name, rank, and serial number. No more. I've done that."

"And there you are mistaken. It is not against the rules at all. Let me show you a copy of the rules, and you can see for yourself." Schneider pulled a ragged copy of the *Articles* from his desk drawer. In English. The leutnant pointed to paragraph 77. "See, there for example. As you can see, you are required to give me your address. Will you do that?"

He stared at the far wall. "No, sir."

"And why not? Do you not plan to write home? How can you hope to send mail without an address?" Schneider rose again, his hands lifted in a dramatic pose.

"Against my orders."

"How am I ever to clear you if you don't provide me with basic information: religion, next of kin, condition, when you were shot down, military unit, age? You must cooperate if you want to be treated well. Certainly you can see I am trying to help you." Schneider looked offended.

He suppressed a laugh, noted the pout and the quick shift from the requirements of the *Articles* to the Nazi forms. "No can do."

"Be reasonable. Surely you can see that the Geneva Convention does not require me to admit you to a Red Cross internment camp if I have no proof you are even military personnel."

He turned, met the leutnant's eyes, displayed a resolve he hoped appeared genuine. "Leutnant Schneider, you know very well I am who I say I am, and so does your lackey, von Felder. You've sniffed through everything I have, seen my pictures, examined my dog tags, for God's sake. You're trying to get information, and I won't knowingly or willingly give you any. Furthermore, you must know we had no contact with the Underground. If we had, we wouldn't still be here after six weeks, now would we?"

Schneider smiled. "A bit over six weeks, Lieutenant. That does coincide with the death of the navigator, Ito."

He hung his head, hoped his slip was sufficient to redirect the leutnant.

"Lieutenant, we also know you were directed to that location by the handkerchief. Rest assured, I will find out who directed you."

His heart filled his throat, and he quickly fought to cover the apprehension he knew would be showing on his face. "What handkerchief? What are you trying to pin on us? We didn't do anything but try to escape. That was our duty." He searched Schneider's eyes, hoped the leutnant hadn't detected his bluff.

"Lieutenant Dremmer," Schneider changed tacks, his voice growing stern, "I believe you have a great deal to think about. Perhaps it is time for you to be ushered to your new quarters. I hope you find your stay... well, short. That would be best for everyone."

He held his tongue. Schneider picked up the telephone, waited, spat rapid-fire German. In a moment, a young private, long-nosed and narrow-faced, appeared at the door looking too anemic to be asked to carry the rifle in his arms.

"Gefreiter Wiesel will take you to your cell as soon as you are dressed." Schneider's words were clipped.

The gefreiter pointed toward the door. David zipped his flight suit, stepped past the clerk in the outer office into the hallway.

"Geh hier hinein!" Wiesel pointed down the hall. Before they reached the end, a rough hand gripped his shoulder, and the guard pointed him to a glass-paneled door. He reached for the handle, and the boy grunted, shook his head, pushed him away and opened it himself. The door opened onto a landing above a vacant set of stairs. They descended one flight, turned and stepped down another. At the last landing, Wiesel pointed to a dark hallway, motioned toward a door on the opposite side, and pushed it open. An effluvium of mildew and urine rose to meet them. He took the lead in front of the rifle, reached the bottom of the steps. Wiesel pushed him back, unlocked the door to an open basement. Straw was strewn across the concrete, and three or four shadowy figures lay sprawled across it. Bear rose from the shadows and hobbled into the pale light.

He caught Bear's eye, shook his head, tried to signal his friend not to acknowledge him.

"What's up, cowboy?" Bear showed only casual recognition.

"Not much of a cowboy, pal." He turned so that Bear could see his face, mouthed "No bandana," and winked. A smile crossed Bear's face.

"Nein! Nicht reden!" Wiesel shoved his chin forward, and David shuffled toward a door opening into a short hallway.

He faced a second door, this one closed. It was grimy and soiled, and he waited for the boy to open it. Wiesel grinned and motioned him forward. He turned the handle, pushed. The heavy stench of raw sewage assaulted him, and he jerked his head away. The gefreiter jutted his chin, jabbed him forward with the rifle and closed the door behind him. A moment later, he heard keys in the hallway door.

"Hey! What do we do for a bathroom?" Bear's protest, muted by the two doors.

"Nein! Hault's Maul du!"

He stood without moving, allowed his eyes to adjust to the dark and pushed down the impulse to vomit.

266

# Chapter XXII

Light, dissolute and fragile, leached from a narrow window high on the east wall— if he still had his directions straight. But for that, the room was dark. David eyed the window, probably at ground level but too small to crawl through. No way of escape that he could see. The stench came from a sewage backup, the floor darker toward one end where the toilet had overflowed. If the window could be opened, at least there would be some ventilation. He looked around, couldn't make out anything clearly except the lavatory, what looked like exposed pipe, and the overflowing toilet. The sink was mounted on the wall in the corner below the window. If it could support his weight, he just might get some fresh air.

He turned the faucets. No water. At least a broken pipe wouldn't mean he'd drown in this cesspool. He leaned his weight onto the sink and lifted himself off the floor. It seemed solid enough. He pulled his feet onto the sides and stood, couldn't see the darkened window frame but felt a thick layer of paint over the iron latch. It would take a claw hammer or pry bar to free it.

He eased himself onto the floor, felt around the pipes and found a discarded plunger, mounted the lavatory and placed his head into the recess of the narrow window. Through the frosted glass, light descended from a single source above, the brightness broken by several vertical lines. Whatever the window opened to, it wasn't the outside.

The plunger handle tucked handily beneath the window latch, but some sense of impending calamity urged him to withdraw it. He would need a cushion or the pressure would likely crack the window frame, and that, if discovered, would be interpreted as an attempt to escape. He unlaced his boot and laid it on the mortar, pulled the handle down, the sole acting as a fulcrum.

He held his breath, worked the handle, gently urged a screw from the frame. If he could loosen the other two screws then slip them back into the holes, the latch might slide out and be returned without breaking the paint and revealing his ventilation system. He pried the other end, rocking the latch away from the frame, laid it to the side and tapped against the wood.

The window creaked open and a stir of air whispered across his face. He slid his head into the narrow recess, narrower now with the window lowered. The air was fresher and cool. He looked into a mechanical room, some sort of skylight above, pulled back and stepped down keeping his one socked foot away from the dark floor. The light was better now, and the floor glistened in the corner with wet sewage. He looked around. A mirror, one corner broken, was held to the wall behind the lavatory by four screws.

He pulled at the screw holding the broken corner and released his breath. It wouldn't budge. *My kingdom for a screwdriver!* He looked around the room, caught the glimmer of his belt and wrested it from his flight suit, found a sharp edge on the catch and inserted it into the screw and twisted. It ground free from the wall; he lifted the broken corner, and replaced the screw in the hole.

From the top of the lavatory, he held the broken piece of mirror through the window. Brooms, pipe, a furnace, a coal chute, two buckets. He rolled his hand, panned with the mirror from side to side. Ductwork ran up both sides of the room which appeared to be the height of the building, likely carrying heat to the offices.

The idea came as sheer delight. If he could identify which duct went where, he just might vent the effluvium from the bathroom directly into Schneider's office. He followed the conduit up the wall where each branched off. On his next visit to the outer sanctum, he would try to get an exact fix on the layout of the building.

For now, he needed sleep. He looked around the smelly hole, frowned. Lying on the floor was out of the question. He'd have to sit on the commode, but couldn't sleep that way and not fall off. He fingered his belt, tied one sleeve of his jacket around a pipe jutting up to the lavatory. It reached halfway to the pipes above the commode. He tied the other sleeve to the belt, slid in behind the pipes and maneuvered beneath the taut jacket draping his arms over the fleece-lined collar.

He sat folded over his jacket waiting for sleep, leaned against the wall and prayed. Scriptures his mother taught him rose from somewhere deep. One, a fragment of a psalm caught him unawares, the words swelling in resonating certainty: "If I ascend into heaven, thou art there: if I make my bed in She'ol, thou art there. If I take the wings of the morning and dwell in the uttermost parts of the sea; even there thy hand shall lead me, and thy right hand shall hold me." The words took root, grew into a celebration in the midst of his tiny hell. Memory flowed, the words transporting him on a holy wind beyond white-chipped boards, rustled the leaves of a cottonwood, stirred the crimson sunset above fresh-tilled earth and drew a dove to hold white and pure against the sky.

Early in the night, someone knocked on the door to the hallway. He kept quiet for fear that Schneider or von Felder might have hidden microphones, unlikely though it was. All grew quiet, and the night passed peacefully, even offering parcels of sleep.

Light began to filter in. He climbed to the top of the lavatory and pushed the window closed, removed his belt and jacket from the wall and hung the jacket over the mirror. He'd replaced the broken piece but didn't know what the light would expose when the door was opened. Or when his captors might come. He prayed for water, for food, a place to sleep, for wisdom in dealing with Schneider and von Felder. He heard boots on the concrete floor outside the bathroom. A key scraped in the lock, and the door swung wide. A young guard, a different one this time, stood with a gun in one hand, two tin cups in the other and motioned for him to step back against the wall. The boy set the cups on the concrete, backed quickly through the door and slammed it closed.

"Danke. And a good morning to you, too." He smiled, sipped the soup first, then water, and eased back onto the commode, keeping his feet as far away from the sewage as he could. He prayed, pushed the fear away each time it mounted in his chest. Waited.

More boots pounded in the hall, these demanding attention. The key jingled in the lock and the door flung open. He stood, stared at the grinning rictus of the weasel.

The boy jabbed his gun into the dark. "Raus!"

He pushed down the fire ignited in his gut. "Raus, huh? Okay, Weasel, I'll raus." He eased in front, placed his left foot even with the door, counted his steps into the larger cell and looked for Bear. The room was empty. He pointed up the stairs. "Leutnant Schneider?"

"Ja."

The bathroom was eleven paces and a few inches north of the wall defining the southern side of the staircase, grimy in the gray light. They stopped at the first floor landing. The private opened the door, and he stepped to the west wall. Two paces. The door closed behind them, and he mounted the second flight, then the third, emerged and counted thirteen paces to the door outside Schneider's outer office.

The mechanical room was four stories high, counting the basement level. He'd have to be inside to determine its width, but it lay slightly to the east of Schneider's outside office. He looked to that side of the hall. Doors stood every fifteen feet or so along its length except across from Schneider's. There the wall was blank. The vent area above the mechanical room, most likely. The gefreiter opened the door, and he stepped inside.

Von Felder sat at the outer desk where the clerk had been sitting the day before. The leutnant seemed surprised, began to cover with bluster, snapped something at Wiesel who went to the file cabinet, pulled out a drawer and retrieved a form. Blondie grabbed it and walked out the door.

Wiesel pointed to a cushioned chair. He seated himself, found it inordinately comfortable, could have been asleep in minutes so worked to stay busy

The ductwork from the furnace downstairs had turned right. That would be west, and at the second floor level. It should have come out here, beneath the hallway and under his feet.

He looked around the room for a vent, saw none and stood up to stretch. The gefreiter's eyes followed him. David grinned, stretched his back, twisting from side to side inspecting the walls and floor as he moved. No vent. If he were required to stay in the hell-hole again, he'd try to figure it out with the mirror.

The hall door opened abruptly and Schneider came bustling in looking fresh and rested. The leutnant nodded at the guard and motioned for David to follow.

"Good morning, Lieutenant. Did you sleep well?"

"Finest Kraut billet I ever stayed in, thank you." He grinned.

"I'm delighted." The German tossed a folder onto his desk. "You're not going to suggest I stay there?"

"Don't think that would be a good idea, Herr Leutnant."

Schneider turned, raised a single brow. "And why is that?"

"Apt to make you homesick."

"I suppose I can understand your feelings, Lieutenant. I'm sorry I had to do that."

It wouldn't do to have Herr Blue Eyes become his benefactor. He grinned. "A Nazi with a conscience?"

"It is because I have a conscience that I became a Nazi."

He scanned the room, remained silent.

"What are you looking for, Lieutenant?"

"The microphone. No one would say something that asinine unless…"

Schneider's ears reddened. He'd hit home. "Lieutenant, I suggest we remain soldiers. Let's leave political arguments to the theoreticians, shall we?"

"Is that verboten, too? How do you keep from thinking, Herr Leutnant?"

"I've given you my thoughts on the subject. Now let's move on."

The exchange put him at ease. He noted the peculiarity of it, but what about this experience wasn't peculiar? Still, his only chance to win at this game was to remain Schneider's equal. If he acquiesced, Schneider would manipulate him into betrayal. He couldn't allow that. "Where are you from, Herr Leutnant?"

"I'm asking the questions, Lieutenant. Since you seem not to have noticed, I should perhaps point out that I have you at something of a disadvantage. So where are *you* from, Lieutenant?"

"Currently, The Berlin Ritz. Chancellor's Suite."

"And prior to that?"

"Can't say."

"Of course you can. You were, until a few weeks ago, stationed at Ridgewell Air Base in East Anglia. You are a member of the 8$^{th}$ Air Force, 381$^{st}$ Bomb Group and the 534$^{th}$ Bomb Squadron. That is also correct, is it not?" Schneider smiled, looked at his papers.

*How did the bastard know?* He yawned, stretched to cover his shock. It was conceivable the Kraut had learned which groups were involved in the raid, but how did he know which group he was from? Someone had to have told him. His neck and ears burned, venting the fire growing in his gut. "You know, I was never very good with numbers."

"Obviously, the information I have is correct. Tell me, do they still have the picture of the Focke-Wulf hanging at Land's End?" Herr Blue Eyes was gloating now. "A beautiful plane, is it not?"

He ignored it. Decided it must look different if you weren't staring at its guns. "Land's End, now let's see. That would be Antarctica? I'm really not as well-traveled as you might think." He forced a grin to hide his unease.

"Really, Lieutenant, we have all the essential information. You have only to sign this document, and we can dispense with this childishness. Do you really want to be shot as a spy?" Schneider was his buddy again.

"Now, that I can answer. No."

"Lieutenant, would you like to go for a walk? I would like to show you around. Perhaps it would afford us an opportunity to chat in more pleasant surroundings."

"Sounds delightful. Mind if I freshen up, quick shower and a shave first? My uniform's a bit mussed." For all the verbal diversion, the prospect of being out of the building was enticing.

"So I observed." Schneider beamed, put a finger to his nose, acted as if he'd won some contest. "You must give me your word as an officer that you will not attempt to escape. I will have you sign a document to that effect."

He nodded. "So long as I can read the fine print."

"It's all quite straightforward, I assure you." The leutnant pulled a doubled form from his desk, placed a carbon inside it and handed it over. It was as he had promised, straightforward, even requiring the Army to return him if he showed up. Not likely. He scribbled his name on the blank

272

line.

Schneider picked up the form and walked toward the door. "Come along, Lieutenant. I'll leave this with my assistant, and we'll be on our way."

He ambled after him, considered whether to count his steps. Schneider was no fool. Little was apt to escape his attention. The leutnant talked with his clerk, the same baby-faced boy he'd seen the day before. They spoke French. *French.* Why? He followed the conversation, except the references to forms. The leutnant was difficult to understand, but the clerk's pronunciation was perfect. Schneider was taking the prisoner for a walk to "loosen" him, and should be back within the hour. He looked at the clock on the desk, stiffened.

A wall vent was perched a few inches above the baseboard, grated with a wide-spaced mesh of heavy steel. The lamp exposed a short section of downward curve in the duct. A pitcher of water sat on the desk. He'd seen it as he came in. If the two could be distracted, he could pour water down the vent. There would be enough leakage in those rusted turn pieces to mark the ducts so he could identify the one going to the sanctums. He looked back at the leutnant.

"Are you ready, Lieutenant?"

He glanced at the pitcher.

The leutnant opened his hand in generosity. "By all means, Lieutenant. Feel free."

He picked up a glass and filled it, would have gladly given up the drink for the chance to pour it down the vent. Some other time.

Schneider rocked on his heels, his hands behind him. "Let's go then, shall we?"

He followed his captor into the hall. The leutnant paused, let him catch up. Side by side. Best of friends, now. Swell. They proceeded north toward the stairwell they had used entering the building the day before.

He needed to set some limits. "Is it too soon to hold hands, Herr—"

Schneider threw his hand up and shook his head. "Outside."

The leutnant didn't speak again until they reached the guard shack. He handed the guard a duplicate of the paper he'd given his clerk, and the unteroffizier opened the compound gate. They walked a hundred yards or so before Schneider turned. "You will remember that you are under oath and not attempt escape, yes?"

"Of course." He only wished it were possible.

"I would like you to make another solemn promise. I need your word as a gentleman. Do I have it?" Schneider turned toward him demanding eye contact.

He refused to flinch or look away. "Not without knowing what you want."

The leutant raised his head, sniffed the breeze. "I am willing to share information with you, but I must have your assurance that you will share it with no one else."

*Audacious SOB.* "Will what you have to tell me endanger anyone's life?"

"It will not increase the danger to those you have allegiance to, no."

He grinned, delighted for the chance to return the greasy charm. "Do I have your word on that as an officer?"

Schneider stared, seemed to find no humor in it. "I am a man of honor. I believe you know this."

"What does honor mean? Does that mean you won't lie to me?"

The leutnant stared. "I promise you that what I am going to tell you will not further endanger anyone you have any allegiance to."

He looked into the blue eyes. He didn't know why, but he believed him. "All right."

"There are factions, Lieutenant, within our military representing differences of approach. They have to do with a wide variety of things. The handling of prisoners is but one of them. As an officer in the Luftwaffe, I treat all flyers with respect. As gentlemen. The Wehrmacht has quite a different approach." Schneider took a breath, scanned the road, began again. "Lieutenant, there is no reason for us to be adversarial. You are out of the war. You have done your duty, and I am not asking you to divulge military secrets."

"Then how did you get the information you gave me? You plied it from someone either by deception or torture."

"I have tortured no one, except, perhaps, by providing them with less than perfect accommodations." Schneider grinned. "You are a difficult case, less obliging than most."

He refused the smile this time. "I'll bet you say that to all the girls."

Schneider raised his chin. "I have some crucial information. If I share it with other Wehrmacht interrogators, you and your comrade will most likely be broken. Or tortured to death."

He refused to flinch, gave a curt nod. "All right. You have my attention."

"What does the name 'Nicole Serat' mean to you?"

A chain clamped around his chest. His heart pounded in his ears. He forced himself to breathe, shrugged. "Nothing. I don't know any Nicole... Serat is it?"

"You're obviously lying. I have reason to believe she was your contact. A guard shot a man trying to escape the night before you were captured. He was quite desperate for medical attention." Schneider stared at the road, let the insinuation lie that Albert had offered information on Nicole. "I asked the guard not to share what was learned with anyone else. For now."

He forced air into his lungs. "What's that got to do with me?"

Schneider waved the question away, a mere fly in his face. "There is more you should know. The Underground is inept. Every week they smuggle boatloads of airmen— American, British, and Canadian— to the Channel, and every week these boats are intercepted by our patrols. I have no desire to interrupt their bungling. They merely collect prisoners for us. The Wehrmacht, however, wishes to make examples of them, hangings along every street. Come, let's walk."

He shuffled at the leutnant's pace, examining a notion. Two could play this game. He pulled a name he remembered from a French tutorial. "And did this man you had shot say anything about Gilbert?"

Schneider thought for a moment. "Of course. Nicole's accomplice."

"Wouldn't be my term. What I don't understand is how you got her real name."

"Her *real* name?" Schneider searched the air, stopped and turned.

"I was given to understand she's gone by Madeline since the beginning. No one knew her real name. Except me, and..." He hoped the leutnant hadn't used the same French textbook.

"Our intelligence sources, Lieutenant, are very thorough. You are up against a great deal more than you guessed."

"Apparently so." He took a deep breath, squared himself, tried to quiet his pounding heart. "Did Armand, the man you shot, did he talk?" He stared into Schneider's eyes.

"I did not shoot him." Schneider blinked, looked away. "Yes, he talked a great deal. He told us little that we did not know. But, of course, he told us of Madeline and Gilbert."

He warmed with relief. Besides Schneider's familiarity with the phony names, Albert— Gerhardt— would never talk. Never. And it was doubtful he could have lived long enough to say anything.

"You are in love with her, are you not?"

Must have been pretty obvious. "Your intelligence sources really are thorough."

Schneider smiled. "Yes, quite. But what about Gilbert? Is he not also in love with her?"

He shook his head, plastered an unsteady grin on his face. "Those two hate each other. You should understand a difference in approaches. Won't even work together unless they have to. That's why they work alone. Live alone. Didn't your sources tell you that?"

The leutnant chuckled.

His gut knotted. Was the kraut being sly, or was he chuckling because he knew he was being lied to? "Is he still alive? Armand, I mean."

Schneider stretched his chin skyward. He could see the leutnant weighing the options. "No, I'm sorry. He expired a few hours ago."

He nodded. The Hun was slimy, but he hadn't promised not to lie.

"We are in agreement then. When you have something to tell me, you will signal me." Schneider tossed him an apple and a piece of cheese. "Likewise, I will be calling on you for additional interviews. If we need to speak further on this matter, we shall go for a walk. We will not, however, discuss this matter in my outer office. Is that understood, Lieutenant?"

He raised his chin, nodded.

"I think you might move into the larger room. I'm holding Sergeant Billington in processing now, and I'm satisfied with your growing understanding of the situation. The sergeant will be sent to Dulag Luft for standard interrogations."

The knot loosened. Schneider was capable of snafus, too. The effort was likely to isolate him, but Bear's absence would make it difficult to compare stories. Unless Bear had talked. But that wasn't possible, either. Bear would never betray Nicole. Or him.

Still the problem remained. Schneider had her name, seemed to anticipate his reaction to hearing it. But if he knew her before, knew she was connected to Gerhardt... He pulled deep from the cold air. "I agreed not to attempt escape and to hold everything in confidence. I haven't agreed to tell you anything else."

"All right, Lieutenant. I believe it would also be good for your morale if you were given a job in the compound. This would entitle you to better rations, of course."

*And enable you to watch me.* He turned the apple in his hand. "Officers aren't required—"

"Officers aren't required to work according to the *Articles of the Geneva Convention*. Yes, that is true. But I believe you will find it more pleasant than staying in your cell all day. If you don't, you will be allowed to return. Is this agreeable?"

"All right." He wasn't sure he didn't prefer von Felder.

"I shall have one of the guards bring you a pail and mop, and you will start by cleaning that sty of a bathroom you call home."

He thought of the mechanical room and smiled.

# Chapter XXIII

The room contracted, darkness shadowing even his thoughts. David bunched hay beneath his head, ignored the stems and relived the conversation with Schneider. Had he made any missteps? Omitted anything? He weighed the leutnant's words, rehearsed details to add if given the opportunity. *Cigarettes.* He needed to ask Schneider for cigarettes.

He scratched his neck, smoothed the hay again, lay his jacket beneath him. The speed of Schneider's investigation was a concern. The leutnant was quick. If presented with too many dead ends, he'd realize he'd been had. Still, the blue-eyed conniver had to be baited, the inevitable held at bay until some opportunity presented itself to keep him away from the partisans. From Nicole.

Boots shook the stairs. Keys rattled, and the door swung wide. Wiesel stood motionless, his rifle high across his chest, his boots spread apart in an obviously rehearsed pose. The gefreiter pointed to the dark corner of the north wall. He rose, slogged across the litter and found a door with hay blocking it. A current of sheer delight trickled up his spine. It had to be the entrance to the mechanical room, not fifteen feet from where he lay.

Wiesel motioned him a safe distance away, stepped forward and began struggling with the keys. The boy tried several before one moved the reluctant lock, then motioned for him to remove the hay.

The room was larger than he had imagined seeing it in the mirror. Two paces brought him just short of the center of the furnace. He guessed it to be five paces wall to wall, maybe twice that in length. Schneider's outer office was above and west of him. He glanced up. The wall narrowed by the width of the hallway above the second floor, a skylight two floors above that.

Wiesel spewed something guttural, jabbed his rifle toward a mop bucket.

He smiled, nodded. "Keep your pants on, Weasel. Herr Blue Eyes told me."

Cleaning supplies and building materials were strewn about, a few tools, a hammer, some wrenches. He avoided the boy's gaze and scraped toward the bucket. No need arousing suspicions.

"Vasser?" The question all but exhausted his German.

Wiesel looked around, shrugged. Must have been his first time in the room, too. He followed the pipes along the wall, looked for a hydrant, paused for a moment and scanned the ductwork. Seven ducts were insulated in a bundle coming from the north side of the furnace, eight on the south. Those eight climbed the wall, three turning west under the hallway. Finding the one going to Schneider's office would be the trick.

"Da drüben." Wiesel pointed to the north wall. A faucet jutted two feet above the floor. He pushed the bucket underneath it and turned the tap. Surges of red sludge and intermittent air sputtered into the galvanized pail. The water began to clear, and he looked around for a place to pour out the slush. The gefreiter pointed to a drain beneath the furnace. He lumbered over, water sloshing. A discarded section of duct, flanges still in place on each end, lay beside the rusty plate screwed into the concrete. He caught his breath, picked up the duct as if it were in his way and leaned it against the wall beneath the bathroom window. One step closer. If the elbows on the ducts were still flexible, it wouldn't be a problem fitting the flange end on the duct. He would need a ladder, a metal saw, and a screwdriver. And time alone in the room. He swayed beneath the weight of his compulsion, refilled the bucket and stepped toward the door.

Wiesel raised his rifle. "Raus!"

"Disinfectant. I need disinfectant." He pointed to the mop bucket.

Wiesel ignored him, motioned toward the door. He took a step, turned. "I need cleanser. You understand 'cleanser'?"

"Raus!" The boy's teeth glistened in the bare light.

"I'll remember you, Weasel." He bowed, smiled as if offering an apology.

279

"Wiesel!" The boy arched his back.

He half expected crowing to emerge from the pinched orifice. "Right. You betcha."

He slipped quietly into the cell. The gefreiter locked the mechanical room door, moved past him to the stairs, shouted something in German. In minutes another guard appeared in the stairwell with a large bottle.

He reached for it. "Danke."

"Nein!" Wiesel grabbed it, placed it out of reach and stepped back, motioned for him to pick it up.

He started toward the bathroom, disinfectant hanging from his left arm. "Nein!"

He stopped, turned. "What now, Weasel?"

The gefreiter growled and pointed up the stairs. "Hinaufgehen!"

He pointed to the bathroom. "Schneider's orders. Supposed to clean it."

"Steig die Treppe hinauf!" Wiesel flailed his free arm toward the stairway.

The fire rose in his gut. "You've got the crust, Weasel."

"Nein— Wiesel!" The boy rammed the gunstock at his head.

He grabbed the rifle, held it, fought the impulse to slam it into the boy's face. But if he hurt the Weasel, he'd have to escape. Or wait around to be shot. Even if he made it, he'd be out of the game. There would be no one between Nicole and Schneider. He looked directly into the Weasel's eyes, held the rifle firmly, let the boy know he could take it if he chose to, then released it. The boy remained quiet for a moment then pointed up the stairs. David stood, let the kid sweat, stared a moment longer before mounting the steps.

"Dreh dich links!" The boy's shout shook him as he reached the top step.

He looked back. "What?"

"Linke Seite!" Wiesel pointed left.

"Which other way could I go?"

The Weasel glared. He shrugged, pushed through the door and slammed it shut behind him, Wiesel still working the key. Boots pounded up the steps behind the door. He leaned against the south wall beside double doors, forced down a smile. The door to the stairway flew open, and

Wiesel stumbled into the hall. He stared into the boy's eyes, caught the panic before it settled.

He wagged his left arm. "Linke? Means left, right?"

Wiesel discharged a blistering stream of German. He leaned against the wall, tried to look unperturbed. Blondie emerged from a door down the hall, hurried toward them, talked with the Weasel for a minute before turning. "He says you have been insubordinate, that you have threatened him. I have given him permission to shoot you if you do this again."

He raised his hands. "Insubordinate? He hollered 'Linke,' which I thought meant 'left.' I was following the little corporal's orders."

Von Felder stiffened. "He is a gefreiter. And I am aware that your military refers to our Führer as the 'The Little Corporal.' You will be shot either for disobeying an order or for insulting the Führer. I will convey this to Gefreiter Wiesel. Do you understand this?"

"Seems pretty unfair. I was doing my best to do what he told me." He tapped the side of his head. "Seems to me 'The Little Private' has some problems. Maybe that's why he reminded me of 'The Little Corporal.'"

The leutnant's hand shot up, a flash of black leather. He jerked his head aside, caught von Felder's arm, shoved it behind him ready to pull the shoulder out of joint. The black baton fell to the floor a moment before a rifle barrel slammed into his skull above his right ear. He sagged, forced down the fever in his breast and loosened his hold on von Felder's arm.

"Schiess ihn doch!" The leutnant wiggled loose from his relaxing grip.

"Nein, nicht schiessen. Wiesel, hör doch auf, mit der Waffe rumzuspielen."

*Schneider.* He released his breath. The leutnant had appeared from nowhere, screamed above them both, pointed a finger at the gefreiter.

"Wiesel, stell dein!" Schneider's voice modulated, appeared to be calming the boy. The barrel pressed harder into his skull then pulled away.

The veins in von Felder's neck jutted above his collar, his face crimson. He spat German at Schneider, pointed at David leaning against the wall. Schneider pressed his chest against Blondie, his jaw muscles quivering. Von Felder shouted an order at the milk-white Wiesel, and the two proceeded down the hall leaving him, Schneider, and a rocking pail of mop water. He rotated slowly, gave the leutnant his full attention.

Schneider stared. "Lieutenant, if you persist in this behavior, it is very unlikely you will survive your stay." Something in the eyes hinted at respect, or maybe the bond created by a common enemy. The leutnant tilted his head, resumed control. "Follow me."

He stepped smartly, carried the bucket and mop, paraded past the open door von Felder had gone into, went on to the stairway and Schneider's office then deposited the bucket at the clerk's desk. Schneider paused at the door to the inner sanctum and turned. "Now, I want to know what caused your little scuffle."

The request was sotto voce, but the import was clear. Schneider trusted him more than von Felder or the Weasel.

He touched the throbbing above his ear, felt the slight stickiness of blood. "That Weasel's a little too eager to use his rifle. One end or the other. He tried to hit me with the stock. I grabbed it, almost took it away from him. Could have easy enough. Guess it hurt his feelings." He breathed, lowered his hand. "The kid started screaming once we were in the hall, got von Felder involved." He decided to test the waters. "Guess I owe you one."

"Yes, you do." Schneider smiled weakly, leaned in. "And you mustn't refer to Gefreiter Wiesel as 'The Weasel.' You can understand this might irritate him."

"He speaks English?"

"No, but he knows his name is being mispronounced. He's likely guessed he's being insulted." Schneider met his stare, turned back and pushed through the door. "Do you also realize that Leutnant von Felder ordered you shot?"

Full voice. So the leutnant was going on record now. He stood just outside the inner sanctum, put a hand to his mouth. "Does that mean he doesn't like me?"

Schneider circled his desk, sat and leaned back in his chair. "I think it would be best for you to work here until tempers settle. You may begin by cleaning the outer office." The leutnant visibly relaxed, his eyes filled with a blue intensity. "If you need further supplies, I'll have them brought up to you. My clerk does not speak English, but he can notify me if you need anything."

He nodded, winced. "Say, where do you go for a smoke around here, Herr Leutnant?"

Schneider's eyes narrowed, his face stone. "I thought you had perhaps decided to quit." The German extended his pack of Turkish.

He stepped forward, took one, allowed the leutnant to light it. "These would make it easier, all right." He let the smoke burn deep, pretended to enjoy it, turned to go to the outer office.

"Have you thought any more about our conversation?"

"I've thought about it." He reached the door without looking back.

"And what have you decided?"

He turned, met the leutnant's stare. "That you can't be trusted. That you're manipulative enough to have coordinated that little scene out in the hall a few minutes ago just to make me beholden to you or something."

Schneider swelled, allowed a slight smile. "If you're asking, I didn't arrange that incident."

He stared a moment longer, nodded. "Yeah, I know." It was a partial truth, implying he'd orchestrated the encounter. Some mutual respect seemed to be in order.


The clerk typed and filed, watched him from the corner of his eye. It was obvious he made the little man nervous. His part for the war effort. Maybe the boy would make a mistake and cost the Reich a few man-hours.

David mopped the floor, cleaned the walls, wiped the baseboard, stopped only occasionally to massage his swelling temple.

Schneider stepped from his office. "My, but you are an industrious fellow."

"Just spiffin' up for the Ivans. Have any red paint? They'd like that." He turned, met Schneider's glare.

"Lieutenant Dremmer, I suggest you watch your mouth. You might find that next time I'll be more reluctant to order Wiesel to stand down."

He turned back to the wall, held his reaction when Schneider addressed the clerk. French again, asking if something were completed, requested it be brought to him when it was finished. Was it all right, the clerk wondered, to leave the prisoner alone?

*Yeah, you bet. Give me thirty minutes.*

The files were what? *Locked.* The files were locked. Schneider was difficult to follow, the clerk's French too perfect for a German, a bit rapid and nasal for a Belgian, like the boy was straight off the Champs-Élysée. Just might be Vichy. So what was he doing here?

He worked in the opposite direction, left the vent area for later. Why had Schneider brought a clerk all the way from France? Had to be plenty available within the ranks. Could be the leutnant *needed* a French-speaking clerk. So why not a Belgian? Tough finding a Belgian sympathetic to the Nazis, maybe.

Vichy Boy pecked at the keys, shuffled papers. The answer came as clear as the soup he'd had for breakfast, almost took his breath. Schneider was polishing his French, too, entering the same game he was in, only on the other side. And likely after the same partisans he was trying to protect. Or maybe just Nicole. His stomach rolled. Vichy Boy played a part in it somehow. Had to. But what was it? Not likely he was just a tutor. But if Schneider was working with material obtained from French-speaking subjects, then maybe… Or it could be that the leutnant wasn't trusted by everyone working with Abwehr. Maybe they wanted their man in his office. The boy just *might* be watching Schneider.

The clerk pulled the paper from the typewriter, began to arrange pages, stood and stacked them, took a step toward the door and glanced back.

He offered an artificial grin. "Want me to clean over there now?"

"Pardon?"

He pointed to the baseboard behind the desk and moved his rag in the air. "Okay?"

"Okay, yes." The little man nodded in obvious discomfort.

He moved around the desk as the clerk marched through the door, grabbed the empty vase he'd spotted on the filing cabinet, filled it with disinfectant water and leaned down ready to pour it in the vent. The hall door swung open. His heart jolted, and he slid the vase behind the bucket, began cleaning the baseboard, fought to control his breath.

"I'm watching you, Lieutenant. Provide me with one opportunity, and I'll have you shot."

He refolded the cloth, continued to wipe.

"Have you no clever response?"

He turned, met his accuser's stare. "I know you're dangerous. Does that make you feel powerful, Herr Leutnant?"

Von Felder lifted his chin, squinted. "Is Leutnant Schneider in his office?"

"Unless he heard you were coming and jumped from his balcony."

Von Felder scowled.

He looked away, didn't want his satisfaction to show. "It's a joke, Herr Leutnant. He has no window, see, so he can't really jump. That's the way humor works. It's simple, really."

Von Felder huffed . "He left you unattended?"

"Even going to the potty by myself, now."

The door creaked open. The clerk backed through, still receiving orders, bumped von Felder, yelped and whipped around.

The leutnant released a torrent of sharp-edged German. Vichy Boy whitened, looked at him then back at the leutnant.

"Kommen sie rherrein, Herr Leutnant." Schneider broke into von Felder's tirade, suspired loudly. Von Felder stepped into the inner office and slammed the door.

He looked at Vichy Boy. "Herr von Blondie needs to cut down on that coffee he drinks. Makes him ill-tempered."

The clerk motioned for him to move from behind the desk. David shielded the bucket, submerged the vase in water. In one motion, he picked up the bucket and mop and moved to the other side of the room.

Vichy Boy shuffled through files. His chair scooted back, and he rose, marched through Schneider's door but left the door ajar.

His heart rattled against his ribs. He wiped the outside of the vase and crawled across the floor, held the rag against the bottom of the grate and emptied the disinfectant. He wiped the wire mesh, polished the glass with the dry end of the rag and placed it back on the file cabinet, then crept to the bucket.

Vichy Boy emerged from the inner sanctum, Schneider at his heels. The leutnant raised his nose sniffing the air. "Did you have nothing to clean with but disinfectant?"

He kept his head down, wrung out the rag to hide the tremor in his hands. "I asked for it to use in the bathroom in the Chancellor's Suite, but the Weasel took me upstairs." He risked a glance.

Schneider nodded, his ears reddening. "You've done quite enough to-day, Lieutenant. Another guard will take you to your cell. We shall talk tomorrow."

Von Felder stepped from behind, glared at David and marched into the hall.

He watched the leutnant leave then turned to Schneider. "Have I missed dinner?"

The German seemed to soften. "I'll have something sent down to you."

"Found any coded messages in my Chesterfields, Herr Leutnant?"

"Are you asking for me to return them, Lieutenant?"

He winked. "That'd be the berries."

Schneider ducked in his door, returned with the cigarettes from David's escape kit. "There you are."

"Thanks. Have any matches?"

Schneider stared, handed him a book of matches he'd held in the palm of his hand. Always the games. The guard appeared at the door, and he turned to follow, bucket and mop in his right hand.

"Sleep well, Lieutenant."

He stopped in the doorway, twisted and snapped a sharp, left-handed salute. "I fully intend to, Herr Leutnant."


David stared at the door to the mechanical room, saw something he'd missed. The hinges were on the outside, an easy way in with a pair of pliers. He kept his eyes roving as he walked in, spotted a wooden box filled with tools behind the furnace. Likely a pair of pliers there if only he could nab them. No chance of that with the guard hovering over him. He poured out the water and wrung the mop, set both behind the furnace next to the wooden box, took a good look inside. Screwdrivers, pliers, a chisel, several wrenches, a sack of nails, all ripe for the picking. He stepped back into the cell and sat on the hay, watched the guard struggle with the reluctant lock.

He shot to his feet, held up his hand. "I can fix that."

The German stared blankly.

He pointed. "I can fix the lock."

The guard shrugged. He strode into the mechanical room, bent over the wooden box and picked up two screwdrivers, a can of oil, and a rag. The guard stood, rifle at the ready.

He took the lock out of the door and cleaned it with a rag, oiled and re-assembled it, then motioned for the guard to try it. The plunger slid smoothly.

The boy nodded but seemed unimpressed. He deposited the tools in a pile, held the blade of the shorter screwdriver and slid the handle up his sleeve, stepped out and plopped onto the straw. The guard trundled past, locked the door to the stairs behind him.

When the stairwell went quiet, David shot to his feet, hurried to the door, unscrewed the housing and slid the lock out. He picked up his ciga-rettes, lit one and laid it on the concrete near the bathroom hallway then scrambled back to the mechanical room. He grabbed the pail and flanged duct, stepped onto the bucket, could just reach the ducts rising out of the furnace. The one left of center on the south side was wet and smelled of disinfectant at the turn. He raised the spare section of duct so that it was parallel to the bathroom window.

His heart sank. Despite its height, the ductwork was between the sky-light and anyone who might walk into the room. It would be far too visi-ble. He stared for a moment, scratched his stubbled face. He'd come too far to abandon the project now, would go as far as he could and work out the remaining problems later. It just might be that he'd have to vent the bathroom into the offices at night and remove the duct each morning.

He placed the flange over the duct, scratched an outline with his finger-nail and returned to the toolbox for the jigsaw. He'd also need something to puncture the duct to start the blade. A nail would do.

A dozen easy taps with the hammer and it penetrated the light metal. He examined the hole, decided it was too small, placed the nail to the side of the first hole, hoping to enlarge it enough to get the jigsaw blade through and raised the hammer, began tapping. The door squeaked at the top of the stairs. He jumped from the bucket, hurried through the door and closed it behind him. Footsteps pounded on the steps. He looked back. The missing bolt hole shone in the dark corner like a spotlight. He pulled again, grabbed the lock, slid it into place, pushed the door to. Keys scraped against the door. He made a quick dash for his cigarette burning outside the bathroom hallway, flicked the ashes and took a drag just as the door swung open. The young guard looked around the room.

"Can I help you, Gefreiter?" His voice shook in the rhythm of his heart slamming against his ribs.

The guard tapped his earlobe. "Klink, klink."

Blood rushed through his ears. Of course. The ductwork carried the sound right into Schneider's office, though he'd assumed everyone had left at this hour. He looked around, motioned for the youngster to follow him as he stepped toward the bathroom. The guard went only to the entry hall, watched from a distance. David picked up the plunger, tapped the pipes above the privy. "No vasser."

The guard shrugged and grinned. German for "tough luck," he guessed. The boy pivoted, stepped back through the door, locked it and mounted the stairs.

Close. He ground the cigarette beneath his heel. He'd been careless, but it wouldn't happen again. He slid the lock out of the hole, opened the door, wiggled it back in place and tightened it. One push and it would be impossible to discern he'd been through. He returned to the hallway, took a breath and pushed the door, lifted the lid to the commode and dropped the screwdriver beside the flapper valve. The guards wouldn't go into the room, much less spend time there looking for contraband.

The skylight was all he had to work by, so working at night was out of the question. What moonlight filtered down the dark, narrow walls wouldn't be adequate, and the project needed to be completed. He rummaged quickly through the tool box, found a pair of tin snips, stepped onto the bucket, slipped the end of the snips into the hole and cut along the faint outline of the flange, held the excised piece and slipped it in his pocket.

*Clicking.* He froze. Vichy Boy's typewriter. His struggled for breath, should have thought of it! Sound traveled equally well in either direction. It just might be more important than any prank so long as he could protect his discovery.

He slipped back into the cell, pushed the door closed, and placed a block of wood on the floor, tapped four small holes in the piece of duct he'd removed. The sheet metal screws would secure it to the flange, create a removable cover.

He eased back into the mechanical room, stood beneath the hole in the duct, began to attach the loose piece of duct to the flange. A door slammed above him, and an angry voice rattled in tinny resonance. *Schneider.* He scrambled to the bucket, put his ear to the hole, heard French, garbled and indistinct.

"If he suspects racial impurity, Heinrich, we won't be spared..." Vichy Boy, his words fading as he paced before the vent. "Heinrich?" How's the boy getting away with calling an officer by his first name? And whose racial impurity?

"Threats are of no use. Élodie could be..." The voice faded.

*Élodie.* His blood curdled. Nicole's friend at university?

"...move her from Düsseldorf, but it doesn't..."

*Stand still, damn you!*

Schneider's voice snarled in metallic rage, the words indecipherable.

"...both want the same thing. Élodie must be kept safe..." Vichy Boy, moving, turning away. "...can't continue to help you pursue an obsession of your passion..."

Was that it? "...continuer à poursuivre une obsession de ton passé..." No. "...continue to help you pursue an obsession from your *past*..." He gripped the sharp edge of the duct. Jagged metal pressed into his flesh. Blood, warm and wet, trickled into his clenched fist.

Could it be that Schneider's obsession was the same as his?

# Chapter XXIV

David shoved his way through the crowd, clawed at the cacophony, pushed against the incessant bass of German. He had to find her, followed her laugh, chimes in the cool air. Her face, head back, her laugh— only for a moment. The crowd moved in, and she was lost beyond the wall of harsh consonance. He lunged, had to get to her. A rifle barrel collided with his skull, brought a pulsing pain.

Laughter. Feet shuffling back, smiles ripe with malice, hands unfolding in presentation. Nicole and Schneider dancing in the center of the room, the leutnant's hands moving up her back, over her breasts, her neck. The kraut held her, pulled her to him, kissed her, and she him. Everyone clapped. He shouted, but the sound was swallowed in a breathless void.

He jolted upright, grabbed air from the milky gray, sought something to hold on to. For a moment, he was back in the cellar waiting for her to come down the stairs. But only for a moment. He smoothed his jacket over the straw and leaned back letting his breath return and his heart still. He trained his eyes above the joists, above anything he could see, fixed his gaze on what was sure.

He reached deep, filled himself with song, a soft, resplendent certainty, listened, waited for the voices outside the white-chipped doors to join the strain. Finally, the peace returned.

Hearing the conversation in the duct had been a gift. That much was sure. But what of the dream? Was that a gift, too? An unwanted revelation, maybe?

There was a connection, something more than coincidence. The way Nicole had referred to Schneider that day in the cellar. She knew the leutnant, had some link to him. Albert knew him, too, knew who she meant when she'd called him Heinrich. She'd been at the University of Munich when Stein was there, had been his student. She'd studied mathematics, the music of the spheres. He smiled. It stood to reason she'd studied physics, too. Élodie, as well. Likely moved in the same circles. But how did Schneider fit in? And was it the same Élodie?

He rolled on the straw, adjusted his jacket, wished for comfort, a clarity he couldn't find. Something had happened. He remembered the conversations, the warm days with Nicole, her telling how her friends had become involved in resistance movements against the Reich, some disappearing, some executed. But what had happened to Élodie? "Gone in the night" was all she'd said. Whatever it was, the memory of it had brought tears to her eyes. God, those eyes!

She'd been in love. He clenched his hands, thought of Schneider. At least she thought she was in love. It was actually his ideas she'd been taken with. So which of the leutnant's ideas would she have been drawn to? It didn't seem to fit.

If Schneider was at the university when his friends became involved in resisting the Reich, maybe the Luftwaffe prodigy had betrayed them. He rubbed his face, wished for a shower. It seemed unlikely Schneider had played the Judas. He certainly hadn't given Élodie over to the Nazis. Vichy Boy said they both wanted her safe, were worried that someone would discover her racial impurity, said he knew they wouldn't be spared. *They* wouldn't be spared. It was *their* racial impurity.

He took a deep breath, tried to slow his thoughts. So maybe it wasn't Vichy Boy's and Schneider's racial impurity. Maybe it was Vichy Boy's and *Élodie's*. But if Vichy Boy and Élodie were Jewish and Schneider wanted her protected, then he cared what happened to her. Was he using his position to protect her? A really dangerous thing for him to do. So he cared a lot. If so, Élodie leaving the university in the night might have nothing to do with her being pursued. Perhaps she'd left willingly. Maybe Schneider knew something was about to happen, had protected her from it.

David breathed deep, felt the tension in his back begin to ease. It just might be that there was nothing between Schneider and Nicole, the dream a creation of his worst fears. Still, something in her silent exchange with

Gerhardt bothered him. They both had some history with the blue-eyed Lothario.

He released the fear, felt the Presence cradle him. There was so much he couldn't know, more than he could carry. He closed his eyes and surrendered to the peace.

* * *

A hard blow took his breath. David came instantly awake, rolled to his knees and out of the path of the returning boot.

"Weasel." He grunted, released a short pant, pain radiating from his ribs. "Thought you'd crawled back under your rock."

"Nein! Nicht reden!"

"And a happy 'Nicht reden' to you." The rifle barrel slammed into his nose. His eyes watered, blurred his vision. He blinked, saw Wiesel's withdrawing rifle. He smiled, tears spilling on his cheeks. "You're scared to death of me, aren't you, Weasel?"

"Ruhe!" The boy clenched his teeth, displayed the repulsive rictus.

"Now that's a face only a mother could love." He coughed, blood trickling down his throat.

Wiesel snarled, drew back the rifle butt.

He rolled out of range, vowed that if a skull were smashed, it wouldn't be his.

"Halt!"

Wiesel froze, his face a chalky white. Schneider approached him from the doorway, his teeth bared in the pale light. The leutnant began a slow growl, churned words that grew into a crescendo, prattled on until whatever seething oaths he uttered had lost their fire and pointed to the staircase. Wiesel ran to the door and up the stairs.

David struggled to his feet, held his side. "You do have a way with words, Herr Leutnant."

Schneider put his hand to his chin. "Are you all right, Lieutenant?"

He nodded, thought of the dream, all he'd struggled with before sleep took him, hoped he'd reached the right conclusions. "Yeah. So what did you tell him?"

"I shamed him, told him he had disgraced the Reich with his cowardice showing the prisoner how intimidated he was, sneaking up on him in his sleep." He chuckled. "And I told him what you said."

So he'd been listening. "Seems I owe you, again. Unless, of course, you had this staged." He tried to read the blue eyes in the uneven glow.

"Not at all." Schneider removed the charge with a wave of his hand. "I merely thought it best to follow young Wiesel to see exactly what was happening here."

He grinned. Things just might be working out. "You saw him wake me?"

The leutnant turned, marched to the corner and retrieved two cups beside the door. "I sent him with soup, then followed to see what happened. He seemed to have an idea you were asleep. He knows he's been discovered, now. I've brought you a little something to supplement the soup." He extracted from his jacket a large, plump sausage wrapped in waxed paper and an apple.

"Ah, thank you, Herr Leutnant." David took a bite, filled his cheek with the seasoned meat. He waved an open palm over the straw. "Pull up a chair."

Schneider sat unceremoniously. "All right, my friend, it is time for us to talk."

He stared at the sausage. "And what would you like to talk about, Herr Leutnant?"

"Have you thought any more about our conversation?"

"I've thought about it." He nodded, took another bite.

"Good. You have, I assume, some information for me."

"I suppose you could say that." He examined the sausage, took his time.

"Let's hear it, then."

"Where to start?" He looked at the ceiling, chewed, tried to keep the food away from his sore teeth. "Well, first, you should be better informed."

The leutnant laughed, waved his hand in the stale air. "How kind of you to be concerned with my education. Please, inform me."

"You've greatly misjudged the Resistance, I'm afraid."

"Oh, have I?" Schneider dropped his head, the bobbing of his shoulders scarcely perceptible.

David spooned up soup, made the leutnant wait. "Very much so. In the first place, their handling of downed pilots, it seemed to me, wasn't a matter of priority. Except, of course, for Madeline. Perhaps that's why the collection system you mentioned is so ineffective." He shook his head. "Quite honestly, she deserves more help than she receives."

"I see." Schneider grinned, circled his hand again. "Please, do go on."

"Well, most of their work is intelligence, as I'm sure you know." He continued to eat, tried to remember the points he'd rehearsed.

"And why would you be telling me this?"

He shrugged. "As it happens, in my short stay with them, in one of the holes they shuttled us to, they were compiling information on local interrogation officers. They had collected a great deal for use at the proper time."

"Had they?"

The leutnant was all ears, the derision an act. He was sure of it, waited before answering. "Your first name. Is it 'Heinrich' by any chance?"

Schneider was quiet for a moment. "You could have seen that in my office."

He shrugged. "I suppose I could have, though I didn't." He took another bite of sausage. "This is quite good. What's it called?"

"Braunschweiger. Please go on with your story. Is that all there is?"

He turned, met the German head-on. "Oh no! Not by a long shot. Of course, this was probably another Heinrich Schneider. The one they had information on had a girlfriend. Do you have a girlfriend, Heinrich?"

Schneider plucked a piece of straw from his trousers and tossed it aside. "A most perspicacious guess, Lieutenant. Of course, it is not unusual for single officers to have an interest in young women."

"True, but there was something unique about this one."

The leutnant's hands bounced in silent rhythm, fingertip to fingertip. "Is that so?"

He looked up from the crumpled waxed paper, held the leutnant's gaze. "Seems she was Jewish. Élodie, I believe her name was. This particular Heinrich Schneider was keeping her in hiding, hoping the High Command wouldn't find out. A very unhealthy thing to do, I gathered."

Schneider stilled his hands, returned the stare, said nothing.

David tossed the last bite of sausage into his mouth and picked up the apple, rubbed it on his flight suit.

"And what benefit do you think this information is to me?" Schneider's voice was strained.

He chewed for a moment, sipped from the water cup. "Since I'm sure this is another Schneider entirely, probably none. But if you were the right Leutnant Schneider, it would be worth a great deal to you. After all, if that Leutnant Schneider were to pick up some of the wrong individuals, it could mean he would be exposed. Or worse."

Schneider's chin rose. "Worse? What do you mean?"

"Well, suppose that Leutnant Schneider were to become zealous in his prosecution of patriotic Belgians— those who had this information. There would almost certainly be reprisals." He bit into the apple, suppressed the flinch from his sore teeth.

The leutnant threw his head back, affected an assurance that clearly wasn't there. "What kind of reprisals?"

"One can only imagine. But I do know this. They were afraid this Leutnant Schneider might move his Jewish lover. The fears were probably unfounded, but the Resistance had considered it serious enough to put her under surveillance. Who knows what these men watching her might do if her Luftwaffe lover were known to be responsible for the death of one of their friends?"

The German rose, squared his shoulders. "So what are you suggesting this Leutnant Schneider do?"

"Me? Oh, I don't know much about this cloak and dagger business, but if this group is causing him no real problem, I think it might be best to let sleeping dogs lie. Don't you agree?" He bit into the apple again, wiped his mouth with the back of his hand.

Schneider clasped his hands behind his back. "And where did you say this other Leutnant Schneider was keeping this woman?"

"I don't believe I said." He waved his hand, imitated Schneider's ridicule. "Somewhere deep in Germany."

The leutnant's smile returned. He rocked onto his toes, settled back onto his heels. "And you're telling me that this little band of hellions has members in Germany?"

"Not at all. I never told you they were a little band. But, yes, they are apparently quite active in Germany. Responsible for a great many things— sabotage, guiding bomb strikes, assassinations. They even have a misin-formation division. Seems they're quite active within the Abwehr." He glanced at the apple, pretended not to see the leutnant wince.

The German frowned. "We'll talk more about this later, Lieutenant. I have a great deal of work to do."

He smiled. "No rest for the wicked, aye Herr Leutnant?"

"Tomorrow, Lieutenant. In the meantime, do give your imagination a rest, will you?" Schneider stepped to the door, reached for the handle.

He snapped his fingers. "I remember, now! It's Düsseldorf!" He took another bite of apple.

"What?" The door banged against the wall. Schneider turned, froze, his mouth open, his skin paler in the gray.

"I just remembered. This other Leutnant Schneider, he's keeping his Jewish mistress in Düsseldorf."

The swinging door broke Schneider's stare.


David finished the apple, lay back in the straw. He was no longer thirsty, his stomach was full, and he had prospects for a good night's sleep. Still, the nagging lack of ease haunted him. So far as he could tell, his de-ceptions were working. He may have been doing it for the right reasons, as Nicole had said, but he had a growing distaste for it all. He'd seen Schnei-der's face, knew the fear, the responsibility for putting Élodie in danger. It was likely no different than what he felt putting Nicole in danger. But there was no joy in being the one to impose justice, if that's what this was.

Justice wasn't a thing he'd ever been comfortable with. It was, in fact, part of what had kept him at arm's length from God most of his life, part of the anger he'd always carried. Could it be that God's justice brought no joy, that it was administered with no satisfaction, that the Almighty's re-gret at allowing pain came with as much disinclination as he now felt? He wished for Nicole, for Bear, for Albert, whose wisdom would never again be shared on earth. Most of all, he wished for Jesse's Bible.

\* \* \*

Morning came quickly. David drank the remainder of the soup, felt a slight skim of grease beneath his tongue, set the empty cup in the straw. He'd saved it, knowing he'd likely be thirsty before the guard showed up. He leaned back, heard the sound of keys in the door only a moment before it flew open.

"On your feet, Lieutenant."

He stood. "Good morning to you, too, Herr Leutnant."

Schneider's face was as pale as ash. "We're going for a walk."

"Good. A morning constitutional. Most salubrious."

The leutnant pulled a piece of paper from his pocket, held out his pen. "Sign it."

"Not another easy payment plan, is it? I'd rather not make any long-term commitments. I don't plan to be in the country that long." He recognized the familiar form, noted that it hadn't been dated and scratched his name.

Schneider stepped toward the stairs, a pistol hanging from his belt, motioned for him to follow. He said nothing as they exited the building and walked across the grounds. The two approached the gate, David in the lead. The leutnant spoke with the guard, offered him the carbon copy of the form. They were waved out onto the road. David set the pace, marched toward the crest of the hill where they'd spoken before.

"We will talk here, Lieutenant."

He turned, offered a shaky grin. "Shoot."

Schneider stood, his face drawn, his right hand resting his Walther. "I have considered that, but there is much I want to know first."

He wiped his hands against his suit. "Such as?"

"Such as how you gained the information you gave me yesterday."

"I told you. When we were shuttled into one of the billets—"

"Yes, yes. What I'm asking is why these hellions would share this information with you. What would they hope to gain by it?"

He was ready, had expected the question earlier. "Can't you guess?"

The muscles worked in Schneider's jaw. "I'm not here to guess, Lieutenant. I'm here for answers." With some deliberation, the leutnant pulled his pistol from his holster and pointed it at David's head. "Why would the Resistance share this information with someone in imminent danger of being captured? Or shot?"

He straightened. It was time for his ace card. "As you apparently suspect, they attempted to recruit me. They want closer ties to Allied Command, more communication with MI5. 'Coordinated efforts' was their term."

Schneider's eyes burned with rage. "Then you are a spy."

He raised his chin, met the leutnant's stare, pleased with the calm that had taken him. "What about Élodie? If I'm shot, I can guarantee reprisals. And you are in no position to ask the Gestapo to protect her."

Schneider's chin trembled. "I don't believe you."

"I think you do believe me. Otherwise, I'd be dead. How could I know if the partisans hadn't taken me into their confidence?"

"And they told you this on the off chance that I would interrogate you if captured?"

He forced a firmness into his voice. "You weren't the only one I was given information on. You were included because, as a flyer, I would be under your jurisdiction if apprehended in this district."

"And who else were you prepared for? Give me their names."

He swallowed, searched his memory. "There's a hauptman, Wehrmacht, that takes quite a fancy to little Belgian boys, then disposes of them discreetly."

"Nonsense!" Schneider was indignant.

He smiled. Schneider truly was a lone sheep in a pack of wolves. "Schmidt. First name Gerhardt. Check it out. When you find I'm right, I'll consider giving you another."

"All right, Lieutenant, but I am not finished with you." Schneider lowered his pistol, turned and began to walk back toward the gate.

"Herr Leutnant." He stood, refused to move. "You guessed correctly the other day that I was in love with Madeline. Nicole, as you called her. Just remember, you pose as much threat to her as I do to Élodie. There is no difference."

Schneider wheeled, his lips pinched. "There *is* a difference! I am not a spy. I am a soldier. This is my duty. You have brought a non-combatant, an innocent into a battle she has no part in."

He stepped forward, stopped a few feet from the leutnant, a holy fury squelching his fear. "You self-righteous— In the name of duty you overrun

298

peaceful peoples, kill innocent women and children because they're racially inferior. When they have the audacity to resist, you call them spies so they will be exempt from your military code of conduct. Then you shoot them like dogs. Or worse. And you accuse me of being a spy because I recognize the injustice of it. You, in love with a Jew and unwilling to confront men who would abuse her, kill her because they deem her defective."

He edged closer, fought to restrain himself, the fear of what he might say pushing at his need to have it said. "Is she, Heinrich? Is your Élodie human vermin? If not, then why in hell are you fighting for a pack of jackals willing to inflict this suffering? And all because of their hatred for the woman you love. You're no man of honor! You're no man at all!"

Schneider stiffened. "She is not a Jew! Her grandfather, perhaps, but she is not."

"Does that make her a quarter vermin, Herr Leutnant? What's the Party doctrine on that? How are you supposed to view her? Are you sure her eyes are blue enough? Her skin fair enough? How much vermin blood before she is no longer human?"

Schneider's eyes blazed. The leutnant wheeled, motioned for him to follow.

He resisted, held his ground. "You know this woman, Herr Leutnant. It appears you love her. You know those are lies the Party has told about her, about those tainted with Jewish blood, like Armand, the man you murdered. A good man. A brilliant man. Still you are willing to die, to kill to defend those lies. What kind of man does that make you, Herr Leutnant?"

Schneider spun about, drove clouds of rage into the morning cool. "I did not have your friend shot. No one knew. He refused to stop. The guards were under orders."

He had slipped beyond fear, quivered with rage. "He was going nowhere. His arms were spread in surrender. And you were there, weren't you? You could have stopped it. You could have saved a good man's life."

The leutnant looked away, squared his shoulders. "Only at the expense of my own. No one could ask that."

"I could."

# Chapter XXV

David turned on his side, the heavy stems scoring his shoulders and waist. How could Schneider believe for a moment he was justified? Of course, *he'd* thought himself justified. And been wrong. He closed his eyes, saw the black Walther trembling in the frigid air. Where had the courage to stand up to the leutnant come from, the certainty greater than death?

He rolled onto his back, laced his hands behind his head and stared at the floor joists. His heart had changed. There was nothing theoretical about it. He'd known Schneider could pull that trigger, and it hadn't mattered. Not that he *wanted* to die. But the grave was no longer a thing of horror. If his body were left rotting in some field or hanging from a light pole, he was at peace. The prospect of being a nameless face swelling in putrefaction and mud with no one to mourn his passing had lost its sting. His life would never be abnegated in namelessness. He was known to God.

Images of Nicole and Dancer drifted in the silence, brought a soft ache. He'd known love. And beauty. His life hadn't been for nothing. Especially if he could keep her from dying.

Keys clattered in the lock. He tensed, looked up from where he lay. The door opened, the movement incorporeal, a shadow within a veil. *Schneider*. His mouth went dry. He gazed into the face, ashen white in the shadows, and let the silence lengthen.

Schneider took a breath, stepped forward. "All right, Lieutenant. We have an agreement. You have your job, and I have mine. We can detest each other, but we are forced into this contract none the less."

He breathed deep, the pounding in his chest quieting, looked straight into the leutnant's eyes. "I don't detest you, Herr Leutnant."

The German waved the words away. "This is the situation. I am unwilling to allow you to leave my jurisdiction. If anything should happen to Élodie, I want to be there to see you hang. However, it is impossible for me to hold you here for more than twenty-one days. Therefore, I am requesting that you be sent directly to a stalag and circumvent Dulag Luft. I will ask for a transfer to that same stalag. It is not a frequent request for an interrogation officer. I am certain it will be granted. You will be under my purview until the war is over. Or until you die. Is that acceptable to you?"

"Does it matter?"

Schneider raised his chin, smiled grayly. "I believe I can have you reunited with most of your remaining crew."

An act of kindness. He picked up a stem, rolled it between his fingers. Schneider was circumventing normal interrogations, following him, would continue to communicate with him. It might appear to the rest of the prisoners that he'd broken, was feeding the Germans information. He tossed the stem away, brushed his fingers on his flight suit. "If you bring suspicion on me, Herr Leutnant, you may cause contacts with the Underground to be broken. It would make it impossible for me to ensure Élodie's safety."

Schneider stiffened. "Then I would be unable to keep Nicole from being investigated. She would, of course, be found. And hanged."

An icy jolt shot down his neck and back. He wanted to pull the Kraut's heart from his throat, but something held him silent. He'd made his point. His problem would be keeping Élodie safe. He didn't know if it would even be possible to make contact with the Resistance from a stalag.

A slight twitch played along the leutnant's cheek as he rocked onto his toes, turned, marched through the door and pulled it shut. He caught his breath when the door closed at the top of the stairs, slipped quietly into the bathroom, retrieved the screwdriver he'd hidden in the commode tank and marched in the dingy light toward the door of the mechanical room.

The lock slid easily from the hole. In seconds, he'd removed the plate he'd installed on the duct and stepped down from the bucket. The last time sound had been detectable from the doorway. He moved everything in place so that he could be out quickly, stood in the door, rested his back against the frame. Nothing, either from the stairs or the duct.

He closed his eyes. Minutes drained into hours. All was motionless, save his thoughts careening one upon the other, chasing shadows, hopes, doubts. Things were out of control. At least, they were out of his control.

He prayed for Nicole, for her to have a full life. He asked to be a part of it, if possible. If not, he was grateful for the part he'd shared.

Clacking. Vichy Boy was in the outer office. He edged toward the duct, heard the filing cabinet open and close, the scrape of heels on the floor, but not a single word. He sat on the bucket, waited.

A door squeaked. He rose, stepped onto the bucket and placed his ear to the open duct.

"Bon matin, Henri." A woman, her voice clear, speaking over the desk and toward the vent, most likely.

"Bonjour, cheri." Vichy Boy, distracted, slow to respond.

"Jules has taken ill, after you left this morning. I think all this... seeing our concern. His nerves, perhaps. He worries so, that little one. Like his mother." Her French was fluid. Belgian.

"We're all frightened, Celeste. I am no less worried than you." Vichy Boy paused. "You left him with grand-mère?" The voice was distant, speaking away from the vent. David leaned closer, put his ear inside the duct. "...good reason."

"What do you mean?" Celeste's voice full of fear.

"Apparently, Heinrich is..." He strained forward. The bucket tilted, and he jerked back. "...requested a transfer to Stalag 17b."

"He has told you this?"

"The paperwork was on the desk when I arrived. It is senseless. Just yesterday he requested several radio interceptions from the 381$^{st}$ be transcribed. Why would Heinrich do all that if he were going somewhere else? He can't just leave us here."

"Mon Dieu!" Celeste's words, barely audible. "Surely he's not leaving Élodie."

"Heinrich is a good man. He would never do anything to endanger her. Or us."

"Shouldn't you speak with Élodie?"

"And how do you propose—"

302

A door opened. Boot heels clacked, and von Felder snapped something in German. Celeste responded timidly. The door closed. Another bark from von Felder. David fought for breath, replaced the cover, slid the lock back into place and tightened the screws. His mind churned. *Intercepted radio transmissions from the 381ˢᵗ*. So that was it. The German interrogators were thought to be minor gods by the Americans for what they were able to pry from the downed pilots and crews. It just could be that their real source of information was intercepted radio transmissions. He remembered exchanges between Dougan and fighter pilots describing everything from positions to known gun emplacements. It was no wonder decoy missions had failed to draw fighters away from the big ones.

And Schneider's questions the night they were captured. All about their mission and crew. The muscles in his neck grew taut. He placed his foot on the edge of the commode, lifted the top onto his leg and slid the screwdriver behind the dry flapper valve. Ito hadn't broken. Schneider had gleaned the information from the transmissions. The psychological value of that was immense. Undoubtedly, it broke men down, persuaded them to give even more, had even caused him to doubt his friends. If only he could get this information back to Allied Command. He *had* to make contact with the Resistance.

He sat on the hay, hungry, thirsty, could have gotten water from the spigot in the mechanical room, but the pipes carried noise. Someone might figure out he was getting in. His secret had to remain just that.

Footsteps tapped along the stairs. The Weasel, most likely. He sat up, didn't want to give the boy a chance to exact revenge. Schneider wouldn't be apt to come to his rescue this time.

The door squeaked open. He felt the stare before he saw the face. "Herr Leutnant."

"Lieutenant." Von Felder looked from side to side, stared into the shadows, sat two tins on the concrete, stood stiff and unnatural and smiled. It had to be a prodigious effort.

He rose, stepped toward the canisters. "May I?" He eyed the leutnant, too wary to turn his back.

"Of course."

He drank the water in a few gulps, then the soup. "Danke."

"Lieutenant, you are quite aware, I am sure, that there exists between Leutnant Schneider and myself a difference of approaches."

He nodded, noted they were the same words Schneider used.

"You are my enemy, not my comrade." Von Felder tucked his chin.

He remained silent, waited.

"Nevertheless, I believe we can treat each other with respect."

"I suppose so." He forced the words, wished he could show Blondie just how little respect he had for him.

"I am quite sure that in your military, you offer no deference to a traitor. Neither do I. On this point, I am certain we are in agreement."

And he was certain he smelled something.

Von Felder scowled, had apparently expected a response. "I believe Leutnant Schneider is a traitor. Furthermore, I believe that you have evidence of this. I can assure you that whatever he has told you, he is unable to secure for you release from a stalag."

He held his tongue, watched the leutnant's scowl deepen.

"Whatever he has promised you, he will not be able to fulfill since it is likely he will soon be shot. If, however, you should wish to present any information that would be of use in our investigation, I can assure you that we will see to your being sent to a place where more food and better conditions exist."

*Ridgewell would be nice.* He straightened, raised his chin. "Leutnant Schneider has said nothing to me that would indicate that he is a traitor. If he does, and if you can demonstrate to me that you are sincere in your offer to provide food, water, a shower perhaps, I would be most happy to apprise you of anything he tells me."

Von Felder appeared confused. After a moment, he smiled. "I shall have another tin of water and soup brought to you." He pivoted and stepped through the door.

David eased back onto the hay. The subterfuge was becoming difficult to keep straight. He'd just been asked to betray Schneider. But Blondie was a true believer. Hardly a desirable collaborator in this game. Schneider, on the other hand, was a man he knew too well. The leutnant was who *he'd* been, just in a different place. Schneider clung to ideas he believed to be workable if not true, but which tugged at his conscience. What was truth, after all? He knew the struggle, understood Schneider's being torn, his desire to protect Élodie. The leutnant was wrestling with his loyalties. But was he any less dangerous than von Felder?

He shifted on the straw, his discomfort growing. He hadn't suffered with this sort of indecision since his experience in the well. Something wasn't right. He rolled, turned his thoughts upward, pleaded wordlessly.

He sat up, sucked in the stale air. How likely was it that Blondie would come to him to ferret out a traitor? Von Felder had said it himself— he was the enemy. If Herr Blue Eyes were defecting, he would be the most obvious co-conspirator. So could von Felder's contempt for Schneider be great enough to urge him to take that chance? Or was Blondie hoping he might tell Schneider of the offer, and Schneider would, in turn, confront von Felder. *That* would prove collusion between Schneider and a prisoner. But it would mean both he and Schneider would have to fall for von Felder's bluff. Again, not likely.

There was another possibility. It could be von Felder was acting at Schneider's request. Herr Blue Eyes just might want to know if he would play the game two ways, team up with von Felder, maybe. He rubbed at the dull ache in his temples. Schneider certainly wouldn't let von Felder in on his relationship with Élodie or the agreement the two of them had reached. Unless von Felder had been playing a role the whole time. In that case, the two Leutnants might have been staging their feud for his benefit. Working him. Certainly possible. Still, the animosity seemed genuine.

He shivered at the immensity of the stakes, the precariousness of his choices. If von Felder was the martinet he appeared, Schneider was taking a huge chance by giving him the opportunity to reveal what he knew about Élodie. Likely, Schneider was betting his fear for Nicole would be reason enough to keep him quiet. But it was risky.

He lay back, stretched. The game was becoming treacherous. He looked above the floor joists, sent up a silent plea and began to work with an idea.

\* \* \*

The sound of the door woke him. It swung open revealing the second young guard, rifle slung over his shoulder. He rose and nodded. The boy nodded back, pointed to the stairs.

"Leutnant Schneider's office?"

"Ja."

David yawned, marched up the stairs, down the hallway, opening doors without intervention. Henri was busy typing, raised his head when they entered, offered a glance from bloodshot eyes then rose and went into the Leutnant's office. The flowing sibilance of his French and the rough irregularity of Schneider's responses were stifled by the door. Henri returned a minute later, nodded for him to go in.

Schneider glanced up, extended a hand toward the chair then waited until Henri closed the door. "Lieutenant, special arrangements are being made for your transfer to Stalag 17b near Krems, Austria. I am currently requesting a transfer and should be following you in a few weeks. In that time, I would expect that you will become reacquainted with your old friends." He paused, stared. "I'm sure you will have a great deal to discuss."

He nodded his understanding. Schneider might not say anything directly, even in the inner sanctum, but it was clear. He was being given time to make contact with the partisans.

"I am having the surviving members of your crew sent there. The 381st has come to be a very special group to me. As have you, Lieutenant." Schneider stared in threat.

"I'm flattered, Herr Leutnant."

Schneider shuffled papers. "I have some things for you to fill out, forms supplied by the Red Cross. They will notify your next of kin that you are alive, provided you cooperate. You realize, of course, that sometimes paperwork takes time to process." His chin rose, and he offered a burning stare. "Next of kin. That would be your wife, I believe."

He hid his shame, returned the stare. "I'd prefer it be sent to my father."

"Unless you are divorced, Lieutenant, that will not be allowed." Schneider fixed his eyes, expectant. "Are you?"

What business was it of his? "Delores Faye Dremmer. Faye, with an 'e'."

"Thank you, Lieutenant. I'm aware of the spelling." Schneider filled out the upper section of the form and handed it over.

He recognized it from training, filled in the requisite blanks and signed it. "Will you be coming by to offer your regards before I leave?"

Schneider returned to his papers. "I believe you are quite aware of my regard for you."

He grinned, felt strangely exultant at the leutnant's contempt.

Schneider signed a form, looked up. "You may go, Lieutenant. I'll have the guard escort you to your cell. There will be no more work detail. You have not earned that privilege."

"You might reconsider. It's hard to find good help these days." He jerked his head toward the door. The Leutnant made no response.

He stepped into the outer office, exchanged a glance with Henri, and crumpled into a chair butted against the wall. He watched the young Frenchman for a moment— if that's what he was— then let his eyes close. Perhaps the boy was Belgian after all, the Parisian accent an affectation. Or maybe Henri had spent time in France, actually cultivated the ability to speak through his nose. One thing was certain: the clerk knew English. He was translating the 381$^{st}$'s radio transmissions. Had to be proficient in the language.

The door squeaked open. Footsteps. Light, timid. He opened his eyes to see a young woman, her hair bound tightly beneath a babushka. Slight, pretty, her dark eyes darted from him to Henri.

The clerk stopped typing, smiled. "Bonjour, Celeste."

"I came only—" She glanced at him.

"It's all right. He is an American. He doesn't understand. I'm happy you came." Henri's face grew soft, his French, too.

"I wanted you to know that Jules is better. He's eaten."

Henri nodded again, smiled. "Good." The clerk lowered his voice to a bare whisper. "He's a fighter, that one. A true Devillier, yes?"

*Devillier.* Élodie's name! A current prickled along his spine, and the hairs on his neck stood up. That was the connection, why both Schneider and Henri wanted the same thing for her, why *their* racial impurity was a problem. It explained so many things— Henri's working in Schneider's office, his calling the leutnant by his first name. They were brothers-in-law, or something close.

"I'll go. I thought you'd want to know." Celeste backed toward the door.

"Merci, Celeste." Henri smiled, glanced at him, the little man's eyes filled with pain, then turned back to his typewriter.

The door closed. David tensed, fought a mounting urgency he couldn't restrain, rose, stared at the hapless clerk. Henri rolled his chair away from the typewriter and stood, ready to bolt.

He put his finger to his lips, moved between the frightened clerk and Schneider's door, used the desk to box him in. "We have to talk, Henri. For the sake of your family, we must talk now."

* * *

Time moved more slowly in the half-light of his cell. It was settled, his course of action set. David placed his head between his knees, stretched his neck and back. He hadn't given much thought to his leg in the last few days. Amazing. He'd been given his youth back and had so quickly forgotten. To be sure, there was still some soreness around the wound, but nothing like what he would have expected. And to be able to walk...

He thought of Bear, offered a quick prayer for his recovery. It would be good to see him again. He had so much to tell him, had already decided to take him into the scheme, to seek his counsel. And he needed help making contact with the Resistance, though this end was covered. At least, he hoped it was. Would making contact from the camp be possible? He'd feared Schneider discovering his ruse, was haunted by it. Should the Leutnant find out, he would lose any power he had, and any reticence Schneider might possess at having Nicole and Charles and Gaston ferreted out and hung. Or him, for that matter.

He stiffened at footsteps on the stairs. The door opened and Schneider blinked, his eyes adjusting to the gray. "You wanted something?"

Herr Blue Eyes had caught the signal. "Did you know I had a visitor earlier?"

"A visitor? Who was it?"

He held back a smile. The leutnant always answered with a question when he was hiding something. He stood, met the blue eyes. "Von Felder. Are you really going to be shot for treason? If so, I'm dealing with the wrong man."

Schneider laughed. "I'm sure he wishes so. But, no, I am not facing execution."

He breathed deep, listened for more than was offered. "You're not surprised he said so?"

The Leutnant's eyes twinkled in the gray. "Not at all. What did he want?"

"Your head on a platter. Or mine. I'm not sure which."

"Both would be acceptable, I'm sure. How did he plan to get them there?"

He waited, searched the German's face. "Wanted to know if you and I were in cahoots. Said you had no authority to offer me whatever it was you were offering. And since you were about to be hung, he thought I might want to reconsider dealing with you. Said I was working with the wrong man. Promised me a seat next to the gallows with soda and popcorn."

The leutnant grinned. "The right man would be him, I suppose?"

"Of course. And he was extremely subtle about it."

Schneider lowered his chin, broke the stare. "I can well imagine."

He nodded, convinced now. "Shouldn't require too much imagination."

Schneider's head popped up. "What do you mean, Lieutenant?"

He watched the smile drain. "You sent him, didn't you?"

"What on earth for?"

The Kraut was slick, but he'd been found out. Showed it. "To see what I would tell him. To see if I would honor our agreement, maybe?"

"And risk him learning about—"

"You assumed I wouldn't go that far. I wouldn't endanger Madeline... Nicole. But I could have implicated you without endangering my friends. I could have had you drawn and quartered before you initiated an investigation."

Schneider's smile returned. "Only if you had believed his story. If you suspected that I sent him, you couldn't take that chance."

David felt his triumph reduced to indignation. "What, in God's name, did you have to gain by it?"

Schneider looked down, the muscles working in his jaw. "I could see what I had to work with in you, how capable you were of comprehending the situation. And I could possibly secure von Felder's loyalty or, at least, mitigate his hostility. He needs to be part of this investigation. I offered him an opportunity to do that and perhaps make him an ally."

"You were taking one hell of a chance considering what I might have said."

"You're far too concerned with your secret lover to tell him anything, Lieutenant." Schneider grinned. "By the way, I checked out Gerhardt Schmidt. He will be dealt with." The German turned to leave.

"Herr Leutnant." His heart pounded, his rage at the edge of eruption.

"Yes?"

"Don't test me again. I have no desire to see any harm come to Élodie. So long as Madeline is not harmed in any way, Élodie won't be either. Unless you screw this up."

Schneider's eyes glinted, his jaw steeled. "Élodie will remain safe. This you must understand."

He ignored the threat. "Don't keep me on too short a rein once we reach the stalag, Herr Leutnant. Give me time and opportunity to make contact. Allow me enough rope to conclude my end of the bargain."

Schneider nodded. "So long as I am certain that you can ensure Élodie's safety."

He breathed deep, took his time. "I have little influence over natural disasters, tidal waves, influenza, storm troopers. Short of that, I believe I can offer you assurances."

"You had best do that." Schneider closed the door and mounted the stairs.

He took a deep breath, felt peculiarly clean. He hadn't had access to a shower or even a sponge bath since leaving the wine cellar, had fancied being able to bathe, scrub, and rinse for hours. But no bath could have made him cleaner than he felt at the moment. He was doing the right thing, and he knew it. He leaned back in the straw.

Heavy steps resounded on the stairs. He turned, faced the door as it swung wide.

"Hello, Weasel." He grinned, let the boy know he hadn't been intimidated.

Wiesel pitched a package on the hay.

He glanced, looked back. "For me? You shouldn't have."

"Leutnant Schneider."

Time to let it go. He dipped his head. "Danke."

The boy stared, waited for something, then turned and slammed the door.

David bent low and examined the package. A Red Cross emblem was stamped on the outside. He tore it open, found cans of corned beef and spam, instant coffee, D-bars, powdered milk, salmon, oleo, cheese, liver pâté, raisins, and prunes. He dug through the treasure. More dried fruit, sugar cubes, something at the bottom wrapped in tissue paper. He pulled it out, took it to the entrance of the bathroom.

A Bible. Not a pocket-sized New Testament, but a leather-bound reference Bible in English with both Old and New Testaments. His heart welled until he could no longer read the words. He wasn't sure, but it appeared to be one like Jesse's.

# Chapter XXVI

The air was sharp and thin. It cut at David's face with a serrated edge. He shivered, stared into the blue ice of Schneider's eyes, breathed from the untainted atmosphere. The faint crispness of the pines brought a sudden longing for home. He folded his arms, captured it within his breast and wished beyond all else he could be there with Nicole.

"There's been a change of plans." The leutnant spat the words, the first he'd spoken since leading him onto the road.

*His voice.* He steadied his breath. "What kind of change?"

"I regret to inform you that the Wehrmacht has petitioned Oberstleutnant Schuster to have you remanded to their custody."

Electricity shot down his spine. He worked to rein in the surge of panic. "And Schuster agreed?"

The leutnant looked away. "We are waiting only for written orders."

"The Wehrmacht." An icy chill froze his lungs. "Leutnant von Felder?"

A faint border of white rimmed Schneider's lips. Tiny beads glistened on his cheeks. "No, the feldwebel that arrested you, though I'm quite certain that they are in league. He will take you into custody when the orders come through." Schneider looked back. "Their request is not to execute you, you understand, only to have you turned over for interrogation."

"But a hanging is what they want." His heart pounded in his ears.

The German shifted, stared at the compound. "I will do everything in my power to have you returned to my custody; however, it is not a simple matter."

"And our agreement, Herr Leutnant? How can I protect Élodie from the grave?"

Schneider's face tightened. "And how do you keep me from Nicole?"

"Yes." He nodded, met the leutnant's blue eyes, could think of no reason to hide his thoughts. "How long before you receive written orders?"

"There is no way of knowing that. They could arrive by courier tomorrow, or it could take a week." Schneider rocked forward. "However, I have an arrangement that I believe you will find satisfactory. Under the circumstances."

Maybe there was a way. "I'm listening."

"I propose that you write a letter—"

Air rushed from his lungs. "Something that can be read after I'm dead?"

Schneider looked away. "You said you had contacts. If you do, you can accomplish this."

He grunted. "They didn't supply me with addresses, and I wouldn't be inclined to give them to you if they had."

"You are a resourceful man, Lieutenant. This much I know." The leutnant raised his chin. "You will make contact, write a letter to whomever you must. I will see to it that it is posted in Switzerland or Spain, and that no one else knows of its existence. You will explain that Nicole has been discovered and is in danger." He raised his hand, drew a line in the gelid air. "She must be removed from Belgium and must no longer work with the Resistance. You will also explain that Élodie is to be left alone. You may tell of her relationship to me. That will ensure that I will involve no one else. Not Abwehr and not Gestapo."

He stared into Schneider's face, needed desperately to believe him but didn't want the desperation to push him into a trap. "Let me think about it."

"Don't think too long, Lieutenant."

He fought to clear his head. "How can they execute me, Herr Leutnant? On what grounds? I'm a prisoner of war."

"Some are not concerned with the rules of war, Lieutenant." Schneider pivoted to return, stopped. "Is there anything I can get you?"

He closed his eyes, prayed he was doing the right thing. "I want two envelopes, paper and a pen."

"Two envelopes?"

He swallowed. "If you can get one letter out, you can get two."

Schneider nodded. "I shall bring you paper and a pen. And two envelopes."

He tried to comprehend that he might soon be dead, fought the image of his body writhing as they kicked the chair from beneath him. Facing Schneider's pistol was one thing; facing a hangman was another. He sucked in the bitter air, hoped for a last scent of pine.

He turned, walked ahead of Schneider through the gates of the compound, waited then followed him to the cellar. The leutnant deposited him at his cell without a word, stared into the darkness and avoided his eyes.

He shook himself, labored to direct his energies into completing what needed to be done, into protecting Nicole and writing Jesse, putting his heart at rest.

Schneider returned a short time later with several sheets of thin paper, two envelopes and a pen. The German stared, the contempt gone from his eyes. "I'm sorry, Lieutenant."

"It's not your fault, Herr Leutnant."

"Please, call me Heinrich."

He felt a sudden chill. "We're not friends, Herr Leutnant."

Schneider's expression was unreadable, the light inexact, but he appeared to smile. "Are you certain of that, Lieutenant? Friends do not always agree."

* * *

The first letter came easily. Albert and Nicole had spoken extensively about WIM being supported by British MI5. His best bet was to address the letter to MI5, ask them to forward the information through appropriate channels, and to refer to no one but the principals by name. David laid the paper on his open Bible and braced it against his thigh, wrote exactly what Schneider had said, explained that an agreement had been reached, that operative Nicole Serat was under investigation, was in imminent danger, and should be taken out of the country, removed from any active resistance to Nazi occupation. When Schneider read the letter, he would learn nothing new. The pen skidded across the paper, the scraping amplified in the stillness. He paused, gathered his thoughts.

Addressing the letter to MI5 would add credibility to his earlier claims that the Resistance group reached into Germany. He resumed writing, asked that surveillance of Élodie Devellier in Düsseldorf be curtailed. Her safety, he wrote, should be ensured while WIM operative, Nicole Serat, was extricated from the country. He added that Serat's associates were also in grave danger and asked that provision be made for them. He offered assurances that Miss Devellier had no Nazi sympathies despite her connections to Luftwaffe Interrogator Leutnant Heinrich Schneider and stated that Schneider was a party to the agreement allowing Serat's escape. He smiled. Little doubt heads would be scratched in London. MI5 would have no idea who the leutnant was, much less his Jewish lover. Until they read his letter.

He stopped. It seemed unlikely he would have another chance to keep his promise to Nicole, so he added a postscript asking that Nicole's aunt, Claudette LeBec in Antwerp, be removed from Belgium as well since it was probable Abwehr would torture her to gain access to Nicole or her fellow operatives.

Jesse's letter. He put pen to paper, pulled it back. So much needed to be said, and he had no words to hold it. What he had to give his father couldn't heal all that had gone before, and he had no desire to increase the old man's burden. He frowned, wrote that he had been captured, that he was being held by the Germans and was being treated well. He was at a loss for anything further. But he needed to say more. Jesse owed him. Even now he ached for what his father hadn't provided, and even now he seethed.

He brushed his hand over his eyes. What was it that angered him? What had Jesse failed to give him that filled him with such rage, pushed him to spend his life fighting the old man's ways, forsaking pleasure and peace and even God to oppose him? He set pen and paper aside. Whatever it was, he vowed to be rid of it, to face his death in peace.

He lay back and prayed. The peace he'd come to expect eluded him. Splashes of memory emerged. He closed his eyes, saw Jesse towering above him, imperious and strong, laughing as he struggled at the keys of his mother's piano, speaking to the darkness beyond his seeing, toward the warm comfort of her hand on his shoulder.

"What is this? What kind of little girl are you raising him to be?"

The shame washed over him afresh. Another memory played. He had built a doghouse from the remnants of Jesse's construction of the tack shed, had waited for hours in front of the finished structure. He'd worked in secret, had anticipated Jesse's approval for days, his edifice a smaller rendition of his father's. When the old man came, his offering leaned in the shadows of the greater opus.

Jesse looked, shook his head. "You're going to spoil that dog, make him good for nothing but getting under your feet. And look at the lumber you've wasted! A whipping is what you need."

David's pulse pounded, and he worked to push the rage away, but another image came, then another. Always his offering had been too small, not having the sweet savor he'd intended, never sufficient to please. Until the breaking came. The cow with mastitis, fevered and mean, her calf beside her, wasting away as the cow's udder swelled. She needed to be milked out, stripped of the infected milk, but there was no way to get her to the pens. She wouldn't be driven, had fought even after Jesse roped her. The old man spurred his horse, circled and tripped her, threw a second loop around an extended back leg and backed the horse until both ropes were taut. The cow bellowed and kicked the air. Jesse hollered for him to strip the udder, warned him not to leave a drop in her.

He'd been sitting on Bess, the paint mare Jesse had bought him, had been worried for the calf standing at a distance, knew the same fear and confusion the calf must have felt but saw no way to approach it's mother. He jumped from Bess, his feet heavy with trepidation, tripped, rose and ran toward the cow. She bellowed, shook his insides with her bawl, and he retreated. He caught his breath, edged back and grabbed a teat. A cannon shot from her free hind leg grazed his ear, and he scrambled for safety. Jesse hollered for him to finish the job, but he couldn't force himself back within range of her lightning kick. The old man's horse was lathered, tired, the effort falling apart while he struggled to prove himself of some worth.

He heard a sigh of exasperation, turned to see Jesse pull his rifle from the scabbard and take aim at the calf. He screamed, begged to be shot instead of the calf, but his plea was quenched by the roar of the Winchester. The calf dropped in its tracks, and Jesse slid the rifle into the scabbard and looked him straight in the eyes. "Let this be a lesson to you. If you can't do a man's job when it's time to be done, somebody always pays the price."

"Then you should have shot me! It was me that couldn't do it!" Sobs had stopped his words. He'd caught his breath, tried again. "I could have taken care of him."

Jesse looked at him, shook his head in revulsion. "I doubt it."

His chest constricted, forced tears from his eyes. He vowed that day to never try to please the old man again, to never seek his approval. He'd understood that he'd been born a disappointment, would always be one. So he chose to embrace it. What Jesse did, he despised. What Jesse believed, he rejected. What Jesse held inviolable, he violated.

He stared at the Red Cross parcel, a POW treasure chest. It meant nothing. What good would food do him now? And what good would it do to rekindle his rage?

He sought the Presence and the peace, but it refused him. The cellar was a brass coffin silencing his cries. He called out, and a violent heave emerged, doubled him over with grief. Heavy spasms held him for long minutes, mined his core. They lingered and purged the deep deposits of smoldering rage. He lay exhausted in the hay. Then the peace came.

He prayed again, asked that Jesse's life, whatever was left of it, be made better. A wave came deeper than thought. Regret, this time, and loss, but it wasn't for himself. He struggled to his knees bearing his father's heart, Jesse's fear of his own weakness stirring within his breast, the disgust that tormented him when he saw it reflected in his son. The old man had wanted more for him, had ached for him not to be consumed by fear and self-doubt, had been desperate for him not to give in to them lest they devour him, too.

David shook with throbbing certainty, tears blinding him to all else. He had loved the old man, admired him, feared him and hated him, but he had never known his pain. The impartation exceeded anything he'd learned, and he grieved for the way he'd handled the old man's anger, for not seeing the hurt behind his severity.

From the bowels of the earth itself, he sought absolution. And from the light that shone within, he came to know it had been given. Whether he saw Jesse again or not, all had changed.

317

He rose, edged to the door of the bathroom to capture the last light leaking through the window and put pen to paper.

* * *

David had waited vainly for sleep, the morning now folding dark and cold about him. He'd prayed and read, even found peace except when his mind quieted. When his thoughts stilled, the image returned, his body thrashing above a toppled chair, wire cutting into his neck. He'd always feared choosing something abhorrent, something irrevocable, had brought his worst fear to fruition stumbling into a marriage he couldn't want. Then, when he'd sought his end as a consolation, he learned he wanted life, yearned for it as instinctively as breath.

Still, what he feared now was not so much death as the way it would come, the knowing it was approaching. How much suffering would the Wehrmacht require of him? Would his dying be something as immediate as a bullet to the brain, something as painless as the calf had known? Would they allow him enough rope to break his neck, or force him to strangle slowly?

Light filtered into the bathroom from the skylight above the furnace, birthed the staccato whisper of boots on the stairs. His heart pounded, and he fought for breath, slipped the letters into his Bible and dropped it on the hay.

A light rapping sounded from the door. Who would knock on a cell door? "Yes?"

Keys rattled. The door opened wide before a face appeared.

He caught his breath, calmed. It was odd. He'd been hoping it would be Schneider. "So, have you decided? Are you going to try to save your sister? Or have you come to deliver me to the hangman?"

Henri edged forward, set two containers on the floor, and left the door open behind him.

David stared, pushed the thought away. He'd only be forfeiting her life for his.

"I will not betray Heinrich. He has—" Henri's English was precise, only slightly accented.

"So you'll leave Élodie in danger, under surveillance by her old compatriots, people she's betrayed. You'll let her—"

318

"She betrayed no one! Don't assume you know her allegiances. Or mine."

He felt a familiar fire. "I don't have to assume. The uniform tells me all I need to know."

The little clerk shifted, edged his feet apart. "I will contact the Resistance for you. But I will do nothing to put Heinrich in danger."

He nodded, listened to the blood surge through his ears. "I didn't ask you to. I know the Luftwaffe has been intercepting radio transmissions." He stopped, waited for a response. The little man stood motionless. "You will inform the man I described for you— he goes by the name of Gaston— that the Luftwaffe listens to everything that is transmitted in flight. Air-to-air and ground-to-air. I'm not asking that Leutnant Schneider's name be mentioned. You know where to find Gaston."

Henri nodded. "Yes, I remember. All right."

"You'll tell him that Nicole will soon be contacted, ordered out of the country. Arrangements have been made with MI5. If she fails to receive that order within a couple of weeks, she is to go on her own, take whatever route her compatriots can arrange."

Henri nodded, seemed satisfied. "Élodie would want me to help Nicole. They were—"

He smiled. "They were friends. I know."

"You know nothing." Henri's face narrowed, his mouth pinched tight.

"So tell me. What was between Nicole and your beloved Heinrich? And how did he end up with Élodie?" He wasn't going to die without answers.

"What has that to do with our agreement?" Henri stiffened.

He wanted to laugh. The little clerk's suspicions seemed so trivial in light of an execution. "Maybe nothing. Maybe everything. I want to know."

Henri shrugged, loosened his shoulders as if he were preparing for a race. "I know only what Élodie confided. I was studying in France at the time. I was in Germany only a few days when my sister was forced to leave." He moved his head to the side. "We had perhaps one discussion about it. Apparently, Heinrich had been quite taken with Nicole, but she had other interests. A professor. A Jew."

His legs went limp, his lungs an instant void. "Dr. Stein?"

Henri looked up. "You know of him?"

He rolled his hand, demanded more, dared not speak.

Henri shrugged, looked straight ahead. "Professor Stein took Heinrich under his wing. They were close. Nicole, too, was one of his 'special ones.' And Élodie. But Nicole's feelings were deeper. It seemed to Élodie rather passionate for just a schoolgirl infatuation. Stein's family left Germany during this time. The faculty was under pressure to be rid of him. He was Jewish, you see, and his being there brought considerable pressure. But the university had no reason to fire him, so, when Nicole's affections for the professor became evident, rumors began to spread, most started by Stein's colleagues." Henri looked up, tilted his head as if all were clear. "Heinrich was in love with her and believed himself betrayed by Stein."

"Is that why he had the professor killed?" It was a long shot.

The clerk's mouth worked silently, his head shaking. "No. He wouldn't have."

*Your turn, little man.* "He did. The night before we were captured. In the meadow beyond the causeway."

"That was Stein? Heinrich was there, yes, but those were Wehrmacht troops." Henri dropped his head, blinked. "He was upset. I didn't know why. No one knew. I wondered at his interest in you. You were together, were you not?"

He held his tongue, let the suggestion take root, too wary of the question to answer it. "Heinrich's pursuit of Nicole, is he interested in seeing her hanged or in renewing a lost love?"

Henri looked away, remained silent for a moment. "I don't know." But the little man had wondered. That much was clear. "I had thought, perhaps, he only wanted to warn her." The clerk stirred from his thoughts. "Lieutenant, I'm truly sorry for what has happened, the Wehrmacht demanding custody, I mean. But you must remember that many of us have faced death for a long time. It has caused us to make choices, to do things we wouldn't otherwise do."

He nodded, the fire within burning low. "I'm afraid of dying, every bit as much as you. But I've learned this. When justice trumps evil, or even when it promises to, it makes the heart homesick for somewhere else.

Somewhere better. Like the scent of rain at the end of winter makes you want spring all the more."

The little clerk smiled derisively. "You believe in such things?"

He swept his hand between them, drew it halfway around the cellar. "You believe in *this*? That's your only option."

Henri shook his head, pinched his mouth tighter. "I came to tell you something else. Heinrich is leaving within the hour, driving to Ghent. To Abwehr headquarters. He's petitioning for custody of all downed airmen in his sector, claiming to be close to a major breakthrough in his investigation. He's feigning illness so the Wehrmacht won't know that he has left. He hopes to see the oberstleutnant this evening, perhaps over dinner and wine. He will drive through the night and should be back midmorning tomorrow." The clerk looked around, offered a twisted smile. "Since you believe in such things, you'd best be praying the Wehrmacht doesn't come for you until he returns. And that Abwehr doesn't discover Heinrich's application for transfer before considering his request."

David nodded. "I will." He'd plant one more seed to see if it sprouted. "Henri, tell me. If Leutnant Schneider should choose Nicole over Élodie, what would happen to you?"

The little man looked startled. "He won't. He loves my sister."

"But does he love her more than he loves Nicole?"

# Chapter XXVII

David abandoned his hope for sleep, rolled onto his knees and dropped his head into the hay. He ached from cold and fear, longed for a hot shower. Laughter rose in his gullet, acid and sharp. He coveted a clean body, a body that might soon be rotting in an open grave or left to hang on some light pole. Not that his death should be of any more consequence than his life. Even to the Wehrmacht. His execution would be a symbol of retained power, a precedent leading one step closer to hegemony in some officer's tiny kingdom. Nothing more.

He sucked in the chilled air, his faith dwindling that the flowing peace, the Presence that overwhelmed his darkest apprehensions, would return. He prayed only because there was nothing left to do. His head bent to the floor. A portion of some passage he'd read drifted through the bleak obscurity. "For thou hast girded me with strength unto the battle." If only he had that comfort, countering those who wanted him dead. Even if he lost the fight, he could die in an effort to save himself, escape this paralysis of deliberation.

But perhaps that wasn't the sort of battle he was in. The thought took him, and he couldn't escape it. He rose to his knees, stared into the darkness, saw clearly for the first time in days. His was a battle for hope, for the quiet assurance that had taken him by surprise only to vanish under the threat of death. But if this gentle knowing he'd been granted had no power to stand against death, what good was it? And if the God who'd shown himself real was no greater than the grave, what sort of god was he?

He clenched his fists, resolved not to turn from whatever answer came. A notion surfaced on rough water, began to still. He'd been demanding the

322

One he'd come to know as benefactor and friend to release him from the threat of death in order to prove himself God. He remembered reading in some epistle the list of heroes of faith. None had been spared death, most dying hideously. Had he a right to demand an end more unperturbed than theirs?

His sat on his heels, his legs beneath him. What was his battle, then, and what victory could he hope to gain? He wrapped his jacket around his shoulders, waited for warmth, wished for light to read the lines again that had ushered in the quiet unity. All he could do was try to recall the flow and cadence, but a phrase returned, resonating in the chill. "If I make my bed in She'ol, behold, thou art there." He repeated the words until they bore wings, lifted and carried him across the meadow below the well. The land was sweet with spring in his mind's eye, and he stopped to place a flower where Albert had fallen.

Gerhardt. Professor Stein. Nicole's first love. A man he'd admired. A man who'd owned Nicole's heart before he knew her. Where had this man gone? He looked into the stillness, was touched by the warmth he'd feared might have vanished forever. Albert had gone home, to his family, with perfect trust that he would. It would have been unjust for him not to have. He slid his legs in front of him, lay back into the hay and closed his eyes.

\* \* \*

Dancer stood on the outcropping of rocks, his head jutting into a frigid gust. The horse was free, master of all he surveyed. David stepped onto the open land, his hand outstretched, ambled on a tack that would take him west of the rocks where Dancer stood. He stopped, allowed the horse to choose whether they would meet. The black sniffed the breeze, flinched in recognition, took a considered step and waited. He stood without motion or doubt. Dancer moved close, smelled the breeze and moved again. He smiled, urged the black closer with a gentle coo. The horse stepped up, offered his muzzle. The silken head settled deep and warm against his chest, the hot breath tinged with sage, then lifted to rest on his shoulder.

\* \* \*

David woke, a hint of light trickling from the bathroom and stairway. He started, remembered where he was, caught his breath and whispered,

"Behold, thou art here." The hay gave way as he turned, the small warmth that cradled him fading into shadow. It was light outside.

His dream emerged bright and whole, Dancer standing on the outcrop of rocks. Why had the horse yielded? His surrender hadn't been coerced but given. A gift. And for his freedom, Dancer became who he was born to be, more than he could ever have been alone. He'd been unbridled from the dictates of the immediate, become a part of something more. In his giving of himself, he'd gained a greater freedom than he'd surrendered, and the truth of it shone in his eyes.

David smiled, settled back on the hay, felt the warmth rise to meet him. Was it in him? Could he, by some like submission, become who he was born to be? It would mean surrendering his life, his hopes. Everything. It might mean this day would be his last on earth, these thoughts the last he'd have here. But wasn't he convinced that life, the new life he'd come to know, was irrevocable? That it was impossible for it not to continue? He released his breath into the gray. He was sure, just as he was persuaded that the One who'd given it would provide more than he could have planned for himself.

He stood, stretched. The weather had changed, the air damp and chilled. Too cold for rain. Snow, most likely. And Schneider in Ghent, possibly having to drive back through fresh snowfall. Could take a while. He pulled his jacket close.

He stared toward the dim light filtering from the bathroom. It was long past time for his morning ration of water and soup. He needed both but was more grateful than thirsty. Every minute that passed without his being summoned brought Schneider closer. He began counting, every sixty-count a minute, but the counting dragged the moments into an endless procession of approach and finality. He rose, stepped off the length of the floor, the two sides free of straw. Almost eleven steps in length; half that in width. By his reckoning, it would take fifty-eight trips back and forth to make a mile. He could travel, with stopping and turning at the walls, at roughly four miles per hour. Two hundred thirty-five trips would make an hour.

A gentle rapping stirred the gray. His heart slammed against his ribs.

324

Too soon for Schneider. "Yes?"

Keys rattled, and the door eased open. He stared into the dark landing.

A dim shadow stood in the doorway. "I did as you asked. I was assured that she would be given your message to escape if MI5 failed to remove her."

He breathed. "Thank you. And you told him of the intercepted radio transmissions?"

"I told him." The little clerk shifted, looked up the stairs, closed the door behind him and locked it.

A frisson tingled down his back. "What is it? Were you followed?"

Henri fidgeted, looked away. "No. Feldwebel Mesche is here."

"The Wehrmacht feldwebel? Does he have orders from Schuster?" He bunched his hands around his mouth and let his breath warm his trembling fingers.

"No, that would come to Heinrich. It seems Mesche and von Felder are old colleagues."

He fought for breath, tried to force a calm into his voice. "They know you're here?"

"No, and I can't stay. I will try to detain them, search for paperwork if they request it. I wanted you to know I had made contact, that they had been informed." Henri looked down, hesitated.

"How much longer before Schneider is due back?" The words came in shallow pants, his heart thundering in his ears.

"An hour. Perhaps longer." Henri refused to meet his gaze. "There's been a snow, though it is melting quickly. It shouldn't delay him long. But the feldwebel and von Felder seem to have concluded Heinrich has gone somewhere. Perhaps they suspect he's trying to have the orders counter-manded. If they assume that—"

"Listen. I have one more message. Will you deliver it?"

The clerk fidgeted, appeared ready to run. "Will it endanger Heinrich?"

"No. And it's not part of our agreement. I'm asking it as a favor." He thought of her hearing the words, was steadied by it.

Henri looked toward the stairs. "I don't know. It's dangerous going there."

"I want Nicole to know I love her." He stared past him into darkness. "I

325

want her to know how much—"

"Yes, all right. But at an appropriate—" Henri flinched, jerked toward the stairs. The door at the top of the staircase swung open. Boots, heavy-heeled. At least two men.

"Quick! Into the bathroom!" He pushed Henri's shoulder. The little man spun and sprinted down the short hallway, slammed the door behind him. David winced at the sound, slipped quickly to the hallway, pushed the outer door shut as cover. His hand was still on the knob when Leutnant von Felder strutted in, the old feldwebel following. Wiesel stood behind in his practiced pose.

He stared, unable to speak.

Von Felder grinned, turned to Mesche. "Your prisoner, I believe." English. They *wanted* him to understand.

"Yes, Herr Leutnant. His pants are dry, but I am sure this is the same young criminal."

Both men laughed.

He was at a loss to assemble a defense, knew only an urgency to stop what was happening. "Uh, I have to wait here for Leutnant Schneider. He said he would return shortly."

Von Felder stiffened. "He has been here today?"

"Just a few minutes ago." His words were unsteady, his breath too weak to fill with voice.

The Germans exchanged a glance.

"He told me to wait." His mind was frozen. "Said you weren't to take me without orders from Oberstleutnant Schuster."

Von Felder ignored him, appeared taken with a new exigence, turned to Wiesel and nodded. The boy closed the door, stood before it and kicked toward the center. The crack echoed through the room like a cannon volley. The door stood. Von Felder turned, pushed the boy aside, backed away, jumped and planted both feet squarely in the middle. The pop resounded, and the center partition splintered into the stairwell. Still, the fissure was small. Von Felder stepped backward, ran two steps and kicked. The door folded outward, the bottom breaking in the center. The leutnant half rose, one foot through the door, propped by his hands. Blondie pulled his leg through the ruptured wood, took a breath and turned to face him.

"It appears you have escaped, Lieutenant. Come, we shall pursue you."

He shook his head, receded into the dark, couldn't let them get away with it. "I, uh, I have to get my Red Cross parcel. I'll need it."

"You will need nothing."

*The letters.* "Please. I want Leutnant Schneider to have my Bible." He forced the words, gave them wind and voice, to be sure Henri heard.

The two men pushed him forward. He reached to open the shattered door.

"No. You will crawl through." Von Felder pointed to the gaping hole.

He ducked, tried to clear the broken panel. Wiesel moved to his side, kicked, slamming him into the jagged edge. Blood oozed around the tear in his sleeve and dribbled onto his hand.

Von Felder said something in German, left the other two chuckling.

He climbed the stairs, the edge taken off his fear by the pain shooting into his left shoulder. He strained to put his jacket over his arm, looked back. Wiesel appeared to be locking what was left of the door, von Felder and the feldwebel waiting on the landing. The strangeness of it lifted in less than a heartbeat. They were offering him a chance to escape, creating an opportunity to shoot him. They couldn't do it here. It would arouse suspicion if he were found so close to his cell. They'd give him space, room to run.

He turned, faced them, put his hands on his head, offered what must have been a poorly executed smile. Von Felder nodded, looked back at the gefreiter and said something in German.

The three started up the stairs, the leutnant motioning him into the hall. He waited. When they were halfway up the stairs, he pushed through the door, looked down the familiar hallway, hoping to see someone, something to offer succor.

The doors were closed. Yellow bulbs tendered a feeble glow against the tiny window at the far end. The rectangular casement glittered in brilliant white, a contrast to the gloom within. It looked inviting, promised escape, but there was no way he could make it to the end of the hall before being intercepted by a bullet. And if he did, what then? Guards would surely be waiting outside.

The door opened, and von Felder appeared, looked toward the windowed door. No question. They had expected him to run. He caught his breath. The leutnant looked back, a dim smile playing at his lips, nodding. A compliment, it seemed.

He started north down the long hall.

"Nein." The feldwebel grumbled something, looked at von Felder.

The leutnant motioned south, toward the darkness, waited for him to shuffle past.

He squinted into the fragile light, made out the pair of double doors that opened into the warehouse and stood in front of them. The Germans groused, their sentiments guttural and harsh. He listened, turned. They were looking from his arm to the floor. He glanced down, saw two drops of blood collect before the doors. He'd made their case, planted tracks they would claim to have followed. He raised his left hand, held it with his right, felt the sodden beginnings of clots forming at his fingertips and scraped the floor with his boot.

Something in their faces… He was taken with a sudden desperation. "I won't leave this building! You don't have written orders. You can't shoot me here. They'll know. Everyone will know you murdered me. Leutnant Schneider needs me for his investigation!"

Von Felder smiled, looked at his compatriot, said something. The feldwebel turned to the gefreiter, shouted orders. Wiesel trotted down the hall, left the two nodding in the dark.

The leutnant stared. "Come now, Lieutenant. Where's the boldness you displayed earlier? Your attitude seems to have changed with no one present to rescue you." Von Felder's arm dropped, the Walther hanging loosely at his side.

"Leutnant Schneider will be here shortly. He said he'd be right back." He fought for air, drew a trembling hand across his face. Dancer. In the chute, pawing at the cold air. He remembered the submission, the freedom, what the horse had gained. He took a breath, tried to slow his mind.

Wiesel ran toward them, the other young guard with him, both holding rifles across their chests. The two boys bustled past von Felder, stopped, one on either side of him, their rifles lowered.

Von Felder grinned. "Open the doors, Lieutenant. We're leaving the compound."

He met the gray eyes, steadied his breath. "You go on without me. I'd rather stay in my cell today."

The leutnant grunted at Wiesel. The boy's rifle barrel slammed into his jaw. From the base of his teeth, pain splintered, shot to the top of his skull and down his neck. He turned the knobs, and the doors swung inward. Wiesel shoved with the rifle, and he fell in a heap on the cold floor.

"Stand up, Lieutenant."

He turned his head. The feldwebel had apparently decided to join in the fun. David pulled himself to his knees, latched onto an idea. It had worked once… "Do you still want that information we discussed, Herr Leutnant? I'm ready to deal if you do."

Von Felder flinched, jerked his head toward Mesche. He grunted something in German, looked guilty, turned back. "All right. What do you have?"

He glanced at the old sergeant. "In front of him?"

Blondie was caught. "Of course. What has Leutnant Schneider done?"

"He's done nothing."

The leutnant grimaced, leaned forward.

He held up his hand, pressed on. "Except investigate some egregious misconduct within the Wehrmacht."

Von Felder's mouth twisted. "The Wehrmacht. Who has he been investigating, and why would he tell you?"

"He didn't tell me. I told him. When I was sheltered by the partisans, they gave me information. Lots of it." He stared at the feldwebel, held his gaze for a moment then looked back at von Felder. "I was to use the information in the event that I was picked up by the Wehrmacht. An insurance policy."

"Go on."

He shifted on his hands and knees and slowly stood. "Have you ever heard of a hauptmann by the name Schmidt? Gerhardt Schmidt?"

"Possibly I have, yes."

"Then possibly you know he's been called on the carpet. Maybe executed by now." He looked away, made the leutnant wait. "You do know about that, don't you Herr Leutnant?"

"Proceed with your story, Lieutenant."

329

"Our own Leutnant Schneider gave that information to Abwehr. He fed them what I gave him."

"Of what interest is that to me? That matter has been dealt with." Von Felder's face distorted in the shadows; his chest moved quickly beneath the folds of his coat. He was hiding something. The fear was palpable.

"But I have more information. On other interrogators. Lots more." He grinned, held the leutnant's stare.

"We haven't the time for this, Lieutenant. You know nothing." Von Felder's hand was up, motioning the boy. "Wiesel!"

It wasn't going to work this way. He'd end up shot. He turned toward the old sergeant. Everybody had a secret. "I know plenty." He looked back at von Felder. "Your friend here, Feldwebel Mesche." He saw the sergeant jerk. "How long have you known him?"

Von Felder grimaced, was likely relieved to have the spotlight redirected. "That is none of your concern. If you have something—"

"You didn't know him before the war, did you, Herr Leutnant?"

Von Felder pulled the blackjack from his belt. "If you have a charge, make it or you will be shot."

Mesche fidgeted, sucked the dingy air.

He weighed it only for a second, threw the dice. "If you'd have known him before the war, you'd know his name wasn't Mesche. It was Mencher."

"Nein! This is not true! Schiess ihn! Wiesel, schiess den!"

"Nein! Nicht schiessen, Wiesel." Von Felder held up his hand, stared at the old feldwebel, looked back at him. "And you have proof of this?"

"Didn't need any. He knows he's Jewish. Knowing it was all I needed." He shrugged, worked to steady his voice. "Given the right circumstances, Feldwebel Mencher, here, could have worked a deal with me. But he was a bit too eager to watch me bleed. Cost him plenty."

"You're assuming I believe you, Lieutenant."

"I'm not assuming anything. Check it out for yourself. Just let me live until you learn how much I can help you."

"And if you are telling the truth, what would I have to gain by keeping you alive?"

"More information, Herr Leutnant. Lots more information."

330

The feldwebel pushed himself against von Felder. His jowls took on a furious flutter, his hands working in the pale yellow as he spoke. Von Felder nodded, jerked his head over his right shoulder. The old sergeant turned back, glared at him in rounded fury, his lips white. He turned and scuttled down the hall.

"He says you're a liar, Lieutenant, and that he can prove it." Von Felder smiled.

David looked into the empty warehouse, began to count the seconds, prayed for Schneider to return before the feldwebel. He stared into von Felder's face, the revulsion rising from his gut. Words bubbled to the surface. It had been years. He remembered his mother straightening his collar before a trip to Aunt Sarah's, teaching him old Simeon's prayer upon seeing the child Messiah. Now it returned, sure and potent. *Lord, now lettest thou thy servant depart in peace, according to thy word: For mine eyes have seen thy salvation, Which thou hast prepared before the face of all people; A light to lighten the Gentiles, and the glory of thy people Israel.*

The words lifted him with surety and power. He repeated them, filled the darkness of the hallway with silent exaltation. They returned again and again, sating him with peace. He was girded, now, with strength for the battle. Here. In the dim hallway.

Boots resounded down the hall. He stood, squared his shoulders, raised his throbbing chin. Mesche jostled against the light, someone following close behind. A young German, tall, blond. They stopped before von Felder, the old sergeant breathing desperately.

The three talked, their hands circling wildly, Mesche interrupting von Felder. The leutnant put his finger to the feldwebel's chest. The old sergeant quieted, dipped his chin. Von Felder nodded, returned the salute of the young unteroffizier who shook the feldwebel's hand, spun about and marched down the hall.

Von Felder turned, bared his teeth. "You have lied to us. You have wasted our time. The officer was a student in Headmaster Mesche's school when he was a boy. The feldwebel has never gone by another name."

David recited Simeon's prayer, felt the chill of its power. He nodded, said nothing.

"You will wish we had shot you on the stairs!" The old feldwebel was unable to contain his rage. David saw the kick coming from the corner of his eye, turned to protect himself. It caught him in the thigh. Then another to his ribs. Wiesel. A second from Mesche, another and he was down, crawling toward the dark of the empty room. Boots struck from all directions. Pain shot down his back from his temple. He scrambled to escape, but the room began to roll. More kicks, a spasm in his groin. Bile rose in his throat, and he drifted into a fresh darkness.

A moment later, there was movement. His eyes slitted, doors hinged wide, a brilliant light shattered the still. He was being held beneath his arms, dragged. Snow. His hand was wet, warm. He let it fall, touched the snow, tried to imagine the cleanness of it. So white. Car doors opened. Pain shot across his head and down his neck. He slammed roughly, face down, against a muddy floorboard. His body quivered, and he wished for the deep comfort of unknowing.

*Lord, now lettest thou thy servant—*

German, shouted somewhere above him.

*—depart in peace, according—*

It wasn't my battle, this making a defense. I was never capable of that.

Von Felder, giving orders. Mesche hollering. "Schiess ihn!" Good. Let them shoot me. No hangings, Lord. Please, no hangings.

*—depart in peace, according to thy word: For mine eyes have seen thy salvation—*

The car lurched, sped across the compound. The brakes let out a piercing squeal. More shouting. The gate. Gears ground behind a screaming engine. How did they keep the rods in this thing?

*—Which thou hast prepared before the face of all people; A light—*

His head slammed against the floor. Pain shot down his neck

*—A light to lighten the Gentiles, and the glory of thy people Israel—*

Never was my battle to figure a way out.

*—Lord, now lettest thou thy servant depart in peace according to thy word—*

The blackness was winning. He felt the sweet comfort of it, was grateful.

Car doors opened. Someone dragged him roughly from the floor. His

332

head hit something, the doorpost. Laughter. How many of them? David forced his eyes wide. Light ripped into his skull. He squinted, felt movement, was dragged again, shivering from the sudden cold.

"Stand!" Someone slapped him. "You will stand!"

He squinted into the light, saw snow beneath him, pine needles where his knees had scraped the whiteness. He smelled the resin, remembered home. Another shout. He raised his head. The feldwebel stood in front of the car, his pistol drawn. Ten, fifteen yards away. All three yelled, motioned for him to turn, to run. *No. You'll have to look at me. Let Schneider see that I wasn't running, that you murdered me.*

An engine whined, was downshifted. Snow flew in a blur of mud and motion. The staff car rocked gracelessly as a second slid into its bumper. He closed his eyes, gave himself to the blackness, wished for the shouting to end. Von Felder screamed, then Schneider— *Schneider.*

He opened his eyes, stared down to the road. Leutnant Schneider ran up the slope, papers in his hand, shouting at von Felder and Mesche.

"Heinrich!" The effort was only breath, far beneath his hearing. "Heinrich. Take my Bible." The dark grew oppressive, took him under.

* * *

"Lieutenant. Can you hear me?" The words cut through the cold and pain.

David inhaled the brilliance. "Heinrich. Take my Bible." Thoughts seemed too heavy to carry, so he clung to what was sure.

"Henri found the letters, gave them to me. Our insurance, yes?" Schneider paused, his voice warm. "You have done well, Lieutenant. You have survived."

He looked again into the burning white, failed to find a face. "Where's... von Felder?"

"They're gone. You're in my custody now, Lieutenant. Come, let me help you to the car. We'll get you to the infirmary."

# Chapter XXVIII

Jesse swayed, was blown by a harsh wind though the day was still. He gripped a push ring in his left hand, held the letter to his breast with his right, waited to be sure that Delores and Morgan weren't coming back. It was addressed to him. No one else.

It had taken a while for it to settle in that the boy was alive. For a certainty— that somewhere he breathed and spoke and walked.

His keeping the letter hadn't been a loss to her. That was clear enough. She'd primped all morning for her shopping trip with Morgan, that schoolgirl grin on her face. She was always taking that child into Brighton, spending the day with Morgan, staying long into the night. And always taking as much of his money as he would part with after she'd gone through David's check. Her need for groceries was out of proportion to her appetite, what with her skimping the way she did and staring at herself in the mirror all day.

He clenched his teeth, had seen her face as Morgan handed him the letter. It took near all the wind out of her. The boy was alive. She hadn't counted on that. And Morgan not knowing what to say, whether to act glad or consoling. No need for either, so far as he was concerned. It was clear enough where everyone stood.

One other thing was sure. There'd be talk about the letter. It had been postmarked in Portbou, Spain. Morgan hadn't said a thing about that, but he'd seen it. Little doubt of that. There wasn't a piece of mail that went through that store he didn't know all about.

Jesse stared at the empty road, listened to the silence. Maybe the boy had made it to Spain, somehow. Hope rose unbidden, wouldn't be hushed

334

for all his efforts to reason it away. It was a dangerous thing, being so full of hope. He pulled out his penknife and sliced through the flap, his fear rising with the paper from the envelope. There might yet be something left to lose, one more thing he held to that could be taken.

He unfolded the paper, mouthed the words slowly, let nothing escape, repeated each sentence, ran his fingers over the letters, felt where the boy's hand had pressed them into the paper.

David didn't explain why the letter was coming from Spain, left far too many things unanswered. It wasn't his way to see more in words than what they said. That was the boy's way. But this time he couldn't do much else. The truth loomed like a dark cloud in the west on a hot August day, the stillness as much a trick as would come from any lie.

He narrowed his eyes, began again from the first line. The boy always wrote that way, the letters fine to look at but hard to make out. Still, he had a fair estimate of what was said. It was what wasn't said that wouldn't loose him from its grip.

David told of being shot down, most of the crew surviving, of being taken prisoner. Said he was being treated well, though only time would tell what would happen. Then the boy got to the meat of it, to what he figured he had wanted to say from the start. "Dad," he wrote— called him Dad. He shook his head, blinked and waited for his eyes to clear. Said he was sorry for having expected so much of him. Said he'd needed more than he had given, more than any man could give, but had found what it was he was missing and was at peace.

The boy went on, said he'd come to see the truth for what it was. His chest swelled, choked off his air. He swallowed hard, waited until his breath came steady and deep. David said he loved him, always had, though his anger hadn't always let him see it. "Dad, I'm asking you to forgive me." Jesse closed his eyes, let his throat unleash its heavy clench.

The boy wrote of receiving a Bible— said he'd wanted one just like his— told how he came to get it in a Red Cross parcel with no reason for it to be there. Just a gift. That held him strong, he said, was a real comfort to him. Said he'd learned so much from it, more than the words alone could carry. Whatever happened now, things would be different. Things were healed. All the hurt was past, and what they had ahead of them was something good, something to cherish. Whether here or hereafter.

Jesse's ribs ached from the pressure in his chest. He tucked the letter away and wiped his cheeks. It was time the black was fed. He wheeled himself through the doorway and across the boards the boy had left lying on the ground between the tack shed and the working pen, filled the bucket with oats and lifted it to his lap. Halfway to the pens the meaning came clear, slammed the breath from his lungs. He knew what the boy was saying, saw why he'd written the letter as he had. He stopped. Dead. The bucket fell from his hands, the oats spilling between the warped boards. He slumped in his chair, his head nearing his useless legs, was taken in a fierce rhythm that curled him like an oak leaf at first frost. A drop fell to his pant leg, then another. He brought his hands to his face, couldn't restrain the wail clawing at his throat. The boy was telling him goodbye.

Jesse waited in the tack shed even after the tears stopped, tried to feel David in the place, stayed until the warm glow of the sun began to fade. Nothing of the boy was left here now. He took enough sugar to make his pockets bulge and wheeled to the gate, held out his hand for Dancer who stepped cautiously forward, sniffed and took the sugar piece by piece. He looked into the deep and shadowed blackness, felt the spirit of his son. There was meaning in those eyes. Light within the dark. The horse had yielded to the boy, done what had been asked of him not from fear but something else, something he'd never learned to trust. But it was sure, this bond between them, surer than fear could ever be.

Jesse shook his head, let the tears come, endured the spasms that threatened to unseat him. He'd only wanted to make the boy stronger the way you would a horse. Teach him to fear you more than anything else until the fear of all else died. He'd wanted to make him strong because the world was hard. Always someone there to take what you'd worked for, bled over, built from sweat and dream. Always someone offering aid, acting as if they had your best interest at heart. He'd only wanted to make the boy strong enough to stand up to that, know it for what it was.

But he'd failed, broken David's spirit as surely as a man could make a horse skittish or a dog cower. The boy had never learned to stand when he knew himself right. Never seemed to know there *was* a right or that he would be able to see it if it brightened before him. He slid his trembling fingers into his pocket, pulled out the folded paper, held it to his chest. The boy knew now.

He looked at the stallion who stared back at him with a curious eye, thought of the way Morgan gawked at the horse, just as he would at another man's wife, wanting to have it for his own. The man would find a way to take Dancer, to crush his life and spirit, seize it with a knife if need be. His chest heaved, and he crushed the letter in his fist, bumped the chair against the pens, raised himself against the wood pressing into his hands, his useless legs willowing beneath him as if blown by a silent breeze. He hooked his left arm over the splintered plank, waited, breathed hard into the failing light. He stared into the black, saw a light, hard-won but proffered, what David must have seen.

"There's nothing left for you here, boy." His words came in slow shudders. "You're alone now. Best you make a new life for yourself— on the Summit place maybe. Gates are open. You're not apt to be bothered there." He strained, held himself with his left arm clenched to the rail, lifted the rope that held the gate against the corner post and pushed it wide.

"Go on, now." Jesse swept his free hand through the air, the letter fluttering with the wave.

Dancer cleaved the hardened loam, tore through the gate, pummeled the earth that had claimed so much. How much blood would it demand before it was satisfied? How much death to spawn new life?

Jesse watched the magic, the silk and silvery motion as Dancer pitched his head into the dying sun. He released his weight, eased himself back onto his chair, touched the letter to his lips then pushed it into his pocket. His eyes grew full and spilled over. He clung to the words with all his failing strength, vowed beyond utterance to hold with his last breath to the dwindling certainty in those dark eyes.

The horse cleared the gate beneath the rattling elms, lunged across the fallow sorghum patch and thundered into the pines shifting slowly from form to shadow.

**A word from the publisher:**

Did you enjoy *Jesse's Seed*?

If so, please head over to the author's web page, www.sampakan.com, and let the author know!

Also, consider leaving a favorable review at sites such as Amazon.com.

Made in the USA
San Bernardino, CA
06 December 2016